Kiss and Tell

ITALIAN STALLIONS
BOOK NINE

MARI CARR

Kiss and Tell

Grumpy/sunshine times three!

Joey is no stranger to romance. After all, his family wrote the book when it came to falling in love and finding their forever partners. There's no doubt in his mind that his soul mate is out there as well. What he doesn't expect is to be struck down with a serious case of instalove the second Lucy Storm steps off the front porch of her family's farmhouse.

Escaping a difficult relationship, Miles is proud of the life he's forged for himself. He's got it all. A hit cable show, amazing friends, and Joey, the greatest cohost a guy could ask for. When Joey throws a curveball into their well-ordered existence, falling for Lucy, the most obnoxiously cheerful person he's ever met, Miles knows he should be supportive. What he shouldn't do is kiss the chatty woman to shut her up.

Lucy's dreams are bigger than her family's farm, but leaving home isn't an easy proposition. When Joey invites her to hit the road, touring the country with him as he films his show, she jumps at the chance. However, travel isn't what entices her most. Because for her, the greatest temptation is the charming Joey...and his infuriatingly grumpy, sexy best friend, Miles.

Chapter One

"What a place!" Joey Moretti did a complete three-sixty, spinning around to take in the gorgeous views surrounding him. The large wooden sign with the colorful words Stormy Weather Farm—the t's in *stormy* and *weather* shaped like lightning strikes—told them they had arrived at their destination.

He and his cohost Miles Williams had just made the three-and-a-half-hour drive from Philadelphia to Gracemont in Northern Virginia, as they prepared to start filming a new episode of their show. He could hardly believe that he and Miles were already hard at work on their third season of *ManPower*.

When he'd first landed the gig hosting a cable show, Joey had no idea *ManPower* would become so popular. These days, it was rare that he could go out in public without being recognized by people. Just yesterday, his sister Layla had texted him a picture of herself standing in the grocery store checkout line, posing with a copy of a home improvement magazine featuring him and Miles on the cover.

Along with the selfie, she'd included a one-word text.
Squeeeeeeee!!!!
Joey felt like he'd stepped back into the past as he took in the

giant white farmhouse with large navy-blue shutters, surrounded by countless well-kept outbuildings, including an honest-to-God red barn. The place was storybook perfect, with rolling hills, a vibrant view of leaves currently in the height of changing colors, and at least fifteen different-size pumpkins adorning the house's wraparound porch, intermingled with bright yellow mums.

In addition to this farmhouse, there were two other homes situated on Stormy Weather Farm's two-hundred-plus acres, as well as several businesses—Rain or Shine Brewery, Lightning in a Bottle Winery, and some rental cabins.

"Shit, man. That was some climb. I wasn't sure the car was going to make it," Miles muttered. "We're not in Philly anymore, Toto."

Joey chuckled, though he agreed the climb had been white-knuckle steep. The rest of the *ManPower* crew would be arriving tomorrow, but he and Miles had made plans to arrive a day early to meet Levi Storm and his brewmaster, Lou, this afternoon for a tour of Stormy Weather Farm.

Joey had done quite a bit of research on the farm in preparation for the show. The Storm family had settled here four generations ago, and they'd created an amazing legacy in the decades since.

After the tour, Levi, the oldest of the latest generation of Storms, had promised them a home-cooked dinner and a chance to meet the rest of his siblings and cousins. Joey and Levi had spoken on the phone a few times in preparation for the filming, and the man had mentioned the fact he had six brothers. Joey, who was one of five siblings, felt a kinship with Levi instantly. It was apparent the man was as close to his family as Joey was to his own, and the branches on the Storm family tree were as weighted down by countless relatives as the Moretti's.

Levi reminded Joey a lot of his older brother, Tony—confident and take-charge. The kind of guy who never met a stranger. For most of Tony's adult life, the family had called him the mayor because the dude seriously seemed to know every single person in

Philadelphia. He suspected the same was likely true of Levi, though to be fair, the population of Gracemont probably didn't reach four digits, while Philadelphia boasted of close to two million inhabitants.

"Never gave much thought to the farming lifestyle but, damn, Miles, imagine waking up here every morning of your life." Joey stared into the distance, amazed by just how many colors Mother Nature had in her palette. The mountain was awash in golden and neon yellows, vibrant reds and bright purples, deep oranges, and at least three different shades of green.

"No thanks," Miles growled.

Joey rolled his eyes, amused by the response though not surprised. Miles was taking in the same view he was, but his best friend was clearly much less impressed, especially when he pulled out his phone to check his text messages.

"Reception sucks up here," he muttered. A city boy from the word go, Miles viewed the mountains and woods and, well, nature in general as space simply waiting to be "civilized" with houses, stores, restaurants, and a fucking Starbucks on every corner.

Miles had grown up in the Ridgewood section of Queens, his playgrounds made of concrete. Joey had spent his childhood in two large cities as well—Philadelphia and, for a time, Baltimore. However, his family had always resided in the suburbs, so he had a working knowledge of how to mow grass, unlike Miles.

When he was little, Joey helped Nonna and Aunt Berta plant seeds in the raised-bed gardens in their backyards every summer. He'd loved watching the tomatoes grow big and turn red, enjoyed searching the sprawling vines for the green beans that Nonna would cook for dinner, and picking the strawberries that never seemed to make it from the yard to the house because he ate them all before he got inside.

Levi had mentioned during one of their calls that on a clear day, they could see all the way to Washington, D.C., the view from here completely unencumbered by other houses or trees. Joey found himself searching the horizon to see if that was true. They were so high, he could almost believe that if he was only an inch or two taller, he'd bump his head on the sky.

Miles scowled at the cell screen, clearly upset, before stuffing his phone back in his pocket.

"Bad text?" Joey asked.

Miles had been uncharacteristically quiet on the drive. He shook his head, then took another cursory glance at the landscape Joey couldn't take his eyes off of. They hadn't made it more than a few feet from the truck because the view had literally stopped him in his tracks. "Should we go knock on the door?"

Before Joey could respond, they heard a female voice calling to them from the porch of the house.

"You're here!"

Joey spun around, blinking several times and even shaking his head. His shocked gasp was audible, drawing Miles's attention.

"You okay, man?"

"It's her," Joey whispered.

"Her who?"

Joey watched as the petite strawberry-blonde woman descended the stairs, walking in their direction, intent on greeting them. She wore faded overalls over a hot-pink long-sleeved tee and her long hair was pulled back in a high ponytail, though a chunk of it had fallen out on one side. She tucked it behind her ear each time the breeze blew it loose again. She wore the girliest Doc Martens he'd ever seen, the boots covered in pink and purple flowers.

She was smiling as she approached—and Joey knew without a doubt, he'd never seen a more beautiful woman in his life.

"Joey?" Miles prodded. "Who is she?"

Joey grinned, unable to look away from her. "The woman I'm going to marry," he replied, only half joking.

Miles turned to look at him, snorting...until he saw Joey's face. Then he looked confused. "You know her?"

"Never met her."

"Jesus," Miles muttered, but before he could give him shit for saying crazy stuff, the woman reached them.

"I can't believe you're both really here," she gushed. "When Levi told us *ManPower* wanted to film a show about Rain or Shine Brewery, we thought he was pulling our leg. Although to be honest, Levi isn't usually the joking type. That honor falls to my youngest cousin, Jace, who's always pulling pranks and cracking us up with his farfetched stories. We're all—the whole family, I mean—big fans of the show. I especially liked the episode where you went lobster fishing in Maine and that big storm rolled up. Oh my God! I suffered some serious secondhand anxiety watching that."

Joey wasn't sure what part of this one-sided conversation he enjoyed more, listening to the woman talk or watching Miles's expressions, which ranged anywhere from awe to horror.

"That was a good show," Joey interjected, amused by how fast the woman was talking. "And terrifying." He crooked his thumb at Miles. "This guy was in danger of puking his guts out the whole time."

Miles grunted because the truth was, they were both green around the gills by the end of filming, and the first thing Joey had done when he got off the boat was beg for ginger ale and saltines to settle his stomach.

"I can imagine. I've seen all the *ManPower* episodes a few times and I still can't watch that one without freaking out. And I know how it ends!" she added, eyes wide with humor. "Oh crap, I'm rambling, aren't I? My grandma always said I was blessed with the gift of gab, but there were times when I'm pretty sure she substituted the word 'cursed' with 'blessed' to soften the blow. She was kind of wonderful like that." The beautiful woman laughed, and Joey couldn't help but join in.

Miles, who hadn't said anything—probably because he couldn't find a break in the conversation—was studying her with furrowed brows. His best friend was a happy-go-lucky guy overall, but during times when he was stressed out or upset, his resting bitch face was fierce. It was in full force right now.

"Well," Joey said. "Obviously, I'm Joey Moretti, and this is Miles Williams."

The woman threw up her arms. "Dear God, I'm an idiot. Just pounced right on you, didn't I? Completely forgot to introduce myself. I'm Lucy Storm, one of the brewmasters."

"Lucy," Joey repeated, surprised. "Wait. You're Lou?"

When Levi informed him that Rain or Shine Brewery had two brewmasters, Sam and Lou, Joey had assumed they were both men.

"You thought I was a guy, didn't you?" she asked. "Lu is short for Lucy, which is the nickname my family insists on using. Fortunately it's not contagious, because everyone else in Gracemont calls me Lucy."

Joey laughed. "I tried for years to get people to call me Joe, but my family refused to conform, and their insistence on adding that damn y *was* contagious. Eventually, I just gave up and embraced it, though every now and then, Miles treats me to the shortened version because he's kind of wonderful like that," he said, repeating her joke.

"How about you?" Lucy looked at Miles. "Any dreaded nicknames?"

Miles shrugged. "My name is straightforward, without much room for creativity."

"That's true, I suppose," she said, her smile wavering at Miles's uncharacteristically gruff tone.

"You have a beautiful home," Joey said.

Lucy looked over her shoulder. "This farmhouse belongs to my cousins, seven guys in one place. My sister, Remi, calls it the frat house."

Joey hadn't lived with his brothers since they were all old enough to move out of their dad's house. He'd roomed with his oldest brother Tony for a time, but that hadn't worked for long as

Tony was a neat freak and Joey was cleaning challenged. Or, as his family put it, "a fucking slob."

"I know Levi said he would give you a tour, but he had some trouble with a tractor this morning, so he's elbow-deep in machine parts, trying to figure out what's wrong with it. I volunteered to take charge." She pointed to a beat-up truck that looked older than Joey with the words *Farm Use* spray-painted on the door. "The property is quite large and spread out. How are you guys for steps?" she asked.

"Steps?" Miles repeated, confused.

She grinned as she pointed to her Apple Watch. "You know, the step counter?"

Miles frowned, his tone downright sarcastic. "We've been in the car all morning."

Joey shot his friend a look, wondering where this asshole attitude was coming from. "Miles and I are gym rats most of the time, so steps aren't something we usually look at."

"Oh. I got this Apple Watch last year for Christmas, and I've become obsessed with hitting a certain number of steps every day. I'm too competitive for my own good, even if I'm only competing with myself. I set these ridiculous goals. Drives Sam crazy when we're at work because we'll be sitting down discussing something, my watch will beep, and then, well, I have to get up and start moving," she said, as if that should be obvious. "So...a gym, huh? You mean like weights, or are you treadmill guys?"

"Mainly weights," Joey said, but before he could elaborate, Lucy continued speaking.

"I have to admit, I've never stepped foot in a gym—except the one in my high school. Wouldn't have a clue how to use all those weight machines. Life on a farm is its own workout."

Joey loved Lucy's voice. It was a weird thing to be thinking, but there was something about it that made him want to smile... like nonstop. There was a cheerful lilt to it, and she had the tiniest bit of a southern accent that he found adorable. "I bet it is."

"Anyway..." Lucy started walking toward the ancient pickup.

"I think we'd better take the truck. Otherwise, we'll end up walking a hundred miles, trying to take everything in. Why don't you follow me in your vehicle to the first stop, which is the cabin where you'll be staying. We can drop off your suitcases and leave your car there."

"Sounds like a plan." Joey looked at Miles, tossing the keys to his car to him. "You can drive, Miles, while I ride with our beautiful tour guide."

Miles rolled his eyes but didn't argue.

Joey crossed around the back of the truck, claiming the passenger seat, grinning when he realized the thing had a long bucket in the front and no backseat at all. He mentally dibsed the middle spot for himself once Miles rejoined them. He liked the idea of spending a few hours sitting pressed close to Lucy.

God, she smelled good, he thought as soon as the two of them were closed in the cab of the truck. Like lilacs and apples, a perfect blend of the best of spring and fall.

"The cabins aren't far." Lucy glanced in the rearview mirror, checking that Miles was behind them before shifting into drive and starting down the dirt lane. "If you guys are tired, we can delay the tour. Maybe Miles wants some time to unwind?"

Obviously, Lucy had picked up on Miles's bad mood. Joey wasn't sure what the hell had gotten into his friend. While he'd been quiet on the drive from Philadelphia to Virginia, he hadn't been the downright grumpy ass he was acting like right now. Miles was no fan of the mountains, but they'd spent a lot of time in places more remote than this during the filming of the show and he'd been just fine.

No. Miles's mood had darkened when he'd looked at his cellphone. And it had only gotten worse since Lucy appeared. Which didn't make a damn bit of sense, because she was charming and sweet.

"We're good to go on the tour," Joey replied.

"Cool." Lucy gave him a sideways glance. "I guess I should

warn you. I tend to talk a lot when I'm excited or nervous, and at the moment, I'm both. I'm going to try to settle down."

Joey chuckled, loving how open, honest, and even self-deprecating Lucy was. There was no pretense with her, no putting on airs.

Lately, Joey had been dating the same type of women—all around his age, professionals in their chosen careers, sophisticated and worldly. He'd been on a dozen dates in the past few months and not one of them had ended in the bedroom, because Joey hadn't felt any spark or connection to the women. Now it was starting to occur to him that perhaps he'd been seeking out the wrong women to date...which might also account for his failed attempts at finding "the one."

Miles would roll his eyes hard if he heard Joey rambling on about "the one" again, but ever since his only other single sibling, Luca, had found his life partners—Conor and Harper—Joey had become even more determined than ever to find the person he wanted to spend the rest of his life with.

Not that he was *so* determined that he'd settle for just anyone, of course. Joey had witnessed too many examples of true love in his family to ever settle for less.

Aaaaand that was another concept Miles would give him shit for. Because Miles did not believe in true love or soul mates or love at first sight or any of those things Joey knew for a fact existed.

Glancing at Lucy, Joey felt a slight stir in his heart *and* his pants. Both had lain dormant for too long, but now they were suddenly waking up.

"Do me a favor, Lucy. Don't stop talking. I like the sound of your voice."

She blushed as she grinned widely. "Okay, but you might regret that request later."

"I'm pretty sure I won't. Have to admit, I'm looking forward to seeing the farm, seeing where you work. What made you decide to become a brewmaster?"

Lucy lifted one shoulder casually. "I guess a combination of things. I've always loved science, and the chemistry behind brewing beer is fascinating. Plus, there are countless chores and jobs that need to be done in order to run the farm and businesses efficiently. Most of the primary tasks fall to the family, though we certainly have a lot of employees who aren't related to us. I've always been most interested in the brewery side, while my sisters tend to work in the winery most of the time."

"Sisters?"

"I have three, all younger."

"No brothers?"

Lucy shook her head. "Nope, but that's probably a good thing, because with seven male cousins, I'm not sure I could have survived with one more overprotective man in my life."

Joey winced playfully. "Damn. I might resemble that remark. My brothers and I have one little sister, Layla."

Lucy laughed. "I'm going to need her phone number. At least I have my sisters to commiserate with when the guys pull their cavemen routine with our prospective dates, while it sounds like poor Layla is adrift and on her own."

Joey snorted. "Not really. She did alright for herself. Settled into a pretty amazing happily ever after."

"What?" Lucy asked, aghast. "You let a man into the inner sanctum?"

"*Two* men," Joey replied with a wink.

She pulled up in front of a cute cabin, also adorned with pumpkins and mums, celebrating the fact that fall had arrived and Halloween was just four days away. Joey wondered if the decorations had been Lucy's doing.

Before they could continue the conversation, Miles was standing next to the passenger door, duffel bag slung over his shoulder.

Joey got out, retrieving his own bag from the car as Lucy climbed the three steps to the cabin's porch and unlocked the door.

"My aunt Claire runs a B&B on the property with my sister, Mila. They also take care of the cabins. You have Mila to thank for the pumpkins and flowers, as well as the stocked refrigerator. She's got an eye for design, and she loves to make everything pretty. One whole shed behind the farmhouse I share with my sisters is filled with every possible decoration for every conceivable holiday on the calendar." Lucy led them inside as she spoke. "Levi told her she was probably taking it too far when she started decking the B&B in lightsabers, Death Star cutouts, and mini Yodas for Star Wars Day."

Joey folded his hands in front of himself, trying to look like a somber Jedi. "May the Fourth be with you."

"And also with you," Lucy replied, giggling as she crossed herself.

"How many cabins are on the property?" Joey was impressed by the homey feel of the cabin they were going to call home for the next five days.

"There are ten, scattered around various places on the farm. The first three are tucked in the woods and were originally used as hunting cabins...many, many moons ago. When my grandfather took over the running of the farm, he started growing grapes with the intention of opening the winery. Once that happened, he stopped allowing people to hunt on the property. Aunt Claire was the one who suggested we refurbish those older cabins and build new ones to rent to guests, so Uncle Rex scoped out seven spots with amazing views. There aren't many weeks that pass where at least half the cabins aren't rented, and we sell out almost every week in the summer and fall, when the leaves are changing color."

"I was admiring your colorful mountain when we arrived, wasn't I, Miles?" Joey attempted to draw his friend into the conversation because, since entering the cabin, he'd been wandering around, looking completely distracted.

"Yep." Miles jerked his thumb toward one of the bedroom doors. "I'm going to take that one, okay?"

Joey nodded, annoyed when Miles walked away from them.

"Um. Okay." Lucy stumbled for a moment, clearly struggling to make this Miles fit with the man who appeared on her TV screen in every episode. That Miles was all smiles and easygoing, everybody's pal, while today, his first impression screamed impatient asshole.

"Sounds like we were lucky to score a cabin then." Joey tried to distract her from his best friend's rudeness.

"Your producer set up the filming way back in early spring, so we made sure to save the best cabin for you. The other bedroom is over here." Lucy pointed to the door behind her.

"Let me toss my bag in there really quick, then we can start the tour."

Lucy nodded, but her smile wasn't as bright as it had been a few minutes ago.

Joey gave his bedroom a cursory glance, placing his bag on the bed without unpacking before returning to Lucy. Miles had already emerged from his room, but neither he nor Lucy were talking to each other.

"Ready?" Lucy asked brightly, though her tone felt more forced than before.

"Can't wait." Joey reached out, clasping his hand with hers, tugging her along, hoping his enthusiasm would re-spark her own.

She laughed when he gallantly opened the driver's side door for her, bowing as he did so. After she climbed in, he jogged around the hood, bumping Miles out of the way. "I'll take the middle seat," he said, acting as if he was making some sacrifice.

Miles nodded, looking annoyed.

Joey shot his buddy a glare, one that was greeted with a regretful sigh. At least Miles was aware of the fact he was acting like an ass.

"Sorry," he muttered.

Appeased, Joey slid into the truck, shifting until he was right next to Lucy. Then he rested his arm along the back of the seat, smiling at her as she shook her head at his obvious flirting.

She didn't call him out for it though, which Joey took as a win. Especially when he realized her cheeks were turning pink again. God, he couldn't remember the last time he'd dated a woman who blushed. It was endearing and cute as hell.

"Okay. First stop is the winery. We'll drive by the grapevines as we go. Let me know if y'all have any questions about them," she offered.

"We're just focusing on the brewery for filming," Miles pointed out, his tone less harsh. Not that it mattered, considering his scowl was still firmly in place.

"Oh. I, um, just meant questions in general. Or we can skip that part if—"

"No, no," Joey quickly interjected. "We want to see it all." He narrowed his eyes at Miles. "Don't we?"

"Yeah. We do." Miles nodded and even attempted a smile. A weak one. Then his cell buzzed. He pulled it out and his frown returned. Joey tried to sneak a glance at the screen, but Miles tilted it away from him. He raised one eyebrow, curious about who was texting him.

Miles grimaced, then put his phone away.

Lucy pointed out various things along the way, her knowledge and love of the farm showing as she spoke. Joey was impressed by her intelligence, and by the time they reached the winery, even Miles had started to thaw a little, asking how they harvested the grapes.

"And here's Lightning in a Bottle Winery. My cousins Maverick and Grayson are our winemakers. Maverick is certified in viticulture and winery tech and has over ten years of official experience, although he worked with our granddaddy from the time he was old enough to walk, learning everything he could from him about our vineyards. I thought I'd show you where we process it, the cellars, then take you to the tasting room to sample some."

"Sounds great," Joey said as they pulled up next to a beautiful building with a massive front porch containing an assortment of tables and Adirondacks, with yet another stellar view from the mountain.

They spent an hour walking through the winery with Lucy and Maverick, who took charge of that part of the tour since it was his domain. Then they enjoyed tasting four of the wines, served with a charcuterie board filled with an assortment of meats, cheeses, nuts, and crackers.

From there, they drove by several of the other rental cabins, then took a quick walk-through of the B&B—the second farm-house—where they met Lucy's sister, Mila, her aunt Claire, and her uncle Rex. According to Lucy, Claire had decided to turn her family's home into an inn after the youngest of her sons, Jace, moved out. Apparently, after raising seven rambunctious boys, Claire found her empty nest too quiet for her liking.

Finally, they arrived at the brewhouse. Joey thought Lucy had been cheerful and happy all day, but once they entered her realm, she lit up brighter than the sun. She introduced them to two more cousins—her fellow brewmaster, Sam, and Theo, who was the brewhouse manager. During the two-hour walk-through of the brewhouse, Joey had been fascinated to learn about the process involved in brewing beer. He'd never considered it a hobby he wanted to try, but after listening to Sam and Lucy, he found himself thinking about buying a kit and giving it a whirl at home.

Just like at the end of the winery tour, Theo, Sam, and Lucy invited them to the tasting room, and the five of them sampled every beer made at Rain or Shine Brewery.

It was nearly six o'clock by the time Lucy drove him and Miles back to their cabin so they could change for dinner. She waited for them in the living room. Despite the fact it had been a whirl-wind day, Joey was full of energy, something he was attributing to Lucy, who seemed truly tireless. He was feeding off her excitement and enthusiasm.

"I hope you're ready for this," Lucy said, as they pulled up in front of the third farmhouse on the property, the one she shared with her three sisters, Nora, Remi, and Mila—all of whom they'd been introduced to during their tour.

"Ready?" Miles asked.

"I tried to tell everyone it would be better for us to meet you in small groups. Unfortunately, a couple of weeks ago, when Mila mentioned hosting the two of you for dinner your first night here, Aunt Claire hopped on the bandwagon, and then let it slip she was making her chili. After that, well…"

"The whole family invited themselves?" Joey asked, amused. Levi had told him about the dinner on the phone last night, but he'd forgotten to warn Miles.

She nodded.

"Sounds like the Morettis," Joey replied, laughing. "The second we hear Nonna is making eggplant parmesan, we crawl out of the woodwork like ants."

Lucy grinned. "Aunt Claire's chili wins the local chili cookoff every single year, and Mila makes homemade cornbread that is literally to die for."

"Sounds amazing." Joey climbed out of the truck on Lucy's side, the two of them waiting for Miles to cross around the front of the truck.

"Do you have a big family too, Miles?" Lucy asked.

While Miles had shed some of his early moodiness, he'd still been quiet and reserved. Joey planned to corner him tonight before they turned in to find out what the hell was wrong with him.

"No," Miles responded. "My parents are divorced, so for most of my life it's just been me, Mom, and my sister. I have an aunt, but she lives on the West Coast, and we don't see her or my cousins more than once every few years."

"Oh," she murmured almost sadly.

Joey and Lucy definitely shared the same love for big families.

He'd been jerking Miles's chain earlier when he said she was the one he was going to marry. He'd taken one look at the gorgeous woman and fallen head over heels in lust because every single molecule in his body was attracted to every molecule in hers.

However, that statement felt less like a joke the longer he'd spent with her today.

Joey wasn't the type to debunk the idea of love at first sight because he'd witnessed it firsthand with his cousin, Aldo, and his best friend Kayden. Those two guys had fallen for their sweet nurse, Hazel, the second they saw her standing outside a burning motel, all of her possessions consumed in the fire. Luckily for them, she'd fallen right back.

Joey had never experienced it himself, but there was no denying he'd taken one look at Lucy and felt as if he'd been struck by lightning. Which was appropriate, considering they were standing in the middle of Stormy Weather Farm.

"Should we go in?" Joey wrapped his arm around Lucy's shoulders, turning toward the house. He'd been infringing on her personal space most of the day, which was out of character for him. Joey respected boundaries, especially those of women he'd just met. But there was something about her that had him wanting to hold her hand, or tug on her ponytail playfully, or tuck her under his arm as they walked across the gravel drive and up the porch steps.

If she'd given him any indication she was uncomfortable with that, he would have backed off instantly, but so far, all she'd done —God help his libido—was lean closer.

Even better, he got the sense she felt the same attraction because she'd matched him touch for touch, grasping his forearm as she leaned close to be heard over the brewery equipment, lightly smacking his upper arm whenever he said something funny, and shoulder-bumping him in the truck to get his attention when they passed something she wanted him to see.

As they walked toward the house, Joey offered her some reassurance. "Don't worry about Miles being overwhelmed, Lucy. He's spent plenty of time with the Morettis. While the first couple of times were a shock to his system, I think we've worn him down enough that he's prepared to meet your family."

"It's cute that you think I'm not still shocked by your family," Miles said in a deadpan voice. It was his first joke of the day, and Joey and Lucy both laughed.

She reached out to Miles, and Joey was delighted when his friend took the hand she'd proffered. Joey was at ease with her after spending so many hours together, and he wanted Miles to be a part of that. The three of them walking side by side like this felt—

Joey shut the thought down instantly. Because there were places he didn't let himself go, not even in his own head.

They stopped just outside the front door, Lucy grinning at them. "Gird your loins, boys, because the Storm family is a force of nature."

Chapter Two

The three of them hadn't even reached the front door before they were nearly deafened by the sound of too many people talking and laughing inside the house.

Lucy resisted the urge to roll her eyes at the fact the whole family had shown up. Not a single Storm was capable of "playing it cool." They were far too passionate about the things they loved, and there wasn't a soul in this family who wasn't over-the-top proud of the farm and the businesses and the things they had created here.

Joey, true to his word, didn't seem the least bit bothered when she opened the door to reveal no less than twenty people milling around between the living room, the dining room, and kitchen. In addition to her family, she spotted a few farmhands and tasting room employees.

The house smelled like bliss, the spicy scent of Aunt Claire's chili and Mila's buttery cornbread filling the air.

Mercifully, her family didn't descend on Joey and Miles as a pack. Since Maverick, Sam, Theo, and Mila had already met the guys, they hung back, helping Aunt Claire in the kitchen, while the others came over in small groups to introduce themselves.

Uncle Rex came out of the kitchen, handing both men a beer with a wink before moving on.

Joey and Levi shook hands, greeting each other like old friends. Levi had spoken to Joey on the phone a few times and said he seemed like a pretty nice guy. Personally, Lucy thought Levi had underplayed how cool Joey Moretti was because the man was miles away from just "pretty nice." He was sexy, smart, inquisitive, funny, sexy, observant, and charming as hell.

Yes, sexy deserved to be mentioned twice.

"Sorry I couldn't join you on the tour," Levi said. "It was one catastrophe after another all damn day."

"Murphy's Law," Joey replied good-naturedly. "And don't worry about it. You left us with a very capable and entertaining tour guide."

Joey reached out, claiming her hand, and tugging her close when she'd tried to move back, not wanting to monopolize him and Miles. She'd had them to herself all day, so it felt as if she should share them with the rest of her family. Even if she didn't want to.

Mercifully, Joey didn't look intent on letting her escape. He squeezed her hand, giving her a smile.

She'd never met such a tactile man. Joey had found ways to touch her all day, whether he was wrapping his arm around her shoulders, nudging her knee beneath the table as they sipped wine, or holding her hand whenever they walked over uneven terrain outside. She was as independent as the day was long, but damn if his overtures—some were gentlemanly, some were flirty—didn't have her melting because they were so hot.

"Our family is thrilled about you featuring Rain or Shine Brewery on *ManPower*. We're hoping it will draw in more visitors to all the businesses," Everett said as he joined their group. In addition to the B&B, rental cabins, brewery, and winery, they were in the process of building an event barn for weddings, anniversaries, and other large celebrations.

Lucy introduced Everett as her "bookworm" cousin, the one

who worked his magic inside on the computer as opposed to outside in the dirt.

Joey smiled. "Miles and I have gotten countless emails from previous guests, thanking us for the exposure. One guest referred to the response from the public as sheer magic. I hope it does the same for you."

Everett soaked up that information, and Lucy could almost see the wheels spinning in his mind as he tried to figure out how to capitalize on their appearance on the show. Her cousin was a marketing guru, one of the most creative people she'd ever known, and an amazing graphic artist. He was the total package, and since he'd taken over—okay, *created* the farm's marketing and IT department—they'd already seen a huge increase in tourism, as people now viewed them as a not-to-miss destination whenever they visited the state. Of course, it also helped that they were only sixty miles outside of D.C.

She, Levi, Joey, and Everett continued to chat for a little while before Lucy realized Miles was gone. She glanced around, wondering where he had wandered off to. She wasn't surprised when she spotted him standing in a quiet corner of the dining room, chatting with Uncle Rex.

She hadn't exaggerated when she told Joey she was a huge fan of the show. She'd watched every episode at least three times, and that was before she'd found out *ManPower* was coming to Rain or Shine Brewery.

As such, it felt like she'd known Joey and Miles before they arrived. It was probably why she'd launched straight into a conversation without even remembering to introduce herself, like a crazy person. In her mind, they were already friends.

Five minutes with Joey proved her ease with him hadn't been misplaced. The real-life Joey was exactly like the guy she saw on TV. He had a boisterous personality, a great sense of humor, a contagious laugh, and she wasn't sure she'd ever been so comfortable with someone after only eight hours together. She was a social butterfly, so making friends had never been a struggle for her, but she'd never felt such an instant strong connection to someone. Being with Joey was almost effortless, and it was like they'd known each other their entire lives.

Although Lucy had to admit her thoughts were a lot more than just friendly when she looked at the man. In addition to that connection, she'd also experienced an immediate attraction to him —a crank-up-the-AC, chug-down-some-ice-water, fan-herself kind of attraction. She'd never truly understood the meaning of hot and bothered before today.

Miles, however, was a different story.

While he was obviously the straight guy on the show, the calmer, quieter host, he still came across as the kind of man you wanted as a friend. The one who would help you move, stop on the highway to help you change a tire, the fella you called when your kitchen sink was leaking.

She'd seen shades of that person today, but only the dimmest variety. For the first hour or so, she'd actually been worried he was doing the show under protest for some reason. Or—dammit— what she'd *really* been afraid of was that he didn't like *her*, and she was going to somehow ruin this chance for her whole family.

He'd become less standoffish as the day wore on, but he was by no means the man she'd been expecting to meet.

"What did you think of the farm?" Levi asked Joey.

"I love this place. I can't imagine waking up every morning to that view. It's just incredible." There was no question Joey meant what he said, and it warmed Lucy's heart because she knew what those words would mean to Levi.

"Quite a few of our now-locals were people who came to visit the town and never left."

Lucy resisted the urge to groan aloud when Scottie Grover joined their group. She hadn't realized he was here tonight. Scottie was one of the few people present who wasn't a relative. His family fell into the category he'd just described, his parents moving to Gracemont when Scottie was in sixth grade, the two of them in the same classes. Back then, Scottie had been a shy boy with a nervous stammer, and the other kids made fun of him.

When Lucy had shared that with her grandmother, Grandma did what she'd always done. Taught Lucy how to be empathetic, explaining how scary it must be for Scottie to be in a new town where he knew no one. After putting herself in Scottie's shoes, Lucy decided Grandma was right, so the next day at school, she'd introduced herself and offered her friendship.

For the rest of that year and most of junior high, she and Scottie had been friends. While Lucy was one of the more popular kids in their class, active in choir and a member of 4-H, Scottie had never warmed up to anyone else at school, opting to keep his circle small.

Small as in just him and her.

As such, he'd been clingy, insisting they didn't need to sit with anyone else at lunch or invite other friends to the movies with them. By the time high school rolled around, Lucy found it difficult being his only friend. She liked doing things with the other kids, or her sisters and cousins, which always pissed Scottie off.

To add insult to injury, he was an only child. A very *spoiled* only child. So whenever they hung out together, they did whatever Scottie wanted to do because he'd never been taught how to compromise or share or take turns.

On the last day of ninth grade, the two of them had a major falling out when Lucy chose to kick off her summer holiday by going swimming at a girlfriend's house instead of playing video games with Scottie. He hadn't taken her rejection well, and when he'd called her selfish, that straw in the camel's back broke for good, and she told him that maybe they should take a break from each other for a while.

Lucy didn't know if it was their fight that prompted it, but Scottie left Gracemont a week later to spend the summer working on his uncle's cattle ranch in Montana. When he returned just prior to the start of tenth grade, he'd sprouted six inches, lost the stammer, and gotten tan and buff from doing ranch work.

Needless to say, every sophomore girl in the school was suddenly very interested in Scottie, which was fine with Lucy. She'd had her fill. Unfortunately, he'd made her last few years of high school difficult because he still harbored a grudge, and he made sure she paid for it by acting like an arrogant, condescending ass every time their paths crossed, putting her down in front of others, treating her like she was stupid...ridiculous crap like that.

After graduation, Scottie went off to college, while she'd taken a few courses to earn her brewing certification before interning on the farm under Sam. She would have been fine if she'd never seen Scottie again, but he returned to Gracemont to join his family's business.

Two years ago, he'd been elected mayor, and now he worked closely with her uncle, who served on the town council.

"I'm Mayor Grover," Scottie said, extending his hand. Lucy resisted the urge to roll her eyes at his use of his title rather than his first name.

Joey shook his hand. "Joey Moretti."

Knowing Scottie, he'd discovered celebrities were in town and invited himself to dinner, believing someone as important as him would be expected to make an appearance. He was just as egotistical and self-important as he'd been in high school, but he was no longer holding a grudge against her these days.

Because apparently, he'd moved on to something worse.

Much worse.

Nowadays, Scottie had rewritten their past like they'd been some kind of childhood sweethearts...who were on the verge of rekindling something that had never been.

For months, she'd been perplexed about why he was suddenly paying attention to her again, until that confusion was cleared up a few weeks ago at a baby shower. That was when his mother had loudly suggested Lucy had the potential to become the future "First Lady" of Gracemont, then started spouting a bunch of bullshit about how close she and Scottie had been growing up, and how she had always noticed a special bond between the two of them.

Until then, Lucy had seriously thought Scottie was just trying —in his cocky, annoying way—to become friends again. With the new information, she'd started looking at his recent attention in a different light, and not liking what she saw. The idea that he thought she would be interested in dating him sent bile to her throat.

Hell would freeze over first.

"How was your first day in Gracemont?" Scottie asked.

"Lucy's been a very gracious and entertaining tour guide." Joey had released her hand when Levi offered him an appetizer, and he hadn't taken it back...dammit.

She was tempted to reach for it now, especially when Scottie stepped closer, looking down at her with that smug smile he thought passed for affection but came off like creepy possession.

"Lucy is the prettiest part of Gracemont," Scottie said, as if her worth was solely wrapped up in her looks.

She gritted her teeth, annoyed by his misogynistic comment, as Joey tilted his head, looking from her to Scottie curiously. She prayed he didn't think she was interested in a giant douchebag like Scottie.

"We're thrilled you've chosen to feature our small piece of heaven on your show," Scottie said.

"Stormy Weather Farm certainly is heaven," Joey agreed.

Scottie nodded. "Well, yes. The farm is nice. But I think you'll find Gracemont offers more than just homemade beer and wine."

Lucy shared a look with Levi, who looked ready to commit murder. No one in her family knew exactly how big a prick Scottie had been to her in high school. Lucy hadn't seen a reason to toss gasoline on that fire, since it was easy enough to dislike Scottie for his personality alone.

"My family owns a very successful and prosperous horse breeding farm down in the valley," Scottie said. "Many of our stallions have gone on to win some of the top competitions in racing, and trainers from all over the country come to see our horses. Perhaps you'd like to stop by for a tour while you're in town, see if you'd be interested in filming your show there."

Joey didn't look impressed. "Miles and I filmed an episode featuring the Wilshire Farm last season. They've had several horses compete in Triple Crown races. It was a good show, great ratings, but I think it's too soon to do something so similar."

If Lucy hadn't already adored Joey, this conversation with Scottie would have sealed the deal. Scottie's disdain for any horse breeding farm that was more well-renowned and successful than his family's was obvious. His eyes narrowed briefly, but he recovered quickly.

Joey leaned over to bump his shoulder against hers fondly. "The brewery is fascinating and the entire farm charming. I have no doubt the episode will be a popular one, especially when Lucy starts talking. She's a brilliant brewmaster."

"Yes. Well," Scottie said, not bothering to hide his jealousy when he wrapped his arm around her shoulders in a proprietary manner, trying to pull her away from Joey. "We'd still love the chance to show you more of our town. Wouldn't we, Lucy?"

Lucy twisted quickly, forcing Scottie's arm to drop awkwardly. "Excuse me while I go see if Aunt Claire needs any help setting the table."

"Be sure to save me a seat next to you, sweetheart," Scottie called out after her.

Lucy didn't even acknowledge his request, though it took every ounce of strength in her body not to toss him the middle finger. Instead, she stomped away, furious.

"I'm going to fucking kill him," she muttered under her breath.

"Need an alibi?" Miles asked in a low voice behind her.

She spun around, surprised by his sudden appearance, as well as the fact he wasn't scowling at her. In fact, it almost looked like he wanted to smile. "Yeah. Actually, I do. And maybe some help burying the body. You look like a strong guy."

Miles chuckled. "Done and done."

"Thanks."

"Unless it's Joey, of course. Then I'm afraid that bro code thing is going to have to take precedence."

"It's not Joey," she reassured him. "Just the mayor."

Miles's eyes widened as he glanced over his shoulder. His gaze focused directly on Scottie. "I'm assuming that's the guy who whipped out his Halloween costume early. Going as rich frat boy this year? I like the boat shoes," he added sarcastically.

Lucy took in Scottie's pale blue button-down shirt, tucked into his khaki chinos, complete with Sperrys, and laughed out loud. "That's him."

"I think we can take him," Miles said with a wink.

Before Lucy could continue the conversation, Aunt Claire called everyone to the large table. Each of the three farmhouses on the property had a similar long dining table, as family meals like this happened at least once a week.

Lucy grinned when she walked into the dining room to see Joey had gotten there early. He waved her and Miles over, the two men offering her the seat between them. Levi, who'd clearly heard Scottie's request, took one for the team, inviting Scottie to join him and Uncle Rex at the other end of the table. He caught her eye and gave her a quick wink. Her oldest cousin was getting an extra Christmas gift from her this year for that sacrifice.

Once the bowls of chili were placed in front of them and the baskets of cornbread passed around, everyone started digging in with gusto.

"This chili is incredible, Mrs. Storm," Joey said to Aunt Claire.

"Mrs. Storm was my mother-in-law. Call me Claire, please. And thank you so much. It's an old family recipe."

Mila snorted. "It's a family recipe that she has yet to share with anyone in the family."

Aunt Claire's grin was completely unrepentant. "It'll be passed on to you...eventually."

"In her will," Levi joked. "She can't take a chance on you beating her in the local chili cookoff, Mila."

Aunt Claire laughed as she tapped her oldest son on the arm affectionately. "What can I say? All those medals look so lovely hanging from the mirror on my dressing table."

"What did you think of the brewery?" Uncle Rex asked Joey and Miles. "Think it will make for a good show?"

"Absolutely." Joey wiped butter off his fingers. Given the litany of moans that slipped from his mouth every time he took a bite of cornbread or chili, there was no denying his compliment about the food was sincere. "Lucy and Sam are both engaging and easy to talk to, which is exactly what's worked so well in our more successful episodes. We've done a few shows where trying to get our guest to talk was like pulling teeth."

Miles grimaced. "We had this one guy who *literally* wouldn't talk at all. We would ask him questions, and he'd reply with one or two words, spoken straight into the camera, never to us. It was painful. For a day or two, we thought we were going to have to scrap the whole segment because nothing was salvageable."

"But you didn't have to?" Lucy's anxiety over screwing up during filming crept in because Everett was right. This show was a good opportunity for the farm.

Miles shook his head. "We were saved on the third day, when the man's adult son stopped by to see how things were going. When he realized how badly his father was doing, he stepped in to do all the talking while his dad did the work."

"The son must've taken after his mother because he was quite a character, cracking jokes, charming. Turned out to be a great show, and we're still in touch with him. The son, I mean. He came to Philadelphia a few months ago for a work trip, and the three of us went out for happy hour," Joey added.

Lucy was touched to learn that Joey and Miles stayed in contact with former guests, hoping perhaps the same might hold true for her. She mentally added Philadelphia to the list of "must see" cities on her extensive travel wish list. Not that she held out much hope for checking any of those places off anytime soon. She had responsibilities on the farm and to her family, so jetting off to see the world would just have to wait until...

Someday.

"I don't think talking is going to be a problem with Lu," Levi said. "Your struggle is going to be getting her to *stop* talking."

She shook her head as everyone laughed, secretly hoping that was true. While she hadn't admitted it to anyone, she'd lost a fair amount of sleep the past few weeks in the lead-up to Joey and Miles's arrival. "I don't know about that. The truth is, I'm really nervous. I might have to let Sam do the heavy lifting when it comes to explaining our process."

"Don't be silly. You're a natural, Lucy," Joey insisted. "The key is to forget the cameras are there. Just talk to us like you did all day and you'll be fine. And if you find yourself getting anxious, just let us know. Miles and I will talk you off the ledge. Promise."

"Besides, it's not like you're new to the camera," Mila pointed out. "You film *Kiss and Tell* all the time."

"*Kiss and Tell*?" Miles asked.

"That's different," Lucy retorted. "I'm always *behind* the camera." Then she quickly explained to Joey and Miles. "I have a little YouTube show I do called *Kiss and Tell*."

"Little," Sam scoffed. "The thing has over ten thousand subscribers, and some of her shows have had over a hundred thousand views."

Joey's eyes widened. "Seriously?"

Lucy nodded, always touched by the way her family bragged about her success, their pride in her so evident it brought tears to her eyes. "It was a hobby that sort of took off."

"And then some," Levi added. "Lu's reaching the point financially where she could make a living from it."

"You could have knocked me over with a feather when that first check appeared," she admitted.

"*Kiss and Tell* is a fine thing for now, but I'm not sure Lucy can keep up with her job on the farm *and* her hobby for the long-term," Scottie added, as if she gave two shits about his opinion.

"She's been doing fine so far," her youngest sister, Remi, replied, obviously as pissed about his comment as Lucy. "I keep telling her that she should go on the road with it. See the world like she's always talking about."

"Remi," Lucy started.

"Don't *Remi* me, Lu," her sister retorted. "While I was plastering my bedroom walls with pictures of Zac Efron, Drake, and Ryan Reynolds in high school, your walls were covered with torn-out pictures from those travel calendars Granddaddy gave you every year for Christmas."

Theo chuckled. "She still does that. Only instead of her bedroom walls, they're the screensavers on every computer in the brewhouse."

"Lucy has too many responsibilities here, Remi. She'd never leave Gracemont," Scottie said with a confidence that made the hair on the back of her neck stand up, even if it was true.

"Never say never," she replied to the idiot through gritted teeth.

Scottie, the condescending prick, just gave her a smile that said he knew he was right. The part that really pissed her off? He was. She wouldn't leave Stormy Weather Farm.

"I'm going to look up *Kiss and Tell* tonight and watch it," Joey said to Lucy. "If it feels like something we could work in, maybe you can mention it when we're filming the show."

Her eyes widened. "Oh my God. Really? That would be huge."

"We'll have to run it by our producer, and there's a good chance it won't make the final edits," Miles warned.

"I understand completely," she said quickly. "But if there's a chance to promote it, it would be great for my show."

"I'm not sure promoting it is such a good idea, Lucy," Scottie chimed in again. "While you have time for your hobby now, that might not be the case in a year or so when your life becomes more settled."

Her temper had hit the boiling point. "Excuse—"

Scottie's phone rang before she could finish calling him to task for presuming to speak for her. He excused himself from the table, claiming it was an important call. Lucy would bet twenty dollars it was his mother, calling to check in on her "sweet baby boo," a nickname that had been horrible in middle school and was even more disturbing now that he was a grown man. Not that Scottie minded. When Mommy called, he answered.

Lucy drew in a deep breath and mentally started counting to ten in her head, trying to calm down. His comments about her work being a hobby and his veiled insinuation that she intended to become "more settled" rankled.

When counting the first ten didn't work, she kept on trucking to twenty.

"You okay?" Joey murmured quietly.

She nodded.

Miles leaned closer. "Say the word and I'll grab the shovel."

She laughed, while Joey looked confused.

Fortunately, Scottie's call required him to leave to deal with an "urgent matter." After that, the dinnertime conversation was much easier, as Levi and Joey started playfully one-upping each other on sibling stories, each tale funnier than the last. Lucy laughed so much her stomach hurt.

And that wasn't the only part of her hurting. Joey's arm rested on the back of her chair, his fingers toying with her ponytail and occasionally brushing the back of her neck.

Why, oh why, did that feel so good?

She liked how big he was. She was used to being around physically large, strong men—aka, her cousins—so his size didn't intimidate her. Joey was built the same as Levi, so she felt comfortable with him, even though she was at least half a foot shorter.

She told herself she should keep her distance from him and not succumb to his charms. For all she knew, Joey Moretti was some big player, jumping from bed to bed and leaving a trail of broken hearts as he traveled across the country.

Given her concerns about doing a good job promoting the farm, she would be wise to be more professional and less flirty, more serious and less giggly. But it wasn't working. Because every time Joey shifted nearer, she couldn't resist leaning toward him, wanting to be as close to him as possible.

It wasn't until she realized Miles had noticed her actions—and was scowling again—that she finally forced herself to... well...behave.

Finally, everyone began excusing themselves, some to do farm chores, others to clean up the kitchen. Lucy led Joey and Miles to the front porch, both with a piece of homemade apple pie in their hands. She'd opted to skip dessert herself, after eating way too much chili.

The guys claimed rocking chairs while Lucy plopped down on the porch swing, all of them slowly swaying, enjoying the unseasonably warm evening.

"Tell us more about *Kiss and Tell*," Joey urged after he finished his dessert, licking the last crumbs off his fork.

"To be honest, I never intended to create a show at all." Lucy considered how much to tell them. "It's kind of a long story."

Joey placed his empty plate on the small table between his and Miles's chair, then leaned back. "We'll call it a bedtime story."

She grinned, then looked at Miles. She'd seen glimpses of the man who graced her TV at dinner, but for the last hour, he'd gone quiet after seeing her flirt with Joey. Once again, she felt like she was screwing up this opportunity.

Miles caught her looking him. "I don't mind a long story."

"My parents were killed in a car accident when I was ten," she started.

"Jesus, Lucy," Joey said, sitting upright. He'd claimed the

chair closest to her, so he was able to reach over and touch her knee. "I'm sorry."

She appreciated his kindness. "It was a long time ago. After they died, Grandma Sheila and Granddaddy Lloyd took us in. We moved from our farmhouse—the one my cousins live in now—to this one with them. They raised us. Aunt Claire and Uncle Rex helped as much as they could, but it was hard for them to do a lot with seven boys under the age of sixteen in the house. They had their own kids to raise."

"You have a great family, Lucy," Miles said. "They really do remind me of the Morettis."

After listening to Joey's stories, she wished she could meet his family because they sounded terrific. "Grandma and Granddaddy obviously hadn't expected to raise four little girls when they were in their late sixties, but they never missed a beat, smothering us in love. We had a lot of happy years. Until..."

Lucy swallowed. This was always the hard part of the story.

"Until?" Joey prompted.

"Grandma was diagnosed with dementia when she was seventy-five. We'd noticed little things, like her forgetting names, losing things, struggling to make a recipe she'd been cooking for years. After about a year, Granddaddy put his foot down and took her to the doctor. She was in the early stage of Alzheimer's at that point, but we were warned it would eventually get worse."

"That's not an easy disease...for the one suffering from it or the caregivers," Joey mused.

"You can say that again. Anyway, Granddaddy was a sucker for romcom movies, watching them with me and my sisters all the time. Or at least whenever it wasn't Remi's turn to pick that night's film. She always chose horror flicks," she said with a shudder. "If I never see one of those godawful *Saw* movies again, it'll be too soon."

Joey and Miles chuckled.

Lucy continued to sway on the swing. "One night, shortly after we learned of Grandma's diagnosis, we watched *50 First*

Dates. I'd gotten a video camera for Christmas that year, and Granddaddy asked if I would make a video of him and Grandma talking about how they met and fell in love."

"What a cool idea," Joey said.

"And because I loved romcoms as much as Granddaddy, I suggested we set it up *When Harry met Sally* style."

She could tell from Joey's smile and Miles's furrowed brow which guy got it and which one didn't, so she looked at Miles as she explained. "In that movie, there are all these snippets from couples sitting in their homes, on their couches, telling their love stories."

"Ah," Miles said.

"So we did the same. Grandma and Granddaddy sat on the couch during one of Grandma's good days and they reminisced, told their story. I was taking a graphics class at the time, and my teacher let me stay after school to edit the footage every day for a month. The first time I played it for Granddaddy, he cried, said it was perfect and just what he wanted.

"Grandma's dementia advanced quickly. For three years, he watched that video with her practically every single day. It always calmed her down whenever she was agitated. When she was having a good day, it made her smile and sometimes even laugh."

"She lived at home?" Miles asked.

Lucy nodded. "We all took turns taking care of her." She tried to quickly swipe away the tear trickling down her cheek.

Joey saw it. He rose, gesturing for her to scoot over, which she did. He joined her on the swing, reaching to take her hand in his. He gave it a gentle squeeze, then held on to it. "You gave them an amazing gift."

She sniffled. "Grandma died when I was twenty-one, then Granddaddy a year later of lung cancer. It took him quick. I think he wanted it that way. He missed Grandma too much to live without her."

Miles leaned forward. "You took care of him too?"

"I'm blessed with a big family. We set up a rotating schedule toward the end so Granddaddy was never alone. We even put a cot next to the hospital bed we moved into his room so there was always someone with him at night."

"You're too young to have lost so many people," Miles mused.

She smiled sadly. "I still have Aunt Claire and Uncle Rex, my cousins and sisters."

"So that video launched *Kiss and Tell*?" Joey asked.

Lucy nodded. "We played it at Granddaddy's funeral. He was well-loved in this area, and the funeral director said it was the largest funeral Gracemont had ever had. I was inundated with requests from people in town to film their stories after that. So, I did. It was easier to share the files on YouTube because they're quite large. One of the first couples I filmed asked if I would make their video public so they could show their kids, grandkids, and friends who lived out of state. It sort of evolved from there because it turned out, everyone in town wanted to watch everyone else's.

"Remi was the one who came up with the idea of calling it *Kiss and Tell*. So, I created an intro, got permission to share the stories, and before I knew it, my views were growing, along with my subscribers. Nowadays, I get a check from YouTube every month, and I've had at least fifty couples travel here from all over the place to sit on my couch and tell their stories."

"Damn, Lucy. That sounds amazing!" Joey lifted her hand to kiss it. Only Joey could make a simple gesture feel both sweet and sexy at the same time.

"And not at all like a hobby," Miles added with a bit of force.

She loved the way Miles didn't bother to hide the fact he didn't like Scottie or his opinions. "I love being brewmaster, but if I'm being completely honest, my dream job would be to travel the country, filming people from all different walks of life on their own couches, sharing their stories on *Kiss and Tell*. Social media is overrun with bad news and contentiousness and anger. I'd like the opportunity to spread a little happiness and show the power of love."

Joey released her hand, but only so he could wrap his arm around her shoulder, tugging her against him. Lucy couldn't resist the warmth of his hold, so once again, she leaned into it.

"I hope you get your wish because that's exactly what the world needs. And I gotta tell you, it's a great dream because traveling is the best part of making *ManPower*. Before working on the show, my explorations had been limited to the East Coast. Now, Miles and I have seen so many places we never would have even known existed before the show."

"You're so lucky." She reluctantly stood when she felt Miles's eyes on the two of them, his frown back in place. "And with that, I think I should drive you back to the cabin now because that was a ridiculously long bedtime story. I'm sure you must be sick of the sound of my voice by this point."

"Not even close," Joey reassured her, following as she led them to the truck. He claimed his spot in the middle, Miles following him in.

She started the engine, the three of them quiet as they drove down the dark lane. Once they arrived, she put the truck in park.

"I'll see you in the morning," she said, turning to look at them.

Miles nodded. "Good night, Lucy."

"Night."

Joey leaned toward her, giving her a quick kiss on the cheek. "Thanks for a great day, honey."

She smiled, her heart racing at his sweet nickname. Earlier in the day, she'd confided that she was utterly addicted to honey, eating it with everything from apples to pita to cheese. God, she really had talked their ears off.

Lucy watched as they walked to the cabin, Joey stopping at the doorway to give her a wave.

Then, she turned the truck around and headed back to her house, praying for the strength to resist this overpowering attraction.

Joey Moretti, with his winks and endearments and charming smile, was temptation incarnate, which was dangerous enough.

But Miles Williams, with his smoldering looks, deep voice, and dry wit, was turning out to be just as deadly to her libido.

This was not good.

Not good at all.

Chapter Three

"So..." Joey drawled the second they stepped into the cabin and closed the door. "What the fuck, man?"

Miles had been expecting this interrogation from his best friend all day. Mainly because he deserved it.

He'd been out of sorts since waking up this morning. And while he'd tried to pull himself together several times, something always happened to darken his mood again.

"What?" Miles might be in the wrong, but he still refused to admit to his assholery so easily.

"Where the hell was Miles Williams today? Because *this* guy," Joey waved his hand up and down in front of him, "is not him."

Miles sighed, fighting back his annoyance. His temper might be banked, but only barely. "I don't know what you're talking about," he lied.

Joey walked across the room, plopping down on the couch, clearly intent on dragging this out. Miles glanced toward his bedroom, tempted to blow him off and call it a night. Maybe he'd wake up on the right side of bed tomorrow.

"Don't even think about it."

He narrowed his eyes at his friend's threat. Even if he *did* make it to his bedroom, Joey would be right on his heels. Which meant this conversation was happening whether Miles wanted it to or not.

Joey leaned forward, placing his elbows on his knees. "You hardly spoke at all today and when you did, you were surly as hell."

"How was I supposed to get a word in edgewise? It's hard enough when it's just you, but Lucy literally never stops talking." Not that Miles had a problem with that, really. Listening to Lucy Storm talk was one of the easiest things in the world. She was entertaining, open, honest, sharp as a tack, and witty as hell.

"That's not true," Joey countered. "And I've never heard you complain about me talking too much before. Jesus, man. Most of the time we're talking over each *other*. So maybe don't throw that stone in your glass house."

Miles didn't bother continuing the argument because his best friend was right. "I'm just tired, Joey. It was a long drive, a longer day, and I didn't get a lot of sleep last night."

That part was the truth.

"Why not?"

Jesus. Miles should have known Joey would ask. If he wasn't truly so tired, he wouldn't have mentioned his bad night.

He shrugged. "No reason."

Joey, the tenacious fucker, was too damn good at smelling Miles's bullshit. "Why not?" he asked again. "I know you, man. Shared too many hotel rooms with you. You sleep like the dead every fucking night and start snoring within a minute of putting your head on the pillow."

"I don't snore." Miles's response was uttered in rote, the snoring debate a common one between them.

"I'm going to record you one night with my phone," Joey threatened, also not for the first time.

Miles glanced at his room once more.

"Forget it," Joey barked. "I'm not letting you escape. Sit down and talk to me. Because whatever this attitude is needs to pass before the cameras start rolling."

Joey had a point. Miles wasn't great at hiding his mood, something that had revealed itself during the filming of the episode with the guest who wouldn't talk. Miles's frustration had grown to the point where he'd only been shown sporadically in the early scenes that were salvaged because his resting bitch face had been out in full force.

"Rhiannon texted me."

Joey frowned. "Your ex-girlfriend Rhiannon?"

"No. Fleetwood Mac's Rhiannon," he snapped. "How many Rhiannons do you think I know?"

Joey raised his hands in surrender. "Take it easy, dude. You just caught me by surprise. I mean…when was the last time you talked to her?"

Weariness won the day.

Miles crossed the living room, dropping down into a large, overstuffed chair. He and Rhiannon had split up shortly before he and Joey met and started filming the first season of *ManPower*. He'd talked about her a few times, but just in broad strokes, mentioning she'd been a former girlfriend, that she'd been his first love, shit like that. He'd placed those little nuggets into conversations with Joey during the early days, when they were getting to know each other and their friendship was growing.

"A few weeks before we started working on *ManPower*," Miles replied.

"Nothing since then?"

Miles shook his head.

"So why now?"

Miles ran his hand over his head, leaning it back against the cushion. "It's been over two and a half years. She was due."

Joey frowned. "What's that mean?"

Miles looked at his friend, and he suddenly regretted never truly opening up to Joey about Rhiannon. If he had, he'd have said all the shitty stuff when he wasn't feeling quite so…

He couldn't figure out how he felt. He hated the words

vulnerable and *weak*, but he couldn't deny those seemed the best descriptions.

"Rhiannon has a way of reappearing in my life just when I think I've got my shit together," he admitted.

"And she ruins it?" Joey asked.

"Not intentionally. That's the problem. Rhiannon isn't a bad person. She's not vindictive or mean, and I understand why she called me last night."

"Fuck." Joey rose from the couch. "Something tells me this chat needs alcohol." He opened the fridge, reaching in to pull out two bottles of Rain or Shine Brewery beer. Joey popped the caps on them, handing Miles the Rainy Day IPA he'd liked best at the tasting, while keeping the Lightning Lu's Honey Lager for himself. Figured the idiot would prefer the one with Lucy's name on it.

Miles didn't miss the way Joey had given Lucy a kiss on the cheek and called her honey in the truck. His friend was smitten, something Miles had never seen before. Joey had accused Miles of being a different guy today, but the truth was, the way Joey acted around Lucy was out of the norm too.

If Miles wasn't feeling so out of sorts, he would ask his best friend what the hell was going on. He'd seen Joey flirt with countless women over the last two and a half years, but it was like he'd turned up the charm to full volume around Lucy.

No. That wasn't right, because Joey's actions were less charm and flirting and more like genuine affection.

For a stranger.

Every time Miles thought he'd finally broken the Joey code and figured out his best friend, Joey pulled the rug from under him, showing him something new.

Joey reclaimed his spot on the couch. "Okay. Care to enlighten me on why Rhiannon called last night?"

Miles took a swig of beer, wiping his mouth with the back of his hand. "Did I tell you Rhiannon and I have known each other our entire lives? Like literally since birth?"

Joey shook his head.

"We were neighbors, our apartments right next door to each other. Our moms have been best friends since they were in elementary school."

"I didn't know that. I always got the impression you met Rhiannon in high school."

Miles knew why Joey thought that. It was because that was what he'd allowed him to believe. "Nope. We grew up together, and for most of those younger years, we were best friends. I was closer to her than I was to my own sister."

Miles had even thought of her as a sister, until one day—one fucking random Tuesday in ninth grade—when the veil had been pulled from his eyes and suddenly, he wasn't seeing the rambunctious, dramatic girl he called "best friend". Instead, he was seeing the beautiful, sexy young woman she'd become...and he'd lost his heart to her.

Between one beat and the next, it was just there.

Love.

He'd started acting differently toward her after that. They'd just started high school, so no doubt his fourteen-year-old hormones had kicked into overdrive. At first, Rhiannon had rebuffed his flirting, thinking he was joking or even crazy. It took most of their freshmen year for him to convince her that his feelings were sincere. Just before summer break started, he'd gotten her to say yes to a date, and then a first kiss, and from that point on, they were boyfriend and girlfriend.

"Obviously, those feelings changed," Joey said, pulling him from his thoughts.

Miles nodded. "We started dating when we were fourteen. Of course, we were teenagers in high school and prone to drama, so there were a few mini breakups along the way. Usually over stupid shit, like her thinking I wasn't paying enough attention to her, or me getting jealous whenever I thought she was flirting with another guy."

"Sounds like High School Dating 101." Joey crossed his ankle over his knee, settling in. It amused Miles because Joey really did love a good story.

"What is this? Another bedtime story?" he joked.

Joey surprised him by not laughing. "No. This is something you should have told me a long time ago."

Miles couldn't argue with that, couldn't even figure out what had held him back. There was very little he and Joey hadn't shared with each other. Rhiannon had been Miles's big holdout.

"What happened after graduation?" Joey asked, getting them back on track.

"We kept dating. Got our own apartment in Queens, not far from where our mothers still live, and we started doing the adult thing. Rhiannon was an aspiring actress with her sights set on Broadway. She waited tables between auditions. I was doing some professional voiceover work, but I made most of the money needed to pay the rent by driving a taxi. We lived together for four years, until..."

"Until?"

"She was waiting for me one night when I got home from work. Said she couldn't do it anymore."

Joey tilted his head, confused. "Why not?"

"We'd been a couple for over seven years. We'd been each other's first kiss, first love, first time, first fucking *everything*. First...and only."

Joey grimaced. "Ah. She wanted to sow her wild oats."

"Yeah. Something like that. She'd been getting constant rejections after her auditions, so she decided she was wasting her time on New York and Broadway. She'd come to the conclusion her dreams were going to come true in Hollywood."

Joey sighed. "So she left?"

"Yep. And that was when she added another first to my list. She was the first girl to ever break my heart. Shit, she's the *only* one to ever do that." He paused, then added, "A few times."

Joey winced. "Damn, man. She kept coming back?"

"We didn't talk for two years after she moved to California.

My heart was shattered, and I dealt with the pain by staying pissed off at her. Then she came home for Christmas. You remember me saying our moms are best friends, right? Part of that friendship includes spending the holidays together. I showed up at Mom's place Christmas Eve, and there was Rhiannon. She hadn't told anyone she was coming, wanted it to be a surprise for her mom."

"Kind of a shitty thing to do," Joey grumbled. "She should have told you, at least."

Miles lifted one shoulder casually. "She knew I'd stay away if she'd told me she was going to be there, and that I wouldn't give her a chance to apologize and tell me how wrong she'd been."

Joey's face proved he knew where this story was going. "Don't give me all the nitty-gritty details. Just say it."

"I accepted her apology, and we spent the rest of the holidays unwrapping each other in bed. Hollywood hadn't been much nicer to her than Broadway, and I thought that meant she was coming home, that we were working on rebuilding our relationship."

"She went back to California?"

"Three weeks later. Her agent called and said she'd gotten a part in some stupid commercial. She hopped on that plane so fast, I didn't even have the chance to say goodbye. She packed her bag and left a note while I was at work."

"Heartbreak number two."

Miles nodded. "Wasn't as bad that time, probably because I had experience with it, and we'd only been together for three weeks."

"Maybe so, but, dude. After all that, why would you let her walk back into your life a third time?"

Miles drained the rest of his beer, debating opening a second. "I didn't think I would. I got that gig, my big break. You know the one. Doing the voice in that animated cartoon. The job was in California. Where I knew no one. Rhiannon reached out—as a friend—and offered to show me around, help me find an apartment, shit like that. I told myself I could handle the two of us just being friends because I missed her, missed having her in my life."

Joey rolled his eyes and looked like he wanted to argue, but Miles cut him off.

"We'd spent our whole lives together," he stressed. "And I had her mom *and* mine chirping in my ear, telling me that Rhiannon missed me too."

Joey groaned.

"They're still convinced that Rhiannon and I are going to get married one day and give them grandbabies."

"Bro."

Miles chuckled sadly. "Yeah. I know."

"So she gave you the 'we'll just be friends' line?"

"And I fell for it, hook, line, and sinker."

"How long were you *just friends*?" Joey's question proved just how well he knew Miles.

"Six weeks."

Joey laughed. "And how long did you date that time?"

Miles grimaced. "Two years. And before you have to ask, she broke it off because she met someone else. Another aspiring actor. They'd run into each other at a few auditions and started talking. One day, they met for coffee."

"She cheated on you?!"

"Not really. They hadn't progressed beyond a couple coffee dates before she dumped me. Said she felt a spark with the guy."

"Jesus," Joey muttered.

"Anyway, it worked out for the best because a week after that, I landed the *ManPower* gig, and we've been on the road ever since." Miles had divided the time he and Joey weren't filming between spending the occasional week with his mom in New York and staying with Joey, who'd maintained the lease on his apartment in Philadelphia.

Joey finished his beer and set the empty bottle on the coffee table. "Guess I see what you mean when you say she was due. It's been a couple years. Why did she call last night?"

"She wound up dating that guy from the coffee shop. The relationship ended a few weeks ago because she finally got her dream, mostly. She's been offered a role in an off-Broadway play. She's moving back to New York. The boyfriend decided to stick it out in California, so they parted ways."

"That still doesn't tell me why she called *you*." Joey really wasn't letting him get away with shit tonight.

"She said she just wanted to catch up, see how I was doing, find out if I was happy. Apparently, she's never missed an episode of *ManPower*. We talked until nearly two a.m., and it was nice. Two old friends reminiscing."

Joey pinched the bridge of his nose, shaking his head.

"I'm not going back there again, Joey," Miles said, trying to reassure himself as much as his best friend. "I'm older and wiser. I swear it."

"Maybe you need to be specific. Not going back where?"

"I'm not dating her again. Ever."

"Yeah." Joey blew out a long breath, clearly unhappy. "That's what I thought you meant."

Miles frowned. "What's that supposed to mean?"

"You planning on starting the friendship back up?"

Miles froze for a moment—because he knew which answer was the correct one. He just wasn't sure it was the *true* one. Rhiannon still held a big piece of his heart, and not just the romantic chunk. He would always love the girl who was also his childhood playmate, his best friend.

Joey lifted his head, held his gaze, and Miles forced himself to remain steady, to keep his poker face firmly in place as he said, "No. I'm not."

Whatever Joey saw must have been convincing. "Okay," he said at last. "I believe you."

Miles did not like that answer. It would have been a hell of a lot easier if Joey had called him a liar. Since he was pretty sure that was all he could live up to.

"But, Miles, you're going to have to dial this grumpiness back a notch or twenty. Because you're taking it out on my girl, and she doesn't deserve it."

Miles's eyes flew heavenward. "*Your* girl, huh? You realize you've known her less than twenty-four hours."

Joey's crooked smile proved he didn't think that mattered one damn bit. "I don't know how to explain it, Miles. I'm thirty-seven years old, for God's sake, and I've dated a lot of women. I've never looked at one and felt like...like I *knew* her. Like she's the person I've spent my whole life looking for. I know that sounds crazy—"

"It sounds very crazy," Miles interjected.

"I was pulling your leg when I said I was going to marry her."

"I figured as much," Miles murmured.

"I chalked my initial response up to lust because you have to admit, the woman is beautiful."

"She is." There was no point in Miles trying to deny it. Joey would know he was lying.

"But," Joey continued, "somewhere along the line today, that joke stopped being funny. Started feeling real. I expected the instant attraction to fade. If anything, it's grown stronger. Which is freaking me out, because we're only scheduled to be here five days, and I know that's not enough time to get to know her, to see if this insanity is temporary or if soul mates are a real thing."

"Joey," Miles said.

Joey held his hand up. "I know you're going to tell me to chill out, but I can't. It's not in my nature when it comes to stuff like this. So I'm going spend every second I'm here wooing the hell out of Ms. Lucy Storm."

Miles wasn't sure how to respond. For one thing, Joey *did* sound insane. And for another, more disturbing reason—he didn't sound insane at all.

He'd spent the entire day with Lucy and Joey, and the truth was, while he'd never really thought his best friend had a type, Lucy was it. As far as Miles could tell, she was perfect for his single buddy.

Not that Joey was a confirmed bachelor, because he didn't

covet his solitary life or try to hold on to it. Quite the opposite. Joey, a true Moretti, had been none too patiently waiting to find what all his siblings had found.

True love.

Of course, none of them had declared they'd found their future wives within five minutes of meeting them, but at least Joey hadn't gone *too* overboard on the flirting and scared Lucy off.

On the contrary, Lucy hadn't been bothered by Joey's attention at all. Instead, she appeared flattered by it, and she'd definitely been flirting back. Miles knew for a fact the attraction wasn't one-sided.

"You like her, don't you?" Joey asked, genuine concern in his tone, as if Miles's disapproval would be a deal-breaker. "You didn't mean what you said about her talking too much, right?"

Miles lifted his hand, palm forward. "I like Lucy. How could anyone *not* like her? She's perfect." He stupidly paused...revealing a hand he hadn't meant to show Joey.

When Joey tilted his head, confused, Miles panicked, grasping for a save. "She's perfect for *you*, I meant to say." He hoped he'd been quick enough.

When Joey didn't press the point, he breathed a sigh of relief.

"Yeah. I think she is. Well," Joey said, rising and stretching. "You can stick a fork in me, because I am *done*."

Miles grinned at his silly, old-fashioned expression, perfectly aware it was one Joey had picked up from his nonno. He followed suit, standing as well. "Me too."

The two of them said good night, then headed to their bedrooms.

Miles closed the door behind him, taking care of business in the bathroom before walking to the bed. Pulling down the covers, he sank onto the soft mattress, wondering when the last time was that he'd been this exhausted—physically and emotionally.

Before he could come up with an answer, his phone pinged. He sighed and considered ignoring it because he knew who was texting him. After a minute or two, he gave in and picked up his phone. Because apparently, he was a glutton for punishment.

Sure enough, there was a photo of Rhiannon. She'd started practice on her new play today. Someone must have snapped the picture for her because in it, she stood on the stage alone, reading from the script, one arm raised dramatically.

She was beautiful with her shoulder-length black hair, dark skin, and expressive eyes that flashed fire when she was angry or in the throes of passion, and while it was hard to admit, there was no denying she took his breath away just as much now as she had that first random day in ninth grade.

For a moment he considered responding, but he talked himself out of it. Then he lifted his finger, intent on tapping a heart on it.

He stopped himself from doing that too.

He'd opened a door when he answered the phone last night. He'd known that even before he picked up his cell, but he still did it. He wasn't sure why. Part of him wondered if it had been loneliness driving his ill-considered action. Or maybe he was suffering from the same fate as his best friend, longing for the kind of meaningful connection every single Moretti had found in the past few years.

He didn't want to be a bachelor any more than Joey did.

Rhiannon was as close as he'd ever gotten to forever, and as much as he hated it, she was still his Kryptonite. Going back to her was a one-way street to heartache. He knew that.

Or at least, he knew he *should* know that.

Hope was a dangerous beast.

So answering the phone last night?

It had been the height of stupidity.

Rhiannon, true to fashion, had seized that open door and walked right on in, making herself at home.

In addition to the picture of her onstage, she'd texted him two other photos today, as if they'd never skipped a beat, as if they were still best friends who constantly shared bits and pieces of their days. The first photo had come through as soon as they'd reached the top of the mountain. It was a selfie of her with his mom. She'd texted, *Look who I just ran into.*

The second had come at the beginning of the farm tour, and it was a photo of their childhood apartment building, with their moms sitting on the front stoop, heads close together, gossiping. With that one, she texted, *Some things never change.*

Miles forced himself to put the phone down without replying to any of her texts. He needed to stop the madness right here.

No replies.

No heart emoji.

He needed to slam the door closed and dead bolt the stupid thing.

He closed his eyes, but unfortunately his body hadn't sent word to his brain that it was time to sleep, because his thoughts wouldn't stop whirling, touching on one topic before moving on to another, then another.

He replayed Rhiannon's call in his mind, then he tried to force himself to think about Lucy's tour of the brewery, considering questions he might want to ask her and Sam during their demonstration.

Unfortunately, thinking about Lucy sent his brain in a different direction...and he was reminded of her story about *Kiss and Tell* and how it had started. It had touched him, and opened his eyes to exactly what Joey had seen in her.

She was sweet and sexy and special.

Curiosity got the better of him, so he decided he'd put his sleepless night to good use.

Grabbing his phone again, he clicked on the YouTube app and looked up *Kiss and Tell*. He was surprised by how many videos were there. Lucy's family was right. Her show had gone well beyond a hobby because he couldn't begin to imagine how many hours of work she'd put into producing so many shows. His eyes widened when he saw the number of views on some of them. He'd venture to guess she was making a decent amount of money each month, enough that she was probably close to earning a living wage from the show.

Scrolling through the list, he searched until he found her first video—the one she'd made of her grandparents. Clicking on it, he smiled as he watched the cute intro Lucy had created for the show. It included a picture of her, sitting on the porch of her farmhouse, smiling that smile that had only wavered whenever he'd said something douche-y today. Tomorrow, he would have to make up for his bad first impression.

The intro was followed by a short clip of Lucy talking about her guests briefly. She didn't speak for more than a minute or two, and he suspected that was because she wanted the true stars of the show to get the majority of the airtime.

He watched as her grandparents talked to the camera as well as each other, holding hands the entire time, telling their story together. It was engaging and touching and, at times, funny. Miles swallowed hard to dislodge the lump in his throat as the video came to an end.

One show in and he was hooked. He hit the subscribe button because he was a fan.

He clicked on another episode, watching Lucy's comments about her guests and a few minutes of their story. Then he clicked on another, and another.

For the better part of two hours—he was going to pay for this tomorrow—he clicked on nearly every episode, no longer watching the lovers "kiss and tell," but instead listening to Lucy's introductions.

He'd let Joey believe his bad mood was solely driven by Rhiannon's reappearance in his life, and for the better part of the day, that had been true. However, by dinner, it was something else putting him out of sorts.

It was Joey himself.

And Lucy.

The way he'd flirted with her at dinner, the way he'd rested his hand on the back of her chair, how he kept inching closer.

Joey had made that joke about Lucy being the woman he was going to marry, and Miles couldn't stop himself from feeling...

Jealous.

Miles rubbed his weary eyes, trying to tell himself that was the wrong word. However, just like *vulnerable* and *weak*, it was the only one that came close to explaining why he'd had to look away when Joey sat down next to Lucy on the porch swing and held her hand.

He tried to tell himself it wasn't the Lucy he was interested in. That his envy was born from the idea that Joey was on the cusp of getting what he'd wanted for so long.

Rhiannon's call had opened a wound Miles had believed long since healed. He could see now he'd merely been living with a scab, one she'd ripped off last night, putting him in one hell of a fucked-up headspace.

Miles sighed, too damn tired to try to deal with so many fucking emotions.

Weakness and vulnerability wrapped in anger and heartbreak.

Jealousy draped in a thick layer of loneliness.

And worse of all, lust and longing enveloped in a desire he shouldn't allow because Joey and Lucy fit together.

When that realization sank in, all the bad feelings morphed into something even worse.

Desperation.

That was when Miles lifted his phone, opened his text messages, and added a heart to all three of Rhiannon's photos.

Chapter Four

Joey ran a brush through his hair, then slapped on some cologne. He'd changed from his recently gifted Rain or Shine Brewery T-shirt into a white button-down one and dark jeans. He didn't have a clue what they were doing tonight, and he didn't care. Once they'd finished filming this afternoon, Lucy had asked him and Miles if they wanted to hang out for the evening and he had been so thrilled by the chance to spend more time with her, he'd said yes without asking a single question about her plans.

Yesterday had been a wash as far as his pursuit of the beautiful brewmaster. She'd been working in the brewhouse all day, while he'd traipsed around the mountain with Miles, their producer, the director, and the camera crew, as well as Levi—who maintained the barley fields and hop yards—shooting hour after hour of B-roll footage.

The workday had run too late, and he and Miles had been so exhausted, they'd opted for a simple dinner in their cabin. Of course, their idea of simple fare and Claire's differed greatly. Miles's eyes had nearly popped out of his head when the kind woman walked in with a picnic basket filled with fried chicken, potato, macaroni, and green salads, as well as two huge slabs of pumpkin pie, complete with whipped cream. It had been a feast fit for at least ten people, but the two of them had managed to put a hell of a dent in it because it was impossible to stop eating such delicious food.

When they were finally able to rise from the table, they'd hit the couch, turned on the TV, and fallen asleep where they sat within minutes. Somewhere in the middle of the night, they'd moved to their beds, but it hadn't been soon enough for Joey, as he'd spent the first hour of this morning trying to work the kinks out of his stiff neck.

Today, they'd begun filming the show, breaking the process of brewing beer into smaller pieces that the editing crew would piece together into a cohesive episode. Lucy had been incredible in front of the camera, just as he expected. She'd done exactly as he advised, talking to him and Miles like the cameras weren't even there. Her personality had shone through, and he knew this episode was going to be their best of the season. When he'd mentioned it to Miles, his best friend suggested they wait until after filming the rest of the episodes before making that kind of call.

Joey still wasn't sure how to deal with the Miles who'd shown up on the mountain because his hot-and-cold demeanor was giving him whiplash. Yesterday, during their tour with Levi, Miles had been back to his old self, laid-back, inquisitive, witty. It was a great day and they'd gotten some awesome footage.

Today had been a mix. When the cameras were rolling, Miles was totally on point, playing straight man to Joey's antics, asking great questions, looking totally at ease.

The problem was when they *weren't* filming. The second the director called cut, Miles drifted away from him and Lucy, conversing with the crew or Sam, and generally ignoring the two of them.

At first, he thought his best friend was giving him time alone with Lucy so he could get to know her better. As the day wore on, however, Joey couldn't help but notice the way Miles was watching them, even while in conversation with others, always with that resting bitch face firmly in place.

Miles had assured him that he liked Lucy, claiming she was perfect for him. But those words didn't match the dark looks he kept shooting in their direction. Miles had blamed his bad mood on Rhiannon, but Joey started to suspect that was a lie. Something else was going on in Miles's head, though Joey didn't have a clue what.

"You ready?" Miles called from the living room.

Joey walked out to join him, throwing a lightweight jacket on. "Yep."

It was a pleasant evening, the setting sun skirting the line of the horizon, so the two of them planned to walk to the main farmhouse to join Lucy there.

He noticed Miles had taken some care with his appearance too, his hair still damp from a shower, his face freshly shaved. He was wearing a lightweight navy-blue sweater, faded jeans, and he'd thrown his favorite leather jacket on top.

Miles was a good-looking guy, with dark skin, black hair, and deep brown eyes. Like Joey, he was committed to his workout routine. Neither of them lifted weights with the goal of looking like bodybuilders. Instead, their workouts focused on definition rather than building mass. Joey had been amused by the way his female cousins and their friends had fluttered around Miles the first time he'd brought him along to meet the family.

"Looking good, man," Joey said.

"Oh, I know." Miles gave him a crooked grin as he flexed one of his biceps. "Eat your heart out."

Joey laughed as they left the cabin, heading down the quiet dirt lane to the farmhouse.

"Filming's going so great, I'm worried we might finish up tomorrow," Joey mused.

Miles chuckled. "Don't worry, Romeo. Even if we do, we're not scheduled to be in Nashville until the beginning of November. I have a feeling the Storms would let us hang out until then. And by the Storms, I mean Lucy. I don't think she's in a hurry for you to leave either."

Joey glanced over at Miles. "You think?"

"She barely left your side all day, bro."

Joey liked what Miles was saying, but damn if his face wasn't all wrong again, his scowl back in place. They fell silent for a little while, Joey enjoying the solitude of their surroundings. Even Miles finally seemed to be taken by the beauty around him, pointing out a fat squirrel, then wondering what kind of bird it was that landed in a tree as they passed.

When they reached the farmhouse, Lucy was waiting for them on the porch swing, looking adorable in her ripped jeans, ankle boots, and V-neck white T-shirt that showed the perfect amount of cleavage. She also wore a blue-and-tan geometric print cardigan sweater that hung past her knees. She was the very picture of fall.

The past few days, she'd worn her hair in a ponytail, so this was the first time Joey had seen her with her long blonde hair hanging loose and wavy over her shoulders. He sucked in a breath when she rose...and for a moment, he thought he heard Miles do the same.

"Hey," she said, giving them a wave. "You guys look great."

Joey's gaze took her in from head to toe, and he had to give his dick the "down, boy" command.

Miles cleared his throat. "So, what's the plan?"

"I thought I'd let y'all decide," she said, drawling the words *you all* in that sweet Southern accent.

"Okay. Hit us with our options. What's fun to do in Gracemont?" Joey asked.

Lucy laughed. "Well, considering you guys are from big cities, I think you're going to be disappointed in your limited choices. Buuuuut...I promise you that what we lack in quantity, we make up for in quality."

Before she could begin her list, Theo and Remi walked out of the house and joined Lucy on the porch.

"These guys are going with us too," Lucy added.

Joey had already chatted with Theo, whom they'd also interviewed today, as he managed the brewhouse, ordering supplies, equipment, and ingredients to make the beer, as well as hiring and training employees to work the tasting room.

As for Lucy's younger sister, he'd only spent a little bit of time with her at dinner their first night here. Regardless, Remi made an impression. The woman had a cutting wit, cussed like a sailor, and laughed loudly enough to shake the rafters. She reminded him a lot of his brother Gio's girlfriend. Keeley was a live wire who kept Gio and their partner, Rafe, on their toes twenty-four seven.

So, needless to say, Joey thought Remi rocked.

"What did you guys decide to do?" Theo asked.

"We're still waiting for Lucy to hit us with our choices," Miles said as the three Storms left the porch and joined them in the yard.

"Well," Lucy started. "We could go bowling. And before you say no," she added, despite the fact neither he nor Miles rejected the idea, "the bowling alley also has an old-school arcade. It's got pinball, Donkey Kong, Galaga, PacMan, and one of those old-fashioned shooting galleries, where things move or squirt water if you hit the targets."

Remi rolled her eyes. "You are ridiculously enthralled by that stupid shooting gallery."

Then Remi quickly added to the list, clearly not down for bowling or arcade games. "Another cool thing we could do is go to the drive-in. Not sure what's playing tonight, but it's always a double feature. If we opt for that, we could throw a bunch of camp chairs and blankets into the bed of one of the trucks and bundle up to watch."

Theo groaned at that suggestion. "You *are* aware the temperature is supposed to drop significantly tonight. We'd freeze our asses off." He turned to Miles and Joey. "The last option is Whiskey Abbey. It's a local bar that plays country music. They have ax throwing and a dance floor—and it's warm."

"You could always take a flask of bourbon to the movies," Remi said. "That'll keep you warm enough."

Theo shoulder-bumped Remi. "Or I can have my bourbon in a glass with ice at the bar."

Joey glanced at Miles. "I'm leaning toward the bar. You?"

Miles nodded, looking relieved they were thinking along the same lines. Joey wasn't a bad bowler, but after three fairly long days, the idea of just chilling with beers and fun people sounded a hell of a lot easier.

"Perfect," Lucy said. "Theo, can we take your car? It's the biggest."

Theo agreed and they all piled into his RAV4.

This was the first time Joey and Miles had left the mountain since their steep climb up three days earlier. The journey down was just as daunting, the near-vertical decline full of twists and turns.

"We've made improvements to the road leading to the farm over the years," Theo told Joey, who had claimed the passenger seat and was resting his hands on the dashboard as they descended. "Used to be nothing but one hairpin turn after another. When we decided to open the brewery and winery to the public, we knew we'd need a better road. We couldn't get rid of all the turns, but at least they're less harrowing."

Joey chuckled. "Good to know you think this is less harrowing."

Then he glanced over his shoulder. He'd intended to climb into the backseat with Lucy and Miles, but Remi had gotten there first, insisting he take the front seat, since he was taller. He tried not to be jealous of the fact that Miles and Lucy were smooshed up next to each other, thanks to Theo making a sharp left turn.

Joey half expected Miles to be uncomfortable with the seating arrangement, since he'd been so hell-bent on keeping his distance from Lucy. So he was surprised when he spotted the two of them grinning at each other when she was tilted into him by centrifugal force, his body pressed against the door. Remi, not to be left out, leaned heavier than she needed to into her sister, so the three of them looked like they were on an amusement park ride together.

When Theo turned to the right, they laughed as they shifted in unison, pushing Remi against the opposite door.

Conversation never waned during the drive off the mountain and along Main Street, especially with Remi, Theo, and Lucy taking turns discussing various points of interests they passed. Joey had never found the idea of living in a small town appealing, but as he listened to their stories, he almost envied the Storms getting to grow up in a place where everyone knew everyone else.

"It's a shame you weren't here two weeks earlier," Remi said. "You guys just missed the Fall Harvest festival. It's always the second weekend in October, and we have a parade and a carnival, pie baking contests, and an eighties dance. They even close schools on that Friday. It's a blast every year."

"Sounds great. We'll have to put it on our schedule for next year," Joey said, serious about adding the event on his calendar. He'd grab hold of any reason to make return trips to Gracemont.

"Well, here we are." Theo pulled into the crowded parking lot of Whiskey Abbey. "Wednesdays are ladies' night, so Abbey—the owner—always pulls in a good midweek crowd."

Joey wrapped his arm around Lucy's shoulders in a friendly way as they walked into the bar. The dance floor was filled with countless people doing a line dance to the old country hit "Watermelon Crawl." Remi didn't miss a beat, racing to the floor to hop in.

Theo shook his head, amused, then pointed to an available table off to the right. "Y'all wanna claim the table? I'll grab us a couple pitchers from the bar. Rain or Shine, okay?"

Joey grinned and nodded. "What do you think?"

"Need a hand?" Miles offered.

"Sure."

Joey and Lucy sat at the table, watching Remi on the dance floor. The woman had some awesome moves.

"Your sister really seems to like to dance."

Lucy smiled. "She loves it, and she's so good at it. Meanwhile, I have two left feet."

Joey chuckled. "Seriously?"

"Yep. I don't even attempt to line dance anymore because I can assure you, if everyone else is going left, my ass will be boot-scooting to the right. Remi's declared me a dance floor hazard."

"Maybe so, but I'm still planning to drag you out there for a slow song," Joey warned her.

Lucy lit up. "I'd love that." Unfortunately, her smile didn't last long as she glanced toward the bar. "Can I ask you something?"

"Of course."

"Did I do something to piss Miles off. I mean...he was cool in the car just now, but most of today during the filming, I got the impression he was avoiding me."

Joey was hoping Lucy hadn't noticed Miles keeping his distance because he'd suspected it would hurt her feelings. Looked like he was right.

"You didn't do anything wrong," he reassured her, wondering if he should offer her more, then realizing he didn't know what he'd say. He couldn't figure out Miles's deal himself.

"Okay," she replied, clearly unconvinced. "But you should probably know something else about me."

"Another confession?" he asked, recalling her first-day admission about talking too much when she was nervous or excited.

"I have a fatal flaw."

Joey shook his head. "I already don't believe you. You have no flaws."

Lucy laughed, delighted. "You sure are a charmer, Joey Moretti."

"That wasn't charm. It was me stating a fact. You're easy to be with, Lucy. I'm really happy for the chance to get to know you."

Her eyes softened. "I feel the same way."

They held each other's gazes for nearly a minute, and for the first time, Joey started to get a sense that he wasn't the only one lost to insanity, falling way too fucking fast.

She gave him a wry smile. "I probably shouldn't say this, but I'm going to be really sad when you leave. Time is moving too fast."

Joey was blown away by her openness, her willingness to share her feelings without knowing if they were returned. "Yeah. I'm not looking forward to leaving either. And you're right, the days are flying by. Looks like we need to figure out a way we can see each other again. Miles and I will be traveling off and on for six months, with a longish break for the holidays in between, but Philadelphia and Gracemont aren't that far away. Maybe you could get some time off to travel to Philly. I could show you the city and you could meet my family."

Lucy's eyes sparkled. "I would love that."

"Then it's a date." He leaned toward her, giving her a kiss on the cheek, enjoying the way it made her blush.

"A date," she repeated softly.

Then Joey recalled the way this conversation had begun. "Although maybe you'd better tell me what this fatal flaw is before we start planning an itinerary," he teased.

She glanced over her shoulder at Miles, who was still standing at the bar, laughing with Theo. "I can't stand it when people don't like me. Or maybe I should say when people I like don't like me back. I don't really care if assholes don't like me," she added, giggling.

He hadn't set her mind at ease about Miles at all. "He *does* like you, Lucy."

She lifted one shoulder as if to shrug off his reassurance. "He seems to have warmed up to everyone else on the farm. With me... he gets a lot chillier."

Before Joey could come up with a response to that, Remi returned to the table and, a couple of minutes later, Miles and Theo arrived with the pitchers of beer.

Remi poured a glass for each of them, claiming she was an

expert pourer, thanks to her experience as a server at the brew-house. Miles and Lucy smiled widely and "hmmed" in apprecia-tions after they took a sip. Something Theo and Remi found hilarious.

"Oh my God, Lu," Remi exclaimed loudly. "Miles is as big a beer snob as you."

"I just appreciate good beer," Miles said, jerking his thumb toward Joey. "While this dude downs Bud Light like it's some-thing special."

Lucy crinkled her nose adorably.

They continued to drink and chat, ordering several appetizers for the table to share. The night was just as relaxing as Joey had hoped for, the Storm family great company. Even Miles had loos-ened up, letting Remi drag him to the dance floor to teach him a country line dance, which was hilarious to watch. Miles was a good dancer, but his skills were of the bump-and-grind variety, not the heel-toe, do-si-do kind.

They'd been at the bar just over an hour when the mayor showed up. Joey had taken an instant disliking to the asshole, and his feelings toward Scottie Grover weren't changing tonight. Espe-cially when the man made a beeline for Lucy.

"Lucy," the smarmy guy said, bending over to give her a kiss on the cheek, one that didn't land because she leaned away quickly. "You should have told me you were going out."

"Why would I do that?" she asked.

"So I could join you," Scottie said, as if Lucy were the igno-rant one, not him.

Lucy's lack of love for the mayor was evident to everyone except Scottie, the clueless wonder.

"How did you know I was here?" she asked.

Scottie pointed to three women sitting at a nearby table, one of them waving at Lucy. "Jess texted me. She and her girlfriends never miss ladies' night." Scottie glanced at him and Miles, chest puffed out with self-importance as he said, "Jess is my PA. I couldn't live without her." He studied the five chairs at the table, all claimed, then glanced around for an extra one at the surrounding tables.

Mercifully, the bar was packed.

"Well, it was just peachy running into you, Scottie," Remi said, her tone making it perfectly clear she meant the opposite. "See you around."

It was the least subtle dismissal in history, and if Joey hadn't already thought Remi was amazing, that would have sealed the deal. Especially when Scottie frowned at her obvious insult and stormed off. Fortunately, someone called out to him, and Joey watched as he pulled on his politician mask to start shaking hands.

"Gotta admit, I'm curious how a guy like that was elected mayor," Joey mused.

Remi snorted, Theo rolled his eyes, and Lucy laughed as she said, "He ran uncontested."

He chuckled. "And now it makes sense."

Lucy had made it clear she was limiting her dancing to the slow songs, so Joey quickly claimed the next two, dragging her out before Scottie could reach their table. The mayor shot daggers at Joey both times, upset at having his prize taken away. The man's annoyance pleased him too much, so Joey countered the dirty looks with smug grins. Theo joined the game, cockblocking Scottie on the third song, but only because Joey had been in the restroom and unavailable.

When another slow country ballad started to play, Joey looked at Lucy and quickly tilted his head toward Miles, who wasn't looking their direction.

She nodded at the unspoken suggestion, asking Miles to dance. Joey tried not to laugh when his best friend shot him an alarmed look, as if he expected Joey to be pissed off.

Lucy wanted him to like her, so Joey was going to make sure she got what she wanted.

"Don't be surprised if she steps on your feet," Joey joked, before leaning close to mutter in his friend's ear. "And act fast. Mayor Douchebag is en route."

Miles rolled his eyes, rising quickly and taking Lucy's hand. "You act like Lucy's the one to blame when the problem is you, Joey. Let me show you how a *real* man leads," he bragged.

Joey pitched a pretzel at him, watching as the two of them made their way to the floor before treating himself to a quick peek at Scottie's irritated face.

Miles took Lucy in his arms, her hands resting on his best friend's broad shoulders as Kenny Chesney's "Take Her Home" played. If Joey had expected the dance to be stiff or awkward, he would have been disappointed.

In fact...

Joey leaned forward, grateful Remi and Theo had found dance partners as well and were also on the floor. Because it gave Joey the chance to make sure he was seeing what he *thought* he was.

Miles was focused on Lucy, who was peering up at him through those long, thick lashes of hers. The two of them were staring into each other's eyes, Miles smiling at whatever Lucy was saying. He sure as shit wasn't looking at her like she talked too much.

Nope. He was looking at her like a man who was hanging on her every word.

He was looking at her exactly the same way Joey had when *he'd* danced with her.

"Jesus," he muttered.

Suddenly, he was reexamining Miles's behavior the past few days...and seeing things in a very different light. Miles hadn't been keeping his distance from Lucy because he didn't like her or because he was distracted about Rhiannon.

Miles was holding himself apart because Joey had expressed an interest in the beautiful brewmaster first. And Miles, good friend that he was, was respecting that, stepping aside, giving him a chance to form a connection.

Joey prayed the couple on the dance floor didn't look his direction because they would think he was drunk as a skunk if they saw him sitting there, watching them with a big goofy grin on his face.

Something Joey never imagined had just presented itself, and rather than shove that thought into a dark corner, he waved it in.

Because the future was right there, spinning around on that floor.

Joey was the last single Moretti standing. Unbeknownst to some, he wasn't holding on to his bachelorhood because he enjoyed it.

He was holding out for something special.

It was true love he was seeking, and he was determined he wouldn't settle down with just anyone simply to be married. He wanted a love like his parents had, one so enduring, his dad hadn't even considered dating another woman after his mother's untimely passing nearly twenty years earlier. How many times had Dad said he couldn't give his heart to another woman when it still belonged to Mom?

Joey wanted *that*. Wanted to meet the person who completed him. He felt like Lucy could be that person. All he needed in order to be sure was the very thing he'd asked her for.

Time. Time and a chance to see if this instant connection he felt was genuine.

So yeah.

True love. That's what Joey had been telling himself he was holding out for. And while that desire was genuine...he could see now that perhaps that wasn't *all* he wanted.

He wanted more.

It was his sister Layla's fault. And his brother Tony's. And Gio's and Luca's.

His siblings hadn't found just *one* true love. They'd found two. All of them living in committed threesomes.

Each of his brothers' throuple relationships varied, but they were all making it work, each of them living with their best friends, as well as the women who'd stolen their hearts.

Joey hadn't considered that was what he wanted as well until this very instant.

Watching Lucy and Miles together, seeing the way they were looking at each other...

He drew in a deep breath because...

God, they were beautiful together. Joey and Miles had been friends for years, but he'd never seen his friend look quite as...

Joey struggled for the word. He'd met Miles post-Rhiannon, so he'd only ever known the Miles who lived with a broken heart. The guy currently swaying on that dance floor with Lucy, looking down at her like she hung the moon, was one he'd never seen before. There was a sudden peace in Miles's expression, as if every sadness, every hurt, every drop of anger had evaporated inside him, leaving this new man behind instead.

Joey had never realized how unhappy his best friend was until right now when he saw him truly happy.

As he considered that, Joey saw two paths open before him.

One where he stepped aside to let his best friend pursue Lucy.

Or one where they pursued her together.

The second was definitely the more difficult to tread, but Joey's Moretti blood flashed hot, that passionate, never-say-die adventurer inside telling him the sweeter reward—a life with Miles *and* Lucy—would be worth the fight.

After all, hadn't that been proven to him time and time again by Layla, Tony, Gio, and Luca. None of them had found their happy ending easily. It had taken a lot of work and courage and commitment. In the end, they'd found not only what their hearts desired but so much more.

When the song ended, everyone made their way back to the table. Abbey, the bartender, shouted last call, and they decided to close their tab and head home. Glancing around, Joey realized Scottie must have cut out right after the last missed dance.

The ride home was quieter, everyone either tired or lost in their own thoughts. Joey was in the passenger seat again, but this time Lucy was behind the wheel. She'd offered to DD because, as she'd said, "I get to sample the goods all the time."

Not that those free samples had held Theo back as he'd consumed the lion's share of their pitchers.

Once they arrived at the farm, they stopped at the girls' house. Remi climbed out of the car. "See you in the morning, Joey? Bright and early?"

Remi had talked him into taking a trail ride with her. Part of her chores on the farm included leading tourists around the mountain trails on horseback. Joey thought it sounded cool and was looking forward to it.

He gave Remi a thumbs-up. "I'll meet you at the barn."

She nodded, said good night to everyone else, and walked inside.

Lucy handed Theo his car keys and he pocketed them, walking down a second lane that led to the farmhouse he shared with his brothers.

"I'll pick my car up in the morning," he told Lucy. "I need to walk this off."

Miles had only had one beer the entire night, so she tossed him the keys to the farm use truck so they wouldn't have to walk back in the dark. Neither he nor Miles climbed into the truck, walking her to the front door instead.

She stopped on the threshold. "I had a lot of fun tonight. Thank you for the dances."

"You're welcome." Joey was aware of how closely the three of them were standing to each other, and because he was high on beer and hope, he decided there was no better time than the present to see if he could steer destiny in the right direction.

He cupped Lucy's cheeks in his hands, bent forward, and kissed her the way he'd dreamed of since the first moment she'd stepped off this porch in those Doc Martens.

He heard her soft intake of breath, aware he'd surprised her. The shock wore off quickly, though, as her hands rose to his shoulders, her fingers stroking the sensitive skin around his ears, then slipping through his hair.

He ran his tongue along her lower lip, her mouth parting to allow him inside. Joey gripped her waist, his hands sliding beneath her long cardigan. He was sorely tempted to untuck her white tee, desperate to touch skin.

Her tongue danced with his for a full minute, the two of them sharing the same air.

Joey was finished questioning these feelings because he was a goner.

Lucy Storm had just claimed his heart.

Sign him up for the Love at First Sight club.

Call him the King of Instalove.

He was tempted to push her back against the door, to explore every luscious curve on her body, but he was hyperaware of the fact they weren't alone. There may be two pairs of lips doing the locking, but there were three people kissing.

At least in his mind.

Joey dug deep and forced himself to break the kiss sooner than he wanted because he was so turned on. By Lucy's soft lips and sweet sounds...as well as the fact that Miles was standing right there, next to them, watching.

He hadn't walked away. He hadn't even stepped back.

It was the one thing that had kept Joey kissing her.

Miles was in this, though he suspected his best friend didn't realize it yet.

When the kiss ended, Joey gave her a quick wink that made her laugh softly. Together, they glanced over at Miles, who remained motionless for a moment.

Joey could read his best friend's desire like it was written in jumbo neon letters. He could also see just as clearly the war Miles was waging in his own head.

Lucy blushed under Miles's scrutiny. At first, Joey thought she was embarrassed for getting carried away in front of an audience, but then...

He looked more closely.

God.

Lucy was slowly closing the distance between her and Miles, issuing an unspoken invitation for him to claim his own kiss.

Joey silently willed Miles to move, to take what she was offering.

For the briefest of moments, he thought Miles was going to do it. Unfortunately, whatever battle he'd been fighting came to a conclusion.

The wrong conclusion.

"Good night, Lucy," Miles said, woodenly.

"I, um…" Her desire evaporated in the blink of an eye, and she shook her head like someone trying to come out of a trance. It was clear she was embarrassed by her actions, aware she'd just kissed one guy and was ready to kiss a second. Lucy didn't realize exactly how much that would NOT piss Joey off. "Good night."

Joey sighed. "Night, honey."

He and Miles waited until she walked inside and locked the door. As they headed for the truck, Joey could feel the heat from his friend's anger.

"What the fuck was that?" Miles asked as soon as they were in the vehicle.

Joey, a smart-ass from way back, didn't bother to hold back. "A good-night kiss. A good one too."

"Way to make me feel like an awkward third wheel, asswipe."

"You didn't have to be a third wheel."

"What the hell does that mean?" he barked.

"Why didn't you kiss her too?"

Miles reared back as if Joey had struck him. "Why the fuck would I do that?"

Joey smirked. "Because you wanted to."

"No, I didn't." It was the quickest protest Joey had ever heard, and the most hilarious when Miles tacked on, "She's not my type."

Joey laughed loudly. Too loudly.

Miles was not amused, and his scowl grew more pronounced as he started the truck in order to avoid eye contact. "And even if she was, which I'm not saying she is," Miles continued, as they drove down the dark lane, "you've made it perfectly clear that you're interested in her, and I don't poach."

"It's not poaching." Joey twisted on the seat because he wanted to see Miles's reaction to his next comment. "It's sharing."

This time, *Miles* laughed, but there wasn't a drop of humor in it. "That's not happening."

"Why not?"

"Because I'm not a Moretti. I don't believe in threesomes. Hell, I'm not even sure I believe in love at the moment because that shit fucks you up."

Joey scoffed. "That's because you've decided to let Rhiannon live in your head rent-free again. Kick her to the curb once and for all."

"That's easier said than done."

"No, it's not."

Miles's teeth were clenched, his lips pursed shut.

"You still talking to her?"

Miles shrugged. "Few texts, nothing more."

Joey hated his answer, but he dropped that line of argument because he had another one he needed to pick up. "Let's put Rhiannon aside for a minute. Because you need to open your eyes and stop lying to yourself."

Miles's hands gripped the steering wheel tightly "About what?"

"I don't believe you when you say Lucy's not your type. I saw you dancing with her. I saw the way you were looking at each other."

Miles shook his head as they pulled up in front of the cabin. He shut off the truck, then turned to look at him. "I know what you're thinking, and it's not going to work, bro."

Before Joey could question him, Miles climbed out of the truck, clearly hoping to make a quick escape to his bedroom.

Like Joey would let that happen.

"What's not going to work?" Joey asked the second they were inside.

Miles stopped in the middle of the living room, crossing his arms. "You're not going to shoehorn me into the kind of life you want."

"I've never said what kind of life I want." Joey hadn't. Because before tonight, this possibility hadn't been a part of his plans.

Miles lifted one eyebrow. "I have eyes, Joey. I see the way you look at your brothers and sister. Every single one of your siblings has found a committed threesome. Admit it. You want that too, don't you?"

Joey hadn't been aware of those looks. It proved just what a good friend Miles had become in such a short time. The man seemed capable of seeing things about him that Joey couldn't see himself. In the end, he merely shrugged, not bothering to deny Miles's comment because, well, it was the truth. "What if I do?"

Miles lifted his hands. "There's not a damn thing wrong with that. In fact, I hope you get it. I really do. But, Joe—it's not going to be with me. And not just because I'm fucked up over Rhiannon."

"What's the other reason?" Joey knew the answer, but he wanted to hear Miles say it. Months earlier, Joey had confessed that he'd gone on a couple dates with guys. Miles had been shocked, to put it lightly.

Since then, Joey couldn't help but notice his best friend had never mentioned it again, obviously uncomfortable with the subject.

Miles looked away, and for a minute, Joey suspected he wasn't going to respond.

When Miles's gaze met his again, he lifted his shoulders. "You like guys."

Yep. There it was.

"And?"

"And I don't."

Joey snorted. "Yeah. Pretty sure I know that, Miles."

He rubbed the back of his neck wearily. "I'm never going to kiss a guy, never feel attraction or arousal for one. I'm not wired like that."

Joey closed his eyes briefly. "Again, I know that."

"So that should tell you—"

"Ask me," Joey interjected.

Miles frowned. "What?"

"Ask me about my experience with dating men."

"That's none of my—"

"Just fucking ask, Miles."

His jaw tightened. He obviously didn't want to, but it spoke to their level of friendship that he forged on anyway. "Fine, Joey. Hit me with it."

"I've gone out with two guys—only two. They were both gay, not bi, and they asked me out. I accepted the dates because I was curious, and I had a good time. I didn't do more than kiss either guy. No sex. The kissing was hot, but it didn't go beyond that."

"Did you want it to go further?"

"Honestly, no. Both guys made it clear they were interested in me for more than a hookup, and while I liked them well enough, I couldn't see myself dating either of them. Because the truth is, I prefer women."

"Oh," Miles murmured.

"I actually didn't realize until tonight that I *do* want to find what my brothers and Layla have. Because you're right. I think throuple relationships are pretty fucking fantastic. But I also know—because I'm not an idiot—that there are all sorts of ways to make a threesome work. In my mind, for the three of us, I envision what Tony and Rhys share with Jess."

Miles fell quiet. He'd spent a lot of time with Joey's family, so Miles knew the lay of the land when it came to his brothers' relationships. He knew the twins, Luca and Gio, were bi, having sex with both of their partners. Just as he knew Rhys and Tony were straight, the two men sharing Jess only.

"Joey..." he started.

"Miles. I swear to you, I don't look at you *that* way. I look at you like I look at my brothers. Because you're my brother too." Joey didn't say anything else, giving Miles time to digest what he'd just learned. A small part of him hoped the information would make a difference.

Finally, Miles broke the silence, saying exactly what Joey expected and feared. "What you told me... It doesn't change things. Because I'm not looking for what you are. I'm not even looking at all."

It was yet another lie, but Joey didn't call him on it.

"Like you said," Miles added, tapping his temple. "I need to evict someone before I even think about starting something new."

Miles claimed the last word as he turned and walked into his bedroom, shutting the door.

Joey stared at Miles's closed door for a moment, then headed to his own bedroom. Dropping down on the edge of the mattress, he pulled out his cellphone, clicking on the number of the one person he could talk to about this.

It was late, but he knew Tony would answer.

"Everything okay?" Tony's gruff voice told Joey he'd woken up his big brother. He heard a rustling that told him Tony was getting out of bed, followed by the quiet sound of a door closing. He'd obviously left the bedroom so he wouldn't disturb Rhys and Jess.

"When did you know?" Joey asked. "That Jess was the one?"

"The second I lifted her out of that freezing-cold car." Rhys and Tony had taken Jess and Jasper in from the street, the young mother and her son homeless and sleeping in a car in the dead of winter. Like him and Miles, his brother and Rhys were best friends and roommates.

Then Tony huffed out a breath that sounded like a laugh. "Who is she? Do I know her?"

"She's the brewmaster at Rain or Shine Brewery. We're interviewing her for the show."

"You sound miserable as fuck. Am I to take it she's not interested in you?"

"She's interested," Joey admitted.

"Then why do you sound like you lost your best fri—" Tony paused, then said, "Oh."

"Yeah. Oh," Joey said gloomily.

"Guess I don't have to tell you it doesn't have to be either/or."

"You don't have to tell *me*," Joey said. "But I think I asked the wrong question. How did you convince Rhys to share?"

"That's still the wrong question," Tony replied. "Because I didn't convince him. We got there on our own. We realized our lives wouldn't be complete without Jess and Jasper pretty early on. Took us a little longer to figure out our lives wouldn't be complete without each other, as well, so instead of pistols at dawn, we decided to share."

Joey wasn't so sure Miles would ever come to that realization.

"What you want is a beautiful thing, Joey. But it's not easy to achieve. Two people finding their perfect half, falling in love, is rare enough. Three hearts fitting together? That's fucking miraculous. You only left Philly a few days ago, bro. Take a breath. Then take about a hundred more. Let things play out a little longer. You can't push this on Miles. He's gotta find his own way there."

"What if he doesn't?"

Tony was silent for too long. "I think you know the answer to that."

Joey did, and it felt like an arrow straight through his heart.

"While you can't push him," Tony began, "that's not to say you can't guide him."

Joey chuckled. "Guide him, huh?"

"Open his eyes to the future you're seeing. Miles is a smart man. I'm betting he won't be able to say no when he understands just how much he stands to gain."

"Thanks, bro," Joey said, nurturing the tiny spark of hope Tony had lit in his soul. "Give Jasper a hug for me, and kiss Jess's belly, tell my future niece or nephew that her uncle Joey intends to spoil them rotten."

Tony chuckled. "I'll be sure to do that. As soon as Jess stops throwing up. Right now, it's a splash zone."

"Gross," Joey muttered, chuckling.

Tony, Jess, and Rhys had sent a big text to the whole family a couple weeks earlier, announcing the arrival of their child in the spring.

"I look forward to meeting this brewmaster," Tony added. "Must be quite a woman to have you and Miles turned inside out after just a few days."

"You're going to love her," Joey assured him. "Sorry for waking you up."

"No problem. I should probably start getting used to sleepless nights. Good night, Joey."

"Night."

Joey hung up the phone, glad he'd made the call. Stripping down to his boxers, he climbed into bed and considered his brother's advice.

Time to start drawing a road map.

Chapter Five

Lucy put four scoops in the filter and filled the water tank, going through the process of preparing her morning coffee before turning it on. She needed it today because last night hadn't been the least bit restful.

If anyone were to walk into her bedroom and see her tangled, twisted sheets and her duvet kicked to the floor, they'd think she'd been attacked. She had tossed and turned and tried to beat her pillow into submission until the wee hours of the morning.

Sleep, when it did come, hadn't been deep. Instead, it was as if she'd been awake with her eyes closed, driving her dreams, which had been epic and vivid and strongly featured *two* men. She was in uncharted territory here because she'd never felt this kind of instant attraction to any man.

And now?

Fuck her.

She was completely attracted to *both* cohosts of *ManPower*.

Who wouldn't be?

Joey Moretti was sex-on-a-stick hot with olive skin, a strong jawline, prominent cheekbones, and those soulful brown eyes that screamed of his Italian heritage. She was a sucker for a beard, and his called to her like a Siren's song, making her long to stroke it. It had felt rough against her mouth as they'd kissed, and she'd spotted the tiniest bit of beard burn last night when she'd been brushing her teeth before bed. That kiss had contributed greatly to her lost sleep as she imagined him doing it again and again.

And then there was Miles, with his dark skin, close-cropped hair, clean-cut face, those eyes that were such a deep, rich brown they sometimes looked black in different light, and that sexy smile she saw all too infrequently. When he flashed it her way, it made her girlie bits wake up and take notice because it was just—*sigh*—perfection.

It was the kiss he *hadn't* given her that had accounted for the rest of her sleepless night.

God, she muttered to herself.

Her attraction to the two men was the height of madness. For one thing, they were leaving in a couple of days. And secondly, she wasn't limiting this newfound obsession to just one cohost, but both.

So yeah...insanity.

She needed to be smart, to move forward with an eye toward self-preservation because she couldn't let herself get carried away with dreams of something that simply couldn't be. Joey had asked for more time to get to know her. She'd been excited by the prospect last night, especially after that kiss, but the cold harshness of morning had a way of shining a different light on things.

Joey and Miles were going to continue traveling around the country filming, and she was going to remain here on the farm. She wasn't exactly sure how Joey intended to move things forward, but he didn't strike her as the pen pal type, content with exchanging love letters like they were some star-crossed nineteenth century couple. And while phone calls and FaceTime and texts were fine, they weren't the same thing as spending time with a person. Eventually, she could see the calls dwindling, the texts becoming less personal, and then...nothing.

Lucy popped out of the kitchen when she heard a knock at the door, grinning when she saw Miles through the glass pane, standing on the porch. The butterflies in her stomach arrived every time Joey or Miles made their appearance, though she knew enough to know that these particular flutters had nothing to do with nerves and everything to do with hormones.

Taking a deep, calming breath—and kicking herself for not running a brush through her hair to tame her wild bedhead before coming downstairs—she opened the door.

"Good morning," she said cheerfully.

Miles lifted his hand to reveal a ring of keys. "Came to return your truck. Wasn't sure if you needed it. I've learned since arriving, you country folk rise early."

She laughed when he said the last in a truly terrible southern accent. "Your timing is perfect, but only for me. My family tends to give me shit for sleeping in."

Miles glanced at his watch. "It's only eight o'clock." Considering she was dressed, it was obvious she'd been awake, and he hadn't pulled her from her bed. His response also told her she wasn't the only one who preferred a later start to the day.

She gestured for him to come in, and she was happy when he did so, following her to the kitchen.

"Levi insists I've wasted half my day not bothering to rise until eight."

"The man is a lunatic," Miles joked.

"If that's true, then I'm the only sane person on the farm. All three of my sisters are already up and out, their days starting much earlier than mine. I like to keep banker's hours, heading to the brewhouse around nine. Sam takes the early shift. Coffee?"

Miles nodded. "I'd love some. Joey made a pot this morning before he left at the ass crack of dawn, but then the bastard filled a thermos with it. Didn't leave me more than half a cup."

Lucy poured them both a cup, gesturing to the cream and sugar. Miles added a dollop of milk, crinkling his nose when he saw how much sugar she added to hers.

"He'll need the coffee if he hopes to keep up with Remi. She could ride those trails for hours and never get tired. She was excited to show him the views from even higher up on the mountain," she said.

"Joey will be fine. He's tireless himself. Besides, he'll have to cry uncle soon. We have a meeting with the director in a couple hours to discuss what we still need to film."

While Joey and Miles were staying in a cabin on the farm, the rest of their crew had gotten rooms in a hotel about twenty miles away, just off the highway that stretched between Gracemont and Henley Falls. According to Joey, their producer's idea of "roughing it" was a hotel without room service, so she wasn't interested in sleeping in a cabin, no matter how nice.

"You didn't want to join them on their morning ride?" Lucy asked.

Miles feigned a shudder. "Nope. This city boy's feet are perfectly happy to remain firmly on the ground."

"Want some breakfast?" she offered. "I was just about to whip up some pancakes."

Miles rubbed his stomach. "I'll never say no to pancakes."

She grinned. "Then grab a seat."

He plopped down comfortably.

Lucy loved the look of Miles sitting there, legs outstretched and crossed at the ankles. She grabbed a bowl and the ingredients, and it occurred to her that while she'd heard a little bit about Joey's upbringing in Philadelphia and Baltimore, she knew a hell of a lot less about Miles. "City boy, huh? What city?"

"New York."

"Wow. I've always wanted to go there. It's in the top five on my list of places to travel."

Miles tilted his head. "Let me guess. Manhattan? Times Square? Broadway?"

She nodded enthusiastically.

"You realize there are a lot of other amazing places in the city, right?"

Lucy pretended to look shocked. "What? Seriously? There's more?"

Miles snorted, then tapped on his chest. "I'm from Queens."

"I don't detect an accent."

Miles never missed a beat, responding to that observation in the strongest Queens accent she'd ever heard, the corners of his lips pushed into a pucker. "Took some dead-ass work, but I managed to learn 'ow to talk basic like the rest of ya."

Lucy laughed. "Oh my God. That sounds horrible."

Miles waved her off with a smirk. "You don't know what you're talking about."

This was the most she and Miles had said to each other since he'd arrived, and she didn't intend to waste a second of this opportunity to get to know him. He was more at ease this morning, and that distance he'd been hell-bent on maintaining had vanished completely.

"So how did you end up hosting *ManPower*?" Lucy placed a dollop of butter on the hot griddle, letting it melt.

"By a series of lucky breaks."

His response was far too short for her. "Not enough details. I'll pull out the real maple syrup instead of the cheap grocery store shit if you make the story worth my while."

Miles flashed her one of those amazing smiles, and her pussy literally clenched. "Can't say no to real maple syrup, can I?"

"No, you can't." She pointed the spatula at him to stress her point.

"Fine," Miles began. "I had a buddy in high school whose dad owned a studio that specialized in voice-over productions. I went through puberty pretty young, so my voice was this deep by the time I was fifteen."

She didn't admit it, but Miles's voice was the sexiest thing about him. While it was Joey's infectious laugh and strong calloused hands keeping her panties damp, with Miles, it was the low, almost rumbling timbre of his voice.

"I spent the night with my friend one evening, and his dad asked if I'd ever considered acting. I hadn't. Acting was Rhian—" Miles paused. It was a quick one, but it still captured Lucy's attention. "My neighbor was the one who'd sworn up and down since we were kids that she was going to be a famous star, but I'd set my sights on a different path."

"Oh yeah? What path?"

"I was going to play center for the Knicks, of course," he replied in the most "duh" tone she'd ever heard.

She laughed at his joke. "Right. Of course. How silly of me."

"Anyway, my buddy's dad convinced me to come into his studio to lay down some tracks. Just to sort of try it out. I liked it well enough to work on cleaning the Queens accent out of my voice, and once I got the hang of it, I became popular with his clients. At first, I was doing commercials, providing the voice for training videos, educational materials, stuff like that. It became my after-school and weekend gig for spending money, and it beat the hell out of bagging groceries at the local supermarket or working in a fast-food chain."

"I'll say. It sounds like a cool job. And you have the perfect voice for it."

He smiled. "Thanks. I know you're not looking for another job, but you'd do well in voice-over roles too. I noticed it the other night when I was watching *Kiss and Tell*. You have a great voice."

"You watched *Kiss and Tell*?"

He nodded, and for a second, she thought he looked almost embarrassed by his confession, though she couldn't understand why. Joey had mentioned the possibility of promoting *Kiss and Tell* during the filming, so it made sense they would watch a few episodes beforehand.

"I did," he admitted. "It's really good."

She flipped a pancake. "Thanks," she said, though she didn't want to waste this conversation talking about her. "So what was your next lucky break?" Lucy placed a pancake on the plate on the warmer burner, then poured another on the griddle.

"I got a part doing voice work for a new video game, one that sold like gangbusters after its release. Thanks to that, I was basically discovered and approached by a production company that was starting to work on a new animated cartoon—*Judge and Rocky*."

Lucy put the spatula down and turned to face him. "Shut! Up! You were a part of that?"

Judge and Rocky was an adult cartoon along the same lines as *The Simpsons* and *Family Guy*. Sadly, it didn't last as long as those, only airing for two seasons. The show didn't take off until a year after it was canceled, becoming one of those sleeper hits like *Rocky Horror Picture Show* and *Clerks*.

Lucy quickly added, "Remi stumbled onto *Judge and Rocky* when she was looking for something new to binge on Netflix. She was instantly hooked and since then, she's made every single person in the family watch it. We're constantly quoting funny lines from it. Which character were you?"

Miles sighed. "I don't usually do this, but..." He cleared his throat—and when he spoke again, she could swear she felt the earth tremble beneath her feet. "Hello, lover. Ready to have your world rocked by Rocky?"

The character of Rocky was an absolute manwhore, who was forever propositioning every female on the show with hilariously disastrous results.

"I, I..." Lucy was literally speechless. Because Miles sounded *nothing* like Rocky. She never in a million years would have guessed he was the voice.

Miles chuckled at her reaction. "Pretty sure that's exactly what Joey said—or didn't say—when I did the voice for him."

"I can't believe it. I *love* that show. We all do!"

Miles grimaced good-naturedly. "Yeah, but I believe I heard the word Netflix. They picked it up after it was canceled, which is how it became such a hit after the fact."

She nodded, then quickly turned back to the stove, scraping the pancake she'd just burned and tossing it into the trash. "Yeah, we found it too late and were super bummed when we realized there weren't going to be any more seasons. By the way, you can never do that voice in front of Remi, or she'll demand you talk like Rocky the rest of the time you're here."

Miles laughed. "Thanks for the warning."

Lucy put the last of the pancakes on the serving dish and brought it to the table. She quickly grabbed two plates, forks, and napkins, setting them down.

Miles cleared his throat, raising one eyebrow. "I believe I was promised maple syrup."

She grinned, grabbing the syrup and butter before joining him at the table.

She held the syrup away from him. "We still haven't gotten to the *ManPower* part."

"I was just getting to it." He reached for the syrup, the two of them engaging in a playful tug-of-war that ended when Miles's arm brushed against her breast, and he abruptly reared back as if he'd touched an open flame.

She blinked a couple of times to try to clear the lust, then handed him the bottle.

Miles recovered more quickly than her. "One of the original producers on *Judge and Rocky* started working on a new cable show, *ManPower*, and she suggested that I audition. I told her I'd never been in front of a camera before, but she insisted I try out. She said someone with my voice and looks should be heard *and* seen."

"Was she flirting with you?"

Miles shook his head. "She's in her late sixties and has been happily married to her wife for over a decade. They'd dated nearly twenty years before that and were probably the first couple in line to apply for a marriage license the second gay marriage was legalized in California."

"Obviously you got the part."

"I did. They'd already chosen Joey, so they were auditioning a bunch of people with him for the cohost position. The second I met him, it was like we'd known each other our entire lives. Joey said he knew within three minutes of me walking into that audition that he wanted me to get the job. Our rapport must have come through because they called to offer me the gig before I even got home from the audition."

"That's so awesome. Now, *that* show I've watched from the start. Swear," Lucy said, crossing her heart. "Sam was watching the trailers on his phone in the brewhouse one day, mentioned we should check it out, and we did. One show in and we were addicted. None of us had a clue that Uncle Rex had written to suggest Stormy Weather Farm for an episode. He said he didn't want us to be disappointed if nothing came of the request. You could have knocked Levi down with a feather when your producer called to see if we were interested and to set up filming. We celebrated our asses off that night and paid for it the next morning. Even so, no regrets."

Miles wiped his mouth. "Joey's family, the Morettis, are big fans of celebrations too."

"What about your family?"

"Not so much. I mean, we do the biggies—Christmas and Thanksgiving—but the rest..." He shrugged. "Even birthdays when I was growing up were low-key. I usually just got a card, a small gift, and Mom made my favorite dinner. I think I told you my parents were divorced."

She nodded.

"Money was always tight. Dad gave her as much child support as he could afford, but he struggled to hold down a job due to some issues with depression."

"Oh. I'm sorry."

"He and Mom split right after my little sister was born. I was only five, so I don't remember a whole lot about him living with us. Truth is, when I think back, all I remember about my dad is him yelling. The house was quieter and nicer after he left."

Lucy rarely talked about her own parents. She'd been young when they passed away, but still old enough to remember the yelling. "My parents were in the process of getting divorced when they died."

Miles's eyes widened. "I didn't realize."

She grinned sadly. "Yeah, I know. The Storms really are one big happy family...now. But it wasn't always like that."

"You said you were ten when they died?" Miles asked.

She was touched he'd remembered that, that he'd listened so closely to her story about her grandparents the other night.

"I was. And just like you, a lot of my memories of them involve fights and yelling."

"That couldn't have been easy for you."

Lucy moved the last few bites of her pancake around on her plate, too full to eat any more. "My mom met Dad by chance. She'd just graduated from college and embarked on a cross-country road trip. She was a photographer. Her car broke down when she was driving through Gracemont. Dad stopped to help her and...she never continued her journey. According to Granddaddy, the two of them had a whirlwind love affair, falling hard and fast, married within three months. Nine months later, I arrived. I was a honeymoon baby," she confided.

"You're not kidding about whirlwind."

"The first six or seven years of my life were idyllic. Growing up on the farm with my sisters and cousins, fishing in the creek, playing hide-and-seek in the vineyard, riding bikes. It was a great childhood."

"What changed?" Miles asked.

"Mom," Lucy said simply. "Farm life isn't for everyone, and I guess she started regretting that she'd never finished that cross-country trip. Once resentment kicked in, things at home were less happy. They would get into these yelling and screaming battles. Dad couldn't understand why she'd married him and had kids if she was so unhappy. He'd grown up on the mountain, and like the rest of my family, he couldn't conceive of anywhere else being better than right here. Mom would yell back, tell him there was more to life, that they weren't tied to the land, that he could get a job anywhere."

"Where did she want to move to?"

Lucy shrugged. "I don't think she even knew or cared. She just wanted off the mountain. That was part of what frustrated my dad, I think. That she suddenly seemed to hate the place he loved so much. The fighting went on until..."

"Until?"

"She left."

Miles frowned. "She left?"

Lucy nodded. "I had just turned nine. Woke up one morning, got ready for school, and came downstairs to find Dad sitting at the kitchen table. He was usually out of the house by that time of day. He told me that Mom was taking a vacation. That was what he called it. A vacation."

"I'm guessing that's not what it was."

She shook her head. "Apparently Mom had hit her limit, and she just took off, left us."

"How long did it take before you realized she wasn't coming back?"

Lucy grimaced. "I'm nothing if not an optimist. I bought the vacation story for four months before Everett sat down next to me on the bus home from school. We're close in age, him just a year ahead of me. He told me my mom wasn't coming back."

Miles scowled, but Lucy cut him off, raising a hand.

"He didn't say it to be cruel. He was worried about me because I'd stopped playing, stopped running around the farm, doing kid crap with him, my cousins, my sisters."

"What were you doing?" Miles asked.

"Hanging out on the front porch, waiting for Mom to come home."

Miles started to take her hand, but then he hesitated and pulled back. "You said your parents died together."

Lucy sighed. "She came home after a year away. Not to stay. She wanted a divorce. By that point, I think Dad was all too happy to give it to her. She'd deserted us, left him on his own with four daughters, all of them missing their mom."

"I'm sorry," Miles said softly.

"They went to town to see a lawyer. On the way home, they hit some black ice and the car ran off the road, smashed into a tree. My sister, Nora was with them."

"Jesus." Miles ran his hand over his head.

"She was seven, and she'd been playing at a friend's house. Mom and Dad picked her up after their meeting with the lawyer. Because the front of the car took most of the damage, she was actually able to walk away from the accident. But…" Lucy hated this part. Hated saying it, hated thinking about it. "It was several hours before anyone went looking for them. She was trapped in the car with Mom and Dad and…"

This time Miles *did* take her hand. "They were dead."

She nodded, even though his words weren't a question. Lucy looked out the kitchen window, taking a minute to gather herself, and wondering why in the hell she'd just told him all of that.

"Wow." She forced a smile, dug deep to turn the conversation around. "Talk about bringing the room down. I haven't talked about any of that in years. Of course, I don't have to because this is Gracemont. Everyone already knows."

"No secrets in small towns, huh?"

She gave him a sad smile. "Not many."

Miles squeezed her hand, then released it. "I'm sorry all that happened to you and to Nora. We don't have to talk about it anymore if you don't want to."

"Thanks," she said, touched by his compassion. "So, new subject."

"Okay. *Kiss and Tell*," he said, grinning.

Lucy groaned playfully. "Oh God. Alright. Hit me with it. What did you think of it? You can be brutally honest."

"It's sappy as shit with all that cheesy talk about love and forever," he said, not cracking a smile until she narrowed her eyes, her spine suddenly ramrod straight as she prepared to defend her show to the death.

Miles quickly held up his hands in surrender. "I'm kidding! I liked it, Lucy. A lot. It's a really cool show."

"Asshole. You really got me there," she said, laughing. Then, unable to resist teasing him back, she said, "Who knows? Maybe one day you'll be sitting on my couch with your true love, telling me *your* cheesy story."

"Don't get carried away."

She rose, clearing the plates. Miles stood too, following her, but she didn't realize that until she turned too quickly and bumped into him. She stumbled a bit, losing her footing.

Miles reached out, gripping her waist to yank her forward, but he overcorrected, and her backward momentum was reversed as she suddenly pitched toward Miles, her hands landing on his chest.

She glanced up just as he lowered his head, their lips inches apart.

She was instantly thrust back to last night on the porch, and Joey's good-night kiss. To that moment when it ended and the two of them turned to Miles as one.

Lucy had never in her dizziest daydreams considered kissing two guys at the same time, but damn if she hadn't wanted to desperately. What felt even crazier was the realization that Joey wanted the same thing. She could see it in his eyes.

He was the one who'd suggested Lucy ask Miles to dance, and he'd initiated the kiss knowing his best friend was standing right there. Now that she considered it, it was Joey who'd turned toward Miles first, as if he was directing her attention toward the other man, encouraging her to look at him.

Miles's breath was warm on her face, and it smelled sweet. Maple syrup. Her mouth watered for a taste.

"Lucy," he murmured. His grip on her waist tightened as the distance between them shrank. She wasn't sure if he was tugging her forward or if she was leaning toward him.

Maybe both.

One second, they were looking at each other, and the next, his lips were on hers.

Her hands were pressed against his muscular chest, so she slid them upward, wrapping them around the back of his neck, part of her terrified he'd come to his senses too soon. She didn't want this kiss to end any more than Joey's last night.

Dear God. Who taught these men how to kiss?

Not that she had much to compare them to. She'd only dated a couple guys because it wasn't like there was a large crop to choose from in her tiny neck of the woods.

Neither of her past boyfriends had kissed her with this all-consuming passion. Miles's hands slid around her back, and he pulled her flush against him, chest to chest, one hand sliding lower, finding her ass. His tongue tangled with hers, stroking inside her mouth before vanishing for a second, then coming back again.

When he lifted one hand to her hair, his fist wrapping around it tightly, tugging slightly, Lucy saw literal stars, her knees going weak, her pussy quivering.

She wasn't sure how long the kiss might have continued, but they broke apart at the sound of footsteps on the porch. Miles stepped away rapidly, putting some distance between them.

Lucy had to reach behind her to grip the edge of the counter for support because the man had kissed her boneless.

She heard Joey thank Remi and listened as her sister climbed the stairs. Three seconds later, Joey walked into the kitchen.

His dark hair was windblown from his ride, his cheeks red from the chill in the air, his eyes were bright and sparkling and—as always—he was smiling. He started to say something to them, then stopped, his gaze traveling from her to Miles and back.

Lucy felt flames licking her face, partly caused by the arousal Miles's kiss had awakened and partly from nearly being caught in the act. She cast a quick glance in Miles's direction, impressed by his far-better poker face. He was giving the perfect impression of boredom. Or he would have, if he'd managed to look Joey in the eye.

Lucy forced herself to face Joey again, clearing her throat, trying to find her voice.

Before she could say anything, Joey's smile grew even wider.

"Sooo," he drawled. "What have you two been up to?"

If Lucy didn't know better, she'd think Joey knew exactly what they'd been doing, and once again, she couldn't help but wonder if he *wanted* her to kiss Miles.

In a normal situation, she might think the guy who'd kissed her last night and asked for time to get to know her would feel jealousy or annoyance, but nothing between her, Joey, and Miles felt normal. The look Joey was shooting their direction was completely devoid of both emotions. Instead, he looked... delighted? Pleased? Happy?

"Nothing," Miles answered, way too quickly.

She huffed out an exasperated breath.

Joey chuckled at Miles's response, then reached for one of the pancakes still sitting on the warming plate. He didn't bother with syrup or butter, tearing the thing into bite-sized pieces he shoved his mouth.

"Nothing?" Joey reiterated after he'd demolished one pancake and reached for another.

"You can have a plate, you know," she said, trying to distract him. "And butter and syrup."

"I'm fine." Joey leaned against the counter, munching on the second pancake, clearly waiting for an answer to his question.

Miles didn't offer anything else, though she noticed his stoicism was slipping slightly, guilt starting to color his features as he continued looking around the room to avoid facing Joey.

"We were just chatting about our families," Lucy said.

It was the truth.

Or at least part of it.

Joey grabbed the last pancake and plopped down on one of the chairs at the kitchen table.

"How was your ride?" Lucy asked, going for distraction.

Joey gestured toward the other chairs at the table, an unspoken invitation for the two of them to join him. They did, and Miles finally seemed to recover enough to revert to his old self.

Unfortunately.

He closed down again, his arms crossed, that scowl back in place.

She instantly missed the engaging and entertaining man she'd just been talking to.

"Great. Not sure I've ever learned so much about trees and birds and bug sounds and woodland creatures. To be honest, I didn't know I *wanted* to learn about that stuff until Remi started talking. Her facts were fascinating."

Lucy grinned. "She's a walking encyclopedia when it comes to subjects that interest her. She was always top of her class in science, just as she was the bottom in math."

"Sounds like my brother, Luca. His report card was a potpourri of hit or miss. I think it's safe to say he'll never be fluent in Spanish," Joey said.

"That's alright," Miles added. "He's got Conor now. His billionaire boyfriend can translate for him."

Lucy was confused because the other night at dinner, Joey mentioned his brother Luca was dating former supermodel, Harper Branson. Needless to say, that tidbit had captured the attention of every single one of her cousins, all of them wanting to know if she was as beautiful in person as she was in the magazines and commercials. Joey told them about her restaurant in Philadelphia, promising to take them there if they ever came to visit.

"Conor?" she asked.

"His partner," Joey quickly responded.

"Oh." Lucy frowned. "I thought Luca was the brother who was dating Harper Branson?"

Joey stood up, walking across the kitchen to help himself to a cup of coffee. "He is. He's in a relationship with both of them."

Aaaaaand that cleared nothing up for Lucy. "I don't understand."

"My brother Luca is happily shacked up in a committed

throuple with Conor and Harper, the three of them currently living in a bougie-ass penthouse in Philly."

Lucy blinked a few times, wondering if Joey was going to hit her with a "just kidding."

Instead, he rejoined them at the table, taking a sip of his coffee. "Harper and Conor recently opened a restaurant together. The one I mentioned at dinner. Luca was their contractor." When she didn't respond, Joey reached over and tapped her hand. "No follow-up questions? Because they're allowed."

Miles rolled his eyes. "Jesus, man. Stop playing with her. Joey's siblings have all found their happily ever afters in threesome relationships."

"Seriously? *All* of them?" she asked, wondering how in the hell Joey had failed to mention that in all his stories of home.

Joey nodded. "It all started with Layla."

Suddenly, a light bulb went on. Joey had mentioned being overprotective when it came to his kid sister. When she acted shocked that he'd let a guy date Layla, Joey had casually dropped in that it had been *two* men. She thought he meant she'd had two different boyfriends, at different times. "Wow, she was the first?"

"Yeah." Joey put his cup down. "And don't think that didn't go over like a lead balloon. Layla was the only one of my siblings upset when the family moved back to Philadelphia from Baltimore when we were kids. So none of us were surprised when she decided to live there as an adult. The shock came when she returned home for a visit with Finn and Miguel in tow. I thought my brother Tony was going to have an aneurysm."

Lucy's eyes widened. "I bet. My cousins probably would have taken a couple swings."

"Oh, we thought about it. Until we got to know Finn and Miguel. Hard to stay mad at two stand-up guys who love your sister and basically worship the ground she walks on."

"As they should," Lucy added with a giggle.

"Damn right. The three of them have been together for years. Layla legally married Finn, but she and Miguel exchanged vows as well. She's seven months pregnant with their first child, and I've never seen three people more excited to become parents."

"That's..." Lucy paused, still trying to digest this new information. "Nice," she finally added lamely.

"After that...I don't know," Joey said, rubbing his beard. "It was like a door opened, and once my brothers took a peek inside, they decided they liked what they saw."

"So they're all in threesomes?" Lucy was having a hard time wrapping her head around this whole conversation.

"It's not as unheard of as you might think," Joey added. "I've read a few articles lately talking about the rise in polyamory relationships. Given the state of the world, sadly, these days it takes three salaries to buy a home and pay the bills."

"Ain't that the truth," Miles added.

"You should plan a trip to Philly to interview some of my siblings and their partners." Joey reached out and grasped her hand, holding it. Lucy saw Miles's gaze locked on their linked hands. "Just think, you could explore different kinds of relationships on *Kiss and Tell*. My brothers all have great stories to tell. The Morettis are masters of romance."

Miles scoffed, his response causing Joey to frown.

"You're really not a fan of romance, are you?" Lucy asked, recalling his jest about her show being cheesy.

Miles shook his head. "Romance novels and romcoms are called fiction for a reason. That shit doesn't happen in real life."

"That's Rhiannon blowback," Joey muttered.

"Rhiannon?" she asked. Miles had started to mention his neighbor's name before cutting himself off earlier.

"My ex," Miles replied, shooting Joey a dirty look. "Who we are NOT talking about."

Joey put his free hand up in surrender, refusing to relinquish his hold on Lucy's. "How can you say romance isn't real after spending the last couple of years with my family?"

Miles crossed his arms. "Those relationships are still relatively new. Your family seems to embrace extended honeymoon phases, all hot sex and hearts in their eyes. Let's table declaring them soul mates and all that shit until they've been together twenty years, faced some hard times, raised a few smart-mouthed brats, and waged countless wars over doing the laundry and washing the dishes."

Joey shook his head but didn't bother to belabor the point. "Looks like it's up to us to show Miles the ways of romance, Lucy. Speaking of, what's the deal with you and the mayor?"

Lucy wrinkled her nose in disgust. "Ugh—that sure as hell isn't romance. There *is* no deal. And there will *never* be a deal."

Joey looked pleased with that response. "Good." Then he released her hand, glancing at his phone and rising. "Shit, we gotta go, Miles. Our director will be here soon, and I want to get a shower first. Wash the horsey smell off."

"The plan is to pick up filming after lunch," Miles reminded her as he stood as well.

"Sam and I will be ready," she assured him.

"We'll see you later, honey." Joey leaned forward, giving her a too quick, too platonic kiss, though she was secretly pleased it was on the lips and not her cheek. When he cupped one side of her face affectionately, she melted. Especially when he stroked it with his thumb, looking at her like she was the most beautiful person in the world.

She gave him a soft smile that morphed to a breathy laugh when he bopped the tip of her nose with his finger.

Lucy expected Joey to leave, so she was shocked when he glanced in Miles's direction, tilting his head toward her with a grin that was the definition of shit-eating. For a split second, Lucy prayed Miles would take Joey up on his unspoken suggestion.

Unfortunately, Miles just narrowed his eyes at Joey.

"See you later, Lucy." Miles's farewell didn't include a kiss, but the way he reached out and slowly stroked his fingers along her arm was just as hot.

They left together, leaving Lucy reeling in their wake.

Drifting to the sink, she started to fill it with water and dishwashing soap to scrub their breakfast dishes. As she did so, she considered what she'd just learned about Joey's siblings. She noticed that when he talked about Layla's relationship opening a door, he didn't include himself when he said his brothers took a peek inside.

Had Joey?

Was he interested in the same kind of relationship?

What would she do if he asked her to participate in a three-some affair? How the hell did a person even reply to something like that?

It certainly wasn't a kink she'd ever considered before.

Her curiosity was piqued, though, and there was no denying she was intrigued by it.

Of course, there was a big difference between thinking about something and doing it. Lucy wasn't a virgin, but she wouldn't call herself super experienced either. Her two longish relationships were both the same flavor. Vanilla.

Picking up one of the dirty plates, she used a sponge to scrub off the remnants. As she did so, her mind drifted, her fantasies of Miles and Joey thus far had been either/or scenarios, but now, she couldn't imagine one man without the other...

"That was delicious," Joey said. "But I'm still hungry."

"You can't be," Lucy said with a laugh. The three of them had just polished off a huge breakfast, gorging themselves on pancakes and bacon.

"I am too," Miles added.

She dismissed their complaints and started to clear the plates.

"Still starving," Joey insisted, rising quickly to band his arm around her middle and tug her onto his lap. "Give us another taste?"

Lucy felt his thick erection hard against her ass.

"Okay," she whispered.

Miles moved to stand in front of them. "You're wearing too many clothes."

Her cheeks flushed with desire when Miles backed that statement up by reaching for her shirt and pulling it over her head.

"Still too many," Joey added, as he unfastened her bra and tossed it to the floor.

"Not finished yet." Miles grasped her hands, tugging her from Joey's lap, so that he could pull her jeans and panties off before lifting her so that she was sitting on the edge of the kitchen table, her legs outstretched, Miles standing between them.

Joey stood, moving to her side. Once there, he reached out, squeezing one of her breasts before bending over to suck her nipple into his mouth.

"Mmm," he moaned. "Delicious."

God, he hadn't exaggerated about being starving. Lucy gasped at Joey's rough suction, and suddenly, she was suffering from the same hunger pangs.

Miles grabbed one of the kitchen chairs, positioning it so that he could sit down between her outstretched legs. Placing the back of her thighs over his shoulders, he wasted no time doing a little tasting of his own.

Her back arched until Joey placed a firm hand on her collarbone and pressed her flat against the table. They weren't holding back their strength, putting her exactly where they wanted with ease.

Joey focused on her breasts, kissing, pinching, and sucking until the peaks were so hot she feared she might have third-degree burns.

Not that Lucy minded. Her hands clenched Joey's hair, holding him tight to her chest.

"God," she cried out, their dual attacks driving her out of her mind. Between Joey's teeth toying with her nipples and Miles's wicked tongue, she was already on the verge of an orgasm, something that typically took a lot more time and work.

Miles, sweet Jesus, was proving himself to be accomplished at going down on a woman. He held her pussy lips apart with his thumbs, as he sucked her clit into his mouth. Then he teased it, tickling it with his tongue.

"Miles," she gasped.

Joey lifted his head, curious to see what Miles was doing to make her so crazy. "Fuck, man. That's hot. Keep going."

Joey cupped one of her breasts, squeezing it firmly, but he didn't lower his head again, too fascinated with watching what Miles was doing to her.

Miles raised his head, slowly slipping two fingers inside her, thrusting in and out a few times before withdrawing completely. They were shiny with her arousal when he showed Joey just how wet and ready she was for them.

"Jesus," she groaned when Joey wrapped his hand around Miles's wrist, sucking those two fingers into his mouth.

She writhed beneath them, on the verge of spontaneous combustion.

Joey released Miles's fingers. "You want more, honey?"

She nodded emphatically. Joey chuckled, but mercifully, Miles responded.

Pushing his thick fingers back inside, he kept his pace slow and gentle as he lowered his head, putting his mouth back in the game as he sucked on her clit.

When he curled his fingers, she was all but lost.

"Fuuuuuuuck!" Lucy's drawn-out curse let them know Miles had found that spot inside that never failed to send her into orbit. The one she'd discovered on her own...with the help of her vibrator.

"I... I..." Her face flushed with heat, her eyes closed tightly.

Joey leaned over until his bearded cheek was next to hers, his lips at her ear. "Come for us, honey. Yell our names and know that you're ours. Ours."

Her mind played over that pronoun, aware nothing had ever sounded sweeter.

She decided right then and there she definitely preferred ours *to* mine.

She wanted to belong to them. To both of them.

"Joey," she breathed, a split second before Miles stroked her G-spot again. "Miles!" she cried louder. She trembled on the table as Miles pushed her over the edge, slamming a third finger inside.

Her orgasm hit her like a two-ton truck, and her vision went gray. At this rate, she wouldn't be surprised to come to and discover broken bones. Miles drew out her orgasm, slowing his thrusts but not withdrawing. Joey added more fuel to the fire, pinching one nipple tightly, sucking on the other.

Several aftershocks rumbled through her before her body finally went limp.

She lay on the table, her skin shimmering with perspiration, as Joey brushed damp hair away from her face, both men looking down at her with such awe.

"Ours," Joey repeated.

Completely exhausted, all she could do was nod.

Lucy's vision cleared and she realized she'd been scrubbing the same plate for five minutes now. She rinsed it off, placing it in the drainer, not bothering to reach for another.

Instead, she reached up, cupping one of her breasts, her nipple so tight it poked through her shirt. If she slipped her hand into her jeans, she knew her panties would be drenched. She'd never—ever—gotten so turned on from a daydream.

Lucy sighed blissfully.

Ours.

Yeah. She liked the sound of that.

Chapter Six

Miles sat on the edge of his bed, thought *fuck it*, and fell to his back, staring at the ceiling. They'd finished filming with Sam and Lucy at Rain or Shine Brewery this afternoon, and Miles agreed with Joey. It was going to be their best episode of the season.

He'd overheard his producer and the director excitedly discussing certain sections that were not only instructive but extremely entertaining. Sam Storm had a quick wit that paired perfectly with Lucy's adorable giggle. Their close family relationship shone through every time her cousin playfully ruffled her hair or she tried to shove the giant man in true Elaine from *Seinfeld* style.

They'd been fun to interview, as they were both very good at sharing their knowledge of brewing beer, while adding amusing anecdotes about failed brews and silly family stories. It had been flawless.

Their producer said she was sorry the schedule for the season was so tight because they could have easily done two episodes on the farm. That was when Joey suggested they add Lightning in a Bottle Winery to next season's schedule. Given the fact their producer immediately cornered Levi after that conversation, Miles would bet a million dollars he and Joey would be driving back up this mountain in a year's time.

If not before.

He rubbed his eyes, sighing heavily. He'd spent the better part of yesterday afternoon and today eaten up with guilt over kissing Lucy yesterday morning in the kitchen. He'd been so careful to keep his distance from her, aware of Joey's interest, but those attempts had been for naught.

The second they'd bumped into each other, and she'd stumbled into his arms, he was lost.

In her eyes.

She had the brightest, bluest eyes he'd ever seen in his life. They reminded him of the Caribbean Sea and made him want to dive in and drown.

So he did.

He'd leaned closer and...

Fuck. He'd kissed plenty of women in his life, but none of those kisses held a candle to Lucy's.

Not even Rhiannon's.

Miles shook his head. He needed to put Lucy and her lips and her eyes and—

Enough.

He was putting her out of his mind.

Clearly, that kiss was a result of Rhiannon's reappearance in his life fucking with his head, making him remember what he thought they'd had and how much it hurt every time she walked away. In his younger years, Miles had been every bit as romantic as Joey, not only believing in true love but certain he'd found it.

Coming home to the apartment he and Rhiannon shared to find her sitting there with her bags packed had ripped his heart right out of his chest. As she stood there asking for her freedom, he felt his belief in true love and forever burst into flames, burning brighter with every painful word she said. By the time she'd finished telling him she wanted more from life, that being with him wasn't enough, everything he thought he'd known about love had been rendered to ash.

Joey thought that being around the Morettis should have proven to Miles that true love *did* exist. Maybe it should have. But self-preservation kicked in whenever he was confronted with the Morettis and their partners, people living the happily ever after *he* had wanted, the one Rhiannon had set on fire. So he closed his eyes whenever he was with them and refused to see it.

Or at least...he had.

Until Joey tried to force him to open them, to set his gaze on something he *really* wanted to blind himself to.

Joey had never alluded to wanting what his siblings had, never professed a longing for a threesome relationship. All his friend had ever admitted to seeking was love. Now it was clear that wasn't all he wanted...and Miles didn't know how to convince his best friend that he couldn't be a part of that sort of relationship.

He wasn't ready to give his heart to another woman. The way that single phone call from Rhiannon had sent him into a downward spiral had proven he was still fucked-up by his ex.

Lucy deserved a man who could give her his whole heart...and his trust.

Miles could offer neither. Rhiannon stolen every drop of his trust. That ability burning up the same day as his belief in true love and forever.

He shouldn't have kissed Lucy. For her sake. And for Joey's.

The worst part of this whole mess was that Miles knew his guilt was completely wasted. Joey had acquired a permanent grin since walking into that kitchen yesterday morning. It hadn't taken his best friend more than ten seconds to figure out what had happened, and he'd made no attempts to hide how fucking happy it made him.

Without a clue what to do, Miles had fallen back on the tried and untrue, attempting to put some distance between him and

Lucy again, reassuming what he was calling his mountain personality, aka, grumpy asshole.

However, his efforts at rebuffing her had failed miserably because neither Lucy nor Joey were content to leave him and his miserable attitude alone. It was as if they'd joined forces and doubled down, increasing the force of their tractor beam and finding humorous ways to shoot down his scowls. He was stuck tight, and because he was a damn fool, he was no longer fighting as hard as he should be.

His phone beeped with an incoming text. Miles didn't even bother to reach for his cell. Rhiannon had texted him at least a dozen times over the past few days—just a series of selfies and gifs and some tiny tidbits about her day—and last night, she called. He'd foolishly hit like on a couple of the texts and, while he'd known he shouldn't have, he'd answered the phone.

It had been a very friendly, run-of-the-mill conversation, Rhiannon claiming she was calling to touch base and see how the filming was going. They chatted for a little while about a lot of nothing, then said goodbye.

After a lifetime of history, it felt like he should be able to maintain a "just friends" relationship with Rhiannon. That was why he kept letting himself fall back in with her. It was easy. They'd talk about old times, all the fun they'd had as kids. While his memory was shit, Rhiannon's was incredible. He would put money down that she could tell him what outfit he wore on the first day of seventh grade. It was uncanny the details she recalled, and it was fun to talk to someone who remembered his childhood better than he did.

These calls where they caught up after a long time apart didn't take any work. God, they could go two years without talking, then she'd call, and they would pick up the conversation like they had just seen each other the day before. The problem was, those early reminisces never included the bad times, never ventured into anything that might be difficult or uncomfortable or painful to recall.

So, they'd strike the friendship back up.

And then...more.

Sex had never been a problem for them, the two of them coming together in a wave of passion and need and desire.

Unfortunately, the "more" was always when the trouble started. Because all those old feelings emerged, giving him hope that things had changed, that this time they would go the distance. Then that hope was sucker punched to the ground when Rhiannon pulled her vanishing act again.

He recalled a quote from *Ted Lasso* that had stuck with him after watching the show. "It's the hope that kills you."

Wasn't that the damn truth.

"Fuck," he muttered, pushing thoughts of Rhiannon out of his head. He had bigger fish to fry at the moment.

Miles glanced at the alarm clock on the nightstand. He needed to get ready for the evening. The second they'd wrapped up filming, Joey had cornered him and Lucy, suggesting the three of them go out to celebrate.

Alone.

Miles had tried to bow out so that Joey could take Lucy on a proper date. He'd used the "I'm too tired" excuse, but of course, Joey had refused to let him off the hook, claiming it was only dinner and he had to eat anyway.

When Lucy joined in, begging him to come along, he'd foolishly agreed—then kicked his own ass the entire way back to the cabin.

It was no wonder Rhiannon kept managing to finagle her way back into his life. He apparently had no self-control when it came to things he wanted.

His entire life, he had wanted Rhiannon.

But right now...

Well, now, he wanted the same girl as his best friend.

Joey seemed to think that was an easy fix. All they had to do was embrace the Moretti way and share.

Miles hadn't lied when he said wasn't wired that way. He'd

spent a lot of time with Joey's brothers, observing their relationships. Never—not once—did he ever look at them and think that lifestyle was the one for him. When he settled down, there was only going to be one man and one woman in his bed. The idea of having sex with another guy present…

Nope. Not for him.

He worked solo.

Miles pushed himself upright with a groan, then managed to get his ass moving.

Twenty-five minutes later, he walked into the living room to find Joey sitting on the couch, looking at his phone.

He glanced up as Miles plopped down next to him.

"I can still stay in," he offered, even though he knew it was wasted breath.

"Nope. It's our last night with Lucy. I want to make it count."

Miles sighed. "It's *your* last night."

Joey studied him. "You know, you can't dodge the subject forever. Just how hot *was* that kiss you and Lucy shared in the kitchen? Because it sure as hell wasn't heat from the stove that made her blush like that."

Joey had been relentless, asking him about the kiss every time he managed to get Miles alone.

He didn't budge. "I told you. Nothing happened."

"Mm-hmm. So, what were you talking about then? Lucy said family."

Miles nodded, quickly recounting Lucy's story about her parents' death and Nora's presence in the car. He didn't feel like he was betraying a trust because Lucy mentioned the fact everyone in town already knew. Plus, well, the woman had proven herself to be an open book on just about everything. Something about her told Miles she wouldn't mind him sharing the story.

"Jesus," Joey muttered when he was finished.

"Yeah. Jesus." Miles's phone pinged, but he ignored it.

"You gonna check your texts?" Joey asked when Miles didn't pull out his cell.

He shrugged.

"Rhiannon still texting?"

He nodded. He hadn't planned to mention her texts to Joey, but his phone had been on the kitchen table yesterday when she'd sent another one. Joey picked it up to hand it to him, scowling when he saw her name and realized it was an ongoing thread.

He wasn't sure if Joey was upset because he thought Miles was caving or—knowing his friend—mad that Miles wasn't focused on pursuing Lucy with him.

"Miles," Joey started.

"It's just a few friendly texts, Joey. I'm not starting things up with her again."

Fortunately, Joey was in a good mood, thanks to their upcoming date—no, not date, *dinner*—so he grinned when he said, "I'm not sure how you can start things up with Rhiannon when we've found our girl right here on this mountain."

Miles rolled his eyes. "Keep it up and I'm staying in tonight."

Joey laughed, gripping Miles's shoulder. "Empty threat. It's our last night. There's no way you'd miss out on spending it with Lucy."

As he spoke, Joey's smile faded, unhappy with the prospect of leaving tomorrow.

"No one is dying, Joe. Tonight isn't the end if you don't want it to be. There's Zoom and FaceTime and texting. Plus, we have that holiday hiatus from filming between Thanksgiving and Christmas. You can come back then if you want."

Joey perked up, realizing Thanksgiving was only a few weeks away. "You're right. We can come back."

"Pretty sure I didn't say anything about me."

"You'll come back too." Joey rose when headlights shone through the front window. Lucy was picking them up in her car for the trip down the mountain.

Miles didn't bother to continue the argument. Joey was a headstrong motherfucker when it came to getting his way. Not that it mattered because once Miles left this mountain tomorrow, he wasn't coming back. If Joey and Lucy were meant to be, they'd find a way...as a couple.

Joey pulled on his lightweight coat, then opened the door. There was a nip in the air tonight. Miles grabbed his leather jacket, following. Lucy waved from the car.

Joey claimed the passenger seat, so Miles climbed in the back.

"Where are you taking us?" Joey asked.

"There's this awesome little French restaurant on Main Street," she replied.

For the rest of the trip to town, Lucy entertained them with stories of Gracemont's first families. Apparently, some of the local families had been living in the small town "since God was a baby," according to Lucy. Miles chuckled at the expression.

"Oh shit," Joey said, pointing when they hit the city limits. The sidewalks were crawling with parents and kids, all venturing from house to house. "I forgot it was Halloween."

Lucy slowed down, just in case any kids decided to dart across the street. "Obviously, we don't get any trick or treaters at the farm, so whenever my sisters and I get the desire to participate, Edith Millholland lets us sit on her front porch with bowls of candy to hand out. Miss Edith lives in a huge house toward the end of Main Street. It's too big for just her, so she rents out rooms. She's a sixth-generation Gracemont local and a real hoot."

She took a right at the next stop sign, then pointed. "Here we are. Café Des Amis."

There was a small parking lot behind the restaurant, which looked like it had been a home somewhere in the past before it was renovated into a French restaurant.

"I called ahead," Lucy said as they got out of the car. "Not that reservations are usually needed, but I figured it was better to be safe than sorry."

"Lucy!" an older woman called out as soon as they walked inside, approaching them.

"Hello, Bridget," Lucy replied, turning to them. She introduced them to the woman, who was also the owner.

Bridget spoke with a soft, lilting French accent. "I was delighted when Lucy called earlier to tell us she was bringing you in. My husband is in the kitchen cooking, but I'm sure he will stop by the table at some point to meet you. He started watching the show when Rex told him you would be coming to film at Rain or Shine Brewery. He's hooked. I must apologize to you both now, but he bought a magazine with the two of you on the cover, and he was hoping to get it signed."

Joey chuckled. "We'd be happy to."

"Let me show you to your table. I saved you the best." Bridget guided them through the quaint foyer. This had definitely been a home because the floor plan hadn't been altered much. Rather than rip out walls to create one large dining room, there were three separate rooms with tables set up. The room they were led to only had two other tables, both empty. Between the dim lighting and the fire burning in the fireplace, the place was downright romantic, something that wasn't lost on Joey, who looked far too pleased.

"It is a slow night," Bridget explained. "Most parents are out and about with their kids, while the rest of town is sitting on their front porches handing out candy. I suspect you will have this room all to yourself."

They took their seats at the round table, accepting the menus as Bridget handed them out, telling them what the specials were. "Now," Bridget said at last. "Let me go get you some glasses of water. Would you like anything else to drink?"

They decided to split a bottle of cabernet sauvignon.

Once they were alone in the dining room, Joey smiled. "This is a great place, honey."

"Wait until you taste the food. Bridget's husband, Jacques, is an amazing cook. He was the chef in a Michelin-star restaurant in D.C. for nearly twenty years before Bridget convinced him to open his own place. A few years back, they came here one Saturday in the fall to look at the leaves and do a wine tasting at

Lightning in a Bottle. They took one look at the view and knew they'd found their new home."

"I'm not surprised at all," Joey said. "There's definitely something special about this place."

Bridget came back with their drinks and to take their orders. All three of them requested the special, when Lucy told them she'd had it before and it was her favorite.

Bridget promised the food would be out soon and left them alone again.

"So where are you guys off to next?" Lucy asked.

Miles groaned. "We're heading to Nashville to film a guy who makes one-of-a-kind catios and birdhouses."

"What's a catio?" Lucy asked.

Joey chuckled. "A screened-in porch for cats."

Lucy laughed. "I can't decide if that sounds cool or insane."

"We've met the guy who builds them, so I think insane is the right guess," Miles grumbled.

Joey slapped him on the shoulder. "He's not that bad."

"Remember you said that in a few days." Miles took a sip of his wine. "The guy is the brother-in-law of one of our executive producers, Sherri. He drove out to visit her once when we were on location close to Nashville. Apparently, he convinced Sherri to add him to this season's schedule."

"Sherri is a self-proclaimed crazy cat lady. I think she has like seven at home," Joey interjected. "Her brother-in-law made a custom catio for her, and she loved it. Now, she's convinced every cat lover in the world will want one for their precious fur babies."

"Doesn't sound too bad," Lucy mused.

Miles scowled. "The brother-in-law literally has the loudest, most obnoxious laugh in history."

Joey grimaced. "To make things worse, he only laughs at his own jokes, which aren't funny. And he keeps laughing until everyone else joins in."

"Oh my," Lucy said sympathetically.

"At least we'll be in Nashville," Joey added, always finding that silver lining. "I love Nashville."

Lucy sighed. "I've never been, but it's another on my list of places I'd love to travel to." She glanced at Miles. "Right after New York, in fact. The real New York, not the one where they have that horrible Queens accent."

"Oh, that's real nice, Luce," Miles pretended to chastise her. Then he whipped out his old accent as payback. "You's know it would serve you right if I used that accent for the rest of the night."

Joey and Lucy both covered their ears, begging him to spare them.

Miles waved them off, grinning.

"After Nashville," Joey continued, "we're heading to Maris, Texas, to film an episode with a rancher, Hank Cooper. Trudy, another producer, was passing through the town and stopped at a local barbeque place that had been featured in a magazine she'd read. You've met Trudy," Joey said to Lucy, "so you probably know by now she can strike up a conversation with a wall."

Lucy grinned. "She does like to talk."

"Understatement of the century," Miles muttered.

"Trudy is the one who discovered you, right?" Lucy asked Miles.

He nodded. "That's her."

"Anyway," Joey continued. "Trudy started talking to the bartender about *ManPower*, and the next thing she knew, the bartender was dragging her home to meet her husband. It must have been an impressive ranch because Trudy decided to film a show there while they're making homemade apple butter. Apparently it's a weekend event, with lots of people chipping in to do the work."

"Sounds like some real *Little House on the Prairie* shit," Miles added.

"Maybe so, but I think it still sounds amazing." Lucy sighed. "God, I'm so jealous of you guys, getting to travel all over the country, meeting different people, experiencing all these cool things."

"You've really never traveled anywhere?" Miles asked.

"One time, when I was seven, my mom insisted that my sisters and I needed to see the ocean. She talked Dad into taking a long weekend and we drove to Ocean City. I can remember standing there at the edge of the shore, the waves lapping around my ankles, thinking I'd never seen anything so big. I'd love to go back one day."

"You've only seen the ocean once?"

She nodded sadly. "You can't just take a vacation when you live on a farm because the chores still need to be done. One day, though, maybe I'll take off on a grand adventure."

It sounded to Miles like Lucy had inherited a bit of her mother's wanderlust.

"Maybe?" Joey asked.

Lucy seemed uncomfortable that Joey had picked up on that word. "It's not a good time for me to leave."

"Why not?" Joey pressed.

Given Lucy's silence, it was obvious she didn't have a response. In the end, she just shrugged.

Joey leaned forward, reaching for Lucy's hand. "You know what I think? You should come with us when we leave tomorrow."

Lucy laughed, thinking Joey was joking. Miles didn't even crack a smile—because he could see the light that had just gone on in his best friend's head.

Shit was about to go off the rails.

Lucy's laughter died when Joey said, "I'm serious."

She shook her head. "Joey, I can't just take off."

"Why not? You know, most employed people get vacation leave, and it sounds to me like you're owed a lot of it."

"I'm not just an employee. I'm part owner of the brewery."

"And you have many very capable people working for you. Plus, Sam and Theo are there to keep things rolling."

"Yeah, but—"

Joey cut her off. "Think about it, Lucy. We're offering you the chance to knock a city off that list of dream trips. I'm not kidding. You'll love Nashville."

"Yeah, but aren't all your travel arrangements made by the production company? I'm not even sure how—"

"We're road-tripping it," Joey said, interrupting her again. "I hate flying. Had a terrifying experience with turbulence once. Swore after I got my feet back on the ground, I was never stepping in one of those death boxes in the sky again."

"You drive everywhere?"

Miles sighed. "Yep. Joey is a firm believer in that old saying, it's the journey, not the destination. The producers have gotten better at setting our schedules, always padding in a few extras days for us to get from point A to point B. Because *this* guy," Miles jerked his thumb toward Joey, "loves stopping at random places he finds on the way. And he refuses to eat from chain restaurants, only eating at local places along the road."

Joey took a sip of wine. "Some of the best meals I've ever had have come from off-the-beaten-path, run-down diners."

Miles couldn't argue with that. "He's dragged me into a few sketchy places, but damn if the food hasn't been killer. And we've seen some interesting sights. Remember that literal hole-in-the-wall in New Orleans?"

"Literal?" Lucy asked.

Miles nodded. "Yep. We entered via hole in the wall. Best damn breakfast I ever had."

"What about Carhenge in Nebraska," Joey said. "I sure as hell had to drag your ass *there*."

Miles grinned, then explained to Lucy, who looked confused. "It's this exact replica of Stonehenge, made completely out of cars and car parts."

Lucy's eyes widened. "No way."

"It was really cool," Miles admitted, hoping he'd changed the subject enough to distract Joey from continuing his campaign to take Lucy on the road with them. Even though the idea of her coming with them sounded more appealing than it should, considering he'd set his mind on leaving and letting Joey continue to woo Lucy long-distance style.

If she joined them on the road...

The tune to "Jessie's Girl" started playing in his head, but Miles found himself changing the name from Jessie to Joey.

Miles and Joey had never fought over a woman, and Miles intended to keep it that way. Since sharing wasn't an option he would consider, what other choice did he have except to step aside?

Of course, that step would be easier to take without Lucy around.

"See what you're missing?" Joey asked.

He hadn't laid down the gauntlet. In fact, Miles braced himself because it looked like his friend was only just getting started.

"Yeah, but—" Lucy started.

Joey steamrolled right over her. "It's a ten-hour drive to Nashville. We'll be there four days before we head on to Texas."

"Nashville," she whispered, clearly tempted.

Miles remained quiet, though the smart thing to do would be to put his foot down, come up with some solid reasons why Lucy should remain on the farm.

"I can't just pack up and go," she said with a lot less force.

Joey leaned toward her. "Why not? You just finished saying you longed for an adventure. We're offering you one."

Lucy took a long sip of her wine, clearly stalling. It looked to Miles like she was seriously thinking about the offer. "So I would just fly home after Nashville? Just one week?" she mused, speaking more to herself than them.

"Or venture on to Texas with us," Joey added. "I saw the way your eyes lit up when I talked about our plans on that ranch. You should be a part of that."

Miles fought hard to swallow his groan.

Lucy shook her head, obviously thinking that Joey was starting to get carried away. "And what comes after Texas?"

Joey's grin proved he was claiming the victory, even though Miles thought it was premature. "We make our way back to the East Coast—Baltimore, to be exact—to film the next show, so it would be very easy for us to drop you off at home on the way."

"Oh," Lucy breathed.

Miles had to hand it to Joey. He'd certainly tied up Lucy's dream trip in a big bow.

"Or you could just pack in the day job and join us in our adventurous lifestyle," Joey joked.

She didn't laugh. "I couldn't do that. I wouldn't... I'm not..."

Miles couldn't tell if Lucy was trying to convince herself or them.

"Come on, Lucy," Joey said. "You've spent your whole life on that farm, taking care of your grandparents, working in the brewery. Do something for yourself. You deserve it, honey."

Lucy toyed with the stem of her wineglass, not speaking for several moments. When she did, Miles knew he was screwed.

"So I'd be gone a couple of weeks?" she asked.

"Plus a few days, yeah," Joey replied.

Miles needed to stem this flood somehow. "If that's impossible, like you said, you could always catch a flight home from Nashville."

Maybe he could survive one more week with her...but two? Three?

Joey flashed him a dirty look. "Or we'll drop you off, like *I* said. You don't want to miss Texas."

Lucy bit her lower lip. "Is there even room for me in the car?"

Joey rubbed his hands together. "That's the best part. This season, the show's providing us with a motorhome to travel in. It arrives tomorrow morning. When we told our producers about the cool side trips we'd been taking, they offered us the RV with the caveat that we record anything from our journey we think is interesting. The idea is to include outtakes at the end of each show, where it's me and Miles recording funny shit on our way to the location."

"That would be fun," Lucy agreed. "An RV, huh? Guess that requires a follow-up question. Where would I sleep in the RV? Because this felt more doable when I thought you guys drove in your car and slept in hotels."

"There's a king bed in the bedroom, a bunk bed, and a loft bed above the front seats. Plenty of room." Joey had an answer for everything. In fact, he seemed so prepared, Miles began to wonder if his friend had only just thought of inviting Lucy to join them or if he'd come here tonight with the plan already in hand.

Lucy took a sip of wine. "Can I think about it?"

Joey reached out and squeezed her hand. "Of course. The RV doesn't arrive until tomorrow afternoon. Take the night, talk to your family."

Bridget returned with their food, which was absolutely delicious. Miles had never had lamb shank navarin, but he was damn sure he was going to want to have it again.

Jacques, the chef, visited their table for a few minutes, the man just as pleasant and friendly as his wife. They signed his magazine and posed for pictures, with Lucy serving as photographer.

Then they wrapped up the meal by splitting crème brûlée, all of them too stuffed from dinner to order their own desserts.

As they walked back to the car, Joey grasped one of Lucy's hands. When she caught Miles looking at their clasped hands, she reached out and took his as well.

Miles should have let it go, but he didn't want to hurt her feelings.

Or at least, that was what he told himself, rather than admitting he *liked* the feeling of her small hand in his.

The ride home was a quiet affair. Miles figured Lucy and Joey were in the same boat as him. Too pleasantly full and lethargic after a long day and a warm, wonderful meal, as well as consumed by thoughts of what came next.

Lucy parked in front of the cabin.

"Nightcap?" Joey offered. "We've got a variety of Rain or Shine beers and a couple bottles of wine. Mila stocks one hell of a fridge."

"I'd love to come in."

Miles kicked himself for being happy by her response. He'd gone to dinner seeing a light at the end of the tunnel. This was supposed to be their last night. Clear sailing come morning.

However, with his invitation to Lucy, Joey had gone full-on Wile E. Coyote, setting off the dynamite and sealing the tunnel.

Joey grabbed the beer while Lucy claimed a spot on the couch. Miles started to sit down on an overstuffed armchair, but Joey bumped his shoulder, practically herding him toward the couch. "Sit with us."

Against his better judgment, Miles claimed one end of the couch, Joey the other, as Lucy curled one leg beneath her, sitting in between them.

Joey handed out the beers and they tapped them together.

"To new adventures," Joey said before taking a sip.

Lucy smiled. "I'm still thinking about it, Joey. I haven't committed to anything yet. In truth, I'm not sure I can make this work on such short notice. It wouldn't be fair to Sam and Theo."

Joey placed his beer on the end table, then turned toward Lucy, his arm draped over the back of the couch behind her. "You deserve a vacation, Lucy. Are you telling me Sam never takes one?"

Lucy's grimace answered that question, so she didn't bother to answer it, but instead lodged one of her own. "Is he always this relentless?" she asked Miles.

"Honestly? Yes," Miles replied. In the past, he'd always considered Joey's drive one of the best things about him because their ambitions lined up perfectly. They were committed to making the show a continued success, hoping to draw this career out for as long as they could. After all, *House Hunters* was still going strong after two decades. They wouldn't mind beating that record.

"You know you want to do this, Lucy." Joey took her beer away, placing it next to his on the end table. "If it helps, call it a work trip. You can bring your equipment and record a few episodes of *Kiss and Tell* while we're on the road."

With that suggestion, Joey managed to slam the last nail in Miles's coffin because his friend had finally dangled the ultimate carrot.

"I *could* do that," Lucy said softly. "I've always wanted..."

"You don't really want the show to be a hobby, Luce," Joey continued. "Why not take the next few weeks to see if you could turn it into a career. Your dream job, right?"

She nodded, clearly overwhelmed by temptation. "It is," she confessed. "I think if I told Sam and Theo I would be filming the show..."

Joey stroked Lucy's hair, and Miles didn't miss her soft intake of air at the touch or the slightest tinge of pink creeping up her neck to her cheeks.

Joey leaned toward her, his lips next to her ear. "They'd encourage you to go."

"They would," she whispered.

Miles tried to ignore the way his body was responding to this conversation.

No. It wasn't the words that were impacting him.

It was their body language. He was reacting to Joey's hand slipping beneath Lucy's hair to gently grip her neck. To the way Lucy's eyelids became heavy. To the way she turned her face just the slightest bit until Joey's lips were a mere inch from hers.

Miles told himself he should get up and walk away, but he couldn't. Just like he couldn't stop watching them.

He was tempted to tell Joey to hurry the hell up and kiss her. Then he wanted to demand he do more. Like unbutton her pretty blouse and run his lips along that elegant neck, down to her breasts. From there, he'd suggest Joey draw her bra down until one of her nipples popped free, so his friend could take it in his mouth and suck until Lucy moaned.

Jesus Christ. He'd never considered himself a voyeur, but he wouldn't mind a show.

To keep himself from speaking, Miles took a long sip of his beer, nearly draining the bottle, before deciding alcohol was the last thing he needed right now. He should keep his wits about him. He put the bottle down, trying again to make himself leave the room.

Joey must have sensed the war he was waging with himself because his friend's gaze darted over Lucy's shoulder to capture his, and Miles saw the subtle way Joey shook his head before turning back to her...and giving her the kiss Miles had been waiting for.

This kiss was much different from the first one Miles had stood witness to on the porch. That one, while hot, had been more tentative, an exploration, a get-to-know-you kind of first-date kiss.

This one surpassed that by far, Joey and Lucy coming together like they'd known each other for years. It was as if they were ravished, their hungry, passionate embrace rivaling those of lovers reunited after a war.

Joey gripped her neck tightly in one hand, the other slipping around her back. Lucy's fists clenched his shirt, tugging him closer with a desperation that took Miles's breath away. He saw their lips part, their tongues touch, and suddenly, Miles was parched for his own taste.

He sat there, still as a statue. Or so he thought.

Between one blink and the next, he realized he wasn't as far away as he'd been a minute ago. Because before...he couldn't feel the heat from their bodies, couldn't smell the beer on their breath as their kiss went nuclear.

Joey released Lucy, rubbing his beard against her cheek as he whispered in her ear, loud enough for both of them to hear. "Kiss Miles. I want to see it this time."

Miles tried to resist, but everything about tonight—the cozy fireplace and romantic atmosphere in the restaurant, the wine, the way Lucy's lips were right there, so full and pink and utterly kiss-able—was just too much. So, he allowed himself to shut down all the thoughts and anxieties and bad feelings that had been swirling around inside him for nearly a week and give in to what he wanted.

One kiss, he thought as he looked at her.

Just one.

Lucy twisted, desire etched in every line on her face, and he was helpless to resist her. They slammed together with the same level of need as they showed Joey exactly what he'd missed yesterday morning. Miles grasped her waist, his fingers itching to pull her over his lap, so that he could feel the heat from her pussy against his denim-covered cock. He hadn't dry-humped since he was a teenager, but damn if he didn't want to do that with Lucy.

She cupped his cheeks in her soft hands, kissing him like...

Fuck. She kissed him like he mattered.

He wasn't sure what to make of that, what to do with it. Like Joey, he was no stranger to dating, to one-night stands, to casual affairs. Neither of them had been living like monks, but it had been a long time—too fucking long since he'd kissed a woman he knew he could...

Care for.

Fall in love with.

Miles's phone buzzed in his pocket, the sound hitting him like a bucket of cold water being dumped over his head. He jerked back, the hands he'd been using to hold Lucy tight, now pushing her away.

Lucy blinked several times, her brows furrowed in confusion over his abrupt actions.

"That shouldn't have happened." Miles had to clear his throat, the guttural words sounded too gruff, even to his own ears.

Lucy bit her lip, suddenly unsure and uncomfortable.

Goddammit. He'd hurt her feelings.

He didn't have to look directly at Joey to see the anger on his friend's face. Less than a week in and Joey's protective instincts when it came to Lucy were already full force.

Lucy nodded, bobbing her head too rapidly. "You're right. I haven't decided what to do about the grand adventure, but if I do decide to go, it's best that we do it as friends. Thank you for being the voice of reason, Miles." She rose as she spoke the last, not looking at him or Joey.

"Lucy," Joey started, when she made a beeline for the door.

"It's getting late, and I need to run the idea of taking some time off by my family."

She was still considering the trip. Or perhaps she was simply pretending she was so that she could make her escape.

Miles wasn't sure if he was relieved or disappointed by the idea that she might turn them down.

Joey followed her to the door, reaching out to grasp her hand before she could get away. "Please come with us, honey."

She smiled at the nickname, but Miles noticed it didn't quite reach her eyes.

"I promise I'll think about it," was all she said.

Joey nodded stiffly, then stood in the open doorway, watching as she climbed into the car and drove down the country lane.

Once she was gone, Joey closed the door with a bit too much force before turning the lock. Miles braced himself for the onslaught, certain his friend was about to read him the riot act.

Instead, he leaned against the door wearily, studying his face for a moment.

"I'm sorry."

Of all the things Miles expected Joey to say, that sure as shit wasn't on his bingo card. "What?"

Joey gave him a guilty look. "I should have talked to you before inviting Lucy to come with us. It's just...the idea popped into my head at dinner and the next thing I knew, I was saying it out loud."

Miles couldn't be angry about that.

Well, he could, but he wasn't.

He knew his best friend very well. Knew Joey Moretti was nothing if not impulsive. It was probably one of the best things about him, since Miles tended to be overly cautious. These last two years with Joey had been the best of his life because he'd experienced things, done things he never would have considered attempting without Joey dragging him along.

"It's okay, Joe," Miles said. "Lucy is great. I meant what I said the other day. She's perfect for you." This time he was careful not to pause after the word *perfect*. "I know you want to spend more time with her, and her coming along will give you that opportunity."

"Us," Joey added.

Miles sighed but didn't contradict him. How could he after what they'd just done on the couch? He didn't exactly have a leg to stand on, but that didn't mean he wasn't going to try to find his footing again.

He had to.

"I'm think I'm going to turn in. Good night." Joey pushed away from the door and walked to his bedroom.

"Night," Miles called out, following suit, heading to his own room.

He sank down on his bed, unsurprised when his phone buzzed again with an incoming text, Rhiannon's name flashing on the screen.

You still up?

He considered ignoring the text until the kiss he shared with Lucy replayed in his mind.

He couldn't be a part of what Joey wanted.

He just...couldn't.

Miles opened the message thread.

Yeah. Just climbed into bed. Been a busy week.

Coming home for Thanksgiving?

Tell her, he thought to himself. *Tell her.*

Tell her you can't be her friend. Tell her you can't talk to her anymore, can't see her. Tell her it's over. All of it.

Miles touched his lips, the taste of Lucy still lingering there.

Then he stared at his phone, the words he should say fading away.

No. But I'll be home for Christmas.

He put his phone on the nightstand, not waiting for a reply. Then he lay down without bothering to get undressed and closed his eyes, closed his mind.

To all of it.

Chapter Seven

Joey watched as Lucy rolled her suitcase behind her, Miles following with Lucy's backpack slung over one shoulder, her laptop case over the other, while he carried her camera bag in both hands.

She was coming with them.

Joey hadn't been able to wipe the grin off his face since she'd texted him less than an hour ago. She'd gone right to the wire time-wise on making her decision. The RV had arrived just a few minutes before her text, and he'd been sweating it, mentally creating a list of ways he could convince her if she said no.

Given the fact she was ready to go, he'd venture to guess she had packed last night, just so that she would be prepared one way or the other. That felt like something Lucy would do.

"Need a hand?" Joey asked as they approached the RV.

Lucy shook her head. "Nope. Miles is lugging the heavy stuff."

Joey reached for her hand as soon as she was within arm's reach, tugging her close to give her yet another kiss on the cheek. "I'm so glad you're coming with us."

She laughed. "So I gathered."

Ten minutes after receiving her text, he and Miles arrived at the farmhouse, anxious to get to her lest she change her mind. Lucy had stepped out onto the porch and Joey had picked her up, spinning her around, then twirling her in a celebratory dance.

Miles's response had been more subdued as he simply rolled his eyes at Joey's antics, then gave her a stiff sidearm hug.

Joey had felt the strong urge to roll his eyes right back at his best friend because, while Miles had a good poker face, Joey saw right through it. Miles was happy she was coming. He didn't want to be happy, but he was.

For a few minutes last night on that couch, Joey let himself believe everything was falling into place as Miles remained there, watching him kiss Lucy, before giving their girl one hell of a kiss himself.

Joey didn't know what was better. Kissing Lucy or watching Miles kiss her. It all felt perfect in that moment because he'd been certain Lucy would join them on the road, and the three of them would take the first steps toward an incredible future.

He should have known better.

Because Miles's damn phone buzzed, his Rhiannon-riddled brain kicked in, and he pushed Lucy away.

Joey's initial reaction was anger. He couldn't understand how Miles could be so fucking blind to what was standing right in front of his face. Rhiannon was the wrong woman, something that should be evident to his best friend. Fool me once, shame on you. Fool me twice, shame on me. Fool me three times? Four times? Jesus Christ. There wasn't a word strong enough to describe that level of absurdity.

However, his anger faded quickly when Joey realized *he* was to blame. Miles had told him he didn't want to be part of a three-some, and Joey had done exactly what Tony had told him *not* to do—force him.

Patience had never been Joey's strong suit, and he was as subtle about his desires as a hundred-person marching band parading through the middle of a living room.

He needed to stop pushing so hard, or he'd end up shoving Miles away. And in the process, he could lose Lucy too.

Miles and Lucy carried her things into the RV, and Joey started to follow, stopping when he heard someone calling his name.

Joey turned around, unsurprised to find Levi and Sam headed his direction. He would have been shocked if he and Miles made it off this mountain without at least one of her male cousins issuing "the warning."

Joey, Tony, Luca, and Gio had warned off many guys when Layla was in high school and shortly after, letting them know their sister was to be treated with respect at all times or else. Fortunately, since he and his brothers were all well over six feet tall, and muscular, thanks to years of physical labor, they'd never had to come up with an actual "or else." The threat had always been enough.

"Are you the elected representatives?" Joey joked.

Both men got it. Sam cracked a tiny bit of a smile, while Levi held steady, his stern expression firmly in place.

"We wanted to have a word with you before you left," Sam started.

Joey nodded. "I would have lost respect for you if you hadn't."

Levi huffed out a grunt that could have been approval or a warning. "We've noticed you and Lucy spending a lot of time together the past few days. Neither one of you has exactly been subtle about your interest in the other."

Joey had wondered why he was the only recipient of this stern talking to. Evidently, Miles was successful in his attempts to appear uninterested, even though Joey knew he was anything but.

Sam ran a hand through his hair. "I have to say, we were shocked when she stopped by our farmhouse last night to ask about taking off for a few weeks. Despite her comments about wanting to see the world, Lucy's never taken a holiday in her life. I can count on one hand the number of times she hasn't shown up to work, and all those absences were due to illness."

"I'm aware of that. Lucy told us last night at dinner. She also shared her desire to travel. I'll admit my initial invitation was impulsive, but the second I issued it, I knew I wanted her to come with us."

Levi sighed. "Lucy loves this farm, and she loves us more than anything. We all know that. Just like we know..." His jaw clenched, and Joey got the sense the other man had been about to say something different than what he finished with. "She deserves to see more of the world."

"She takes her responsibilities seriously—*too* seriously. This is the first time she's ever asked for time to do something she really wants," Sam added. "We couldn't let her miss the opportunity."

Damn. Lucy really did have an amazing family.

"Her dream to travel was the main reason I invited her along. That, along with the chance to record more episodes of her show. We're driving back by here in three weeks, so it felt like a decent amount of time for her to dip her toe in the water, mark a couple of cities off that travel list of hers. And she can always fly home any time before that if she gets homesick," Joey reassured them.

"We're going to need your word that you'll look after her, Joey," Levi insisted.

"You don't even have to ask. Lucy will be safe with me and Miles. I swear," he vowed.

While Sam seemed convinced, Levi still looked uneasy.

"Levi—" Joey started.

"You said you have a sister, right?" he interjected.

Joey nodded.

"Would you feel good about putting her in an RV with two guys she's known less than a week?"

Joey frowned because... Well, damn. He sure as fuck wouldn't. His silence must have been enough of an answer.

Levi grimaced. "Yeah. That's what I thought. But I'm going

with my gut on this because it's telling me that you and Miles are good guys and you won't hurt my cousin."

"We won't," Joey swore. God, if he had his way, he'd spend every day for the rest of his life making Lucy happy.

Levi nodded, just as Lucy and Miles stepped out of the RV.

"Okay, then." Levi reached out to shake Joey's hand, then Miles's. Sam did the same.

The handshake must have been the equivalent of the Bat Signal going up because Storms started filing out of the farmhouse, joining them in the yard.

There were lots of hugs and laughs, and even a quick tour of the RV for Remi, who was dying to see inside.

None of the other men gave him or Miles the stink eye, which proved Joey had guessed correctly about Sam and Levi being charged with the task of laying down the law.

Joey was almost sorry to leave. While they'd only been on the mountain a short time, he and Miles had been truly welcomed and treated like part of the Storm family.

Finally, after everyone said their goodbyes, he, Miles, and Lucy climbed into the RV. Miles climbed behind the wheel, volunteering to drive the first stretch. Joey and Lucy waved from the windows until they made the first turn, the farmhouse and her family now out of sight.

Lucy gave Joey the passenger seat, while she claimed the one behind it.

For the first ten minutes or so, they were quiet as Miles maneuvered his way down the mountain. Joey stole a few peeks over his shoulder at Lucy, who was looking out the window with a pensive expression. Joey was slightly concerned she might change her mind and ask them to take her back home.

Which didn't make sense to him. It was clear Lucy wanted to travel, so her reticence felt misplaced. Then he recalled this was her first trip, so she was probably just nervous.

"Can we talk for a second about how bougie this RV is?" Joey asked as he spun the seat around so he could see Miles *and* Lucy without having to twist his head at an awkward angle.

His jaw had hit the ground when the RV was dropped off, he and Miles marveling over how large it was inside. They'd seen pictures of it, but those hadn't done justice to just how massive the thing was. The network had been careful to provide an RV that didn't require them to get a special license to drive, but it looked like they were skirting the line.

It was a mammoth. The interior was cozy and spacious, with recessed lighting, a widescreen HDTV, comfortable seating, tile flooring, an induction cooktop, and tons of storage. Lucy had already claimed the bunk bed, maintaining she was the "hitch-hiker" and the shortest. No amount of insistence on his or Miles's part would change her mind.

Miles grinned. "I think it's safe to say we're riding in style. The refrigerator is even fully stocked."

"No way." Lucy spun her seat around, taking in the rest of the RV. Then she shook off whatever was bothering her, giggling glee-fully. "I'm sorry," she said, as if she had to apologize for laughing. "It's just... I can't believe I'm doing this."

Miles chuckled, and Joey noticed that right after getting Lucy's text that she was coming, his friend immediately started to relax.

"It's definitely going to be an adventure," Miles added.

They had mapped out their route this morning, opting to spend tonight in a campground by Claytor Lake. It was a nine-and-a-half-hour drive to Nashville, but they were only tackling about a third of that today. Given their late start, they figured they'd save the bigger portion of the driving for tomorrow. Lucy pulled out her phone to look at the campground as Miles took the on-ramp to I-81. Joey was tasked with serving as deejay, all of them marveling at the state-of-the-art audio system.

For the first couple of hours, they took turns suggesting songs, anxious to share their favorites. Joey grinned when Lucy sang along loudly to Noah Kahan's "Dial Drunk." Because none of them had eaten lunch prior to hitting the road, Miles pulled over at a rest stop so that they could stretch their legs and make sandwiches. As they ate, the three of them sat around the table, engaging in a heated discussion about *Star Wars* movies, debating which were the best and whether the newest generation lived up to the reputation of the old.

Miles had glanced at his phone a couple times while they were making lunch, frowning at the screen. If Rhiannon was texting, it appeared his friend wasn't responding. Or perhaps she wasn't texting at all, and *that* was what was bothering him. Both those scenarios sucked.

Joey wasn't sure where Miles's head was regarding his ex because history seemed to be repeating itself. Miles said he wasn't interested in resuming a friendship with her, but that was certainly ringing false, given their regular communication. Miles also seemed to believe Rhiannon wasn't interested in getting back together, but Joey wouldn't bet the farm on that, given how often she was texting and calling.

As far as Joey was concerned, if Miles was as over the woman as he claimed, he should tell her to lose his number. Maybe not that harshly, but it was clear her texting and calling was blurring some lines for Miles.

In the middle of the meal, Joey pulled out his phone, firing up the video camera, panning around the table to show their first meal in the RV. He was certain the video wasn't interesting enough to be used as an outtake for the show, but that wasn't why Joey was recording it.

He wanted to preserve this memory for himself. Wanted to be able to look back one day at what he prayed was not only the beginning of a road trip adventure but of a lifetime one. Miles and Lucy were smiling, hamming it up for the camera, cracking jokes. They looked good together. Really good.

After a minute or two, Joey flipped the camera, reaching out to pull Lucy closer so that she was in the frame. "So tell the fans,

Lucy Storm, what are you most looking forward to as we start this big adventure?"

Lucy tapped her chin, playfully considering the question. "I think I'm most excited about meeting new people and seeing new places."

Joey nodded, then flipped the camera back around. "And you, Miles?"

"I'm looking forward to the food. Hot chicken in Nashville. Barbeque at Sparks."

"Oh," Lucy said excitedly. "I want to change my answer to that."

Joey laughed. "Too late."

Lucy grabbed his phone, pointing it at him. "And what are you looking forward to, Joey?"

Joey didn't hesitate for a second as he gave them his honest answer. "Spending time with my two favorite people."

Lucy smiled and said, "Aww."

Miles smirked, shaking his head. "Ass-kisser," he muttered.

Even though they were finished eating, none of them made a move to clean up so they could get back on the road.

"So you grew up in Philadelphia and Baltimore?" Lucy asked Joey.

"I did. But Philadelphia is the only city I call home." There must have been something in his tone that gave away his feelings for Baltimore.

"Not a fan of Baltimore?" Miles asked, clearly surprised. The two of them had spent a good bit of time there, usually visiting Layla and her partners, always taking the time to stop at Pat's Pub for a pint and a chat with the Collins clan. It made sense that to Miles, all of that looked like Joey enjoying time in his old stomping grounds. But the truth was, he went back for the people, not the place.

"Baltimore is fine. The only reason we ended up there was because Dad was offered a really good job when I was eleven. It was one of those too-good-to-pass-up deals. Believe me, that was the only reason he would uproot us and leave his beloved Philadelphia."

"Never met a bigger Philly fan," Miles admitted. "I don't think I've ever seen the guy dressed in a shirt that wasn't emblazoned with the name of one of his Philly sports teams."

Joey chuckled. "Tell me about it. I had to take the old guy shopping for a dress shirt to wear to my cousin Elio's wedding to Gianna. He bitched the entire time and bought the thing under duress, insisting Elio wouldn't mind if he wore his Flyers jersey."

Miles frowned. "Elio played for the Baltimore Stingrays."

"He sure did, but Dad insisted that Elio's allegiance to 'that other team,'" Joey air-quoted, "ended the second Elio retired and moved home."

"It's a fair point. I'm sure Elio wouldn't have minded the jersey," Miles added. "He only had eyes for his bride that day. Never seen a guy so in love, with his wife *and* his daughter."

"That's because Sofia is so stinking adorable," Joey added, grinning when he thought about Elio and Gianna's one-year-old daughter. "And while Elio wouldn't have cared, Nonna would have had Dad's head if he'd shown up in a jersey. I was trying to save Dad from one of her long-winded lectures about proper attire."

"How long did your family live in Baltimore?" Lucy asked.

"Five years." Joey was delighted that she was interested in learning more about them.

"And what made your dad decide to come home?"

Joey sighed. "My mom died."

"Oh, Joey." Lucy leaned closer, reaching out to touch his knee. "I'm sorry. I didn't know."

"Cancer," he said. "I think that's probably why I'm not fond of Baltimore. Too many bad memories in that city."

Lucy squeezed his knee. "I'm sure there are."

"I spent most of my last year there at Johns Hopkins. After she passed, my dad was struggling to deal with five grieving kids on his own. Nonno and Nonna told him to come home, and he did. That was the summer right before my junior year of high school."

"That's a hard time to move," Lucy observed.

Joey shook his head. "It wasn't that bad. I reconnected with friends from elementary school, and I was back home with my cousins. I'd missed the hell out of them. And best of all, after we came back, Dad and my uncle Renzo opened Moretti Brothers Restorations. Which set me up for," Joey waved his arms around, gesturing at the RV, "this sweet life."

"Guess we have something in common. We both lost our moms when we were young," Lucy pointed out.

"Miles told me about the car accident," Joey said. "About Nora."

Lucy took a sip of water. "It was a bad time for our family."

Joey nodded. "I'm sure it was. Grief is a bitch. Takes a long time to shake her off."

"Yeah." Lucy was quiet for a moment, but she bounced back quick, a smile crossing her face. "You know...I looked up your bio online after that first season of *ManPower*. Both of your bios, actually. I was curious about the two of you. When I saw that you were offered the hosting gig after Moretti Brothers was featured on a couple episodes of another cable show, I watched them. Seeing you with your brothers reminded me so much of how my cousins are together. By the way, how bad was the Levi and Sam speech?"

Miles looked confused. "Speech?"

Joey chuckled. "Levi and Sam were elected representatives for the Storm men, sent to make sure I minded my manners."

Miles blinked a few times, and Joey could almost read his thoughts, could see him wondering why he hadn't gotten the same warning.

"Were they mean?" Lucy asked, concerned.

Joey shook his head. "I've had worse. Hell, I've *given* worse. They just wanted to make sure their sweet, innocent, impressionable baby cousin was safe."

Lucy's eyes narrowed. "Please tell me they didn't use those words."

Joey considered drawing out the joke, adding a few more words that would get under her skin, but Lucy looked annoyed enough to fire off a text to both men if he didn't let them off the hook. "I might have inferred those words."

Lucy slapped his arm playfully. "You're in for a rude awakening if that's how you see me. Like I said, when I watched those shows with you and your brothers, I saw shades of my cousins. You guys are all birds of a feather. Oh, and FYI, I think Aunt Claire might have a crush on your brother Tony. She watched the shows with me, and she fanned herself every time he came on the screen."

Joey laughed loudly. "It's the hair, isn't it? Fucker always gets all the attention because of that hair."

Lucy smirked. "Right. It's just the hair. It has nothing to do with his firm, muscular body or his—"

"You can stop there." Joey reached out, wrapping his arm around her shoulders to hold her in place so he could tickle her, when she tried to continue listing his big brother's attractive attributes. Then he cast a glance in Miles's direction. "Our girl is thinking about other guys, Miles. Seems like we should do something about that."

"Not other guys," she argued. "Just Tooonnny." She drew out his older brother's name, working overtime to make it sound dreamy.

To Joey's surprise, Miles stood from the table with a grin. "I think you're right. We'd better take care of that."

Lucy's gaze traveled from Joey to Miles, though there wasn't a trace of nervousness there. If anything, she looked turned on.

Joey just hoped it was him and Miles pushing those buttons and not thoughts of his brother.

"I'm a free agent," she taunted, shaking off Joey's arm and rising from the table. "I can look at Tony if I want. After all, he has that chiseled jaw and—"

"Hmm," Joey interrupted, shaking his head. "Thinking about my brother. Yeah, that's not gonna work for us, honey."

"And those dreamy eyes," she added, ignoring him.

Miles chuckled darkly as he crossed his arms. "You're poking the bear, Luce."

"Oh yeah?" Lucy tilted her head. "And which one of you is the bear?"

"Tread carefully, little girl," Miles warned.

There was no missing the way Lucy's nipples made an appearance, the tight nubs poking through her T-shirt or the way her eyelids slipped lower at his words.

Joey wiggled his eyebrows, enjoying the game. "We might need to teach her a lesson about teasing us."

Miles snorted.

When Lucy offered him a fearless, wicked grin, Joey knew he was in trouble.

"Have you ever considered letting your hair grow longer?" she asked.

Miles barked out a laugh, clearly amused by her jab.

"Lucy." Joey laced his tone with a sensual threat.

She tapped her chin. "No. I guess that wouldn't look good on you. Hair like Tony's requires special bone structure."

"A chiseled jaw?" Miles tossed one of her own descriptions back at her, just to get under Joey's skin.

"I don't need long hair to be hot, honey." Joey stood and took two steps toward her as Lucy moved away, inching closer to Miles. While the RV was roomy, a game of cat and mouse wouldn't last long.

Lucy glanced at Miles, as if seeking help, mistakenly thinking he was on her side because of his jest. He remained where he was and shrugged. "I told you not to poke the bear."

"A gentleman would protect me," she retorted.

He reached out and tugged her against him. "Who said I was a gentleman?"

She looked up at Miles, her cheeks pink, her breathing shallow. Joey could already cut the sexual tension between them with a knife when she added more fuel to the fire, stroking her free hand over her chest.

"I warned you about that bro code," Miles murmured, his comment piquing Joey's curiosity. "I gotta have my boy's back."

Lucy lifted her hand from his chest, shoving her pointer finger into Miles's pec.

"Poke, poke, poke," she teased, letting Miles know she'd decided he was a bear too.

Miles laughed, catching Lucy off guard when he gripped the wrist of her poking hand and twisted her until her back was flush against his chest, his arm wrapped loosely around her upper body.

Joey seized the opportunity, moving until he was right in front of her. Lucy squirmed in Miles's arms, but he soon realized she wasn't seeking to escape as much as she was trying to drive his friend crazy.

Given the way Miles stiffened, his jaw clenching, he'd guess her "struggles" were having the desired effect. Her ass was rubbing right against his friend's crotch.

Hell, Joey was fighting his own arousal, and if either of the people in front of him looked down, they'd see he was losing the battle, his erection pressing against his jeans.

Joey caught Miles's gaze. "Hold her hands. I think we need to show our girl what happens when she teases us." He started tickling her before Miles could capture her wrists. Not that it took his friend long to restrain her.

Lucy squealed with laughter, struggling in earnest to get away as Joey tickled every part of her that he could reach.

"Tell us we're hot," Joey demanded.

She shook her head, even as she gasped for air, laughing louder. "Never!"

Joey doubled his efforts, driving his fingers into her waist, and when Miles lifted her arms over her head, he dove in, tickling under her arms.

"Tell us we're hot," he repeated.

Lucy put up a hell of a fight, twisting to the left and right in an attempt to free her hands before she finally relented. "Fine! You're hot!"

Joey stopped tickling her, his hands resting on her midriff. "Say it again."

She narrowed her eyes, but her wide smile proved she wasn't annoyed. Rather than speak, she wiggled her wrists until Miles released her. Then she reached out, pinching the hair of his beard between her finger and thumb, using it to pull him closer.

"You're hot," she whispered when their faces were just an inch apart. She backed her words up with a quick, hard kiss before releasing his beard.

Then she twisted around, cupping Miles's cheek in her palm. "You're hot too." She gave Miles the same kiss.

While her lips on his had guaranteed Joey's blue balls, Miles appeared to double down on his efforts to resist Lucy's appeal.

The grumpy ass returned. His smile faded and a crinkle appeared between his eyes. "You're going to be trouble, aren't you?"

Lucy, the irrepressible, perfect woman, shrugged unapologetically. "What can I say? You poked the bear."

Chapter Eight

"Time is going too fast," Lucy complained after they were dropped off at the campground.

Since they were traveling in the RV, one of *ManPower*'s cameramen, Mack, had been tasked with driving Joey's car to Nashville and serving as chauffeur while they were filming, so they weren't driving around the city in the monstrous RV.

"You're not kidding." Joey wondered where in the hell the last four days had gone.

He and Miles had been dreading this trip to Nashville ever since receiving the production schedule. Not that they didn't want to travel to the city but because they hadn't been looking forward to interviewing their guest.

While Jeff Barber, King of the Catio, had proved to be just as annoying as the last time they'd met him, the filming wasn't as unbearable as Joey might have expected.

Probably because Lucy was there.

It was impossible to be in a bad mood around the woman. Once she shook off her initial brief bout of reticence, her enthusiasm for the road trip hadn't waned. If anything, her excitement grew with each passing day as they took in the sights.

Joey didn't realize when they invited Lucy to come along that she didn't just have a list of dream cities she wanted to see, but a detailed itinerary for each one as well. He had been to Nashville a handful of times and considered himself fairly well versed in what the place had to offer. Lucy had shown him the error of his ways quickly, introducing him to attractions he didn't know existed—like Marathon Motor Works and Printers Alley.

Then she'd started playing a one-dollar-sign, five-stars game on Yelp, searching out affordable places for them to eat. According to her rules, they couldn't eat anywhere that didn't have a four-point-five rating or above and it could only have one dollar sign. Joey had protested, assuring her their food budget was more than sufficient to feed them in style, but Lucy wouldn't be moved. And damn if she hadn't found them some of the best food in the city.

She also seemed to attract people like flies to honey, striking up conversations with random strangers whenever they went out. Strangers who felt like friends by the time they parted.

Their first night in Nashville she had befriended a woman, Emily, at the bar where they'd stopped for a quick dinner. When Lucy told Emily about *Kiss and Tell*, she'd begged Lucy to do an interview with her and her wife of twelve years, Tate, which was how he, Lucy, and Miles had found themselves in the living room of a quaint little townhouse in Germantown their *second* night in Nashville.

Joey had insisted on accompanying Lucy for the interview, just to make sure she was safe. He'd told Miles it wasn't necessary for both of them to go, but he refused to stay behind.

Watching Lucy work had been eye-opening, as he and Miles quietly discussed the way people naturally gravitated toward her. She was approachable and funny and an incredible listener. It was probably why her show was such a success. She took a genuine interest in the love lives of her guests, asking insightful questions.

Lucy had accompanied them to Jeff's workshop each day while they were filming, either watching them work or finding a quiet corner to edit her new interview for *Kiss and Tell* on her laptop. The entire crew had already fallen in love with Lucy, the cameramen even teaching her tricks she could use while doing her own interviews.

Joey had expected Miles to push back after that initial flirty tickle fight in the RV on their way to Nashville, and his friend had sure as hell tried. Unfortunately for Miles, Lucy had proven herself to be a worthy adversary. Every time Miles tried to disengage himself from them, she found a way to reel him back in.

The last couple of days, Miles had stopped trying to distance himself, going so far as to start seeking out his own restaurants that satisfied Lucy's game requirements. Last night, they'd taken Miles's suggestion and eaten at an amazing Greek café that was out of this world.

They were four days into their adventure, and Joey never wanted it to end. As far as he was concerned, he and Miles had found their third Musketeer, their third Stooge, their third Amigo. She was the perfect partner in crime, sliding into place with him and Miles like she'd always been there.

They walked into the RV, Miles placing the take-out bag of hot chicken they'd picked up on the dining table. Even though it was their last night in Nashville, they'd opted to eat in since the past few days had been a whirlwind of nonstop activity.

Lucy grabbed plates, utensils, and napkins, while Joey pulled a beer for each of them from the fridge. Miles unpacked the food. In addition to the chicken, pickles, and bread, they'd ordered sides of macaroni and cheese and coleslaw.

The three of them had become comfortable companions, so for a few minutes, they ate in silence, enjoying the delicious chicken with a chorus of "mmms" and happy sighs.

"You were right about Nashville, Joey," Lucy said, breaking the silence. "This place is amazing. I hate the idea of leaving tomorrow. Even if we did have to spend four days with Jeff." Lucy followed her comment with a spot-on imitation of Jeff's braying laugh, which cracked up him and Miles.

"You've perfected it." Joey applauded her, while Miles covered his ears, pretending to wince in pain.

"Never do that again," he begged.

Lucy crossed her heart, though she was mischievous enough that neither of them believed her promise.

"We'll come back to Nashville one day when we have more time and don't have to work." Joey had been talking about their future lately like it was a done deal, making lots of plans. Every time he did so, Lucy's smile wavered, while Miles either sighed or shook his head.

What neither of them did, however, was correct him.

So Joey was calling that a win.

"I guess we're getting up and out tomorrow?" Lucy asked.

Miles nodded. "Yeah. We've given ourselves three days to get to Texas, but it's still a twelve-hour drive. We figured if we put each day's four hours behind us early, we'll have the afternoons to either relax at the campground or explore wherever it is we decide to stop."

Lucy wiped her hands. "Sounds perfect."

"You sure you're finished shopping for your family?" Joey teased.

Lucy had insisted on buying every single Storm a tiny trinket from Nashville since they were, as she said, "carrying her load" at the farm.

Lucy's eyes twinkled as she reached for the backpack sitting on the floor near her. "I know you're joking, but I better check."

He and Miles exchanged amused glances as she pulled out a pile of shot glasses, magnets, bags of hot peanuts, bottles of barbeque sauce for Aunt Claire and Mila, and a large bottle of Tennessee whiskey for her cousins to share. Lucy appeared to do a mental checklist as she tried to remember which souvenir went to which family member. She frowned for a second before she dug back into the bag, finally pulling out a guitar pick.

"Phew. Thought I'd lost the pick Billy asked me to get for him." Lucy started tossing everything back in her bag.

"Billy?" Miles asked.

"Yeah. You met him when we were filming. He works in the brewery."

"Tall, thin guy, blond hair?" Joey asked.

Lucy nodded. "That's him. He started playing guitar in high school. We were dating at the time, and he insisted on learning my favorite song, 'Just the Way You Are.' The Bruno Mars song, not the Billy Joel one. He's got a really great singing voice. He plays at the brewery tasting room one Saturday a month."

Joey frowned. "You dated Billy?"

Lucy nodded. "Yeah, for most of our junior year."

"Was he your first boyfriend?" Miles asked, his arms crossed. He didn't appear pleased to discover Lucy was working with an ex. Joey could relate. He'd never been a particularly jealous guy… until now.

Lucy added another scoop of the macaroni and cheese to her plate, oblivious to their sudden black looks. "Yeah, he was."

Miles must have realized he'd asked the wrong question because he went back in with a follow-up. "As in, your *first time* first boyfriend?"

Lucy blushed and giggled. "Well, yeah. But things didn't work out. In the end, we realized we were better off as friends, so we split the summer before we were seniors."

"And now he works at the brewery?" Joey asked.

Lucy's smile began to fade under their third degree. "To be fair, he's always worked at the farm, started part-time when he was a sophomore. After he graduated, he came on full-time."

Miles leaned back in his chair. "And that's not awkward?"

Lucy's nose crinkled up adorably whenever she was confused. "Why would it be awkward?" She paused a second before her expression cleared. "Oh, you mean because we had sex? No, it's not awkward. For one thing, it's ancient history, and for another, I was serious about us being great friends."

"Is he dating anyone? Married?" Joey hoped she'd throw them

a bone because, while she didn't have a problem working with her former lover, he wasn't so sure he felt the same way.

"Nope. He's single."

Joey blew out a slow breath, trying to get his shit together, knowing his reaction was super misplaced. Especially since he and Lucy hadn't kissed since their first day on the road, and it wasn't like they were a couple. While he'd flirted with her nonstop, he'd been hesitant to push the envelope until Miles was on board.

He was trying to follow Tony's advice by being patient, while showing his friend just how well the three of them fit together. There were moments—like now—when he felt like he was making progress. Because Miles was as hot under the collar about Lucy and her ex working together as he was. Unfortunately, so far, those optimistic glimpses had been too few and far between.

Miles ran a hand over his head, and Joey got the sense he was doing the same mental exercises—talking himself off the ledge before he said something stupid.

"Do you work with any other exes we should know about?" Miles was going for levity, but his husky, almost grunting tone belied the forced smile.

Lucy laughed and shook her head. "Nope. Only Billy. My other ex lives in Chicago."

"Other..." Joey repeated quietly. "You've only dated two men?"

Lucy gave him an exasperated look. "You've seen where I live, Joey. It's not like there are available guys hanging out on every street corner. I grew up in a small town, so I know every single man in Gracemont who's my age. The pickings are slim, believe me."

"So who was the other ex?" Joey was aware they hadn't really engaged in the standard past relationships conversation yet.

Which might be the only topic they'd missed in the past few days, because God knew they'd talked about every other thing under the sun. Joey would have bet money that he had already learned everything there was to know about Miles, but damn if

Lucy hadn't drawn out no less than twenty new stories about his best friend's childhood, his most embarrassing moments, as well as his philosophies about life and death that Joey had never heard.

"Marco," Lucy replied. "He was also a Gracemont guy, but we didn't start dating until after graduation. I didn't go out a lot socially after high school because I was helping take care of Grandma, and then Granddaddy. I went to Whiskey Abbey on my twenty-third birthday and Marco was there. We ran into each other around town from time to time, and we were always friendly, but that night he asked me to dance. Then he called me the next day and invited me to the movies. We dated for a couple years."

"Why did you break up?" Miles asked.

"He left town in search of greener pastures. One of the things we had in common was our desire to see more of the world. Marco went through with it, packing up his car and heading west. He asked me to come with him, but I couldn't leave my family and the farm."

Joey wasn't sure how to feel about that response. Lucy was close to her family, and she took her responsibilities at the brewery seriously. He'd hoped the fact she'd come out on the road with them meant she was open to the possibility of a different kind of life than the one she was living. The fact that she'd said no to Marco left him wondering if the only reason she was here now was because they had couched their invitation as a vacation, not a lifetime.

"He's doing really great in Chicago. Got engaged last Christmas. We catch up whenever he comes back to Gracemont to visit his family."

Joey grinned. "You stay in touch with your exes."

Lucy took a sip of her beer. "Neither of my breakups were bad, and they're both nice guys, so why not? So do I even want to ask about the millions of ex-girlfriends in y'all's pasts?"

Miles jerked his thumb at Joey. "This guy could probably entertain you for a few years on that subject."

Joey shook his head. "Actually, I think I could tackle my list quicker than yours, Miles, because she asked about ex-*girlfriends*. While I've gone on lots of dates, I've only called a few women girlfriends, and those relationships happened so long ago, there's not much to tell."

"No broken hearts?" Lucy asked, eyes wide.

Joey shrugged. "Sure. A couple. First big one was in high school. Got dumped by Mandy Preston, the head cheerleader."

Miles rolled his eyes. "Of course, you dated the head cheerleader."

Joey reached across the table and punched Miles on the shoulder. "Jealous bastard."

"What happened with Mandy?" Lucy placed her elbow on the table, resting her chin in her hand.

"We dated for a few months my junior year. I thought it was love. She felt otherwise. I remember thinking it was the end of the world when she dumped me for another guy, but when I look back now, I wonder if my overblown reaction was because of my mom."

"You were still grieving," Lucy said.

To be honest, this was the first time Joey had considered the connection between his broken heart and his mother's death, though it made sense. "I suffered from an extreme broken heart, crying in my room, swearing off women forever. Drove my brothers crazy for weeks talking about Mandy nonstop, wavering between ways to get her back and bemoaning my lonely state. Finally, Tony stormed into my room one afternoon and told me to suck it up."

Miles chuckled. "That sounds like Tony. Did you do it?"

Joey nodded. "Yeah. Of course, it helped he'd also set me up on a blind date with the sister of the girl he was dating at the time. Nothing helps mend a broken heart like the captain of the volleyball team."

Miles and Lucy laughed.

"Since high school, it's been a lot of casual relationships.

Nothing to write home about, I'm afraid to say." Joey hated to admit just how bad his track record was. "But that hasn't stopped me from looking for the one." He looked at Lucy as he spoke, grinning when she blushed. He wasn't exactly hiding the fact he hoped she might *be* that one.

"How about you?" Lucy asked, turning to Miles. "How long is your list?"

Joey wondered if Miles would answer her question. Rhiannon certainly seemed to be a taboo topic for his best friend, considering Joey hadn't even heard the nitty-gritty details of their relationship until just over a week ago.

He was surprised when Miles wiped his mouth, then said, "There's only one woman on my list."

"Rhiannon?" Lucy asked. Joey had mentioned the other woman's name the other day in the kitchen. Obviously, Lucy had been paying attention.

Miles nodded...and then, to Joey's relief, he opened up, telling Lucy everything he'd shared with *him* about their ups and downs. Lucy listened attentively, asking questions throughout.

"So you're texting and calling each other now?" Lucy asked as Miles's story wound down.

Miles didn't seem pleased with his own answer when he said, "Yeah."

Lucy quickly waved her hands. "I didn't mean that as a judgment. I mean, I'm still friends with both my exes, and you and Rhiannon had an even longer history."

"I'm just not sure..." Miles hesitated.

"That you're over her?" Lucy asked gently.

Miles shook his head. "No. I'm over her. I'm just not sure I should be opening the door to friendship."

Joey didn't point out that Miles had told him point-blank he hadn't intended to. He was curious why Miles hadn't held firm to that assertion.

Lucy seemed to understand. "Maybe not. But I can't imagine it helps that your mother still wants you to be with her."

Miles frowned. "I'm a grown man. While I don't go out of my way to disappoint my mother, this is one time when I can't give her what she wants. I've moved on."

"Have you?" Joey asked.

"I have. Jesus, man." Miles rubbed his jaw wearily. "I played the dumbass the last three times we were together. Fourth time is *not* going to be the charm. Besides, I can never trust her again. Ever."

Joey tried to be appeased by Miles's reassurance, but he wasn't wholly convinced.

Lucy reached out to take Miles's hand. "Only you know what you're capable of handling, Miles. If you think you can be friends with Rhiannon, you should be. If not, then walk away. Just make sure to protect yourself...and this." She reached over, placing her other hand on his heart.

Miles covered her hand with his. "I will." His fingers grabbed hers so he could lift her hand, placing a soft kiss on her palm. "Thanks for listening."

Lucy gave him an adorable grin. "It's sort of what I do. Romance guru and all that shit."

They laughed, then fell quiet again as they finished their meals.

Joey considered everything they'd just shared, enjoying the contentment he felt with them, the closeness. It was as if every time the three of them were alone together, they peeled off another layer, revealing bits and pieces of the things they typically held inside.

"What do you say we clear the table and watch a movie?" Joey suggested.

Miles rose, grabbing his plate. "Sounds good."

The three of them worked to pack the leftovers, then wash and dry the dishes.

Twenty minutes later, they settled together on the couch, as Joey flipped through their choices on Apple TV while they debated which movie to watch. In the end, Lucy made the choice, insisting Miles needed to see *When Harry Met Sally*, so he would better understand why her couples sat on their couches for the *Kiss and Tell* interviews.

Lucy was curled up in between them for the first half, until Joey decided he didn't like the distance between them. Shifting toward her, he placed his arm around her shoulders, crowding her closer to Miles.

Miles shot him a knowing look over her head, smirking.

Joey liked the smirk because it felt like permission to keep going. He played with Lucy's hair, enjoying the way she nuzzled against him. He was debating how to move things up another level, when Lucy took over for him, pushing her bare feet beneath Miles's thigh.

Miles glanced at her, grinning when she said, "My feet are cold."

Joey chuckled. "Oh yeah? How about your hands? Are they cold?" He reached for them as he asked, cupping them between his before lifting them to his mouth to place warm kisses on her skin.

"That helps," she murmured.

From his peripheral vision, he could see Miles's hand resting on her calf, his thumb slowly stroking it.

They pretended to watch the movie for a little longer, even as they continued to touch each other.

Lucy shifted her feet to Miles's lap, groaning softly when he deepened his massage of her calves, his hands slipping under the legs of her jeans to do so.

Joey ran his fingers through Lucy's hair before gripping her neck, using his hold to pull her toward him so that he could place a kiss on the top of her head.

Lucy wasn't idle, her hands digging into Joey's thighs, her feet into Miles's, giving each of them a massage of their own. She giggled briefly, capturing Joey's attention, and he realized Miles was tickling the sole of her foot.

Before long, the movie was completely forgotten as Joey did what he vowed to himself he wouldn't.

He stepped over the line.

Guiding wasn't working.

Time for some force.

Tilting Lucy's face upward, he cupped her chin and kissed her. It was a long, slow kiss that drugged his senses as time stood still. Lucy's hands drifted higher, her fingers brushing over the crotch of his jeans. She drew in a quick intake of breath when she felt his erection tenting the denim.

Joey broke the kiss, placing his forehead against hers briefly before letting his gaze travel to Miles.

Lucy followed it, turning to face Miles, who remained still. While he didn't seek to close the distance, he didn't move when Lucy shifted toward him. Joey figured his friend was going for plausible deniability. If Lucy made the move, Miles could feign innocence.

Or he could have if Miles hadn't grasped her shoulders at the first touch of Lucy's lips on his and tugged her body against his.

"Lucy," Miles whispered against her mouth. "Sweet Lucy."

Joey watched until he couldn't resist joining in. God only knew how Miles would react, but his strength was gone, and he doubted it was ever coming back.

Moving across the couch, Joey wrapped his arm around Lucy's waist, drawing her long blonde hair over one shoulder, baring her neck. As Miles consumed her lips and her soft cries, Joey placed a long line of kisses down the side of her neck, nibbling and licking every luscious inch.

He felt, rather than saw, Miles still when he realized just how close Joey was, but that response was mercifully brief as Miles deepened the kiss, moving a hand to grip her hair in his fist.

When Lucy whimpered, Joey lifted his head, watching as Miles tightened his hold, pulling her hair. Joey wanted to produce one of those whimpers himself.

Slipping his hands under her sweater, he drew his fingers up her stomach, cupping her breasts over her lace bra. Lucy wasn't overly endowed, but she had more than enough to fill his hands. Her back arched, silently demanding more.

Miles continued to kiss her, and Joey had a front row seat. Miles stroked his tongue along her lower lip before nipping it.

Lucy jerked slightly, though he didn't know if it was from Miles's love bite or because Joey had slipped his fingers beneath her bra to pinch her nipples.

They were offering her smalls tastes of pain, testing to see if they added to her pleasure. Given the sounds she was making and the way her body was writhing between them, Joey would say they'd found one of their girl's hot buttons.

Lucy was the first to break the kiss, sucking in deep breaths even as her hands kept a tight hold on Miles's head.

Miles was gasping as well, his eyes closed. When he opened them, they landed first on Lucy's flushed face, then on Joey.

Something shuttered in his expression, and Joey had to bite back a curse when his best friend disentangled himself from Lucy's arms, scooting away from them.

"I..." Miles started. "We..." He frowned, clearly unhappy with himself for getting carried away.

Lucy stiffened in Joey's arms.

No. Fuck that.

He wasn't going to let this moment turn awkward, wasn't going to let Miles pretend this is wrong.

"That was hot," Joey murmured in Lucy's ear. "You're so beautiful, honey."

His words penetrated, Lucy giving him an almost shy smile over her shoulder. "It *was* hot." She held Joey's gaze, and he got the sense she was avoiding looking at Miles.

Joey wasn't going to let his friend off the hook that easily. He exchanged a glance with Miles, lifting one eyebrow, a clear invitation for him to say something.

Miles remained stubbornly silent.

Sighing, Joey reclaimed his side of the couch, Lucy scooching back to the center. The movie was almost over, but none of them were interested enough to rewind it.

Joey took Lucy's hand in his, giving it a squeeze as they pretended to watch the movie.

After another fifteen minutes, the credits began to scroll.

Joey expected Miles to make a quick escape, but Lucy spoke before that could happen.

"Can I ask you guys something?"

He and Miles nodded.

"Have the two of you ever..." Lucy waved her hand in the air, clearly uncomfortable with her question. "I mean, I was wondering... Never mind."

"Ask your question, Lucy," Joey demanded.

"You told me about your siblings, Joey. About their relationships. Is that something that, um, the two of you are looking for?"

Miles shook his head, saying, "Absolutely not."

At the same time, Joey replied, "Yes."

Her gaze traveled between them. "So the two of you have never..."

Lucy never struggled to speak what was on her mind, so Joey wondered if her issues now were based on embarrassment or something else.

"What just happened on this couch is as close as Miles and I have ever come to sharing a woman." Joey's response took Lucy's cheeks from pink to bloodred in an instant.

"I shouldn't have let things go that far," Miles added.

There was no denying the hurt in Lucy's expression at his comment. "Because you don't want—"

"Don't," Miles interjected, lifting his hand. "Don't even think that, Lucy." Softer, he added, "But please don't ask either."

Joey stared at his best friend, grateful Miles wasn't attempting to lie, to tell Lucy he didn't want her. Of course, that was where the gratitude ended because the bastard also didn't want to confess to his feelings either.

"So you don't want to be part of a threesome?" Lucy asked Miles.

"I'm a one-man, one-woman kind of guy. There's no way in hell I can take off my clothes and have sex with a woman while another man is lying in the bed. I'm not wired that way. I'm not saying there's anything wrong with what Joey's brothers and sister have, nothing wrong with Joey for wanting it too. It's just not what *I* want."

As much as he hated what Miles was saying, it also opened the door for Joey to probe a bit deeper. "Is your hesitance a jealousy thing?"

Miles didn't answer immediately, which told Joey he was seriously thinking about the question. When Miles's gaze drifted between him and Lucy, Joey realized Miles had found his answer. And he didn't like it.

Finally, Miles shook his head. "I...I don't think it is."

"Can I ask you something else?" Lucy asked.

Joey got the sense Miles wanted to refuse, his friend struggling with the conversation as much as Lucy.

"Sure," he said, somewhat begrudgingly.

"Did you like it when the three of us kissed?"

Joey had been looking at Lucy, but at her question, his eyes flew to Miles.

Miles dodged the question by asking one of his own. "Are you asking that because you want to participate in a threesome?"

Lucy bit her lower lip. "It's not something I've ever thought about before Joey told me about his family."

Joey leaned forward. "But you've been thinking about it since?"

"It's pretty hard not to. I like kissing both of you," she admitted.

She had to be the bravest woman Joey had ever met, to be so willing to lay out her feelings without reservation and in the face of rejection.

"I like kissing you too," Joey said.

Miles grimaced, then admitted, "Fine. I liked it. But, dammit, kissing is a hell of a lot different from sex, Lucy."

She nodded. "I know that. And I have to admit that while I love what we just did on this couch, I'm not a hundred percent positive I wouldn't freak out or freeze up if we tried to take things any further."

Joey kissed the side of her head. "We would never ask you to do something you weren't comfortable with."

She gave Joey a sweet smile. "I know that too. I trust you." Then she turned to Miles. "I trust both of you. So..." She lifted one shoulder, her adorable expression letting Joey know that while she might not be totally on board, she wasn't ready to jump ship like Miles. "Maybe we could extend this grand adventure, just a little bit, and keep kissing."

Miles bowed his head and rubbed his temples. He didn't agree outright, but in some ways, Joey thought what he said next was even better.

"Trouble," he muttered under his breath.

Joey was reminded of their first afternoon in the RV, and he chuckled. "Grand adventure, huh?"

"I only have this limited amount of time to pack in as many experiences as I can," she said.

"We could have more than just this trip." There was no way in hell Joey was letting this end after Texas. "We can come visit you over the holidays. Or you could come see us in Philly."

Lucy shook her head. "No. I have too many responsibilities at home. I can't take any more time off and even if you came to visit, I would still have to work. I think it's best if the adventure has an end date. The one we already agreed on."

"End date," Miles muttered in disgust.

For the first time, he saw Miles waver. Joey had been approaching this thing with forever in mind, and his best friend had balked. Big-time.

Now...

Joey sighed. One step forward, thirty-two back. He stood up and held his hand out for Lucy. "Come on."

She placed her hand in his as she rose. "Where are we going?"

He pointed in the direction of the bedroom. "To bed."

When she tried to jerk her hand from his, he clarified, "To sleep. *Just* sleep."

"Then why not stay in our own—" Lucy started.

Joey cut her off. "Because you've started a damn countdown, and I'm tired of keeping my distance from you, honey. I want to lay down next to you and watch you sleep."

"Perv," she joked.

Joey winked. "Guilty as charged. Miles?"

He fully expected Miles to refuse to join them.

The fact that he didn't sparked something dangerous inside Joey. Something stupid. Because he was a million miles away from getting what he wanted.

But that didn't stop him from feeling...

Hope.

And it kept growing when—after each of them took a turn in the bathroom to change—they returned to the bedroom.

Lucy climbed in first, sliding to the middle, as Joey claimed the right side. He held his breath until Miles blew out a long, slow sigh and slipped under the covers on the left.

Joey had lived in a lot of different places, laid his head down on a lot of different pillows.

Tonight was the first time he ever felt like he'd finally found home.

It wasn't this RV.

It wasn't this bed.

It was them.

Chapter Nine

Miles pushed into Lucy from behind as he bent her over in the shower, closed his eyes, and groaned. She was so wet and hot and tight. There was no way he could draw this out as long as he wanted. Lucy met him thrust for thrust, pushing back toward him, silently urging him to take her harder, to go deeper.

His eyes flew open when he heard Joey's voice telling Lucy how pretty she was, how perfect. Lucy's lips were wrapped around his cock as she gave Joey one hell of a blow job.

Miles slowed his own movements, spellbound by the image of Joey and Lucy together. Joey's fists were closed in her wet hair, and he used that grip to guide her, to encourage her to go faster.

She hummed around his dick. His friend was close. Miles could tell by the way Joey clenched his teeth, the stuttered staccato of his breathing, the expression that could be confused for pain if one didn't know it was driven by pure pleasure.

"Lucy," Joey panted. "Honey."

Miles was still moving inside her, her pussy clenching tightly around him. He wasn't going to last much longer either.

Joey cursed when his orgasm struck. Miles watched it take him *down, enthralled by the sight. Joey's climax triggered Lucy's, her back arching as she went over the edge.*

He'd never seen anything more beautiful than Lucy and Joey in the throes of passion. The image was too much, and Miles came as well.

God help him. It was the most powerful orgasm he'd ever had, the pleasure of it almost blinding.

He grunted, and then...

Miles caught his come in the hand wrapped around his dick, the other hand pressed flat to the shower wall. He sucked in some much-needed air as the hot water pulsed over his head.

Once he recovered, he let the water wash away the evidence of his fantasy.

His fantasy.

What. The. Fuck?

Miles grabbed the body wash, scrubbing himself roughly, as if that might wash away what he'd just done. He'd *never* had a fantasy like that, never imagined himself having sex with Joey there.

He lifted his eyes heavenward and mentally cussed out his best friend. Fucking Joey! He was planting seeds all over the place and now they were taking root.

The worst part was, he couldn't heap all the blame on Joey's doorstep because Miles hadn't scorched the earth. Nope. What he'd done was worse. He'd put water on those damn seeds, maybe even a little Miracle-Gro.

He never should have agreed to the three of them sleeping together in the same bed. The second Joey made that suggestion, Miles should have put his damn foot down. And honestly, he thought he might have if Lucy hadn't given him an out.

While Joey was determined to see this thing between them go the distance, Lucy had put more manageable parameters on it. Parameters Miles could handle. All she asked for was a casual, just-kissing affair with an end date. No commitment, no relationship, no sex with another man in the bed, no feelings, no broken heart.

Lucy made it clear she wasn't leaving the farm or her family. After all, her ex, Marco, had asked her to hit the road with him and she'd refused. The only reason she came with them was because it was a vacation, not a new life.

Sure, long-distance relationships existed, but Miles knew Joey wouldn't be happy spending long periods of time away from Lucy. He also knew Joey hadn't given up the hope that Miles would be a part of the equation.

Weird fantasies notwithstanding, Miles had not—and would not—change his mind on that.

Probably.

Jesus.

He couldn't sort his shit out about Rhiannon, which, to be perfectly honest, should be the easiest goddamn problem on the planet to solve. So how the hell was he supposed to figure out how to walk through the Lucy/Joey minefield without blowing his life to smithereens in spectacular fashion?

If he was smart, he'd take a step away from *all* of it. Stop texting Rhiannon. Stop sleeping in the same bed with Joey and Lucy.

Miles did an internal eyeroll. Like the last was going to happen.

He turned off the water and grabbed a towel, drying off before wrapping it around his waist.

He was going to get calluses on his hand at this point because the last two nights had been an experiment in sensual torture. Apparently, Joey and Lucy considered sleeping in the same bed the new norm, the two of them donning their pajamas, crawling beneath the covers, and then waiting for him to do the same. Which he did.

Then they spent hours making out like teenagers who'd just discovered what hormones do.

Kissing Lucy was quickly becoming Miles's favorite thing

ever. She kissed like she lived—all in and with exuberant joy. So yeah. He was a big fan of the kissing.

What he hadn't anticipated was how much he also enjoyed being an observer. Voyeurism was a previously undiscovered kink for him. Typically, when Miles was kissing Lucy, Joey wasn't content to sit on the sidelines, his friend always touching her in some way. Either stroking her hair, running his fingers over her body, placing soft kisses on the back of her neck.

It didn't work that way for Miles when Joey was kissing her. His arousal was off the charts when he watched them together. He felt no attraction toward Joey, but he loved seeing him kiss their—

Nope. Record scratch.

Lucy wasn't *theirs*.

Miles lathered his face with shaving cream and tried to focus his attention on the task at hand. Nothing good would come from overanalyzing unwanted feelings.

Rhiannon had called twice since they'd left Stormy Weather Farm, but both times he'd sent the calls to voicemail. He should tell her to stop calling, tell her that he couldn't be friends with her. Too much water had flowed under that bridge. The only reason he hadn't picked up the phone was because the conversation was going to be a hard one, and he didn't want to have it while Joey and Lucy were within earshot, which was pretty much always.

So instead, he shot off the same lame texts in response.

Busy. Talk later.

That was him. King of the Cop-outs.

He winced when he nicked himself with the razor.

"Shit," he muttered, blotting the blood with a piece of toilet paper.

They'd gotten up extra early this morning so that they could get the driving part of their day over quickly. They had pulled into tonight's RV park an hour earlier, hooking up the water and electric so that Miles could take a shower. Finishing up, he stepped out of the bathroom. The space was really too tiny to dress in comfortably, so he'd laid out his clothes in the bedroom. He'd taken two steps in that direction when he heard Lucy's wolf whistle.

He turned around, grinning, until he spotted Lucy on Joey's lap.

His dick twitched, the hand job he'd just given himself to blow off some steam forgotten like it had never happened. It could not be good for his health to live with a hard-on twenty-four seven.

Miles changed direction, walking toward them. "What's going on out here?"

Lucy pointed to her laptop on the table in front of her. "I was trying to upload my new *Kiss and Tell* episode, but Joey keeps distracting me."

"If you don't want to be distracted, you need to stop looking so adorable." Joey's arm was wrapped around her middle, holding her in place when she playfully squirmed. Her attempts to rise were merely for show because it didn't look to Miles like she really wanted to get off Joey's lap.

When she wiggled her ass again, Miles caught Joey's wince. Clearly, his friend was suffering from the same prolonged erection problem.

Lucy stopped moving, sighing deeply.

"What's wrong?" Miles asked.

She closed the lid on her laptop, her gaze drifting down to his towel.

He probably should have gotten dressed before venturing out here because this was the first time he'd revealed so much of his body to her. He hadn't even slept shirtless—though that was his norm at home—donning lounge pants and a soft cotton tee both nights before their make-out sessions. While Lucy's hands had slipped beneath his shirt to touch him, she hadn't seen his bare chest.

"I think I might sleep in my own bed tonight," she said softly.

Joey made a buzzer sound. "Wrong."

Miles schooled his features, trying hard not to acknowledge how disappointed he was that she wanted to call a halt to their kissing adventure, even though he'd just been thinking the exact same thing.

"Joey..." she started, turning to look at him over her shoulder.

"Why?" Joey asked.

She blew out a frustrated breath. "Because blue bean is real, and it hurts."

Joey burst out laughing.

Lucy, unamused, narrowed her eyes. "Aren't you guys...like..." Her eyes drifted to the towel wrapped around Miles's hips again. Because yeah, he was. And the towel was doing a shitty job hiding just how much like *that* he was.

Her gaze, *there*, was as potent as if she'd wrapped her hand around it, because his dick was ready for round two.

Miles jerked his head toward the shower. "I gave myself a hand," literally, "with that."

Joey grinned. "I did the same thing this morning before we got on the road."

Lucy rolled her eyes. "I'm not usually like this. I mean, sex with Billy and Marco—"

"You're going to have to stop reminding me that you work with someone you slept with," Joey grumbled.

She giggled. "Jealous?"

He didn't even bother to lie. "Insanely so."

"Fine," Lucy relented. "With those two ex-boyfriends, who shall remain nameless, the sex was nice, but I never had this desperate need to jump back into bed with either of them. Sex has never felt like something I would die without."

Joey shook his head. "The fact you just described the sex as *nice* tells us exactly why you weren't desperate."

"Yeah. Well. I feel like I'm about to come out of my skin. It's like there's a lightning storm making me feel all staticky and fluttery." Lucy bit her lip as she glanced toward the bathroom. "Maybe I should take a shower too."

"No," Miles said, louder than he'd intended.

She looked at him in surprise for a moment before anger set in. "So you guys are allowed to find relief, but I have to suffer?"

Joey rested his chin on her shoulder, nuzzling her cheek with his. "I'm sure that's not what Miles is saying."

"Sorry. I didn't mean to snap," she apologized. "I'm seriously regretting not packing any of my toys."

"Why didn't you?" Joey asked, amused.

"Um, because I'm never more than ten feet away from you guys in this RV, and like I said, sex isn't something I've missed much the last few years. When I get an itch every few months, I scratch it, and then I'm good to go for a while."

Joey reared back, shocked. "Every few *months*?"

Lucy rolled her eyes.

As they talked, Miles stood there, fighting like the devil to get control of himself. He hadn't told Lucy she couldn't take a shower because he wanted her to suffer. He said it because hell would freeze over before he let her take care of herself.

Before he could talk himself out of what came next, Miles said, "You're not taking care of your blue bean in the shower." His gaze rested on Joey's face, wondering if his friend would be on board for what he had in mind.

Then he snorted to himself. Of *course*, Joey would be on board.

Miles moved toward the couch, tightening the towel around his waist before sitting down. "Joey is going to take care of you."

Joey sat up straighter.

Miles was tired of pretending he didn't want Lucy, tired of making excuses. Because they were starting to run dry. Even worse, they were starting to prove false. His fantasy in the shower proved he wasn't as resistant to sharing Lucy with Joey as he'd thought.

He still wasn't one hundred percent sure he could go all the way...but perhaps it was time to test the waters, see how deep he could go before the need to return to shore became too strong.

Miles nodded. "You are. We're going to play a little game of Simon Says. We'll call it Miles Says. I tell you what to do, Joey, and you do it." Then he looked at Lucy. "And if I give any directions you don't like, all you have to do is say so. Okay?"

Lucy readily agreed. "As long as this ends with me having an orgasm, I'm down for anything."

Joey groaned. "Maybe don't say *anything* because I'm painting way too many pretty pictures in my head, Luce."

Miles was too, and he planned to kill two birds with this stone —exploring his newfound interest in voyeurism while determining how far they could take this thing.

"Stand up, Joe."

Miles was slightly surprised when Joey did exactly as asked. His best friend was an easygoing guy, but he'd been around him enough to know he wasn't the type to follow orders blindly. His take-charge nature was one of the reasons he excelled as host of *ManPower*. He was very good at leading their guests in the direction he needed them to go.

Since Lucy had been on Joey's lap, she stood as well, both of them looking at him, waiting for his next command.

Fuck if that wasn't a heady thing.

Moment of truth.

"Take off her shirt."

None of them had shed any clothing the past two nights, all of them wearing tops and bottoms to bed. Lucy's cheeks pinkened, but she didn't demur when Joey reached for the hem of her thin sweater and pulled it over her head.

Miles took a second, sucking in some much-needed air as he studied Lucy in her pretty floral bra. Her wardrobe was as colorful as her personality. She was a fan of bright colors and bold patterns, so it shouldn't be surprising her underwear was the same. Her bra was adorned with pastel flowers and was one of those with half-cup deals that pushed her tits up perfectly.

He lifted one leg, resting his ankle on his knee, hoping that position shielded just how hard his dick was. He adjusted the towel, but there was no hiding the tent he'd pitched.

Joey raised his hands, clearly intent on cupping Lucy's breasts.

Miles stopped him midway. "I didn't tell you to touch her yet."

Joey glanced at him with narrowed eyes, unhappy about being denied his treat.

"Lift her bra straps over her shoulders, let them fall down her arms." Miles was confident gravity would take care of the rest.

Joey shifted one strap, then the other, and as Miles expected, her bra dropped enough to reveal the tops of her pink areolas. The bra might have fallen completely if not for her nipples. They were budded tight, so the material caught.

"Tug her bra down, Joey, until it's just under her tits."

Joey had the bra down before Miles had even finished making the demand.

Lucy's hands raised, like she intended to cover herself. Then she reconsidered and dropped them back to her sides.

"Good girl," Miles praised, recalling the way she'd responded to him calling her little girl a couple nights earlier.

Her breathy whimper was music to his ears.

Miles gestured to Lucy with a nod of his head. "Cup her breasts, Joey. Suck on those pretty nipples."

Joey bent his head, squeezing one of her tits in his hand, drawing the nipple into his mouth as Lucy's head fell back and her eyes drifted shut.

Miles watched for several moments, captivated by the two of them together, suddenly understanding how much he missed when it was just him alone in bed with a lover. There were so many fascinating facial expressions and physical reactions Miles had never noticed because he was too wrapped up in his own arousal.

Watching the two of them allowed him to not only see but hear things he'd never observed before, like Lucy's soft whimpers, the rise and fall of her chest as she struggled to breathe, the heaviness of her eyelids that drifted closed only to rise again whenever Joey did something different. She was literally the most beautiful woman he'd ever seen.

After a minute or two, Miles cleared his throat. "Unfasten her jeans."

Lucy took a shivery breath that he didn't mistake for fear. Miles was intent on soaking up every detail of her deep-seated need, studying it closely for future reference.

Joey unbuttoned and unzipped her jeans, tugging them down as Lucy's hands flew up, gripping his thick, muscular arms, her fingers digging in.

Joey shoved the denim as far as her knees, and Miles noticed he hadn't taken her panties down with it.

Miles knew how much Joey wanted this, knew that his friend was viewing what was happening here very differently from him and Lucy. While neither Miles nor Lucy could see a way for this to work in the long-term, Joey, the confident bastard, refused to agree.

It was then that Miles understood why Joey was playing along. He was being careful to take this at a pace both Miles and Lucy could be comfortable with, unwilling to do anything that might spook them.

He couldn't decide if he was annoyed or impressed by his friend's cleverness.

"Lift her up on the edge of the table." Miles tried to remain apart, tried to keep his participation to that of narrator, but when Joey grasped Lucy's waist, placing her on the table before stepping between her outstretched thighs, he lost the battle. Slipping his hand beneath the towel, Miles wrapped his fist around his thick cock. He didn't stroke, merely holding it instead.

"You've been such a good girl," Miles said to Lucy. "So patient, even though you've been hurting. Stroke her clit, Joey. Reward her for not touching what belongs to us."

Joey released a guttural groan that was one of the hungriest sounds Miles had ever heard. He'd been a fool to use the word *us* because he'd just triggered a key part of Joey's desires.

Lucy jerked as if zapped by electricity when Joey dipped a finger beneath her panties and ran the tip over her clit.

"Please," she whispered, when his featherlight touch continued. "More."

Joey didn't give in to her request. Instead, his gaze drifted over to Miles. It was the first time his friend had looked at him since they'd begun the game. He took in everything at a glance. Miles's clenched jaw, his labored breathing, his hand gripping his cock—hidden from view by the towel.

"What next?" Joey asked, his voice husky.

Miles held his gaze. "Finger her. Give her what she needs."

Joey responded like a captive man freed from his bonds. He slipped her panties down, stroking up and down her slit, his fingers slick from her undeniable arousal.

Lucy began to tremble, her hands still locked around Joey's biceps in a white-knuckle grip.

She groaned softly when Joey pushed two fingers inside her.

It was several seconds before Miles realized he'd begun rubbing his cock at the same speed Joey was fucking Lucy with his fingers. He was matching him stroke for stroke, imagining and wishing he was inside her.

"So wet and hot," Joey murmured, his lips brushing the side of Lucy's cheek, not kissing her as much as rubbing his face against hers. "So fucking tight."

When Joey added the last description, Miles clenched his dick harder, added more force. He liked rough sex, liked his pleasure to include a taste of pain.

Lucy shifted on the table, pushing herself harder onto Joey's fingers. Her cheeks were red with exertion, her body writhing, her whimpers and moans the only sound in the RV.

"Add another finger," Miles demanded through clenched teeth, as he increased the speed of his hand job.

"Ahh!" Lucy cried out, her tone telling Miles that Joey had obeyed him.

"Fuck, honey. You're so sweet, so perfect. You're almost there," Joey whispered in her ear. "Come for us. Show us how pretty you are when you come. Let Miles watch you gush all over my fingers."

Jesus. Christ.

Joey had been relatively quiet during all of this, letting Miles take the lead. Listening to his deep voice, hearing his dirty talk...

It was working for Miles.

What the *hell* was going on? Miles's mind was at war with his body because while he kept thinking he shouldn't like this, shouldn't *want* this, his dick was all-fucking-in.

"Oh my God." Lucy's body responded to Joey's demands. Her back arched as she cried out Joey's name. Then Miles's.

The moment his name flew from her lips, Miles was a goner, his climax striking hard.

"So. Fucking. *Good*." He used his free hand to catch his come, some of it splashing against the towel. He was going to need another shower.

The second his climax waned, his brain kicked in, and he tried to convince himself what they'd just done was a far cry from actual sex. For one thing, Joey was fully dressed, and Miles covered by the towel. Not that nudity was his problem, necessarily. He and Joey had been traveling together a couple of years now and sharing an apartment during the off months, so it wasn't like they hadn't seen each other's junk. The difference was, they'd never seen each other with an erection.

In his mind, sex was meant to be shared between two people.

Now, he was forced to reconsider that idea. Because what they'd just done?

Miles wanted to do it again.

No, he wanted to do that and more. Much, much more.

None of them spoke, the silence between them dragging out. Miles suspected Joey was too afraid to break the spell to say anything, and Lucy, quite frankly, was still trying to catch her breath.

As for him...he didn't know what to say. He'd been the biggest naysayer, the one insisting this couldn't happen.

He pulled his hand free from the towel, rising. "I need a minute to clean up." He pierced them with a gaze. "Don't move."

Lucy nodded, while Joey frowned, clearly anticipating kickback.

He hated that his friend's mind had gone there, though he could hardly blame him. Miles had been fighting against this tooth and nail.

He quickly walked to the bathroom, washing his hands before grabbing a clean towel. He tossed the old one in the corner. He'd deal with that later. He didn't want to leave Joey and Lucy alone for too long.

Once the clean towel was wrapped securely around his hips, he returned to the main living space of the RV. Lucy had risen from the table. Joey had washed his hands in the kitchen sink and was now helping her pull up her jeans. She'd already pulled her bra up and her thin sweater back on.

Miles should probably put some clothes on, but he didn't want to take the time. He gestured to the table, each of them claiming a seat.

"Miles—" Joey started.

He lifted his hand, cutting him off. He had a pretty good idea how Joey felt about what happened, so Lucy was his main concern. "You okay?"

Her cheeks were still a faint pink, her eyes somewhat glassy. It must have been one hell of an orgasm.

"Yeah. I... I didn't expect... I didn't know..." She blinked a few times, searching for the words. In the end, she just shrugged. "That was freaking amazing."

Miles laughed. The sudden loud, joyous sound taking Joey by surprise.

"Miles?" he said again.

"Freaking amazing," Miles said to his best friend, grinning widely.

Joey released a long, slow, steady breath, looking like a balloon slowly deflating. "I was worried I had pushed..." He paused.

Miles knew exactly what he was worried about. "You do remember I was the one who started that, right?"

Joey gave him a small grin. "The three of us are good together."

He'd been saying that since the night he'd watched Miles and Lucy dance, and Miles knew he hadn't been honest about his feelings. He'd continually brushed the words aside, refusing to acknowledge them.

Even now, he couldn't take those final steps, getting to the place where Joey hoped they'd end up.

"I still think we should take things slowly," Miles said, glancing at Lucy. "At whatever pace you're comfortable with."

She gave them a wicked grin. "Slow is okay, but a hard and fast pace works a hell of a lot better."

They laughed, then stood up and started fighting over what to make for dinner.

While they playfully debated which meal was easy to make, yet still tasty—soup and sandwiches or frozen pizza—Miles found himself replaying Joey's words.

They *were* good together.

Chapter Ten

"Mmm." Lucy rolled to her back and lifted her hands above her head when the alarm went off. "Morning."

She giggled when Joey's hand slipped under her pajama top to cup her breast, tweaking the nipple. Last night, they'd reverted to simply making out for a little while before curling up to sleep. She'd begun using one of her guys as a pillow, resting her cheek on their chest, her arm wrapped around their waist, while the other one spooned her.

At home, she had a full-sized bed all to herself. She'd always thought that was the most comfortable way to sleep, but she was wrong. Dead wrong. She was already dreading returning to the farm and sleeping alone.

Lucy had expressed her concerns about taking things to the next level, but as the nights passed with her as the cream filling in a sexy man sandwich, her restraint was gone. She loved being the center of attention, the recipient of their touches and kisses and dirty talk.

She wasn't sure she'd ever had anyone pay so much attention to her. That wasn't a complaint against her family. It was just that she'd been one of many, many kids growing up on the same farm.

Between that and her parents' contentious marriage, Mom's desertion, then Mom and Dad's untimely deaths, Lucy had stopped being a kid around the age of eight, taking on more and more adult responsibilities. Whenever Mom and Dad fought, Lucy rounded up her younger sisters, taking them outside to play or to Grandma's house for a snack, anywhere they would be out of earshot of the arguments.

After her parents died, Lucy's sense of responsibility was already well-entrenched, and while Grandma and Granddaddy were excellent caregivers, she'd tried to lighten the load as much as she could because they were older and hadn't expected to spend their golden years raising four little girls. When Grandma was diagnosed with Alzheimer's, then Granddaddy with cancer, Lucy had tried once more to bear the brunt of the duties. She was determined her sisters should have as comfortable a life as she could give them.

She couldn't ever recall a time when *she* was someone's primary, sole focus, when there was someone taking care of *her*. The past week with Miles and Joey had given her that, made her feel special, happy, and best of all, carefree. With them, she could let go because she knew they were there, watching out for her, giving her things she never would have asked for on her own.

Her physical attraction to both men had flashed hot from the day they'd met, burning brighter the longer they were together. She'd held back at the farm, making the typical excuses, like she didn't know them well enough or—the biggie—she couldn't have both.

Obviously, she'd heard the term menage a trois before. She'd read a few polyamory romance novels from Mila's stash of books, but she'd always placed that concept in the column titled fiction. She'd never met anyone who was part of a committed threesome. God, she suspected such a relationship would set the sleepy town of Gracemont on its ear.

Lucy had adopted the mindset that everything happening on the road was a break from reality. One where she could indulge in kisses and a dream job and travel without any repercussions. And while she was enjoying every second, she was also careful to remain cognizant that this wasn't something she could hold on to forever.

Because she had responsibilities at home—to the farm and to her family.

Because she had a job—a real one at the brewery.

Because she hadn't known these men more than two weeks, so these feelings she had couldn't be anything more than fondness wrapped up in a healthy layer of lust.

Because this wasn't the real world. At least, not *her* real world.

She worked hard to convince herself that, one day, when she was old and gray, she would look back on this grand adventure— the trip and the men—with nothing but fond memories and without an ounce of regret.

Or at least...she hoped so.

Miles stirred at the sound of her voice and the alarm Joey turned off. He twisted to his side, smiling at her.

Lucy hadn't realized just how much Miles had been holding back during those first two nights of kissing. Not until last night, when he came to bed, drew her into his rock-hard embrace, and kissed her senseless. He'd turned a corner during their interlude after his shower, his reserve all but gone.

They were all mostly clothed. She was in her pajamas, while Miles and Joey had opted to sleep in lounge pants. Last night was the first that they'd eschewed wearing T-shirts. It had given Lucy the perfect opportunity to explore their chests. Miles's was smooth and bare, his dark skin silk over steel. Meanwhile, Joey's chest was hairy. Not gorilla levels, but there was enough there for her to play with.

"How's the blue bean today?" Miles asked, grinning as he used her expression.

She sighed. "It's a chronic condition, I'm afraid. Treatable, but not curable."

Joey chuckled behind her. "Sounds dire."

"Not really. Because apparently all I need to do is take a shower," she teased.

Miles narrowed his eyes. "Thought we established that was *not* the answer for you."

Joey tsked. "Sounds like we might need to teach our girl another lesson."

"Yes please," she replied enthusiastically.

Miles laughed. "Hard to punish the willing. Besides, we don't have enough time. We need to be on the road in the next hour. Got that meeting with Hank Cooper set for lunchtime, and Maris is still four hours away."

Lucy sighed. "Spoilsport."

Miles cupped her cheek, giving her a soft kiss. "Remember you said that after."

She frowned. "After what?"

Miles moved before she'd finished asking her question, ducking under the covers. Her pajama bottoms and panties were off within seconds. Then Miles lay between her outstretched thighs.

"Punishment takes time to do right. But this little bean..." Miles stroked her clit with his thumb. "Well, I think we established that we can fix it up in minutes. Besides, I didn't get a taste yesterday."

Joey, not one to be left out, lifted the covers, stealing a peek as Miles ran his tongue along her slit. "*Fuck* that looks hot." He reached for her shirt, tugging it over her head, and Lucy was thrown back to that day in her kitchen when she'd indulged in her first fantasy starring both of them together.

"God! I've dreamed about this," she admitted.

Joey cupped her breast, running his forefinger over her sensitive nipple. "Oh yeah?"

Lucy nodded, unable to speak when Miles drove his tongue inside her, his thumb wreaking havoc on her clit. He was right. This wasn't going to take long.

Joey added more fuel to the fire, sucking her nipple into his mouth, pinching the other with his free hand. Then his lips traveled upward, as he planted kisses along her neck, her cheek, behind her ear.

After three nights of kissing, touching, and exploring, Miles and Joey had officially found every hidden erogenous zone and hot button on her body. Even some she hadn't discovered.

Kiss the back of her neck? Check.

Nip her earlobe? Check.

Tickle the crook of her knee? Check.

Suck her finger into their mouths? Check.

Pull her hair? Hell fucking yeah. Check.

Lucy's hands drifted under the covers, her fingers sliding over Miles's tight curls, the broad shoulders holding her thighs wide apart. Any shyness she might have harbored around them had vanished yesterday on that dining room table, when Joey finger fucked her to one of the strongest orgasms of her life.

At this point, modesty be damned because she was a junkie, willing to burn every piece of clothing she owned if it meant another hit of Miles and Joey.

"God," she breathed, when Miles's mouth replaced his thumb, sucking on her clit. Her hips lurched upward as she sought more. He didn't disappoint, pushing two thick fingers in deep.

His groan was music to her ears, especially when he lifted his head, the covers rising enough to let her see his face, his mouth shiny from her juices. "So sexy," he murmured. "And tight. You're going to strangle our dicks, honey."

It was the first time Miles had ever used Joey's term of endearment, and it sounded just as sweet coming from him. Especially when combined with dirty talk.

Marco and Billy had been passive in the bedroom, more apt to ask permission or make sure she was alright than to take charge. Neither of them had ever used such graphic terms when they told her what they wanted from her.

Joey's lips were wrapped around her nipple again, but he

stopped sucking after Miles's comment. He didn't move otherwise, didn't give any indication that he'd heard the same thing Lucy had.

Miles had been resistant to the three of them having sex together, but given his words, it appeared he thought that was a foregone conclusion now. Not that Lucy was complaining. Any concerns she had about engaging in a threesome affair vanished that first night they'd made out, then cuddled in this bed together.

Their first week together was already over. Time was going way too fast for her.

So, she needed to make every second of these next two weeks count.

Miles didn't appear to realize what he'd said, or the impact it had on her and Joey, because he lowered his head and sucked on her clit like it was his fucking job.

His fingers thrust in and out several times before he curled them, finding her G-spot.

Lucy went off like a bottle rocket, her climax coming out of nowhere and taking her down hard. "Jesus!" she gasped, her back arching, stars exploding behind her closed eyelids.

Miles didn't relent, didn't give way. Instead, he continued thrusting, stroking that spot over and over until Lucy feared she would pass out from the prolonged orgasm.

While Joey still cupped her breast, he'd shoved the covers off the bed and lifted his head so he could watch as she came completely undone from Miles's talented touches.

"Fuck, man," Joey murmured.

His words captured Miles's attention, the other man finally pausing.

Miles slowly drew his fingers out, her pussy clenching around them, trying to hold them in. Apparently, it hadn't gotten the memo that Lucy was on the verge of death by orgasm.

Kneeling between her legs, Miles sat back on his haunches, then licked his wet lips. "Delicious."

She felt flames lick her cheeks. God, what these men *wouldn't* say. Perhaps what was most surprising was how much she liked it.

Lucy lay there boneless, shocked when both men rose from the bed.

"You want to take the first shower?" Joey asked Miles. "You earned it."

The two of them laughed, Joey slapping Miles on the shoulder as they left the bedroom together, leaving Lucy lying there so blissed out, she couldn't speak.

She was still there when Miles returned to the room after his shower to dress. "You okay, Luce?"

Lucy raised one hand, giving him the thumbs-up.

Miles chuckled as he dressed and headed back out of the room again.

She was just managing to recover her wits when Joey showed up, his hair wet from his own shower.

He bent over the side of the bed to kiss her. "I'm going to scramble up some eggs, honey. And Miles is demanding bacon. Want some?"

Lucy blinked a few times, suddenly concerned that none of this was real. Because there was no way she was lying in bed after the longest, most satisfying orgasm ever, given to her by the two sexiest men on the planet, who now wanted to make her breakfast.

"Shh," she said to Joey. "Don't wake me up because I'm having an amazing dream."

He gave her another kiss, this one deeper, with tongue. His breath was minty fresh from brushing his teeth.

"Best dream ever," he agreed.

It was.

It really was.

* * *

Lucy stretched as she stepped out of the RV, grateful they'd divided the drive from Tennessee to Texas into thirds. She was used to moving around a lot at the brewery, and completely unaccustomed to sitting for long periods of time. As such, even their short four- or five-hour stretches left her stiff. So much for hitting her daily steps. Her Apple Watch was going to give up on her at this rate.

As she stood on the sidewalk, she glanced down Main Street, feeling oddly at home. Maris, Texas, reminded her a great deal of Gracemont. They were both small towns with a unique down-home feel. This Main Street mirrored the one that ran down the center of Gracemont almost perfectly, right down to the coffee shop—not a Starbucks—on the corner, the local pharmacy, and the smattering of family-run restaurants. There wasn't a single McDonald's, Cracker Barrel, or Taco Bell to be seen.

Joey stepped up next to her, placing his hand on the small of her back. Just that one light touch sent heat to her cheeks.

Miles joined them, glancing around as well. "This place reminds me of Gracemont."

"I was just thinking the same thing," Lucy confessed.

"I suspect Maris, Texas, wasn't on your list of dream cities," Joey mused.

Lucy shielded her eyes with her hand, wishing she'd thought to grab her sunglasses from the RV. "It wasn't, but that's just because I didn't know it existed."

Joey tucked her closer. "That's one of the benefits of our lifestyle. Seeing little corners of the world others never get to enjoy."

Lucy was jealous every time Joey mentioned their adventurous existence. When Marco had asked her to take off with him in search of greener pastures, she'd refused without giving it a moment's thought, unwilling to leave Gracemont and her family.

Now, when she thought back on Marco's invitation, she wondered if maybe it wasn't the leaving that had felt wrong, but the person who'd asked her to come along.

God knew there hadn't been more than a few minutes of hesitation when Joey asked her to come with them. Of course, he had offered a short-term adventure, not a lifetime. It was the only reason she'd agreed, even though that little voice in the back of her head spoke up, telling her she'd been a fool to rip the lid off Pandora's box.

Lucy had avoided leaving the farm because she'd always known if she did, if she took one tiny bite of that apple, she'd never want to go back. And she *had* to go back. Leaving the farm felt too much like betraying her father's memory, of doing the same thing her mother had. He'd loved the farm so much he couldn't conceive of leaving it, even if it would have saved his marriage. Lucy knew her sisters felt that same devotion to the land, so it was only her who felt out of step when it came to home.

She'd talked to at least one of her sisters every single day since leaving. Each of them had assured her everything on the farm was running fine and she should enjoy herself. Hearing that helped a little, though she still felt a fair amount of guilt. Especially in regards to Sam and Theo, who were holding down things at the brewery on their own.

Remi had called when they were en route to Maris this morning, to say she'd watched the latest episode of *Kiss and Tell*. Lucy had finally managed to put it up last night after dinner. She had been touched by Emily and Tate's love story, and anxious to share it with her viewers. The second it finished uploading, she'd texted Remi, who was her second set of eyes and typically the first viewer, the one who made sure everything uploaded correctly and Lucy hadn't messed anything up in the editing.

Lucy had been too distracted by Miles and Joey this morning to check the views, so it was Remi who'd told her it was a hit. The views were already significant and, according to her sister, there were several comments from people wanting to know if Lucy planned to travel through their hometowns.

The second she said goodbye to Remi, Lucy had done a search on her phone and discovered her sister hadn't been exaggerating.

For so long, she'd called *Kiss and Tell* a hobby...but she was starting to genuinely believe she could turn it into a career. Her royalties from subscriber numbers and advertising continued to grow, and she was already making a living wage.

Not that it mattered.

She had a permanent job at the brewery and a home. Her life was on that mountain. It had to be.

She didn't mention the success of the most recent episode to Joey or Miles for two reasons.

One, she was a firm believer in the jinx. Saying something out loud felt like a great way to ruin it. She didn't want the views to stop.

Secondly, she feared Joey would hop on that information and press her to spend more time on the road with them. While she was doing an okay job at holding her emotions at bay, too many more days—and nights—with the guys would ensure she lost her heart to them entirely.

Miles reached for the front door of the restaurant, the words Sparks Barbeque painted in bright red letters across the large storefront window. A bell tinkled from above, announcing their arrival.

The heads of several older gentlemen sitting in front of a long counter swiveled in their direction. She caught the look of recognition on a couple faces when they saw Joey and Miles walk in. The guys had, what Lucy considered, just enough fame to live comfortably. In Nashville, they hadn't been swarmed by rabid fans, but over the course of the three days, they were approached by at least a couple dozen viewers who'd kindly asked for autographs or taken selfies with them.

"You made it!" a woman exclaimed, walking around the counter to greet them. She slapped one of the guys on the shoulder as she passed. "Stop gawking, Bucky, or they'll think we're nothing but a bunch of rednecks."

Lucy couldn't help but laugh, even as the woman stretched her hand out to shake theirs. "I'm Macie Cooper. It's really nice to meet you," she said to Joey and Miles before looking at Lucy, eyebrows lowered. "Damn, you've got a familiar face. How do I know you?" she asked.

Lucy took Macie's outstretched hand. "Maybe I just have one of those faces? I'm Lucy Storm. It's nice to meet you."

Macie's eyes widened. "You're that *Kiss and Tell* girl!"

Lucy was taken aback by the fact Macie knew who she was. While people very occasionally traveled to the farm to meet her because of the show—which was pretty freaking cool—she'd never been recognized out in public.

Lucy was so stunned, all she could manage to say was, "I am."

"You're famous, Luce," Joey said, bumping his shoulder against hers.

"You are around here," Macie said. "My dad TJ—the lazy ass—surfs YouTube regularly, usually when he's supposed to be working a shift here. He stumbled across your show and shared a link to one of the episodes with me and my sister. Said we should write to you to see if we could be featured on your show."

"No way!" Lucy's feet hadn't touched the ground since Remi told her how well her new episode was doing. With this, Lucy was in danger of hitting her head on the ceiling.

Macie guided the three of them toward a booth. "Dad's very fond of my and Adele's husbands, mostly because they took us off his hands. Loves to tell anyone who'll listen how lucky in love his girls are."

Lucy wasn't sure what Macie's love story was, but she would die to hear it because it was clear Macie would be an entertaining storyteller.

She slid into one side of the booth, Joey following her in. Miles claimed the opposite bench seat, while Macie grabbed some menus from another waitress who was passing by.

"My husband, Hank—everyone around town calls him Coop —called a few minutes ago. He's running a little bit late, but he wanted me to tell you he's on his way."

Joey and Miles had made plans to meet Hank Cooper here, as

the man insisted they couldn't come to Maris without sampling Sparks Barbeque's famous sandwiches. If the smell was anything to go by, Lucy already knew it would be the best she'd ever had. Her mouth started watering the second they walked inside.

"Oh, hey." Macie waved as a man entered the restaurant. "There he is."

Lucy had never seen a real live cowboy up close and personal, but Hank Cooper certainly fit the bill of what she imagined one looked like, with his darkly tanned skin, loose-fitting, faded jeans, cowboy hat, and dusty boots. When he reached their table, he tilted his hat back, giving Macie a kiss on the cheek. "Hey there, Whiskey."

Lucy practically melted at the sound of his slow Texas drawl and the nickname. They were in Maris to film Hank on his ranch, but Lucy decided right then and there, she was going to ask Macie and Hank to do a *Kiss and Tell* episode as well.

Hank tipped his head toward them as Macie did the introductions, then he claimed the spot next to Miles while Macie took their drink orders. After exchanging a few pleasantries, they got down to business, Joey and Miles discussing what they would need from Hank over the course of the next few days.

Lucy listened with half an ear, feeling a bit like a *ManPower* expert after filming her own episode, then hanging out behind the scenes as Joey and Miles worked with the catio guy. While they talked, she was more interested in looking around the restaurant, which was busting at the seams as the lunch crowd rolled in.

It appeared pretty much everyone in the place was a regular, considering Macie greeted them all by name as they walked in. Macie had mentioned when she delivered their drinks that all the employees were family, as she, her sister, and several female cousins ran the place.

Lucy felt a kindred spirit in the woman, watching Macie and her sister Adele cracking jokes behind the counter. They were clearly as close as Lucy was to Mila, Nora, and Remi. She hadn't felt homesick once on this trip, but a small wave of it passed through her now. This was the longest she'd ever been away from her sisters, and a familiar wave of guilt hit, *hard*.

Lucy had been busy—and distracted by two hot men—every single day since leaving home, so she hadn't had much time to think about her life when she returned to the farm.

Or maybe it was safer to say she was trying not to.

She'd been young when her parents died, but she recalled her mother enough to recognize that Lucy took after her in a lot of ways. Her mother had a zeal for life, a strong sense of adventure, and more than her fair share of wanderlust. Mom had felt trapped on the farm, and with each passing day she spent there, her light dimmed a bit more.

Granddaddy always used to say Lucy was the spit of her mother, looks and personality-wise. That never felt truer than at this moment, when her own wanderlust was in full force. Lucy loved the farm. Hadn't she said those words at least a million times in her life? While she knew they were true, it occurred to her now, as she watched Maris and Adele, that it wasn't so much the place she loved, as much as the people.

She had chosen to work in the brewery after high school because her family needed her. Grandma had just been diagnosed with dementia, and Granddaddy was working overtime to take care of her. As such, Lucy stepped up so that she could be there for her sisters, who were all still in school, helping them with homework, offering them advice about boys—she'd been the one to give them "the talk"—and taking care of the million other little day-to-day things a mom would have.

She'd just turned twenty-two when Granddaddy died, she and her sisters essentially orphans again. By that time, working in the brewery had become second nature to her, something she got up and did every day without giving it much thought, and any dreams she harbored about leaving the farm had long been snuffed out.

If someone had asked her a month ago, she would have said she loved her job.

Now...

Now, the idea of returning wasn't sitting as comfortably as it should. There was a pit in her stomach that told her she didn't want to go back.

God, this was why she'd never left to begin with. Ignorance was bliss. And she'd just shattered her unawareness to a million pieces.

"Lucy?"

She blinked when she heard her name, realizing Miles had said it a couple of times.

"Sorry," she said. "You caught me daydreaming."

Miles jerked his head toward Hank. "He's seen *Kiss and Tell* too."

Lucy smiled at the handsome cowboy. "Did Macie make you watch it?"

Hank chuckled. "Only the first time. I really liked the episode that featured your grandparents."

"That's my favorite too," she confessed. "I was actually wondering if you and Macie would let me record your story while I'm here."

Hank grinned. "Oh, I don't think that would take a bit of convincing. Macie's a huge fan. I also don't think I'll have to do much more than sit there. Not sure if you noticed or not, but my wife likes to talk."

Lucy pretended to be shocked. "I hadn't noticed that at all."

All four of them laughed as they looked toward the bar, where Macie was basically holding court, weaving a tall tale that had no less than seven people sitting nearby enraptured.

"Truth be told," Hank said, "Macie's whole family could be on your show. Lots of interesting romances in the Sparks family."

"Really?" she asked.

Hank nodded. "Yep. I have a feeling that once they find out you're filming me and Macie, you're going to have them lining up for their turn."

If Hank thought that might concern her, he'd missed the

mark by a mile. Part of the appeal of this trip was the opportunity it offered to meet and interview more people. If the rest of the Sparks clan was as entertaining and funny as Macie, she'd be set up for a string of great episodes. With the success of Emily and Tate's show, she was anxious to keep the momentum going.

After they finished eating, Miles and Joey walked to the counter with Hank to pay, while Macie came over to clear the table. "So, what did you think of the food?"

Lucy gestured at the plates, which they had all but licked clean. "So freaking good. Seriously. Have you considered bottling that barbeque sauce? Because I swear you'd make a killing."

"It's been discussed many times, believe me. My cousin, Paige, has put out some feelers about how we might get started. She's the brains of this organization, while my cousins Jeannette and Sydney create their masterpieces in the kitchen. The rest of us—me included—provide the entertainment."

Lucy had just spent nearly two hours watching Macie and Adele work the room, serving drinks and food, along with a hearty helping of humor. She'd joked earlier that it was almost like dinner and a show, and Hank, who'd been a widower, confessed he'd fallen in love with Macie while eating dinner at the counter, listening to her stories. The more she watched the couple, the more excited she was to record them.

Lucy gestured at the still full dining area. "Can I just say? You're *very* good at your job."

"So...inquiring minds want to know," Macie began. "And by minds, I mean mine, because I'm a nosy bitch from way back. How in the heck did you wind up traveling with Joey Moretti and Miles Williams? Are you dating one of them?"

Lucy wasn't sure how to answer that question. "Um..."

Wow.

She probably should have worked on some sort of explanation for being with the guys. Joey had told the *ManPower* crew that Lucy was joining them because she'd always wanted to see Nashville, and because she was interested in learning more about the makings of a show. Luckily, they'd bought it, no one questioning if she, Joey, and Miles were anything more than friends and travel companions.

"They filmed an episode at my family's brewery, featuring me and my cousin, Sam. We hit it off, and when they invited me to join them for the next leg of their journey, I couldn't say no."

Macie studied her face, the observant woman obviously aware there was more to it than that. "So, Joey or Miles?" she asked again. "Or both?"

Lucy's eyes widened, wondering why in the hell Macie would leap to that conclusion. She, Joey, and Miles had simply sat in the booth, eating together in a completely platonic fashion. "Um," she said again, resisting the urge to slap her forehead for sounding like such an idiot.

"Both. Got it," Macie said, as if they were discussing something as casual as the weather.

"I didn't say both," she hastily replied.

"Nope. But your face did."

Lucy reached up, touching one of her cheeks, wondering if she was blushing and didn't realize.

"Not right now," Macie added. "During lunch. I'm not even sure you know you're doing it, but whenever one of the guys speaks to you, your eyes light up and you lean toward them. Hank tells me I'm good at reading body language, which is a nice way of saying I'm meddlesome, with a talent for sniffing out good gossip. Not that I intend to pass on any of this conversation."

Lucy wasn't sure why, but she trusted that was true. Macie had stumbled onto her secret—a juicy one at that—but Lucy wasn't worried she'd tell anyone else.

"You like them," Macie said, not bothering to pose those words as a question.

Lucy nodded. "Very much. Maybe too much. To be honest, I'm not this kind of girl," Lucy said, feeling like she should defend herself.

"What kind of girl?"

"The kind to hook up with two men at the same time."

Macie waved her words away with a quick swish of her hand. "Screw that. You can be any kind of girl you want, Lucy, and you don't owe anyone an apology for being who you are. Besides, anyone with eyes can see those guys have got it *bad* for you."

Lucy couldn't stop herself from hoping that was true. "It's just... Well, you have to admit threesomes aren't exactly a normal thing."

Macie pointed toward the counter. "See those two good-looking guys at the end of the bar?"

Lucy glanced over, even though she already knew who Macie was talking about. She'd seen them walk in, both wearing identical Maris Fire Department shirts. "Yes."

"They're living with my cousin Jeannette. And when I say living with, I mean *living with*."

Lucy blinked, shocked. "Seriously?"

"Seriously."

"Back where I'm from, no one has ever engaged in a threesome as far as I know—not for one night, and definitely not forever." Lucy wasn't sure why she was confiding in a woman she'd just met, but something told her Macie wouldn't just understand, she would offer some much-needed insight. "The thing is..." She paused.

Macie wouldn't let her hesitate or stop. "Yes?"

"I'm only on vacation. This entire thing—the trip and the guys—is a break from the norm for me. I've never left the family farm before, so when Joey and Miles offered me a chance to see a bit more of the world, I jumped on it."

"So you came for the travel, not for the guys?"

Lucy grimaced. "Well, I'm not going to say they weren't a bonus, but I guess I didn't expect things to progress..." She sighed. "As far as they have. We only just met a couple of weeks ago, and yet when I'm with them, it all feels strangely natural."

"I think that's great. You're falling in love with them," Macie said.

Lucy jerked back as if she'd been struck. "No. Not at all. I mean, I barely know them."

"So?" Macie asked.

"So you can't fall in love with someone that fast," Lucy insisted.

"Of course you can. I'm pretty sure I was head over tits for Hank about ten minutes into our first date. And while you're worrying about being some sort of girl, let me tell you, that man had me out of my panties before the date was over. I think if you know, you know. So stop trying to set up some sort of timeframe."

Lucy considered that, wondering if perhaps Macie was right. Because she'd felt this feeling even before getting on the RV. It was what had prompted her to get on in the first place even though her brain was screaming, "Abort! Abort!"

"Even if I *am* starting to get feelings for them, I can't follow through on them."

Macie frowned. "Why not?"

"Because this isn't forever. It's for now."

Macie scoffed. "I'm pretty sure most forevers started as a for now."

"I have to go home to the farm, to my job, and my family, and Joey and Miles have to, well...they have to keep going."

Macie didn't seem to like that answer. "Maybe that's true, but I think you owe it to yourself to at least consider some other resolution. Especially since being with them feels right. If you ask me, it sounds like the beginning of one hell of a *Kiss and Tell* episode. You're a lucky woman, Lucy Storm."

Macie loaded the rest of the dirty dishes on her tray and walked back to the kitchen, just as the guys reappeared.

"Ready to go?" Joey asked as she stood, wrapping his arm around her waist.

She nodded.

Joey and Miles discussed their plans for interviewing Hank Cooper. It was obvious they were excited about the show. Joey climbed behind the steering wheel of the RV, while Miles rode shotgun. Lucy was happy to claim the backseat because it gave her time to consider what Macie had said.

She wasn't in love with Miles and Joey...yet. She hadn't known them long enough. However, there was a big part of her that suspected she could fall very hard for both of them if she let herself.

No. Macie was wrong. This wasn't *Kiss and Tell*. This was a casual-shrug kind of what-the-hell.

She wanted them, and they wanted her. She was going to keep it as simple as that. To do otherwise would be the height of stupidity.

Lucy watched the houses fly by as Joey took them out of downtown Maris, following the GPS that would lead them to the campground where they'd reserved a spot for the next few days. Once they arrived, they set up the RV. After so many days on the road, they were professionals when it came to arranging the campsite.

While the guys put down the RV jack pads and hooked up the electric and water, Lucy turned on the appliances and pulled out all the loose items they tucked away during long drives.

Mack was staying with the rest of the crew and producers at Maris's lone hotel, and as always, he would serve as their driver, transporting them to and from the ranch.

Lucy turned at the sound of the RV door opening, Miles and Joey returning.

The moment the door closed behind them, Lucy stepped in front of Miles, gripped his shirt in her hands, and pulled him in for a kiss.

If he was surprised by her impromptu, hungry kiss, he sure didn't show it, his hands gravitating to her ass, gripping it tightly.

Joey remained where he was, less than two feet away, watching them kiss. He didn't reach out to touch her. Probably because this was the first time Lucy had initiated anything physical. It felt as if he was still tiptoeing around them, careful not to push too far, lest he push them away entirely.

She was starting to hate that. Lucy had turned the corner on this affair, and now that she was there, she wanted them with her. All in.

Tonight, they were diving into this adventure with both feet.

Lucy broke the kiss, reaching over to draw Joey closer.

He leaned toward her, clearly expecting a kiss, so he frowned when she took a step away.

She turned her attention to Miles. "I liked you giving orders yesterday."

Miles grinned. "Is that right?"

"I was hoping you would do it again," she purred in her sexiest voice.

She knew what Joey and Miles were thinking, loved the way they both offered her an enthusiastic grin. So far, they'd taken care of her little horniness problem for her, while dealing with their own issues alone.

"Of cour—"

Miles stopped mid-word when Lucy dropped to her knees in front of them.

"But this time, I want you to tell *me* what to do."

Chapter Eleven

He and Miles exchanged a glance, Joey aware that they were mirror images of each other at the moment because Miles looked just as shocked and thrilled as he was.

Joey was also instantly hard. He wasn't sure he'd even gotten erect so quickly in his whole life. Lucy dropped to her knees and that was fucking it. Immediate erection.

Unfortunately, Joey had to put his impulsive nature aside for once and use his head—the smart head, not the dumb one. There was too much at stake.

He needed to be sure this was what she truly wanted. Like Miles, Lucy had been hesitant to take things to the next level, content to move forward in baby steps. Hence their super-hot make-out sessions. Kissing and touching her was incredible, but it had all been very vanilla, with him and Miles taking turns, none of them doing anything they hadn't done before, with the exception of the extra body in the bed.

Yesterday and this morning, they'd taken things a step further as he and Miles each gave her an orgasm.

It had been incredible, but again...it was a hell of a lot tamer than what Lucy was suggesting. In all their encounters, he and

Miles had left their pants on, and Lucy's hands hadn't ventured below their waists. So they were entering dick-infested waters for the first time, and Lucy was attempting to jump into the deep end without water wings.

While it would be difficult, it would be smarter for Joey to step away and remove himself from the equation this time. He would let Lucy test her limits with Miles, while he watched. That was going to be enough of a challenge for both of them.

Miles was resistant to "performing"—for lack of a better word—in front of another guy, so that was another reason he would be smart to slow things down.

Joey hadn't admitted it aloud, but the truth was, he'd never participated in threesome sex either. He wasn't concerned about it. The thought turned him on a lot, but it wasn't like he had any experience in this realm.

So.

Yeah.

Blue balls it was.

"Lucy." Joey reached down, cupping her cheek to tilt her face up so she was looking at him. "I'm going to sit this one out."

"What? No," she rejected outright.

He cast a sideways glance at Miles, looking for support. He was surprised to find his best friend was scowling. Actually, Miles looked downright pissed off.

Joey ignored both of them, forging on because he was determined to do this right. "We promised to take it slow. You don't know what you're ask—"

"I *do*. I want to do this, Joey. I want it so badly," she reassured him before looking at Miles. "But I want you to direct it, tell me how. In my past relationships, I…" She stopped, aware neither of them liked hearing about her exes. "I mean I…"

"We're not looking back, honey," Miles said. "Not talking about or thinking about the past. All that matters is right now."

She seemed to like that. "Okay."

"And none of us is sitting this one out," Miles stressed.

"I just thought—" Joey started.

"I know what you thought," Miles said, no heat in his tone. Joey was starting to wonder if his friend wasn't actually angry at him for trying to back away, but mad at *himself* for hesitating in the first place. "But I'm with Lucy. I want this. I'm sorry I told you that I didn't."

Joey didn't realize until this second that he'd been walking around with a pile of bricks on his chest. While he'd loved every minute of this trip, enjoyed the tiny steps they'd taken toward each other, he'd still worried about pushing them too hard, so he'd gone a hell of a lot slower than he wanted, measuring every step, every action, every word.

Now, he felt free.

"Before we start..." Joey stepped over to the couch. He grabbed a cushion, placing it on the floor and helping Lucy up so that she could kneel back down on it.

"Thank you," she whispered, obviously touched by his thoughtfulness.

"There's something else we should discuss, too." Miles stroked Lucy's hair, pushing it back behind her shoulder. "How far are you willing to go? Because while I'm all in on blow jobs, gorgeous girl...is that all you want?"

Lucy shook her head. "I want it all. I've taken the time, thought about it, and there's nothing I want more than to be with you. With both of you."

Joey didn't even bother to hide his smile.

Especially when Miles added, "That's what we want too."

Life. Made.

With his question answered, Miles seemed to morph into a different man. Joey recognized this guy as the same one who'd issued all those commands yesterday from the couch, dressed in nothing more than a towel.

Joey wasn't surprised to discover his friend had a dominant personality in the bedroom. It was just one more way they were alike, and another reason why Lucy was perfect for them. Joey had seen the way she blushed when Miles called her a good girl, and the way she'd enthusiastically reacted to the mere mention of punishment this morning. She was a natural submissive, ready and willing to do whatever they said.

"Unzip Joey's pants," Miles said, looking down at her.

Lucy's quick movements told Joey she hadn't lied about wanting this. Once his pants were open, she started to reach inside his boxer briefs to grasp his dick, but paused. Her eyes lifted to Miles, as if seeking permission.

Perfect. She was fucking perfect.

"Touch me," Joey said, his voice husky with need.

Yesterday, he'd let Miles call the shots, but he wouldn't do that again. He wanted Lucy to look to *him* for the permission she sought.

Her eyes flicked over to his, a soft smile crossing her face. Then she did what he said, dipping her fingers inside his boxers, her eyes widening slightly as she gripped his cock in her small hand.

"Shit," she murmured. "That's...uh..."

Joey chuckled. "You're good for the ego, honey."

Lucy licked her lips, and that was when he realized it wasn't nerves he saw in her expression. Instead, it was a blend of hunger mixed with a desire to please him. Her teeth nipped at her lower lip as she drew her hand up and down his cock, her grip too loose.

"Tighter." Joey shoved his pants and boxers down to his ankles, giving her unhindered access. If she wanted a lesson in blow jobs, in how to please him, he was going to give it to her. He covered her hand with his larger one, showing her exactly what he liked.

While his gaze was focused on Lucy, he was hyperaware of Miles's presence.

"Move faster." Miles stepped closer to them. There was a part of Joey that had expected him to keep his distance, despite what he'd said about wanting this. After all, his main concerns regarding the threesome seemed to involve being in close contact with another naked, aroused man.

Joey hadn't lied to Miles about his dates with other men, hadn't downplayed them. He'd tried it because he was curious. He'd always felt an attraction, so it seemed right to act on it, to see where that pull would lead.

What he'd learned was exactly what he'd told Miles.

While he could look at a man and feel aroused, he much preferred kissing and touching and fucking women.

Joey picked up the pace, moving their hands faster, sparing a quick glance at Miles, whose gaze was locked on their hands wrapped around his dick. A bead of precum slid from the tip, Joey too fucking turned on by Lucy's touch and his friend's hungry look.

Miles gripped Lucy's hair in his fist, closing it tightly enough that her eyelids lowered with desire. They'd done a lot of exploring and testing the waters the past few nights. Lucy had expressed surprise when she learned how much she liked it when Miles pulled her hair, or when Joey wrapped his hand around the base of her throat. She'd been sleeping with lambs, men who hadn't deserved her, hadn't known how to draw out the sensual woman lurking beneath the surface.

As far as Joey was concerned, those two discoveries had opened the door to more intense sexual play and added yet another item to the column titled, "Why Lucy is perfect for us."

"Lick his cock," Miles demanded. "Take a taste."

Lucy must have been listening for the command because her tongue darted out instantly, the tip of it lightly circling his slit. Once again, her touch was too light, too much of a tease.

"God," Joey said through gritted teeth. "Suck it, honey. Take the head in your mouth. I need to feel those pretty lips of yours wrapped around me."

Lucy opened her mouth, giving him exactly what he wanted and then some. While he continued to drive the pace and force of their combined stroking, she took some control for herself. With her free hand, she reached between his legs, cupping his balls lightly.

He hissed in pleasure. "Fuck, Lucy. Baby."

"The two of you together... So hot," Miles murmured, his hand still fisting Lucy's hair. He was using his grip to push her mouth farther down Joey's dick. At first, his movements were slow, her mouth taking him shallowly, but gradually Miles pushed her harder, faster.

Lucy's cheeks were flushed with desire, and Joey groaned when her tongue brushed a sensitive spot beneath the head of his cock. She was a quick study as she marked the spot, stroking it with her tongue repeatedly, quickly driving him out of his mind.

"Fuck, baby. I need..." Miles muttered.

Joey's attention slid over to where his friend was unfastening his own jeans.

Lucy released Joey with a pop, frowning when Miles quickly dropped his pants and started to stroke his own dick.

"Mine," she said simply.

Miles narrowed his eyes. "Thought *I* was in charge?"

Joey reevaluated his initial impression of Lucy as submissive because the raised eyebrow she shot at Miles was one of sheer challenge.

"I asked you to direct what I do to you. Wasn't that the deal yesterday? My orgasms come only from the two of you. If that still stands..."

"It still stands," Miles grumbled sternly.

Lucy obviously liked that answer. "Fine, then the same is true for you. No more showers to take care of business alone. You're all mine. Both of you."

Miles released his cock and crossed his arms. "You think you're up for that, little girl?"

Lucy's eyes drifted closed briefly. "Why is that so hot?"

Miles chuckled but didn't relent. "You didn't answer my question."

Lucy lifted her gaze to them. "Bring it."

Joey had to lock his knees to keep himself upright when Lucy punctuated that statement by reaching out to grip Miles's dick, tugging him closer.

If she still didn't have a death grip on his cock, Joey would have stepped back to give Miles more space, because as it was, they were now standing shoulder to shoulder, pressed right against each other.

Miles must have read his intent because he shook his head at Joey. "Don't move," he said gruffly—before grunting.

Lucy's lips were wrapped around the thick head of Miles's dick.

"Shit, now *that* is hot," Joey observed. He loved Lucy's mouth on him, but watching her suck his friend's dick was proving to be a close second in turn-ons.

Miles gripped Lucy's hair tighter, taking over once more, directing her pace and depth. Joey pumped his own fist up and down his dick, his rough, almost frenetic stroke the same one he employed when getting himself off. He'd never been a slow and easy lover, too big a fan of going hard and fast.

Joey kept his hand over Lucy's, matching Miles's speed. And she'd clearly been sincere about accepting the challenge. Soon, she began alternating, taking Joey, then Miles into her mouth, back and forth, until Joey's vision went gray around the edges.

This was too fucking much. Too fucking good.

It hadn't taken the three of them more than a minute to find their rhythm, working in tandem. The only sounds in the RV were his and Miles's groans, Lucy's deadly hums vibrating over their cocks, and the light slapping of skin on skin.

Any direction Miles intended to offer disappeared, his friend no longer capable of saying anything more than Lucy's name and a string of gasped curses.

"Shit, Luce. So good," Miles said.

Lucy shifted back, taking Joey inside her mouth. If he had his way, he'd drag this out all damn night, but Lucy was proving too skilled.

"I'm close," he admitted, his breathing labored, his balls tight.

"Me too," Miles gritted out. Given his pained tone, Joey thought he might already be there.

Joey released his dick and gripped Lucy's cheeks, pulling himself out of her mouth with a willpower he didn't know he possessed.

She frowned, perplexed, then turned toward Miles, ready to resume his blow job.

Miles must have understood Joey's intent because he shifted away, not allowing her to take him back inside her mouth.

Lucy still clenched their dicks in her hands, though her movements halted. "What—"

"Not this time," Miles said.

Lucy tilted her head in confusion. "But you're not finished."

He didn't respond. Instead, he clasped her wrist, pulling her hand off his dick, before reaching beneath her arms to lift her from the floor. Miles gave her a quick, hard kiss. "When I come, I'm going to be buried deep inside that tight pussy of yours."

Understanding dawned, and Lucy's cheeks flushed a deep red. "God," she breathed. "Yes. But next time, you finish in my mouth."

Miles ran a hand over his head, and for a second, Joey thought his friend was going to say fuck it and give Lucy what she was asking for.

Joey wrapped his arm around her waist, drawing her into his arms. His kiss lingered longer than Miles's had. When they parted, he rested his forehead against hers. "Best blow job ever."

She giggled, waving his words away as nonsense, so Joey gripped the back of her neck, forcing her to see how serious he was.

"The best, honey. My head nearly blew off my shoulders." He kissed her again before she could attempt to demur.

Joey might have gone on kissing her all night if Miles hadn't tugged her out of his arms. "Let's move this to the bedroom.

Because if I stand here watching you two for much longer, I'm not going to be able to stop myself from coming."

Joey was pleased—if shocked—by Miles's confession. He liked the idea that his friend was as turned on by the watching part as Joey was.

"Apparently I have a voyeur kink I didn't realize was there," Miles confessed.

"Ditto." Joey toed off his shoes, jeans, and boxers. He probably looked like an idiot standing there in a long-sleeved Henley and socks, with his erection pointing straight at the ceiling, but he couldn't summon the energy to give a shit.

"Come on." Joey grasped Lucy's hand to drag her to the bedroom. "Let's test our guy's willpower by giving him a show."

Miles groaned. "I'm serious, Joe. It's not going to take much."

Lucy giggled as she passed Joey, jumping up on the bed and kneeling in the middle, crooking her finger for them to follow.

Joey pulled off his shirt, then leaned against the dresser to pull off his socks. Miles finished undressing as well.

Once they were both naked, they stood side by side as their adorable Lucy looked her fill. That was when Joey realized she was still completely dressed.

"Your turn." He pointed to Lucy. "Take off those damn clothes."

Whatever shyness Lucy had possessed at the beginning vanished without a trace because she lost no time pulling her shirt over her head, tossing it their direction. Miles caught it, placing it on the dresser.

When her bra came soaring toward them, it was Joey who scored the prize. He placed the colorful lace on top of her shirt.

Miles stepped toward the bed, clearly intent on taking over, but Joey's palm swung out, catching him mid chest to hold him back.

Miles gave him a curious look.

"She's not finished."

Miles smirked but stopped, his attention returning to Lucy.

She gave them a grin that was pure seduction as she crawled off the bed, turning her back and looking at them over her shoulder briefly. Then she unfastened her jeans, shimmying them and her panties off in the slowest, sexiest ass wiggle Joey had ever witnessed.

"*Goddamn*, your ass, Luce," Miles murmured. He had confessed last night to being an ass man.

She smiled, pleased by his compliment.

The second she kicked her jeans away, he and Miles pounced.

Miles pushed her forward. "Bend over the end of the bed." She was halfway there already, guided by his strong hand in the middle of her shoulder blades.

This new position gave them a bird's-eye view of just how fucking hot her ass was.

Joey recalled Miles's threat this morning to punish her. Unable to resist, he lifted his hand and swatted her ass. There was no real force behind it. This, like so many other things they'd tried, was just a test. A way of seeing if her desires ran the same direction as theirs. He spanked her again, harder.

Lucy moaned.

Joey was no stranger to sexual spankings, and given the way Miles reached out to run his fingertips over Lucy's now-pink skin, it looked like he and his friend had found another shared kink.

Lucy wiggled her ass, silently inviting him to spank her again. Never one to look a gift horse in the mouth, Joey swatted her on the other cheek.

Not to be left out, Miles added his own slaps to her ass. Unlike Joey, Miles didn't hold back. And Lucy did not disappoint.

"Oh my God! That should not feel so good." Her voice was muffled from where she'd buried her face in the duvet.

Joey gripped her inner thigh, drawing her legs apart before sliding his fingers along her very, very wet slit. When he looked at Miles, he knew his friend was on the same page. He wasn't sure when they had developed this telepathy, but Miles responded as if Joey had told him exactly what to do.

He gave Joey a slight nod, then lifted his hand, spanking Lucy again.

As Miles swatted her ass, each blow varying in placement and force, Joey added his own form of sexual torture, circling Lucy's clit, teasing her with a touch that never quite landed.

"Please," she cried. "Joey. Please!"

"Please what, honey?" he asked, as if he didn't know exactly what she wanted.

Her blow jobs had pushed him and Miles right to the brink, but they'd chosen to hover there rather than go over. Because they wanted Lucy with them. Standing at the edge of that cliff, staring out into the abyss, so ready to leap in with them.

Miles alternated between spanking her and rubbing her hot ass cheeks. "I'm never going to get enough of this."

After another minute, Joey gave in to her pleas, applying pressure directly to her clit.

Lucy jerked like she'd been struck by a live wire, and he didn't doubt for a second she would have come...if he hadn't pulled his fingers away.

"Don't stop," she protested.

"We're not coming until we're inside you, remember?" Joey asked. "That means you're not coming either, unless it's around one of our dicks."

"Then one of you better get inside me! Now!"

Joey laughed. Yeah, he might have been wrong about that submissive thing.

"Are you on birth control?" Miles asked.

Lucy shook her head. "Not much need," she replied, somewhat sheepishly.

Miles ran the back of his fingers along her ass. "It's okay. We got this part covered."

Joey didn't have a clue when or where Miles had grabbed the

condoms, but he was grateful as hell when his friend slid one into his palm.

"You first," Miles said.

"You sure?"

Miles nodded. "I want to watch the two of you together. Then I'm going to show you how it's done."

Lucy giggled when Joey punched Miles on the arm. The two of them were trash-talkers from way back, constantly giving each other a hard time. It was their friendship love language. The fact that Miles was bringing it into the bedroom only added to Joey's conviction that the three of them were meant to be.

Joey opened the condom, sliding it on. "Yeah, right. Make sure you pay attention, bro. Cause I'm about to teach you a thing or two."

Joey reached for Lucy's arm, guiding her onto the bed, positioning her in the middle on her back. He couldn't resist smirking when she winced as her sore ass hit the mattress.

She narrowed her eyes, but there was no anger behind the glare.

Joey bent low, giving her a soft kiss on the cheek before whispering in her ear, "You loved it, and you know you did."

Her breathy laugh was all the reply he needed.

Joey and Lucy looked over when they felt weight on the mattress. Miles was sitting on the edge, twisted so that he was facing the same way as Joey, both of them looking at Lucy's beautiful face.

Joey knelt between Lucy's outstretched thighs, positioning his dick at her opening. Then he lifted his gaze to meet hers.

Her soft smile was all the permission he needed as he slowly slid inside. He rested his elbows by her sides because he was overwhelmed by the need to kiss her when he reached the hilt.

"Honey," he whispered.

She cupped his cheek. "This feels so good."

Joey gave her another kiss, then lifted his upper body until he rested his weight on his hands. He hadn't started thrusting yet, wanting to give her a few seconds to adjust. Given Lucy's limited sexual experience, as well as the fact it had been years since she'd been with a man, he didn't want to hurt her.

He glanced over, surprised yet again when Miles shifted, closing the distance. He lay down next to Lucy, stretched out fully on his side. Reaching over, he cupped one of her breasts as he placed a soft kiss on her shoulder.

Joey shifted, withdrawing until only the head of his cock remained inside her—then he pushed back in with one hard, rough thrust.

Lucy gasped with pleasure. "Yes," she hissed, lifting her legs and wrapping her ankles around his waist. With her hips tilted, Joey slipped in even deeper on the next return, and Lucy's fingernails scored his shoulders and upper arms.

"Joey!" she cried out, when he took her the way he'd dreamed. His pent-up desires broke free of the reins. He didn't worry about that because Miles was there, watching her. He would stop Joey if he took it too far. It was that knowledge that allowed him to give in to his hunger.

Lucy met him thrust for thrust, which was saying something, considering he wasn't holding back. He pounded into her like a jackhammer. All the while, Lucy gripped his arms in a viselike hold, demanding more and harder.

"I can't hold off," Joey gritted through clenched teeth.

Lucy was close too. He could feel it in the way her pussy tightened around his dick.

When Miles reached between them, stroking Lucy's clit, he sealed both their fates as she threw her head back, her hips lifting a good five inches off the mattress. Her pussy squeezed his cock so tightly, he saw stars as his balls emptied, filling the condom.

For the first time in his life, he was sorry he wasn't riding bareback, wasn't coming inside a woman with the intent of making a baby.

He had no idea what had prompted that thought. All he

knew was he wanted to see Lucy pregnant, wanted to watch her belly swell with new life, wanted to create a family with her and Miles.

Apparently, he wanted everything his brother, Tony, had. The partners, the children, and the happily ever after.

He shut those thoughts down because it was way too soon to go there...even if only in his head. Especially since neither Lucy nor Miles seemed to believe this was a forever thing, both of them still regarding it as an adventure. One with an end date.

Once he and Lucy caught their breath, Joey sluggishly pulled himself out of her, dropping down to the free side of the bed. He tugged off the condom, tossing it in the trash can in front of the nightstand. One benefit of staying in an RV, everything was fairly close at hand.

Miles still lay facing them, resting his head on his hand. His fingers had moved from her clit and were now drawing slow circles on her flat stomach.

For a second, Joey wondered if Miles was having the same thoughts he was about future babies.

He dismissed the idea immediately. Most likely his friend was giving Lucy time to regain her wits.

When her eyes opened, she looked over at Joey, smiling. "Wow," she whispered.

He chuckled. "You can say that again."

Then she turned her attention to Miles, lifting her hand to cup his cheek.

"We can stop here, Luce," he offered.

Joey's eyes slid down to Miles's painfully erect dick, appreciating the strength it must take to make that offer. Especially since Lucy had taken hand jobs in the shower off the table.

She shook her head. "Come here." She parted her thighs, making it clear she was nowhere near finished.

Miles slipped on a condom, claiming the spot Joey had just vacated.

Finding his second wind, Joey pushed himself up, placing a pillow behind his back, so he could rest against the headboard.

"Show me how it's done," Joey teased, and Miles rolled his eyes.

His words had been a joke, but damn if Miles wasn't giving him what he requested. Because while Joey's style was fast and furious, his friend's had everything to do with going slow, savoring.

Joey wouldn't have thought that was something he'd enjoy, but given the look of pleasure etched on Miles's face with each careful entry and retreat, it was apparent Joey had been missing out on something.

Lucy trembled in his friend's arms, her labored breathing as well as the flush that covered not just her cheeks, but her chest proving Miles was pushing all the right buttons.

"Oh God!" she cried on one thrust.

"There it is," Miles murmured.

Joey had been watching Lucy, so he missed the way Miles had repositioned himself, tilting his own hips as he sought out her G-spot. Then he tossed gasoline on the fire, lifting Lucy's legs, throwing her calves over his forearms to achieve an even better position, one that allowed him to stroke that spot every single time.

Lucy came quick, the orgasm apparently surprising her. "Holy. Fuck! I just..." Her words gave way to panting breaths.

Joey ran his fingers through her hair. "Miles has mad skills."

Lucy didn't laugh. Not because she disagreed but because she was currently trying to fill her lungs with air.

Miles, meanwhile, gave him a shit-eating grin and a wink. "Hope you were taking notes. Because our Lucy..." Miles withdrew. "Likes it..." He started slowly sliding back in. "When we touch her..." Lucy gasped when Miles dipped his hips slightly. "Right *here*."

Lucy slapped her palms against Miles's chest. "I can't take anymore!"

Joey knew if she truly tried to push Miles away, he'd stop, but she wasn't applying pressure. And after a few seconds, her fingers started caressing his friend's bare chest.

"You can give us one more." Miles bent to kiss her.

Joey liked the way Miles's pronouns had changed so he was always included as well, loved hearing him say *our* and *us*.

He slid down, leaning toward her until his lips brushed the shell of her ear. "Just one more, honey. Then we'll let you sleep," he promised. "For a few hours."

This time, she *did* laugh, though it was all air, no sound. "I'll be dead by dawn."

Rather than reassure her, Joey decided to take a page from Miles's book, sliding his finger down the middle of her body, through the valley of her breasts, over her stomach, not stopping until it rested on her clit.

"Oh God," she cried, as Miles started thrusting again, hitting her G-spot over and over as Joey stroked her clit.

Her third orgasm left her shaking, her body writhing out of control.

"Lucy," Miles gritted out. "God. *Fuck.* So good."

Joey glanced up just in time to see Miles's expression of pleasure and pain mingled together as he came too. His finger stilled, though he kept it there, amazed by the way he could almost feel their orgasms pulsing together.

There was so much he wanted to explore, discover, do.

Miles withdrew from Lucy's body, rising to go to the bathroom to clean up. Joey considered doing the same, but he couldn't summon the energy. Especially not when Lucy rolled toward him and nuzzled against his chest. He wrapped his arm around her shoulders and placed a soft kiss on the top of her head, aware she didn't even feel it. She'd already drifted to sleep, not even stirring when a drowsy Miles climbed back into the bed, spooned her from behind, and immediately followed her into dreamland.

Joey would always be jealous of his best friend's ability to fall asleep so quickly. Especially as he lay there, wishing he could find the same peace.

Because he had finally found everything he'd ever wanted.

Now he just had to find a way to keep it.

Chapter Twelve

Miles leaned back in his chair, watching Lucy and Joey attempt to do a Texas two-step to Kenny Chesney's "American Kids" on the dance floor. What they lacked in ability, they were making up for in enthusiasm, the two of them laughing as Joey stomped his feet and spun Lucy around like a rag doll while she hung on for dear life. Joey had gotten a cowboy hat from somewhere—probably borrowed from Hank— so he looked the part of...well, an Italian trying to pass for a redneck, Miles thought with a chuckle. He made a mental note to give him shit for it later.

Their camera crew was set up in the corner, capturing footage that would serve as B-roll and make a nice ending to the episode. The past four days had passed by in a blur as he and Joey spent all day, every day, filming for *ManPower*, their time on the ranch starting at an ungodly hour each morning.

Meanwhile, Lucy had traveled from one Sparks house to another, interviewing several of Macie's relatives for her YouTube show. In addition to recording Hank and Macie on their couch, she'd also filmed a cousin, Sydney, and her former soldier husband, Chas, as well as another cousin, Gia, and her husband,

Logan—who built beautiful custom-made furniture, and had been booked by Sherri for a show next season.

Logan was currently pounding out a beat on his bass with the band Ty's Collective, onstage. The other three members of the band—Caleb, Tyson, and Harley—had been the last of Lucy's *Kiss and Tell* interviews. Miles had been shocked to learn they were a committed throuple. Apparently, the Morettis didn't own the market on threesome relationships, the Sparks family giving them a run for their money.

Miles noticed Lucy had been decidedly quiet after returning from that interview, only offering the barest of responses to his and Joey's questions about how it had gone. He hadn't seen any of the footage, so Miles wasn't sure what to make of her reaction, trying to decide if she'd been concerned about their relationship, bothered by something they'd said, or perhaps...jealous?

Miles had never coveted what Joey's brothers had, never wanted to be a third of a menage a trois. Not until this week, with Joey and Lucy.

Now, he couldn't shake the green-eyed monster sitting on his chest.

Every night for the last four, they'd returned to the RV at the end of each workday, where they ate dinner together then climbed into bed, he and Joey taking turns with their beautiful girl. Nowadays, Miles struggled to remember why he'd been so against participating in the threesome to begin with.

Actually, he remembered exactly why. But it turns out, having Joey in bed—naked and erect—hadn't bothered him as much as he'd expected. Hell, it hadn't bothered him at all, really. Miles didn't think that would be the case with another man. But with Joey, it felt natural, and even easy. Probably because he was closer to Joey than anyone else in his life. There still wasn't any sexual attraction—at least on his part. Though he wasn't sure if Joey felt the same.

That was just one of about a million things the three of them weren't talking about when it came to this...this...

Miles sighed.

Affair.

He hated that word, but self-preservation wouldn't let him use another, not even in his own head.

Every night, they fell into bed, never speaking a word about feelings or the future. As soon as the two F words popped into his head, he shut them down.

No feelings. No future.

Just fucking.

Guess it was obvious why none of them had broached the subject.

They'd wrapped up filming at the Cooper ranch that afternoon. It was a long day that started before dawn as countless people—family, friends, and ranch hands alike—gathered to begin the process of making the apple butter. They'd spent hours the day before peeling bushel after bushel of apples. There'd been a bit of a chill in the air today, everyone bundled up in fall jackets, hats, and scarves. They took turns stirring the apples, butter, cinnamon, and sugar in the huge copper kettles using long wooden paddles, while a bunch of kids ran around playing tag and hide-and-seek.

Growing up in the city, Miles had never experienced anything like today. It was as if he'd stepped back in time, and he'd enjoyed the peacefulness. The whole thing had felt like an episode ripped out of *The Andy Griffith Show*, and he'd joked with Mack, the cameraman, that he'd be shocked if the footage didn't show up in black and white.

By the end of the day, they had made an ungodly amount of apple butter, probably enough for every resident in Maris, Texas. He, Joey, and Lucy had all been gifted with a couple quarts each of the sweet spread. Miles intended to give his to his mom and sister for Christmas because he knew they'd never had it and was certain they would love it.

According to Macie, it was tradition that Maris's apple butter making was always followed by a barn dance. Miles wasn't sure where everyone found the energy after such a busy day, but the place was hopping. Ty's Collective was a bluegrass band, and while it wasn't Miles's kind of music, he had to admit they were really good.

All in all, it had been a great day, so Miles hated that he was now in this funk. Even though he knew the cause.

Their time in Texas was over. The sand in the hourglass was almost gone. Tomorrow, they'd start the three-day journey back to Virginia, where they would drop Lucy off at Stormy Weather Farm before he and Joey traveled on to Baltimore to film their next episode.

Joey had suggested interviewing Killian Collins, Layla's uncle by marriage, and his partner Justin, who ran their own construction company. He and Joey had been thrilled when the producers agreed not only to that interview but to allowing the two of them more input on who they featured on the show.

Before this week, the two of them had been looking forward to the trip to Baltimore and the chance to hang out with friends and Joey's sister.

Now?

He was dreading it.

Miles had known before crawling into bed with her that leaving Lucy would be hard. There was simply no way to be around her and not feel happy. Her optimistic view of life reminded him a lot of Joey's, which was why Miles was so drawn to both of them. He wouldn't call himself a pessimist, preferring the term realist, but spending time around such genuinely positive people was pleasurable and contagious.

Lucy was sweet and thoughtful, attentive and fun. Miles had thought her just Joey's type when he'd first met her, never suspecting she was his as well.

He also thought he'd prepared himself for the inevitable end, but he didn't expect it to be this hard.

They'd declared this time their brief escape from reality or, as Lucy called it, an adventure. It was that idea that had convinced

Miles to lower his walls and give in to the undeniable desire growing inside him. Idiot that he was, he thought he could keep things between them casual, indulging in sex while holding his emotions at bay. He'd never had trouble doing that in the past. Miles hadn't fallen in love even once since Rhiannon, and he'd wondered countless times over the years if he'd lost the ability.

Or if his heart simply refused to let anyone in besides his ex.

Lucy Storm had found the key.

To add insult to injury, Rhiannon hadn't stopped texting or calling, despite the fact he hadn't responded to her in over a week.

Today, Rhiannon had doubled down, his phone pinging no less than two dozen times as she sent him photo after photo of the two of them together, starting from when they were toddlers, holding hands as they walked through the New York Zoo. She'd included their junior and senior prom pictures, another of them standing outside their first apartment building dangling the keys, and countless other "couple" photos that included them dancing, cuddling on the couch, or making silly faces at the camera.

She said she'd finally found time to finish unpacking her things since moving back to New York. Apparently, the pictures had been in one of the boxes, so she'd flooded his phone with a lifetime of memories.

He should have blocked her number because with each new text, his mood got blacker and blacker.

There was no room for Rhiannon in his life anymore.

Period.

Not since Lucy came into his life and claimed his heart.

Miles picked at the label on his beer bottle and let that realization sink in.

In the past, whenever he and Rhiannon reconnected, he'd felt like a besotted teenager embarking on first love, always checking his phone for messages, lighting up whenever she called, counting down the minutes until they were together. She would sashay back into his life, crook her finger, and he'd go panting after her.

The fact that he didn't want to talk to her...*at all*...

God, he was finally—FINALLY—over his ex for good.

That insight should have made him feel like a million bucks. But all it did was drive home another fact.

He'd just set himself up for another heartbreak. One that would be a million times worse than the ones he'd suffered over Rhiannon.

His gaze traveled back to the dance floor, where Joey and Lucy were swaying together to "Make You Feel My Love." Miles loved the song, but he'd never really considered the words until this moment. When Lucy turned her head to find him, offering him one of those sweet smiles of hers, Miles realized he'd done it again. Fallen in love with a woman he couldn't have.

Not that he could fault Lucy for that. She'd been very honest about her commitment to her family and the farm. Even today, as they were standing by the fire, she'd gotten excited about incorporating some of the flavors of the apple butter into a new beer, making notes in her phone and even texting Sam her thoughts. She'd admitted that her favorite part of working as brewmaster was developing new recipes, playing with ingredients to achieve a certain flavor profile.

Her life was on that farm, and try as he may, Miles couldn't see a way to make her world blend with his and Joey's. Not for the long-term.

His phone buzzed in his pocket and, despite his better judgment, he pulled it out.

Sure enough, Rhiannon had sent another photo, this one of the two of them kissing on New Year's Eve, streamers falling over them. He stared at it for a long time before flipping his phone over and placing it face down on the table in front of him.

When the song ended, Lucy and Joey stepped apart. Lucy left the dance floor, drifting over to a table where Macie sat with the other women who ran Sparks Barbeque, including the ones Lucy had interviewed with their spouses for *Kiss and Tell*.

Joey returned to their table, dropping down next to Miles. "You're scowling."

Miles shrugged.

"Rhiannon still blowing up your phone?"

"Yeah."

Joey had walked up behind Miles earlier and caught him scrolling through some of the photos his ex had sent this afternoon. He hadn't said a word about it. Instead, he'd shaken his head sadly and walked away.

"I think we should ask Lucy to stay with us." Joey's comment came out of left field, but it didn't really take Miles by surprise.

His friend wasn't any happier about leaving her behind than Miles was.

"We can't do that, Joe. It wouldn't be fair to her. Her life is on the farm, running the brewery with her family."

Joey ran his hand through his hair, and Miles could almost see his friend compiling a list of ways they could convince her to stay with them. Tenacious didn't even begin to describe Joey when he set his mind to something.

Miles's phone buzzed again, but he didn't reach for it.

Joey stared at it for a second, then looked at him, concern in his expression. "Do you want to ask her to stay?"

He hated that Joey thought he didn't, that his friend thought he was dismissing this because of some latent feelings for Rhiannon.

Although...

Miles spied a way that might make this easier for the two of them. Because his best friend was obviously feeling as low as he was.

"This was just an adventure, Joey. Not forever. Besides, things still aren't settled between me and Rhiannon, and I'm in a shitty headspace. It wouldn't be fair to drag Lucy into the middle of that."

Joey scoffed. "Bullshit. Don't use Rhiannon as an excuse, because you and I both know you're over her."

Sometimes Miles thought Joey knew him better than he knew himself.

"This thing with Lucy..." Joey continued. "It's different. It's special."

Miles shook his head. Not because he disagreed but because he didn't know how to argue against something that was true. God. What the three of them shared wasn't just special. It was fucking perfect.

"Lucy had an offer to leave home before," Miles reminded him. "She turned down Marco. Chose to stay on the farm. That woman is as close to *her* family as you are to yours. But more than that, she feels a sense of responsibility to that place, to those people. I mean, for God's sake, she's not just an employee at the brewery but an owner. She has a financial stake in their success."

"I know that." Joey reached for his beer, taking a long drink. "And you're right. She can't leave. At least not right away. We have time off between Thanksgiving and Christmas. We already talked about the possibility of returning to the farm to see her. We'll set that up, get the details solid before we head on to Baltimore."

Miles sighed, aware that Joey's suggestion was a short-term solution at best. More than that, prolonging things would only make this harder later on.

"Could you really do a long-distance relationship?" Miles asked. "And if so, for how long? Because even when our *ManPower* days are over, you have a vested interest in your family's business in Philadelphia."

Joey didn't reply to that for a long time. Probably because he didn't like the answers he was coming up with. "I'm away from Moretti Brothers more than I'm there these days. My brothers are making it work without me. Maybe I could become a silent partner."

Miles knew just how much Joey would hate that because he missed working with his brothers. It was exactly why he and Miles spent the off months in Philadelphia. So Joey could get his fix of Moretti family time.

"And then what? You move to the farm?" Miles hated saying these things aloud, but they'd been rattling around in his brain for the better part of this week. He wasn't sure Joey was thinking through exactly what it was he was asking for.

"I love that farm, but…"

Miles's grimaced. "But you're a city boy like me."

Joey nodded. Just once.

"What we've been doing with Lucy," Miles said, "it's incredible. I mean…the sex…"

Joey grinned, but it was a sad one. "This is where I'm going to drop that 'I told you so' I owe you."

Miles chuckled. "I deserve that. This past week has been amazing, but there's a big difference between a threesome in the bedroom and a committed menage. It's hard enough making a relationship work with two people. You're proposing the three of us try to build a life together while not even living in the same state."

Joey's jaw tightened, but he didn't argue.

Then Miles brought up something else that had been bothering him. "Besides, while your family accepts the threesome relationships, my mom and sister never will."

"You don't know that," Joey started, but Miles waved off the dispute before it could start.

"I know them, and I know they wouldn't approve. And it wouldn't just be them. What do you think would happen to our careers if word got out that we were sleeping with the same woman? We've already gotten a couple comments from Sherri about Lucy's presence in the RV. I think she's trying to figure out which one of us Lucy is sleeping with."

"Who we sleep with is no one's business," Joey said hotly.

"I'm not saying it is, but our jobs thrust us into the limelight. There's a chance society will judge us for our relationship, and that could have a negative impact on us remaining employed with the show. Our image matters to the production company and the advertisers."

Joey scowled because he knew Miles was right.

He reached over and placed his hand on Joey's shoulder,

hoping to console him. "We head back to Virginia tomorrow. I think we'd be smart to end things with Lucy when we arrive there. We need to cut our losses now, bro, because..." Miles swallowed heavily, trying to dislodge the lump forming in his throat. "I know what heartbreak feels like, and I can't face that again. The longer we drag this out, the more it will hurt. All of us. Lucy included."

Joey frowned. If there was one thing he knew about his friend, it was that he'd cut out his own heart before he'd hurt Lucy.

"Let's make the best of the time we have left."

Before Joey could agree or disagree with that suggestion, Lucy returned to the table.

"I cannot believe how much fun I'm having!" she said, swaying slightly as she sat down.

"Are you drunk?" Miles asked.

Lucy shook her head. "Tipsy at best. And maybe a little concussed from that Texas two-step."

Joey laughed. "I wasn't swinging you that hard, honey."

"By the way," Miles said, "Where's your hat, cowboy?"

Joey gestured toward Hank. "Returned to its owner. Just borrowed it for the two-step. Wanted to look the part."

Miles grinned. "Well, if you were going for Guido, you got there."

Joey rolled his eyes and punched him on the arm. "Asshole."

"Did you guys want to hang around a while longer?" Lucy asked, while trying to hide a yawn behind her hand.

Miles shook his head. "No. It's been a long day, and we need to get on the road fairly early tomorrow morning. We're facing eight, nine hours of driving."

Lucy made a face. "Ugh."

Joey rose. "Let's go say goodbye to Hank and Macie."

Lucy took Joey's hand, the two skirting the tables between them and the Coopers.

Miles picked up his phone, intent on following. He glanced down when it pinged, expecting to see another picture.

Instead, Rhiannon had sent a message.

When are you going to be in Baltimore? I was thinking I might drive down to see you.

Shit. His mother had informed him a week ago that Rhiannon was interested in his filming schedule for the show, so she'd shared it with her. At the time, he'd been more resigned than pissed, but now? Now the anger he should have felt then arrived with a vengeance. Because it wasn't just Rhiannon he needed to set things straight with. It was his mother too.

Great. Another fun conversation to look forward to.

After saying goodbye to approximately fifty-seven members of the Sparks family, Mack gave them a ride back to the RV.

"Last night in Maris," Lucy said with a sigh as they walked in.

Joey wrapped his arm around her waist. "So we need to make it count."

Lucy had looked exhausted on the ride back to the campground, but with that one comment from Joey, her tired eyes brightened.

Miles found his second wind as well when they made their way to the bedroom.

They'd developed their own routine the last few nights, each of them stripping off their clothes before diving beneath the covers. While Lucy had grown more comfortable being naked in front of them, her skin still flushed the prettiest pink. Originally, Miles had chalked it up to modesty or shyness, but he knew now it was a sign of her arousal.

For someone with limited experience, Lucy matched him and Joey right down the line as far as sexual appetite.

So far, they hadn't done more than take turns, though that was by no means a criticism. The truth was they hadn't needed to expand their horizons because just being with her—then watching Joey push their beautiful, sweet honey over the edge— was all Miles wanted. He could get lost inside Lucy's body and never want to be found again.

Once they were naked, Joey drew back the covers, intent on climbing in.

Lucy stopped him. "Wait. We're making it count, right?"

Miles stepped behind her, wrapping his arm around her waist to pull her back flush to his chest, his erection brushing her ass. "What did you have in mind, little girl?" he murmured in her ear, loving the way she shivered with need.

Her long blonde hair tickled his nose, but he didn't care. She smelled like apples and cinnamon and the faintest hint of woodsmoke, despite the fact they'd all showered before the barn dance.

"Something different."

It was a vague answer, her wicked grin telling Miles it was her intent to make them guess.

"You have a plan?" Joey asked.

Lucy nodded.

Miles placed a kiss on her bare shoulder. "Sounds like you're the one directing things tonight."

Ever since the afternoon when Miles had taken charge, directing Joey as he brought her to orgasm, narrating the action had become part of their sexual games. And neither he nor Joey were quiet observers when the other was making love to Lucy. Instead, they laced their voyeurism with commands and dirty talk, guiding the play, driving it to the next level.

"Get on the bed, Joey," Lucy said, taking charge. "Sit with your back against the headboard, your legs spread."

Joey did as she asked, grinning widely, clearly all in. The guy was always up for anything, and damn if Miles didn't follow in his wake every single time. Mainly because Joey had never led him into anything other than a good time.

Lucy joined him on the bed, crawling between Joey's outstretched legs.

Joey groaned when she licked the underside of his cock from root to tip, not touching him with anything other than her tongue. She did the same thing half a dozen times, licking his dick like it was a cone of delicious, rapidly melting ice cream.

"Shit, Luce," Joey breathed.

She gave him the cutest smile, obviously pleased by his response. Then she looked over her shoulder at Miles. "I want to give Joey a blow job while you take me from behind. I want both of you at the same time tonight."

Miles had foolishly thought his dick was as hard as it could get. He was wrong.

"You're going to come in my mouth," she told Joey. While she'd given them other blow jobs since those inaugural ones, they still hadn't come in her mouth, always too anxious to fuck her to even consider recovery time. "And Miles is going to fuck me like he means it. He's going to make it hurt."

Joey's head fell back against the headboard, his eyes closing. "Jesus. I'm not going to last long if you keep talking like that, honey."

Miles climbed onto the bed, kneeling behind Lucy, who was sitting on her haunches. He gathered her hair, holding it in one hand in a loose ponytail before tightening his grip and tilting her head back and to the side. His rough kiss, combined with him pulling her hair, produced the desired result. Lucy whimpered with need.

When he released her, he reached around her midriff to pinch one of her nipples. "Since your mouth will be occupied, dirty girl, I'm taking over as far as making demands. We're going to give you what you want, but you're going to give us what *we* want too."

Lucy nodded, then cleared her throat. "Okay," she whispered.

Miles tilted her forward with a firm hand in the middle of her back. "Hands and knees."

Lucy, the little minx, gave him exactly what he asked for, wiggling her ass provocatively, her mouth a mere inch from Joey's cock.

Joey cupped her cheeks. "Open your mouth, honey, and let me in."

She'd just taken Joey into her mouth when Miles spanked her ass, swatting each cheek three times until her pale skin turned red.

Lucy hummed around Joey's cock. Spankings were a surefire way to get her sex drive revving.

Joey slid his fingers through her hair, his fists closing around the long, blonde tresses. "I want to fuck your mouth, Lucy."

Miles couldn't see her face, but he saw her neck bend as she looked up at Joey while still holding his dick in her mouth, before giving him a very slight nod.

Miles had grabbed a couple of condoms from his wallet while undressing and tossed them onto the nightstand. Reaching for one, he pulled it on, pumping his hand up and down his hard length as Joey used his grip to push Lucy farther down his dick.

She jerked instinctively when Miles touched her opening, covering his fingers with her wetness, then sliding lower to stroke her clit.

She moaned, arching her back, tilting her ass higher, a silent plea for more.

He loved how uninhibited Lucy was with them, never shying away from her desires, never holding anything back. It made him want to push her limits. Dragging his fingers back to her pussy, he gathered up more of her body's juices before traveling a different direction.

Lucy's mouth popped off Joey's dick when Miles pushed the tip of his forefinger into the tight pucker of her anus.

Her sudden withdrawal and gasp drew Joey's attention. He looked at where Miles was touching her before lifting his gaze, meeting Miles's even as he spoke to Lucy.

"I didn't tell you to stop sucking me, honey." Joey started to push her head back down, then paused for just a moment. "We'd never hurt you. You know that, right?"

Lucy nodded, casting a quick glance over her shoulder at Miles.

He wiggled the fingertip inside her ass. "No more than this," he reassured her, regretting that promise when she looked almost disappointed.

Then she turned around and took Joey back into her mouth.

Regardless of what Lucy might think she wanted, they were in the beginning stages as far as threesome sex was concerned, so Miles pulled his finger out, trying not to let her muffled mewl convince him to push it deeper.

Instead, he gripped his cock, guiding the head to her oh-so-wet opening.

Once Joey resumed control of her mouth, drawing her lips along his dick, Miles pushed inside in one hard, relentless thrust.

Joey had proven himself to be a passionate, sometimes even rough lover, so Miles had taken the opposite role. He enjoyed taking his time with a woman, paying attention to her sounds and her body, both letting him know what turned her on. Lucy was a vocal lover, not so much in volume but in groans, moans, hums, and hisses. Miles was sure she didn't realize how much she revealed with those quiet sounds.

Once he was buried to the hilt, he slowly withdrew, his gaze connecting with Joey's. Their newfound telepathy came into play as they began to fuck Lucy in unison, Miles's inward thrusts matching the speed and force that Joey used to push her mouth down.

They continued to take her—use her—as she cried out around Joey's cock, trembling as first one, and then a second orgasm blew through her. They paused after each of her climaxes. It was that or lose control, and there was no way Miles was letting this end too quickly. It was the most intense sexual experience of his life, staring at his best friend as the two of them drove their woman out of her mind with pleasure.

Lucy's strength deserted her as she dropped from her hands to her elbows, her cheek resting on Joey's muscular thigh. Joey released his hold on her hair, stroking his fingers through the long tresses instead, massaging her scalp, which was probably sore.

Neither of them had come yet. A fact that wasn't lost on

Lucy, who, despite being wrung out from her own orgasms, seemed determined to bring them to their knees.

Miles could have told her she didn't have to try so hard. She'd had him on *his* knees the first time she flashed that sunny smile his direction.

When he reached around her waist, touching her clit, intent on claiming a third orgasm, she lifted her head, looking back at him.

"With me," she demanded.

Miles nodded because he didn't have a choice. Feeling her come around his dick twice had been sheer fucking bliss, and as much as he wanted to experience that sensation a million more times, his self-control was hanging on by a thread.

Given Joey's harsh breathing and the tight clench of his jaw, it was safe to say his friend was as close as he was, if not closer.

Miles resumed his thrusting, stroking her clit, while Lucy took Joey back inside, and he began to fuck her mouth in earnest.

"Fuck!" Joey's voice was hoarse as he came. He closed his eyes and his head fell back, banging against the headboard with enough force it probably hurt. "Shit! Honey. Lucy."

Lucy never lifted her head, swallowing every drop of Joey's come.

The image of Joey and Lucy together sent Miles over the edge as well, his hips pistoning as he took her at her word, giving her exactly what she'd asked for.

Lucy came a split second behind him, her body jolting so roughly he had to grip her waist to keep himself inside. Miles's vision went black for a few seconds as he filled the condom, hoping the damn thing could hold it all because he'd never come this much.

The three of them remained frozen in place. Lucy's head rested on Joey's thigh again, his now-soft dick close to her face as he clumsily patted her hair. His head was still thrown back against the headboard, his eyes shut, as he tried to catch his breath.

Miles remained tucked inside Lucy, not ready to give up the warmth of her body.

For several minutes, they stayed just like that. Miles wasn't even sure if Lucy and Joey were awake. She stirred slightly when Miles forced himself to withdraw, and Joey lifted his head as soon as he felt Miles's weight leave the mattress.

Miles walked to the bathroom, where he disposed of the condom and washed his hands and face. When he returned to the bedroom, Joey and Lucy had shifted, though not much. Joey was now lying down, Lucy tucked against his chest.

A sharp pain pierced his heart as he faced the future that loomed before him. One where neither of these people were in his bed.

He climbed onto the mattress but they didn't stir.

Miles lay on his back, staring at the ceiling for a long time as they slept. Too many things were rattling around in his brain for him to find peace. Considering the long drive that lay ahead of them, he'd pay for the lack of sleep tomorrow.

His frustration over everything he was about to lose grew until his chest ached with helplessness. Feeling the need for control over one tiny fucking part of his life, he decided to take charge of what he could. Ready to do something he should have done weeks ago.

Carefully climbing out of bed, he tiptoed out of the room, sitting down at the table and opening his laptop.

It was nearly two a.m. in Texas, so he opted to say what he needed to in an email rather than by text or phone call because Rhiannon would most likely be asleep.

He considered waiting until morning and calling, but they were getting on the road early for the first day of three nine-hour drives, and he wanted this over with *now*. And he didn't feel the least bit bad about doing it in email instead of in person or over the phone because the second time Rhiannon had dumped him, it was via a note written on the back of a take-out menu.

Firing up his email, he said all the things he should have told her when she called him that first night three weeks earlier. He told her they both needed to move on, and to do that, they couldn't be friends, couldn't be *anything* to each other. He asked her to stop texting and calling, then told her he hoped she would be happy—because he *did* want that for her—even if it wasn't something they could find together.

Miles prayed the email would be the end of things, but he knew her well enough to know Rhiannon wouldn't accept his words at face value. She'd launch into all the reasons why they should and could be just friends because she'd done it before. Why *wouldn't* she think she could wear him down? He hadn't exactly gone out of his way not to look like a fucking pushover, letting her slip under his defenses too many times in the past.

Hitting send, he closed the lid to the laptop, blocked Rhiannon's number on his phone, and returned to the bedroom, looking down at the two most important people in his life.

A wave of sorrow washed through him at the thought of walking away from Lucy in a few days.

Apparently, his life was never going to be *Kiss and Tell*.

It would always be Hit and Miss.

Chapter Thirteen

ucy tried to ignore the ever-growing ache in her stomach as they crept closer and closer to Northern Virginia. It had been a long journey back, traveling halfway across the country, while the three of them continued to exist in their little bubble, none of them talking about what happened next. Probably because they all knew, even if they didn't want to say it aloud.

Last night had been their *last* night. Lucy ran her fingertips over her lower lip as she closed her eyes and replayed it in her mind.

Joey and Miles had taken turns removing her clothing, kissing, licking, and stroking every inch of newly bared skin. She'd never felt so adored, so worshipped, so... God, almost powerful. Being with them was a heady experience. Especially when Joey eased her back on the bed, kneeling on the floor between her outstretched legs. He'd given her three orgasms with just his tongue and fingers, playing her body like a concert violinist, hitting all the right notes and driving her to heights she'd never reached before. Her body still tingled at the memory.

When he rose, Miles stepped forward, pressing his impressively thick cock inside her. Normally, Miles was a slow, thorough lover, but last night was on another plane entirely as he pounded into her body like a man hoping to imprint himself on her—*in* her. She was fairly certain it had worked because she swore she could still feel him inside her today.

She lost count of how many orgasms they'd given her throughout the night. After Miles finished, Joey was there to take his place. They'd woken her up two more times during the night and repeated the whole heavenly process.

The trip *to* Texas had been exciting and fun, and she barely recalled the hours spent on the road as they'd talked about anything and everything under the sun. She had never shared so much of herself, never felt comfortable doing so. That wasn't a problem with Joey and Miles because they listened to all her stories with genuine interest. Then they offered her the same, giving her their own secrets and dreams.

This return journey had been more brutal, nine hours of driving each day with only brief stops to eat. They still passed the time by talking, but the stories were less personal, more of the surface-y stuff, like favorite movies, books, and shows, gossip about other people in their lives. Lucy wasn't sure if it was intentional or not, but it felt as if they'd slowly started distancing themselves so the goodbyes wouldn't be as painful.

As if.

While their conversations had dwindled, the same wasn't true for the language they spoke with their bodies. The closer they got to Gracemont, the stronger the sexual tension grew, all of them painfully aware that time was running out.

By the time they pulled into the campsite each night, they clashed together, a rush of kisses, touches, fucking. Some nights, they didn't come up for air until late, not eating dinner until well after ten and always in bed, where they took turns feeding each other.

Lucy had just had the best time of her life, and now...

She sighed as Joey took the exit off the interstate that led to Gracemont.

Now, it was over. She was home.

She tried to dismiss how wrong the word *home* suddenly felt.

Miles was in the passenger seat, staring at his phone, while Joey was driving the RV. Both men had been uncharacteristically quiet since they'd woken up this morning. Of course, she hadn't said much either. At first, she blamed exhaustion. None of them had gotten much sleep. Now, she could see from the strained expressions on their faces they were experiencing the same melancholy she was. Today, there'd been no chatting, no car games, no music.

"Do you have time to stay for dinner?" she asked, breaking the long silence. They'd gotten a later start than normal, none of them in a hurry to get out of bed, aware it was their last morning together. As such, it was nearly six o'clock at night as they neared the farm.

Joey glanced at the dashboard to check the time, but Miles was already shaking his head in response.

"I'm afraid not. It's another two hours to Baltimore. We're parking this beast," Miles said, in reference to the RV, "on our friend Leo's farm. Layla is going to pick us up there and drive us back into the city. We're meeting Justin and Killian tonight for a late dinner and drinks at Pat's Pub, then we start filming in the morning. The schedule is tighter here as we're trying to finish filming in Baltimore before Thanksgiving."

The guys were staying with Joey's sister Layla while they were in Baltimore.

"Pat's Pub?" Lucy asked.

"Finn's family owns it, and a bunch of them work there," Joey explained, mentioning Layla's husband.

"Joey and his brothers actually renovated the entire place after a fire," Miles added. "Ever since then, Finn's mother, Riley, has referred to the Moretti boys as the Italian Stallions."

Lucy had seen all of Joey's brothers, and she had to admit the name fit.

"Between Layla marrying into the family and the rebuilding

of the pub, I've gotten really close to the Collins family," Joey said. "Especially the bartender, Padraig. He's become a good friend. I set him up with his wife."

Miles snorted. "Is that how you're spinning that tale?"

Lucy leaned forward, happy for the distraction as the RV rolled down Gracemont's Main Street. In a few minutes, they'd make the turn that would take them up the mountain to Stormy Weather Farm. "How did you set them up?"

"I asked Emmy, who's now his wife, out on a date. She and Padraig were just friends at the time," Joey said.

"According to Padraig," Miles interjected, "they were just friends until Joey strutted into the pub with his arm around Emmy. That was when he realized he was in love with her."

Joey laughed. "I figured that out about three seconds after Emmy and I walked in. Padraig was shooting daggers at me across the bar. So, I did what any self-respecting matchmaker would do in the same situation."

"Which was?" Lucy prompted.

"I kissed her."

Lucy giggled. "Oh my God. Did Padraig throat-punch you?"

Joey shook his head. "No. He probably *would* have if I'd put up a fight for Emmy, but I could see she was in love with him too."

"That's so romantic...for them." Lucy had paused before adding the last two words, making the guys laugh.

"Theirs is definitely a story worthy of *Kiss and Tell*," Joey said. "Might be fun to get a cameo in one of your episodes. Because I would insist on being recognized for my efforts on their behalf."

Lucy bit her lip, because it was on the tip of her tongue to suggest Joey turn the RV back toward the highway just so she could meet the couple and interview them.

She didn't, because there were too many people relying on her at the farm. She couldn't adopt Miles and Joey's adventurous life-style, no matter how much she might want to.

Joey made the turn, and she leaned back, this winding road as familiar to her as the back of her hand. She had hoped that somewhere over the last few days, she'd find a spark of excitement over returning, but if the unbearable weight pressing down on her was any indication, she'd say that wasn't coming. Perhaps she'd feel better once she was home and saw her family again.

Once they crested the hill and her farmhouse came into view, Lucy literally had to fight back tears. She blinked rapidly because she refused to ruin this goodbye by becoming a blubbering, inconsolable mess. She'd save the tears for later, when she was alone in her own bed.

Joey parked the RV in the driveway, turning it off. She glanced at the porch, sort of surprised no one was there. She'd texted Remi around lunchtime to give her their ETA. She'd been so wrapped up in her misery that it didn't occur to her until just now that Remi hadn't replied.

She stood up and stepped out of the RV, stretching her back. Joey joined her, his hand gripping the back of her neck in that familiar, hot way she loved.

"Home again, home again, jiggety jig jig," she said, repeating a silly line her granddaddy had always used whenever they returned home from town.

Miles climbed down the steps from the RV with her suitcase in his hand, and Lucy had to swallow down the lump in her throat.

"Thanks," she said, when he placed it on the ground next to her, aware her voice sounded thin. She was about to return to the RV for the rest of her stuff—her backpack, laptop, and camera case—when the screen door slammed and her sister, Nora, stepped out onto the porch.

"You're home," Nora said in a weary tone, walking toward them.

"Is everything okay?" Lucy asked, suddenly concerned.

"Not really. We've been struck down by the plague," she said in a monotone voice. Lucy frowned until her sister explained, "Half the family is in bed with the flu."

"What? Who? Since when?" Lucy panicked, wondering who was running the farm and businesses if everyone was sick.

Nora rubbed her neck, the dark circles under her eyes revealing just how exhausted she was. "Aunt Claire and Uncle Rex got hit with it first. They've been in bed since the day before yesterday. Yesterday, Sam, Remi, and Mila all went down. It's a nasty-ass bug. High temperature, vomiting, diarrhea, the works. I'm pretty sure Theo and Levi are coming down with it too, but they refuse to go down without a fight. You know how those guys are."

Lucy hated that so many people in her family were suffering. "Oh my God. Why didn't you call me?"

Nora gave her a tired smile and shrugged. "I didn't want you to worry. And besides, you were already on your way back. Those of us still functioning," Nora added, "have divvied up all the chores, pulling double and triple duty. We've moved everyone who's sick here and I'm playing nurse. We've called in all the employees, offering overtime if they'll work more hours. Unfortunately, a lot of them have the flu too. Luckily, there were only a handful of guests scheduled in the B&B and cabins, so I've been taking care of them, while the rest of the guys are handling everything else."

"What about the brewery?" Lucy asked.

"Theo and Billy have been running things, with Sam coaching from bed—or the bathroom. But with Theo feeling bad now too, I'm glad you're home to take over. Maybe now I can get Theo to rest."

Lucy was racked by guilt. "Of course, I'll take over at the brewery. And I can do whatever else you need too."

Nora grimaced. "Sorry, Lu. Didn't mean to hit you with this before you even made it into the house. Things are fine. Truth is, I got excited when the RV pulled up. I missed you."

Lucy reached out to grip her sister's forearm. "I'm sorry I wasn't here when you guys needed me."

"It's just the flu. Nothing hugely dire." Nora gave her a hug, then reached for the handle of Lucy's suitcase. "I'm going to head back inside. I was making some tea for my patients," she joked, "when I saw the RV." Her sister returned to the house, wheeling her suitcase behind her. It spoke to her level of exhaustion that she didn't remember to say hello to Joey and Miles.

Lucy turned back toward the RV, intent on grabbing the rest of her stuff.

"What do you need from us?" Joey asked.

"What?"

"We can help," Miles added.

She shook her head, touched by their offer. "You don't have time," she reminded them. "You're on a tight schedule, trying to finish the next episode before Thanksgiving. Filming starts tomorrow."

"Yeah, but—" Joey began.

"It'll be fine," she reassured them. "I'm just going to be busy for the next few days until everyone gets better."

Lucy thought that might be a good thing because she was going to need the distraction if she hoped to get through the next few days—weeks, months, years—without falling completely apart.

"We hate to leave you like this," Miles said.

She shook her head, trying to alleviate their guilt. None of this was their responsibility. It was hers. "Don't worry. I'm sure things will be back to normal soon."

The realization that returning to normal felt like a life sentence wasn't something she wanted to acknowledge.

She pointed to the RV. "Give me a second to grab the rest of my things."

Joey and Miles followed her, closing the door of the RV behind them. She didn't want to say goodbye. God, this was going to kill her.

Lucy reached out, intent on picking up her backpack, but Joey's hand gripped her wrist, stopping her.

"I really should get inside. Poor Nora looked exhausted," she insisted. The best way would be to rip this off quickly, like a Band-Aid.

"In a minute." Joey tugged her toward him, wrapping his arms around her back, gently stroking up and down while he hugged her. Her arms remained bent between them, her hands resting on his chest. She considered pushing him away because his embrace was too warm, too comforting, too tempting.

How could she have fallen so hard, so quickly? Lucy had been in love before...with Billy and Marco. But her feelings for those guys, whom she'd dated much longer, felt lukewarm to this raging inferno of emotions threatening to boil over and burn her from the inside out.

When Joey released her, Miles was there, taking his turn, though he wasn't interested in a hug. He cupped her cheeks, giving her the softest, sweetest kiss of her life. Miles's kisses always made her feel drunk—light-headed and fuzzy.

He placed his forehead against hers. "We can pull an all-nighter if you want. Stay here to help you at the brewery or with the family. Whatever you need."

She smiled sadly, so tempted to take him up on the offer. "No. You heard Nora. They called in extra employees, and everyone who's well is pitching in. One of the best things about a big family is there are plenty of people to share the load in an all-hands-on-deck situation."

"I hate saying goodbye to you," Miles murmured, his lips touching hers as he spoke.

Lucy had to blink a few times, willing away the waterworks.

"We have a break from filming between Thanksgiving and Christmas," Joey said. "You can come to Philly and—"

"No," she said, interrupting whatever he might say next. Lucy and Miles pulled apart, the two of them turning to face Joey.

While Joey, the eternal optimist, refused to give up on this, she and Miles knew the score.

"I can't leave the farm again so soon. It wouldn't be fair to my family," she continued.

"Then Miles and I will come here. We can—"

"Joey," she said softly. "We agreed that this thing between us would end here."

He shook his head. "I didn't agree to that."

Miles reached over and placed a hand on his shoulder. "Joe."

"I *didn't*," he reiterated hotly.

"My place is here. It will always be here." Lucy wished her tone was powerful enough to sell her words. Sadly, she feared she was missing the mark, so she stressed, "*Always*," as she said it a second time.

Joey looked at her like he was waiting for more. If she was a good person, she'd explain why she felt so strongly about staying on the farm, but the truth was, she had a hard time understanding this compulsion, this neurosis herself.

"Lucy," Joey started again. "Honey."

She drew in a shaky breath. "Please," she whispered. "Please don't do this."

Joey frowned, studying her face closely.

She didn't have the strength to hide her feelings from him, so she didn't. She laid it all bare there for him to see. Their life was on the road. Hers was here. Remi hadn't even graduated from high school by the time she'd lost Mom, Dad, Grandma, and Granddaddy. Lucy needed—wanted—to be a constant in their lives, someone they could rely on to be nearby if they needed her.

Joey sighed, running a hand through his hair before looking away, his jaw clenched.

"We understand," Miles said, wrapping his arm around her shoulders, pulling her against him.

Joey shot Miles a look that made it clear he didn't understand a damn thing, but he didn't say it aloud.

"It was a great adventure," Miles said, tightening his hold. He looked every bit as upset as Joey, but he was doing his best to keep this moment light.

Lucy loved him for it. Just like she loved Joey for wanting more.

"It was," she said, her throat tight. "It was the best time of my life."

"Mine too," Miles confessed, leaning down.

Lucy met him halfway, kissing him with every bit of the desperation and sorrow she felt. His hands were strong on her back, her fingers clenching his upper arms, wishing she could drag this kiss out forever.

When they parted, she looked over at Joey, who was leaning against the wall, his arms crossed. She'd felt his gaze on her and Miles as they kissed. She was grateful he wasn't so angry at her that he looked away.

"Joey," she said softly.

He pushed away from the wall, grasping her with an aggression that was zero parts scary and a hundred parts hot as hell. "I'm going to miss the fuck out of you." He backed those words up with a rough, hungry kiss that fired her libido to dangerous levels. Her girlie bits were about to be in for a whole world of disappointment because all she had to offer them from now on was some alone time with a lousy vibrator.

When they parted, she placed her hand on the side of his beloved face, soaking him in, drawing her thumb over his scruffy beard that tickled her whenever he kissed her.

"Thank you for everything," she said.

Joey swallowed heavily, nodding. This time, he did look away.

Lucy grabbed her backpack, camera, and laptop cases, tossing them over her shoulders. She wanted to say more, but her throat had closed completely. What else was there to say besides...

"Goodbye," she whispered, opening the door to the RV and walking to the front porch, refusing to look back.

She couldn't. If she did, Lucy knew there was no way in hell she'd be able to stop herself from running back to them.

The second she stepped inside, she heard the RV engine start and the crunch of gravel as Joey turned it around in the driveway.

She remained in the front foyer, leaning against the closed door as if barring herself from leaving to chase after them, not taking a breath until she couldn't hear the vehicle anymore.

Lucy dropped her bags on a chair near the door.

She glanced up when Nora came downstairs, carrying an empty tray.

"What do you need me to do?" Lucy said, shutting down all thoughts of Joey and Miles, ignoring the painful thudding of her heart, digging deep to wrap herself up in the numbness setting in. Shutting her mind to all the misery, she opted to focus on her family. They needed her.

Nora, God bless her, had a list.

For the next five hours, Lucy rushed around the farm, checking in with Levi and Everett regarding the vineyard, winery, and hops yard, taking temperatures and giving medicine to her sick relatives, feeding dinner to the guests at the B&B, and relieving Theo from his brewery duties because he really did look like shit.

By the time she made it to her own bedroom, it was well after eleven. While she was utterly exhausted, she couldn't bring herself to crawl into her lonely bed just yet, so instead, she unpacked and even started a load of laundry.

When there was absolutely nothing else to do and every part of her body ached, she finally gave in to the inevitable. Crawling between the sheets, Lucy stared up at the ceiling, not bothering to stem the tears that slid down her face.

All the thoughts and bad feelings she'd managed to hold at bay since Joey and Miles drove away hit her, dropped into her mind like a barrage of missiles.

She should have invited them to come visit over the holidays.

They should have given the long-distance relationship a chance.

She should have continued the adventure.

Every single one of those wishful thoughts was destroyed by reason and logic.

They'd known each other less than a month. Upending their lives over a short affair would be the height of madness.

She shoved the insanity aside and forced herself to view things from a practical angle, to look at it without emotion.

Occasional visits would never be enough for any of them, and at the end of each one, she would have to go through another painful goodbye like the one she endured today.

When she recalled their conversations about what came next, she realized they hadn't *asked* her to keep traveling with her. Not really. Joey had only said it once in jest. All they'd truly offered her was the road trip and future visits.

None of them had used the L word or referred to themselves as boyfriend or girlfriend.

They'd engaged in a casual threesome affair.

Neither man had asked for or promised more, but she wasn't sure if that was because they didn't want more or because they thought she didn't.

She had let herself get carried away, had built this up to something much bigger in her heart and in her mind, and while Joey and Miles hadn't admitted to feeling the same, she felt like they had.

Lucy wiped her eyes, wondering if things might have ended differently if she'd told them how she felt.

She dismissed that idea immediately because she knew it wouldn't have made a damn bit of difference.

Her place was here.

Theirs was on the road.

It was as simple and as difficult as that.

Chapter Fourteen

M iles shook Killian Collins's hand. "That was a great show."

"Thanks," Killian replied. "I have to admit, I enjoyed that more than I thought I would. I'm not one for standing in front of a camera, but Justin refused to let me say no when your producer called to set it up. That guy is happiest when he's front and center."

Miles chuckled, glancing across the construction site to where Killian's partner, Justin, was chatting with Joey, their producer, Sherri, and the director.

He and Joey had been in Baltimore for four days. Four long, painful, lonely, miserable days.

They'd tried to fill every minute of their waking hours with activities, be it filming the show, hanging out with Layla, Finn, and Miguel, touring around Baltimore, or watching a hockey game at Pat's Pub. Neither he nor Joey allowed themselves a second of downtime.

Because downtime was bad. It gave them too much time to think about...

Fuck it.

That was his current internal mantra. Every time that blonde-haired, blue-eyed beauty's name tried to sneak into his head, Miles just closed his eyes and thought "fuck it."

The only time that intonation failed was when Miles allowed himself to stop moving. Every night, when he crawled into bed alone, he was forced to remember what—who—they'd left behind. Consequently, Miles was running on fumes after four shitty, restless nights spent tossing and turning and regretting every single one of his life choices. This was why he'd stayed away from relationships after Rhiannon. He had sworn to himself years ago, he'd never put himself through the gut-wrenching pain of loving and losing ever again.

What a joke.

Less than a month. That was all it had taken for Lucy to revive his dead heart, for her to stake her claim. He'd missed her every single one of the 345,600 seconds that had passed since he and Joey said goodbye and left her on that damn farm.

And if that wasn't bad enough, Joey was in the same state. His typically jovial, good-natured best friend was currently absent, replaced by a shell of a man who was simply going through the motions.

Considering the two of them had been about as much fun as dental surgery, Miles was surprised this week's filming had been so successful. They had Killian and Justin to thank for that. What the hosts lacked in charm and wit, the guests had more than made up for. At this rate, he and Joey would be lucky if the production company didn't *replace* them with Justin and Killian.

"I enjoyed getting to know you, Miles. I spent quite a bit of time with Joey when he and his brothers were helping me and Justin rebuild the pub after the fire, but you and I have never really had the chance to talk. My family was thrilled when we heard Joey landed the hosting gig, and we haven't missed an episode of *ManPower* since the debut. The two of you are a good fit."

Miles had met Layla's uncle-by-marriage a couple times in the past two years, but he was right; they'd never had a real conversation before this week. Killian was a bear of a man, size-wise, which was saying something, considering the Moretti men weren't exactly known for being small. Killian dwarfed Miles and Joey, as well as his partners, Justin and Lily.

Like all of Joey's siblings, Killian was also in a committed threesome relationship. A *very* committed one.

When they were at Stormy Weather Farm, Miles had told Joey that his siblings' relationships didn't count because they were all still in the honeymoon phase. He didn't really mean that. After all, Tony and Layla had been with their partners for years and he had eyes, and he could see they were very much in love. But at the time, he'd been shaken by Rhiannon's reappearance in his life and trying to ignore his growing attraction to Lucy.

Killian, Justin, and their wife, Lily, had been married for well over thirty years, the three of them raising a son together, Fergus. So it was safe to say their honeymoon period was over. Though... maybe not. He and Joey had been invited to dinner with the trio last night at their house. The bloom was definitely not off their romantic rose.

When Miles had complimented Lily's cooking, she'd grinned, telling him she'd been slaving in the kitchen the entire afternoon. Justin had taken great delight in outing her, claiming she'd ordered takeout from Pat's Pub, then putting the food in her own dishes to make it look home-cooked.

Lily laughed as she slapped her husband's shoulder, chastising him, though it was obvious she'd intended to confess herself. Killian had leaned toward her, placing a kiss on the side of her head, assuring her they didn't marry her for her cooking. Justin, the jokester, couldn't resist chiming in to say they'd married the successful marine biologist for her awesome 401K and health benefits.

The love the three of them shared for each other was almost palpable. And again, while it should have been a great night, one he and Joey would have enjoyed under regular circumstances, last evening they'd been subdued. He wasn't sure what had been going through Joey's head, but Miles had spent the entire meal wishing it was him, Joey, and Lucy sitting at that table, hosting guests together as a married throuple.

Killian glanced over at Justin and Joey, deep in conversation now that their director and producer had moved on. "Can I ask you something?"

He nodded.

Killian gestured toward the construction trailer. They'd been filming at the site of J&K Construction's latest project; their team was expanding the habitats of some of the larger animals at the zoo. The locale had been ideal because it gave them the added opportunity to capture some awesome footage of bears, tigers, and gorillas to include in the show. With the exception of the catio guy episode, which was a fairly meh interview, this season was shaping up to be one of their best with the brewery, Hank's ranch, and now Justin and Killian at the zoo.

The two of them climbed the steps into the trailer, Killian offering him a chair. They sat down as Miles glanced around, noting the photos on Killian's desk. One of him, Justin, and Lily, another of his son Fergus, with his wife and their baby.

"I hope you won't think I'm out of line, but..." Killian paused. "Is everything okay between you and Joey? I'm aware I don't really know you from Adam, but I know Joey, and *that*," Killian pointed out the window to where Joey was standing, "isn't him."

Miles considered making up some excuse for why Joey was so subdued, but Killian had opened a door, and he wasn't going to waste the opportunity to talk to someone who would truly understand.

"I'm sorry Joey and I haven't been ourselves."

Killian waved his hand. "Not asking for an apology. I'm just concerned."

Miles wasn't sure what to say, so he just started at the beginning. "A few weeks ago, we filmed an episode at a brewery. The brewmaster, Lucy, is…" Miles grinned. "She's amazing. Sweet, funny, beautiful."

Killian nodded. "I see. So you and Joey are fighting over a woman?"

Miles shook his head. "Not exactly. Not at all, actually. We, um… Well, you know all of Joey's siblings have relationships similar to your marriage. It turns out, he's interested in the same."

Killian's eyes widened. "Oh. I see. It makes sense that he'd be open to that kind of relationship, considering he's around it so often. But it's new for you. Are you uncomfortable sharing?" he asked, searching for some understanding. "Jealous when he's kissing Lucy?"

"Jesus, not a drop. I love watching them together."

Killian laughed. "That was a quick answer. If sharing isn't the issue, what is?"

"The production company set us up in an RV this season as we travel around the country to film. They're including outtakes of our travels as part of the show."

Killian smiled. "Sounds fun."

"We convinced Lucy to join us on the road. The three of us traveled to Nashville and then Texas. Things between us…" Miles ran a hand over his head. "Joey wants a *committed* threesome. He's not looking for a casual affair, but I…"

"You aren't sure if you want the same?"

"I was pretty damn sure I didn't want the relationship *or* the affair, but Joey can be a sneaky, persuasive bastard. He kind of inched me and Lucy toward his vision for our future."

Killian tilted his head. "No one can inch you toward anything if you don't take those steps yourself."

Obviously, he wasn't going to let Miles get away with downplaying his own role in everything that went down between him, Lucy, and Joey. He respected that as much as it annoyed him.

Miles leaned forward, resting his elbows on his knees, looking down. "You're right. Joey opened a door, let me see inside. I'm the one who made the decision to walk in."

"What was holding you back to begin with?" Killian asked.

Miles lifted his gaze, wondering how forthright he should be. In the end, he just said it. "I'm straight, and Joey admitted a while back that he'd gone on a couple dates with guys. I was worried…" He blew out a breath, not wanting to sound like a homophobe or an asshole. "I'm not wired that way."

Killian crossed his arms, nodding slowly. "Neither am I."

"Justin?" Miles asked, before quickly raising his hands. "Ignore that. Out of line. That's none of my bus—"

"He's straight too, though his line might have one or two curves in it. We've never explored that because he knows I'm not interested in him sexually. To be perfectly blunt, I'm closer to Justin than I am my twin, Tristan. Justin's my brother, so the idea of us being together that way feels almost incestual."

As soon as Killian said the words, Miles realized that was how he felt too. And hadn't Joey said basically the same thing? They were brothers. "That makes sense."

"Did Joey put a move on you? Is that why you two are out of sorts?"

Miles shook his head. "No. Joey knows where I stand, and he says he's okay with it."

"You don't believe him?"

Miles didn't even need to think about that question. "I do. He *is* okay with it."

Killian leaned back in his chair, crossing his ankles. "I'm struggling to see the problem. Was it Lucy? Was she uncomfortable about the idea?"

Miles smiled when he thought about Lucy's outright enthusiasm. Once the three of them made up their minds to hop into bed together, Lucy was all but leading the charge.

"Okay," Killian said. "The smile answers *that* question. Lucy was in."

"Oh yeah," Miles murmured. "The thing is…she approached our time together as an adventure. One with a time limit. She lives and works on the family farm. Her future is tied to that land, while, God willing, Joey and I will continue to host *ManPower*."

"Long-distance relationships aren't unheard of. If the two of you care about this woman as much as you say—"

"Well, that's part of it too, isn't it?" Miles interjected. "We've known her less than a month. We haven't had enough time to get to know each other, to see if this is something that will go the distance. Committing yourself, giving your heart to someone is hard enough when it's just two people. There are three of us, all new to..." Miles waved his hand.

"A threesome," Killian helpfully supplied with a grin, clearly amused by Miles's reluctance to say the word.

"Yeah. A threesome."

"Love always comes with risks. Doesn't matter if there's one person in the bed with you or two."

"How have you, Lily, and Justin held it together for so long?" Miles asked.

"The same way every other married couple in the world has. By putting in the work. Supporting each other through the rocky times, fighting our way through the bad stuff, remembering that, even when we're arguing, at the core of everything is our love for each other. No marriage is perfect, but if you're with the right person—or people—it's perfect enough."

Killian's words soothed a part of Miles he hadn't realized was so ragged. He'd been pushing away the idea of a committed threesome because, in his mind, it was a more difficult relationship to maintain. He'd genuinely believed that if he couldn't make Rhiannon happy for the long haul, what chance did he have with Joey and Lucy?

"Thanks, Killian." Miles had put the brakes on him and Joey seriously pursuing Lucy because of his own baggage, his own insecurities. Joey had wanted to find a way to make things work with Lucy—even if that meant a long-distance relationship—but Miles had piled on one excuse after another because he was afraid of getting hurt again.

"Not sure I helped much," Killian said, rising.

Miles reached out and shook his hand. "You did. More than you know."

Now Miles had to figure out how to fix what he'd broken.

* * *

Sitting at the bar at Pat's Pub a few hours later, Miles was no closer to an answer about how to proceed from here. All he knew was that he wanted to. With their interview of Justin and Killian completed, he and Miles were basically off the clock for the holidays as far as *ManPower* was concerned, until early in January, when they hit the road again.

Tomorrow, they were heading on to Philadelphia for Thanksgiving. Something that would take them even farther away from Lucy.

Loud laughter had him glancing over his shoulder. Joey was sitting with Layla, Finn, and Miguel, splitting a huge plate of cheese fries while chatting with Finn's mother, Riley, and her best friend, Bubbles. Given the way Riley was waving her hands around as she spoke, Bubbles interjecting something every few words, it must be one hell of a story.

It was the first time in days he'd seen a genuine smile on Joey's face. Miles hated that he'd played such a big role in robbing his best friend of his happiness.

Padraig placed a pint of Guinness in front of Miles. "Why aren't you sitting with them?"

He shrugged. "Thought Joey might like some time alone with his family."

The bartender frowned. "Pretty sure he considers *you* family."

Miles liked Padraig Collins. The man had definitely found his calling because on top of being a great listener, he was astute and a straight shooter.

"He does," Miles admitted. "I just needed some quiet time. I've got a lot on my mind."

Padraig nodded. "Want to talk about it, or should I just keep the Guinness coming?"

Miles chuckled. "How about both?"

Talking to Killian this afternoon had helped a lot, so Miles decided to go for broke. See if Padraig could drive him the rest of the way home.

"Hit me with it," he offered, leaning his elbows on the bar.

"I've never had much luck with love. Fell for the wrong girl in high school and basically let her play racquetball with my heart for the better part of my adult life."

Padraig winced. "Ouch."

"Yeah. I've been trigger-shy about relationships ever since Rhiannon. We grew up together and were best friends literally since birth. We started dating in high school, thus beginning too many years of me being the yo-yo, dangling from the end of her string."

"Yo-yo, huh?" Padraig pulled off the towel draped over his shoulder and wiped some condensation off the bar.

Miles sighed. "She has a way of reappearing in my life just when I think I've got my shit together. She's not a bad person. I think if she was a heartless, cruel woman, this would be easier, but we had a lot of great times together. And to make matters worse, our moms are best friends who are absolutely convinced we're going to get married and give them grandbabies."

"Ouch again."

Miles grimaced. "Yeah. So when Rhiannon calls after a couple of years and we start reminiscing, it takes me back to happier times. For a little while, anyway."

"Then you remember she hurt you too." Padraig was a clever guy.

Miles tapped the end of his nose, letting the bartender know he got it in one. "Unfortunately, those bad memories never manage to resurface until she and I have embarked on something new, and I'm convinced that *this time* we'll go the distance. She was my first love, my first everything, and she has this uncanny skill for turning me into a complete idiot."

"Women can do that," Padraig agreed with a grin. "So is that what's happening? You're being an idiot again?"

Miles shook his head. "No. I'm over Rhiannon. For good."

"Oh yeah?"

"I met someone a few weeks ago. Lucy." Miles couldn't say her name without smiling, even though the thought of being without her had his insides tied up in knots.

Padraig glanced down to the end of the bar where his wife, Emmy, was typing away on her laptop, and he grinned. The bartender had fallen head over heels for the romance writer, who'd set up camp at Pat's Pub a few years ago.

He turned his attention back to Miles. "So tell me about Lucy."

"Joey and I interviewed her for an episode of *ManPower*. She's a brewmaster. You'd love her."

Padraig looked intrigued. "Cool job. I've always been interested in brewing my own beer. I'll have to be sure to catch that episode."

"She's an amazing woman," Miles said. "I haven't felt like this about someone in a long time. Rhiannon did a number on my head and my heart, so…"

"You're worried about being hurt again," Padraig said, not bothering to make his statement a question.

Miles nodded. "Rhiannon started calling again about the same time I met Lucy. I didn't want to get dragged through all the emotions that come with my ex, so I shut down. Or I tried to, at least. Lucy's a hard person to push away. I only spent a few weeks with her, which is way too fast to fall in love—"

"No, it's not," Padraig interjected. "I fell for my first wife in a single night."

Miles had heard all about Mia, who'd died of a brain tumor. "And Emmy?"

Padraig rubbed his jaw, stealing another glance down the bar.

"Probably fell just as fast for her, but, like you, I was afraid to admit it. Broken hearts... They take a long time to heal."

"They do," Miles agreed. The two of them fell silent for a moment. Then he glanced over his shoulder at Joey. "I shouldn't have been such a coward about acknowledging how I feel because I'm not just hurting me."

Padraig followed Miles's gaze. "Joey?"

"He's in love with her too. We, uh... I mean, the three of us..."

Padraig chuckled. "I'm well aware of the Morettis' penchant for sharing. Two of my cousins married Moretti girls with their best friends, remember?"

Miles laughed. Because Layla was currently sitting between Padraig's cousin Finn, and their partner, Miguel. At a nearby table, his cousin Oliver was sitting with Erin—also a Moretti— and *their* partner, Gavin.

"Fair enough," Miles conceded. "Joey and I fell for Lucy Storm. And like a dumbass, I gave my best friend a million reasons why we couldn't be with her because Rhiannon had gotten into my head, and I was too afraid to open myself up to another heartbreak."

"What kind of reasons?"

"The lame kind. I told him we didn't have the right to ask her to give up her job or her life on the farm with her family. I said it could negatively impact our jobs. I told him I didn't want to be part of a threesome beyond the bedroom."

Padraig tilted his head. "Wow. That really was quite the grocery list. You were fighting your feelings hard."

Miles rubbed his temple. "Yeah. The worst part is, it's the first time ever I convinced Joey to do something he didn't want to do. Leave Lucy behind."

Padraig grinned. "That guy really isn't very easily swayed."

"You can say that again," Miles grumbled. "Of course, there's a very good chance Lucy won't leave the farm."

"Long-distance relationships aren't unheard of," Padraig pointed out.

"You're right. They're not."

"You're over the first love, right?" Padraig asked.

Miles nodded.

"You're in love with Lucy, and you don't mind sharing with Joey, right?"

Miles nodded again.

"So?"

"So…" Miles mused.

"So stop drowning your sorrows and go get the girl," Padraig summed. "Because I'm really not seeing a problem here."

And just like that…Miles didn't feel quite so down in the dumps.

He was in love with Lucy. Joey was in love with Lucy. The three of them fit together—and they deserved a chance to see if this thing really *was* as special as he believed.

He was ready to take a chance on love again.

Miles laughed. "You're right. There *isn't* a problem."

Or, there *wasn't*.

Until Miles heard a voice he really—REALLY—didn't want to hear.

"Hey, Miles."

He spun the barstool around, gritting his teeth. "Rhiannon. What are you doing here?"

Rhiannon looked over his shoulder, her forehead creasing. He could just imagine what Padraig's face must look like. It almost felt as if Miles had summoned her like fucking Beetlejuice, simply by saying her name too many times.

"I was wondering if you and I could talk," she said before shooting another glance behind him. "Alone."

Miles knew when he'd sent that email, he hadn't heard the last of Rhiannon. But after so many days of silence, he hoped that maybe she'd taken him at his word and was ready to move on as well.

He gestured toward the front door of the pub. They could grab a table in here—there were plenty of empty ones—but he didn't want to drag this out any longer than he had to. While it was November, Baltimore was having unseasonably warm weather this week, so they wouldn't freeze outside.

She led the way, Miles following. He didn't bother to glance in Joey's direction, hoping his best friend hadn't noticed Rhiannon walking into the pub. His plan was to reiterate what he said in the email, then send her on her merry way.

The two of them walked away from the entrance of the pub.

"How did you know where I was?" Miles knew she had his filming schedule, courtesy of his mother, but it sure as hell didn't say he'd be drinking a pint at Pat's Pub tonight.

"Your mother. She knew I'd traveled down to see you. I was hoping to reach the construction site where you were filming before you finished, but apparently I missed you. When I called your mom to see if she had the address of where you were staying, she mentioned she'd spoken to you."

Mom had called just after he finished talking to Killian. Typically, she didn't reach out when he was filming, but he hadn't thought anything of it at the time. Now, he wondered if she'd been fishing to see if Rhiannon had arrived. No doubt Rhiannon's mom had been sitting there with her, the two of them working themselves up into a frenzy, hoping for his and Rhiannon's reconciliation. Mom had been hands off since he graduated high school, letting him make his own adult decisions about everything.

Except Rhiannon.

When it came to her, Mom always took a very keen and sudden interest in his life, offering lots of advice, constantly dropping her name into conversations, keeping him abreast of his ex's life even though he never asked. He'd planned to talk to her about Rhiannon in person over Christmas, but clearly he should have approached it on the phone.

Miles had told Mom he'd call her back tonight because he and Joey were heading to the pub for dinner and a drink. He'd thought it odd when she asked the name of the pub, but he brushed it off as no big deal.

"She told you I was here."

Rhiannon nodded. "I didn't tell her or my mom about your email."

"Why not?"

"I knew it would upset them and—"

She stopped talking when Miles scoffed. "This has nothing to do with them."

Rhiannon sighed, taking a different tack. "Why are you so angry at me all of a sudden? I thought the other night, when we talked, things were cool between us, but now, I can tell you've blocked my number."

"I'm not angry, Rhiannon."

She crossed her arms. "It feels like you are. You know, I wasn't proposing we get back together, Miles."

He scoffed. "I've got at least a dozen photos and countless texts from you that suggest otherwise."

Rhiannon had looked sad at the beginning of the conversation, but he saw the brief flash of annoyance in her eyes when he called her on her bullshit. She recovered quickly, tempering the anger and resuming the role of injured party. She really was a wonderful actress.

"I've missed you, Miles. I'm back in New York now, and being there without seeing you feels wrong. I mean, we should be getting an upside-down slice at Rosa's, hanging out at Grover Cleveland Park, and watching a Mets game in the nosebleed section. And I don't mean as a couple. Just as friends."

He tilted his head at that lie, letting her know he'd already called her on that. "We can't be just friends, Rhiannon. Past history has proven that."

She sighed. "We're older now, Miles. Wiser. I think we can. I'd like to try anyway."

"No."

Miles was already over this conversation. He had a million

things he could say to her, things he probably should say, but anger like that takes a lot of energy. He was tired of being mad. Tired of being sad and depressed and bitter and vulnerable.

Lucy and Joey had washed all those shitty feelings away and replaced them with emotions that felt good. Happiness, humor, peace, a feeling of truly belonging, and of not only being accepted for who he was but also loved for it.

Rhiannon blinked a few times, frowning in confusion. He got why. He'd never told her no, always letting himself be swept back. "I don't understand. I swear I'm not asking for more."

She never was. Until she did.

Miles gave her a sad smile. "I know you believe that, but it doesn't matter. I'm putting myself first this time, which means I'm moving forward. I'm not interested in looking back."

Those words seemed to hurt her, her eyes suddenly glassy with tears. The less generous part of himself wondered if they were sincere or if this was more acting on her part.

Rhiannon looked away, swiping at her eyes. "You're my best friend, Miles. Even during the times when we aren't talking, I always know if I need you, if I call, you'll pick up the phone."

In the past, he would have. Hell, even just a month ago...he did. But he couldn't do that anymore. "I'm not going to pick up the phone again."

This times, tears flowed down her cheeks, and he understood this was no act. He hated hurting her, but if that was what he had to do to convince her once and for all, then that was what he had to do. "You need to move forward too," he said gently.

Her eyes narrowed slightly. "You've met someone else."

He refused to answer that. He hadn't even told Joey about his change of heart, so he wasn't going to tell Rhiannon first.

She sniffled. "You know, a small part of me always thought it would be you and me at the end of the day."

He chuckled and shook his head. "No, you didn't. I was just the consolation prize, the thing you held onto until something better came along."

Rhiannon scowled. "That's not—"

"I deserve better than that. I've found better," he admitted.

True to form, Rhiannon proved she wasn't going down without a fight. "I love you, Miles. I've always loved you."

"You'll get over it," he said. "I did."

It was a cruel thing to say, but he needed her to understand, all the way to the depths of her soul, that what they shared—the good, the bad, and the ugly—was truly over.

For the first time, his words seemed to truly sink in, Rhiannon showing true remorse over her actions. "You're right, you know. About all of it. I've been terrible to you."

He didn't respond to that. Maybe if he was a better man, he'd forgive her, but he wasn't there yet.

She reached out to touch his forearm. "You did deserve better from me. And I'm sure I could—"

"No," he repeated. He crossed his arms, dislodging her touch, putting a period on this conversation. If he didn't, Rhiannon would stand here until the end of time, pulling out every trick in her bag to get her way. "Goodbye, Rhiannon."

Rhiannon stood there and held his gaze, as if she was waiting for him to tell her he was just kidding or for him to come to his senses and go back to her.

When it was clear those words weren't coming, she whispered, "Goodbye, Miles."

He stood there a minute longer, watching as she crossed the street. When she reached the driver's side door, she glanced back at him and once again, he knew she was waiting for him to call her back.

Hell would freeze over first.

Her shoulders slumped when he simply stared her down, then she got in the car and drove away.

One problem down, four hundred and thirty-seven more to go.

Miles walked back into the pub, surprised to find Joey

standing by the door. He'd clearly been watching Miles with Rhiannon through the front window.

"What's she doing here?" Joey asked, anger lacing his tone.

"What do you think?" Miles said.

Joey scowled. "She wants you back."

"She said she just wants to be friends. But yeah, ultimately, I think she thought we were starting over again."

Joey rubbed the back of his neck wearily. "What did you say?"

Miles placed his hand on Joey's shoulder, squeezing. "I said no thanks. I've already got a best friend. Besides, I'm not sure my new girl would like it if I was friends with my ex because I sure as fuck don't like her being friends with her exes."

Joey froze for a second, and Miles could almost see him replaying those words, trying to decide if he'd heard him right. Then he grinned. "You got a new girl?"

He nodded. "We both do."

"I was talking to Justin about us today," Joey admitted.

He laughed, wondering if the older men had decided on a divide-and-conquer tactic, Justin pulling Joey aside, Killian claiming Miles, in an attempt to help them to pull their heads out of their asses.

"I talked to Killian."

"Oh yeah?" Joey said.

"He showed me the error of my ways. All relationships take work. Doesn't matter if there are two people in the bed or three."

Joey crossed his arms. "Thought you weren't interested in a long-distance relationship?"

"To be honest, I'm not. I'm hoping we can convince Lucy to come back out on the road with us because having her with us was fucking perfect."

"What if we can't convince her?" Joey asked.

Miles sighed. "Then I guess we'd better learn how to till and hoe and shit like that because we'll be spending a lot of our year on that farm. How's your southern accent?"

Joey laughed. "Yeehaw!"

"That was terrible," he said, shaking his head.

Joey wrapped his arm around his shoulders. "So I guess there's only one thing left to do."

"What's that?" Miles asked.

"We get another round to celebrate, then we get a good night's sleep. Because tomorrow morning, you and I are driving back to Stormy Weather Farm to get our girl."

Miles grinned.

Yeehaw!

Chapter Fifteen

Lucy rubbed her forehead wearily, stepping out of the back door of the farmhouse, trying to summon the energy to walk to work. The first couple of days she was home were super busy, alternating between pulling double and triple duty at the brewery and winery and caring for relatives who'd been knocked down by the flu. Yesterday, they appeared to have rid the farm of all the bad germs—or the plague, as Nora called it—because everyone was finally out of bed, and they were back to business as usual.

Which left her with too much time on her hands. She'd made more than a few mistakes in the brewhouse over the past couple days, too distracted to keep her mind on the task at hand. Theo and Sam cornered her yesterday afternoon, concerned.

Theo had point-blank asked if Joey and Miles had been gentlemen, he and Sam more than ready to hop into a car to drive to Baltimore to open a can of whoop-ass, depending on her answer. She reassured them that Joey and Miles were wonderful... but she wasn't sure she'd *convinced* them. Probably because it was hard to say their names aloud without her throat closing.

With the entire family well again, they turned their attention to her, holding a "welcome back" dinner last night, everyone inundating her with questions about her trip, where she'd gone and what she'd seen. After they cleared the table, she gave her family the silly souvenirs she'd bought in Nashville.

Unfortunately, with so much focus on her, it hadn't taken her sisters and Aunt Claire long to figure out she wasn't as cheerful as she was pretending. They'd each taken her aside at one point or another to ask if she was okay. She'd lied and told them she was just tired, but Lucy knew none of them were fooled.

"Where the hell have you been?"

Lucy twirled around, frowning when she spotted Scottie storming across the yard. She'd gotten a late start this morning, after yet another shitty night of sleep. She couldn't understand how a person could sleep like a damn baby for twenty-eight years of her life, then have that ability wrecked in just three short weeks. Sleeping alone sucked.

"Excuse me?" Lucy didn't have the energy for Scottie today. Hell, she *never* had the energy for him. But, perhaps more than that, she didn't have the right temperament. She was already late for work and trying to deal with him was going to set her back even later.

"Where have you been?" Scottie repeated when he reached her.

"You're going to have to be more specific. I was just at the farmhouse, and now I'm on the way to the brewhouse."

"When did you get back in town?"

Lucy wanted to tell the prick her comings and goings were none of his business, but then she decided it would be quicker to just answer his question. "Four days ago."

"Why didn't you call me?"

"Why would I?" This conversation felt like déjà vu, Scottie of the opinion lately that she had to check in with him for some reason.

Scottie put his hands on his hips, giving her that condescending sneer she knew far too well. "You want to explain to me what the hell you were thinking, leaving town with two men you barely know?"

Lucy crossed her arms. "No."

"I think I deserve an explanation, Lucy."

She scowled, the lid she'd barely been holding on her temper flying off. "Why the hell would you think that? We aren't dating, Scottie. We aren't even friends. You're just someone that I used to know. So back off and get the hell away from me."

She turned to head to the brewhouse, but Scottie surprised her, gripping her upper arm and spinning her around.

She shoved his hand off, furious. "Don't you dare touch me!"

"I don't know what kind of stunt you were pulling by leaving town with those guys, but enough is enough. I've made it perfectly clear how I feel about you, Lucy. I get that you want to punish me for some perceived slight in high school, but don't you think it's time to get the hell over it?"

"Really? You've made it perfectly clear?" Lucy was aghast. "You hovering and acting like some possessive, jealous asshole, all while never saying a fucking word to me about your feelings isn't perfectly clear, Scottie. You don't just get to decide I'm your girl-friend without asking me."

"Lucy. You have to see how perfect we are for each other."

Her mouth fell open because...*what*?

"I don't like you, Scottie. And while you haven't bothered to tell me your feelings, I know for a *fact* I've made my disdain for you as clear as a cloudless sky."

Scottie rolled his eyes, like she was being unreasonable. She hated when he treated her like she was some stupid little girl.

"You're just being emotional. You've always been that way. You get upset too easy and it's always over nothing."

Lucy narrowed her eyes. "I know you're not trying to mansplain my feelings to me."

"I'm tired of the continual temper tantrums, Lucy. I don't know what happened between you and those guys, but it's obvi-ously over, considering you're here and they're gone. I was wrong to give you so much space. I'm not going to make that mistake again."

Lucy balled up a fist, but before she could throw it, Scottie grabbed her shoulders, pulled her toward him, and kissed her.

She pushed at his chest and started kicking his legs, twisting her head to get away from his sloppy, disgusting kiss. "Get your hands off me!"

Scottie was stronger than Lucy might have expected, her anger turning to fear when he reached around her body and grabbed her ass, dragging her lower body against his, letting her feel his hard-on.

"It's always been you and me, Lucy. Ever since we were kids." Scottie kept trying to kiss her, his fingers gripping her so tightly she knew he was leaving bruises. "Why are you fighting me?!"

"Let go!" she yelled loudly.

"What the fuck is going on?!"

Lucy was besieged with instant relief when Levi's booming voice bellowed from across the yard. She'd been pushing hard against Scottie's chest, so when he released her suddenly, she teetered, trying to regain her balance. She failed, falling backward and landing on her ass, hard.

Neither Scottie nor Levi seemed to notice, her oldest cousin charging the mayor like a bull waved on by a red flag. Scottie threw his hands up, though whether it was in defense or surrender, Lucy couldn't tell. Not that it did him a damn bit of good.

Levi swung hard, catching Scottie partly on the hand covering his face and partly on the jaw.

"What the fuck do you think you're doing?" her cousin roared.

"You can't hit me!" Scottie insisted. "I'm the mayor!"

"I don't give a shit if you're the King of England. You were hurting Lu!"

Scottie rubbed his jaw. "No, I wasn't. We're a couple."

Lucy pushed herself off the ground in a fury. "Are you fucking insane?!"

Levi grasped the front of Scottie's shirt. "I heard her saying no. Heard her telling you to let go."

"It was just a misunderstanding," Scottie insisted, his hands on Levi's wrists. Lucy didn't know if he was trying to pry them off his shirt or if he was just hoping to keep Levi from taking another swing.

Levi shook Scottie roughly. "I didn't misunderstand a goddamn thing. My cousin said *no*, and you ignored her."

"Lucy." Scottie looked at her from the corner of his eye. "Please. Tell him to let me go."

"Like I told *you* to do?" Lucy spat out.

Levi glanced her direction. "You okay?"

She nodded.

"Lucy," Scottie tried again. "Why are you acting like this? I know you have feelings for me. The way you always hung out at my house when we were kids. How jealous you were of the girls I dated in high school. The way you tried to get my attention by dancing with those guys then leaving town with them. You didn't stay with *them*. You came home. Because you want *me*."

Was that how Scottie viewed their past?

Lucy took a deep breath, fighting like the devil to calm down. It didn't work. She'd never met a more self-centered person in her life because he genuinely seemed to believe he was at the center of everything she'd ever done. "I'm only going to say this one more time, Scottie. I am not your girlfriend. I'm not interested in dating you. I don't even *like* you. We. Are. Nothing."

For the first time, Lucy got the sense her words were actually sinking in.

"But... I... You were always so nice to me."

"I'm nice to *everybody*!" she shouted back.

"No." He shook his head. "I was different. I was special to you."

It occurred to Lucy that Scottie's parents had always lifted him up on a pedestal, told him he was the most important person in the world. As such, he didn't hear the word "no" often. He also wasn't accustomed to not getting something he wanted.

Neither of those things gave him the right to come at her the way he did, and she refused to think about how bad things could have gotten if Levi hadn't shown up. Lucy really hadn't been able to break free from his grip.

"Did you hear what she said?" Levi asked, keeping a firm grip on Scottie's shirt. "Mayor or not, you're not welcome on this property. Show your face here again and I'll have the sheriff arrest you for trespassing."

Scottie looked from Levi to Lucy, then back to Levi.

"Fine," he said stiffly.

Levi released his shirt, and Scottie ran his hands over the front of it, trying to press out the creases with his palms, then he rubbed his injured jaw again. Finally, he turned to her, lifting his chin in that way he had that let people know he was looking down his nose at them. "You're not worth the trouble."

Levi reared his fist back, but Lucy grabbed her cousin's arm, holding on tight.

"He's not worth it either," she told him.

Scottie sniffed. Then—wisely—he walked away.

Levi cupped her cheek, doing a quick visual scan of her face. "Did he hurt you?"

She shook her head. She was definitely going to have bruises on her arms and ass, but Levi was still a man on the edge, so she thought it wise not to bring that up, lest he chase Scottie down for round two.

"What the hell was that about?" Levi raked his fingers through his long hair, shoving it out of his face.

"Scottie seemed to believe we were a couple."

Levi snorted. "Right. As if you'd settle for a douchebag like that."

She smiled. "Thanks for coming to the rescue. For a paper pusher, he's surprisingly strong. I..." She stopped when her voice quivered at the end.

Levi heard it, of course, because the big teddy bear of a man reached out to pull her in for a hug. She wrapped her arms around him, soaking in the comfort.

"Is Scottie the reason you've been out of sorts since coming back?"

Lucy took a step back, then shook her head before realizing her negative answer would require her to come up with another.

"Are you out of sorts *because* you came back?"

She blew out a long, slow breath. "Yeah."

"Always suspected if you ever left the farm, you wouldn't want to return."

Levi was the oldest of her cousins. He'd been sixteen when her parents died, so he probably knew and remembered them the best. She was curious how much he knew about their divorce.

"My mom certainly didn't." She would never have said such a thing if she weren't feeling so low, so lost.

"Do you remember a lot about that?" Levi asked, cautiously. "You were pretty young."

Lucy wasn't sure why she'd opened this door, but now that she had, she didn't have the strength to close it again. "I remember them fighting a lot. How she left for a year. How happy I was when she came back."

The sympathy in Levi's gaze told her that he knew all of that. Lucy had been a mama's girl. Her early memories of her childhood filled with images of her trailing along in her mother's wake, listening to her stories, longing to be just like her.

"The night before..." Lucy swallowed heavily. "Before they died, they had a bad fight. The worst one I'd ever heard. Usually when they got like that, I'd grab the girls and go to Grandma's or to your house, but Nora, Mila, and Remi were already in bed. Mom and Dad were screaming at each other. I couldn't make out a lot of the words, but I heard my name. I always wondered, always worried that maybe I was the reason they—"

"No," Levi said loudly. "No. It wasn't anything like that."

Then he rubbed his chin, his brows furrowed. Lucy got the sense he was debating over whether to tell her more.

"What do you know?" she asked.

"I didn't know you thought that, Lu. I'm sorry. Maybe I should have told you. Your dad came to see mine the morning..." Levi sighed before saying, "That last morning. I overheard them talking. Uncle Ronnie said that your mom wanted a divorce and she wanted custody of you."

"Me? Just me?"

"Mila's been my mom's shadow since birth, and there was no denying, even back then, that Remi and Nora would wither away and die if they weren't breathing this farm air."

Lucy smiled, though her heart was aching. Levi's description of her younger sisters was accurate. None of them would ever call another place home. Stormy Weather Farm was it for them. They'd never felt trapped here.

Maybe this would all be easier if anyone else in the family had ever left the farm, but they'd all remained, let their roots sink deep into the soil. It made her feel like the cuckoo bird who'd been left in someone else's nest.

"You and your mom..." Levi paused.

Lucy batted away a stray tear. "She was my idol. My world. I wanted to be her when I grew up. And then she..."

"She left."

Lucy nodded. These were memories she'd purposely shut away for years because she couldn't understand how even now, she could still love her mother so much, miss her so intensely after she'd willingly walked away from them, from *her*.

"Uncle Ronnie wanted to fight for you," Levi continued. "Couldn't imagine letting you go. But he was worried that maybe—"

"I'd want to go with Mom."

"You were only ten, Lu. If it had come to that... Well, it would have been a really shitty decision for a kid to have to make."

"I would have stayed."

The second she said the words, she knew they were a lie.

Levi gave her a sad smile. "I'm not so sure you would have."

Lucy lowered her head, staring at the ground until Levi lifted it up with a calloused finger under her chin.

"And that would have been okay," he said. "You're not tied here, Lu."

She knew that. Or at least, she wanted to.

God. She needed to put this new information about her mom away for now because, holy fuck...it was way too much to unpack. Especially when she was already on the verge of a complete meltdown, thanks to zero sleep and a severely broken heart.

Lucy didn't know how to respond to any of it, so instead, she just held on to the lie. "This is home. I'm happy to be back."

Levi looked like he wanted to push the issue, but something in her face must have told him she was too close to the edge because he backed away. And since he was wonderful, he changed the subject.

Unfortunately, the one he chose didn't lighten the mood like he clearly expected. "You know, we've all got a pool going."

"Oh?" Lucy asked.

"Half the family thinks you have the hots for Miles. The other half, Joey."

Lucy forced a laugh, even as her heart split in two at the sound of their names. Steeling herself, she took a deep breath and forged on. "Who did you guess?"

Levi never missed a beat. "Miles."

"Not Joey?" Lucy was surprised. After all, she and Joey had been flirty during their time here at the farm, so she thought he'd be the obvious choice.

"Caught you casting a few sideway glances at Miles while they were here filming. The more he kept his distance, the more you looked. Am I right? Because I'm in the minority, so my cut of the pot would be pretty sweet."

Rather than respond, Lucy gave him a noncommittal shrug that he mistook for her being coy.

"Are you going to see them again?" Levi asked.

She shook her head.

Levi frowned, his brows furrowed with concern. "Lu, are you okay?"

Lucy swallowed deeply, anxious to get away. If she stayed here much longer, listened to the compassion in her cousin's tone, she'd shatter.

"I better head to the brewhouse." Lucy turned that direction. "I'm really late now."

"Lucy," Levi started. "Wait."

She paused, surprised when he reached out and gave her another hug.

"I'm around if you ever want to talk about it." He placed a brotherly kiss on her forehead and let her go.

Lucy wouldn't be able to avoid the subject of Joey and Miles forever, but she wasn't able to tackle that subject today any more than the one about her mother.

So she pulled on the mantle of numbness she'd been wearing since returning, hoping it would get her through.

Because it was going to be a long day.

And a long life.

* * *

Lucy stared at the ceiling, fighting to make herself get up. She couldn't be late for work again. She'd already sucked enough at her job this week. At this rate, Sam and Theo were likely to fire her worthless ass.

She'd retreated to her room last night right after a simple dinner of grilled cheese sandwiches and tomato soup with her sisters, claiming she had a headache, which had been true. Too little sleep was taking its toll. When she paired that with the Scottie drama, the new information about her mom, and the broken heart she'd been stupidly trying to convince herself she didn't have, it was safe to say she was completely overwhelmed and overwrought.

She rubbed her scratchy eyes, then looked up when she heard a knock on her bedroom door.

"You okay?" Mila asked, opening the door without waiting for an invitation. They were sisters, which meant those kinds of niceties were nonexistent. If Lucy or her sisters wanted privacy, they simply locked their doors.

"What are you still doing here?" Lucy asked. Typically by this time of the morning, she was alone in the house as all three of her sisters were already putting a dent in the list of duties around the farm.

"We were worried about you," Mila replied.

"We?"

Rather than answer, Mila opened the door wider, stepping inside, allowing Remi and Nora to enter as well.

Lucy was shocked to see them. "You're late for work," she said stupidly.

Remi laughed. "That's the best part about working on a family farm. No one can fire us."

Lucy sat up, sitting with her legs crossed beneath the duvet as her sisters walked over and perched around her on the sides of her mattress.

"I'm fine," Lucy said. "My headache is all better."

Nora pursed her lips. "You still have dark circles under your eyes."

Mila, ever the caregiver, reached out to place the back of her hand on Lucy's forehead. "You sure you aren't coming down with the flu?"

"I'm not," Lucy was quick to reassure her.

Mila picked up the silly little stuffed cat that Lucy always kept on her bed. It was the last gift her dad had ever given her, and she couldn't seem to make herself put it away, even though at twenty-eight, she was too old for stuffed animals.

"Well, that's good. Because I wouldn't wish that plague on my worst enemy." Mila, along with Aunt Claire and Uncle Rex, had suffered the worst case of the flu, all three of them down for the count for several days, while the rest of the family rebounded quickly, most only laid up for a day.

"So, let's have it," Remi said. Her youngest sister was no fan of small talk. If her sisters came here with an agenda—and it appeared they had—Remi would be impatient to get down to business.

"Let's have what?" Lucy asked.

"What happened when you were away, Lu?" Remi asked. "Every time one of us talked to you on the phone, you sounded blissfully happy, like you were having the greatest time of your life. Were you just pretending?"

Lucy shook her head. "No. It really was an amazing trip. I loved every second of it."

Remi nodded, as if she'd been expecting that answer. "Good. So I guess that leaves one of two other possibilities. One, you're sad to be back, or two, you fell for one of the guys and now you're nursing a broken heart."

Lucy mentally checked the box that said, "All of the above," but didn't say it aloud because damn.

She needed to find a way to ease them into the fact that she had indulged in an honest-to-God menage.

"I'm happy to be back," she lied. It spoke to how close she and her sisters were that not one of them bought it.

"Lu...you know you don't have to stay here if you don't want to," Mila said softly. While Lucy was most like their mother, Remi and Nora more like their dad, Mila took after Aunt Claire, a gentle soul with a kind heart and a born nurturer. Lucy wouldn't be surprised if, like Aunt Claire, Mila had a big brood of kids that she raised right here on the farm.

"Millie," Lucy said, using the nickname her dad had given Mila when she was little. Lucy, Remi, and Nora were the only ones who still used it on occasion. "I have responsibilities here."

Remi and Nora rolled their eyes in perfect unison.

"Jesus Christ," Remi muttered.

"What?" Lucy asked. "I do."

Remi pierced her with a hard look. "You don't mean *us*, do you?"

Lucy wasn't sure how to reply to that because she didn't want her sisters to think they were the reason she wasn't leaving. Even if it was partly true. "I mean the brewery."

Nora snorted. "You are hands down the worst liar on the planet. You always have been. Theo and Sam are perfectly capable of running the brewery on their own."

Lucy threw her hands up in frustration. "I left you short-handed when you needed me. You were all sick and I should have been here to help."

"It wasn't all of us and it was the flu, for God's sake. No one was dying," Nora pointed out. "Prior to that, we were doing just fine—*without* you."

Remi picked up the argument. "There are a million Storms, plus no less than two dozen employees on the property. We weren't short-handed, and you know it. You just won't admit it because you're operating under some misguided notion that you still have to take care of us." Remi gestured at her, Nora, and Mila.

Mila reached out and took Lucy's hands. They were the closest in age, Mila only a year younger than Lucy. "You're not Mom, Lu."

Lucy froze. "What do you mean?"

"You're not abandoning us."

Like Mom did.

None of them said those words aloud, but it was clear they were all thinking it.

Lucy let Mila's words sink in, uncertain how to feel about them. To the little girl who'd always aspired to be just like her mother, they hurt. To the bitter girl who'd been abandoned by her hero, they freed her.

Lucy had cried herself to sleep every night since Joey and

Miles left. To be honest, she wouldn't have thought she had any more left to shed.

Her sisters found a new well. Lucy had spent most of her life trying to convince herself she was happy here, that living here, working here, was enough. It was one of the reasons she never took a vacation. She'd always suspected that if she ever left for parts unknown, she wouldn't want to come back and she'd been right.

But perhaps more than that, she was afraid that leaving would prove she was just like her mother, and Lucy's heart couldn't make up its fucking mind if that was a good or bad thing.

"You were just a kid too when she left, you know?" Nora pointed out. "I know you tried to protect us, tried to shelter us from their fights."

"You were so young." Lucy always hoped Nora and Remi didn't remember much about that time. Especially Nora.

"I remember it all," Nora confessed quietly. The two of them held each other's gazes, too many painful memories flowing between them, as Lucy recalled her sister's face the night their parents died, the vacant look in her eyes, the way Lucy had climbed into bed and slept with her every night for the next month, not because Nora needed that but because *Lucy* had.

"But that's my baggage to carry. Not yours." Nora crawled across the mattress, sitting down next to Lucy, placing her arm around her shoulders. "You have to stop fighting against your true nature. Because Millie is right. You're your own person with your own dreams and ambitions, all of which you should follow without worrying about what anyone else thinks."

Nora was right. They all had baggage. The difference was, Lucy wasn't just lugging hers around; she was holding it in front of her like some kind of shield.

Mila squeezed her hand. "You don't have to stay on the farm out of a sense of obligation, or some misplaced guilt, or because you're afraid leaving will hurt us. We want you to be happy... wherever that is."

Lucy sniffled, swiping at her eyes. "Thank you."

"And whoever it's with," Remi said, a wicked twinkle in her eye.

Lucy wasn't getting out of this room without answering the question of which man had captured her heart, and now that her sisters had given her the green light to follow her dreams—as well as a fuck ton of shit to think about, like finding a therapist—she felt brave enough to tell them.

"So..." Nora prodded.

"I *did* fall in love, with..." Lucy drew in a breath. Her sisters loved her, and she was ninety-nine-point-nine percent sure nothing she was about to say would change that, but what if they didn't understand? Or worse, approve?

"With?" Mila asked.

"Both of them," Lucy confessed.

Her sisters were silent for a moment—then all three of them spoke up at the same time.

"Did you tell them?" Mila asked.

"Did they fight over you?" Remi looked way too excited by that prospect.

Nora frowned. "Were they upset you couldn't choose? Is that why you're home?"

Lucy looked from sister to sister as she answered their questions in turn. "No. No. No. No."

Mila tilted her head, clearly confused. "They knew you were into both of them, and they were okay with that?"

Lucy nodded. "The three of us..." Heat licked Lucy's cheeks, and she knew if she looked in a mirror, her face would be bloodred.

"Shut the front door!" Remi shouted, rising from the bed. She was the sister Lucy had been least worried about telling because Remi was a wild child from the word go. God help the man who fell in love with her.

"You slept with both of them?" Lucy couldn't tell if Nora was impressed or horrified. Part of her thought it might be the first.

Mila studied Lucy's face hard. "At the same time?"

Lucy bit her lower lip, then lifted her shoulders slowly. "Yes."

"Holy. *Fuck!* I won the pool! All by myself!" Remi started doing the Running Man dance, laughing with glee.

"What are you talking about?" Lucy was shocked, yet she couldn't help laughing. "You bet I'd fallen for both of them?"

Remi pointed to Mila. "You owe me a twenty." Then Nora. "You owe me a twenty." Then she waved her hands in the air. "Everyone owes me a twenty!"

Lucy shook her head, smiling widely. "You're a lunatic." She was relieved that Nora and Mila were both laughing as well.

"So this really was love and not just some sex thing?" Leave it to Mila to dig right down to the heart of the matter.

"It felt like way more than sex, but none of us really talked about our feelings because we knew our time was so short. I haven't known them for very long."

"Who cares?" Mila gushed. "It's so romantic!"

"God, it has to be love, because I've been a wreck since they left," Lucy admitted.

"Why did they leave?" Nora asked, before answering her own question. "Oh shit. You dropped the damn R word, didn't you?"

Lucy grimaced. "Regardless of what y'all say, I *do* have responsibilities here."

"Ones that can be farmed out to someone else," Remi replied, like Lucy's concerns were completely unfounded.

"I own a third of the brewery," Lucy reminded them.

Remi sat back down on the bed. "Pish posh. This is your time, Lu. I can feel it."

Lucy wanted to believe that was true, but she'd been playing a lot of logic tag with her dreams the past few days, which meant she had a long list of concerns. "They didn't ask me to come with them."

Nora scoffed. "Because you told them you needed to be *here*. I saw the way they looked at you when they dropped you off.

Neither one of them was happy. They want you with them. I'm sure of it."

"What if I show up and that's not true?" Lucy asked.

Remi rolled her eyes. "In that extremely unlikely case, you hit the road on your own. You don't need a fucking man to check off all those places on your list. *Kiss and Tell* is a success. You're making good money from it, and let's face it, you're tapped out on material here."

Lucy truly wanted to follow that dream, but she couldn't help but wonder if that was a risky venture. "Is it stupid to plan my future around a YouTube show? I mean, nothing lasts forever."

"You're a clever, creative woman," Nora said. "Once the show dries up, you move on to the next adventure."

The weight that had been pressing down on Lucy lifted when her sister used the word *adventure*.

"They're right," Mila added. "Follow the guys, hop back on the RV, and give this thing between the three of you a chance. And *when* it all works out, think of how cool your *Kiss and Tell* story will be. You can talk about how you chased after them, and they saw you and hugged you and told you they loved you."

Lucy laughed. "You read too many romance novels, Millie."

Mila shrugged, not bothering to deny something they all knew was true.

Lucy felt a wave of excitement wash through her at the thought of going through with this. "I should talk to Sam and Theo first. Because this would impact them the most."

"Fine. Be a boring adult first if you have to. It won't make a difference," Remi scoffed, like that conversation would be no big deal. Lucy tended to agree with her. She was closest to Sam and Theo, the three of them together day in and day out at the brewhouse. If she told them how important this was to her, they wouldn't stand in her way.

"They're going to say the same thing we are," Nora replied confidently.

Lucy glanced at her phone. "Should I call Joey and Miles to ask if I can join them? If they say no, then—"

"Hell no," Remi interjected. "That ruins the story. This requires a dramatic entrance."

Lucy laughed nervously. "Am I really doing this? Chasing after two guys?"

Remi clapped her hands together. "You bet your sweet ass you are. Do you know where they are?"

"Baltimore. They're staying with Joey's sister, Layla. I don't know where she lives, but it shouldn't be too hard to find the pub her in-laws own. Joey told me about it. Pat's Pub. I guess I just start there."

"Perfect. You've got your plan. Now go talk to Sam and Theo, then come back here and start packing."

"I'm leaving today?" Lucy asked, even though she was perfectly aware her ass would be headed to the car this minute if she didn't have to prepare.

"Of *course* you are," Remi said. "We're not taking a chance on you changing your mind."

Now that she'd made her decision, wild horses couldn't keep Lucy from getting to Baltimore.

* * *

"Okay," Lucy said, several hours later, closing the lid on her suitcase and taking one last look around her bedroom. "That's enough to start with. If I need more clothes or if there's something I forgot to pack that I want, I'll just grab it over the holidays."

Lucy had spent an hour this morning in a meeting with Theo and Sam, as they tried to hammer out her new position at the brewery. The three of them owned equal shares, splitting the earnings three ways. They'd discussed Theo and Sam buying her out, but none of them wanted that. It felt too permanent. Instead, it was agreed she'd be a silent partner, the profits divided up differently, with Theo and Sam getting equal larger portions, hers smaller. This left the door open for her to return if she decided to.

After that meeting, she stopped by the B&B to say goodbye to Aunt Claire and Uncle Rex. Her sisters had done a good job spreading the word about her departure, so her quiet goodbye turned into a larger one as Levi, Jace, Maverick, Grayson, and Everett were there, waiting to see her off. The fact that no one seemed shocked by her sudden exit told Lucy just how shitty a job she'd done at hiding her misery over returning.

What her sisters *hadn't* shared with the family was her feelings for both Joey and Miles. They'd all decided to keep that a secret until they saw how things panned out.

Lucy was grateful the goodbyes were all joyful ones, not a single tear shed. Her family was truly happy for her, their support going a long way toward convincing her she'd made the right decision.

Remi grabbed her suitcase, while Lucy slung her backpack and laptop case over her shoulders before walking downstairs. Mila and Nora were waiting for her at the foot of the staircase.

Mila had a brown paper bag in her hands. She lifted it. "Peanut butter and honey sandwich for the road."

Lucy smiled as she took the bag. "My favorite, Millie."

She and her sisters had just stepped out onto the porch when the sound of an approaching car reached them.

"Maybe someone else wants to say goodbye," Nora suggested.

"I've already said goodbye to everyone who—" Lucy gasped when the car turned the corner, coming into view.

Remi stepped around her so she could see the vehicle. "Who is it?" Then her sister glanced her direction. "Is that..."

"It's them," Lucy said with a huge grin. "They're here!"

Chapter Sixteen

oey stepped out of the car, smiling when he spotted Lucy and her sisters standing on the front porch.

He suffered a serious case of déjà vu when Lucy yelled, "You're here!"

He turned to look at Miles, his expression suddenly serious.

"You okay, man?" Miles asked.

"It's her," Joey whispered.

Miles glanced past Lucy, obviously confused by who Joey was talking about. "Her who?"

Joey watched their petite strawberry-blonde descend the stairs, walking in their direction with a huge smile on her face. She wore painted-on blue jeans with a deep purple sweater under her brown leather jacket. Her hair was loose and hanging over her shoulders, the way he loved it. Just like the first day he'd met her, she was wearing her favorite pair of Doc Martens, the ones covered in pink and purple flowers.

"Joey?" Miles prodded.

He grinned, unable look away from her. "The woman we're going to marry," he replied, fixing the pronoun from that first day they were here, when he'd made the same pronouncement.

Miles laughed. "Yeah, I think we are."

Joey rolled his eyes. "No thinking about it." Then he turned and headed toward Lucy, who picked up her pace, now racing across the yard.

He'd just gotten his arms open as she reached him, leaping into his embrace. He didn't have a chance to say a single word before her lips were on his, and she was kissing him like he was the very air she breathed.

Joey had anticipated things starting much differently, with he and Miles sitting her down to roll out all their reasons why she should leave the farm and come with them. Failing that, their backup plan was to chisel out definite ways to make a long-distance relationship work. Either way, the two of them had decided on the way here that they weren't leaving without Lucy in their lives, however they could get her.

When they parted, Joey smiled, then picked her up and spun her, just as he had the day she'd told them she was coming on the road with them.

"You're hogging her," Miles complained, when Joey placed her back on her feet.

Lucy laughed as she disengaged from his arms, giving Miles the same warm—okay, scorching—welcome. Joey spared a glance toward the front porch, where all three of Lucy's sisters were smiling widely. Given the lack of surprise on their faces about the hardcore kisses Lucy was planting on them, he'd guess she had come clean about their change in status from just travel buddies to travel buddies with benefits.

With any luck today, they'd be upgrading that status again to boyfriend/girlfriend/boyfriend.

Joey waved at them when they caught him looking. Mila and Nora returned the wave, while Remi simply grinned and gave him two thumbs-up.

"You're a sight for sore eyes," Miles said, when he and Lucy parted.

She giggled. "We saw each other five days ago."

"Felt like forever," Miles grumbled.

Joey silently rejoiced when Lucy replied, "Tell me about it."

Unable to keep his hands to himself, now that she was so close, Joey stepped behind her, wrapping his arms around her waist while she faced his best friend. Miles had taken hold of one of her hands so he could kiss every single one of her fingertips.

"Why are you here?" she asked.

Miles countered her question with one of his own. "What's the suitcase for?"

As they'd driven up, Joey had noticed her backpack, laptop, camera case, *and* suitcase all piled up beside her on the porch, and he was wondered the same thing.

"I was about to take a little trip," Lucy said coyly. Given the playfulness of her tone, Joey thought he had a good idea where she'd been headed.

"Oh yeah? Where are you off to?" Joey asked, as he placed a kiss on the top of her head.

"Oh, you know. Here and there." She was deliberately keeping her answers vague to tease them. "So, it's a surprise to see the two of you here."

While Joey got a kick out of their silly back-and-forth, Miles clearly wasn't in the mood to play. He'd been chomping at the bit ever since they'd woken up this morning, ready to get here and get things settled. Joey was glad he'd been the one driving because there was no question Miles would have broken every speed limit in his haste.

"We know we don't have a right to ask you to leave your home and your family, Lucy, but we're doing it anyway. You belong with *us*. On the road. We film our show, you film yours, and then we head on to the next city. World travelers. Together." Miles was still holding her hand, and as he spoke, he pulled it to his chest, her palm resting flat against his heart.

"You want me to come with you?"

Joey couldn't see her face clearly, but he could hear the joy and maybe a touch of disbelief in her tone.

"We don't work without you, honey," Joey admitted. "We've

spent the last five days just going through the motions. You didn't just take your girly underwear and questionable cooking skills with you when you left. You took all the fun, all the happiness, all the life right out of us."

"I have zero questions about my cooking skills," she said. "They suck. As for the rest..."

Joey hated the pause, so he filled the silence with the words they should have said to her the last time they were together.

"I love you, Lucy," Joey murmured in her ear. His gaze lifted to Miles. He'd been deliberate to keep his words just about him. Because it wasn't his place to speak for his friend when it came to something as meaningful as this.

"You love me?" she whispered, looking over her shoulder.

"*We* love you," Miles stressed, smiling at Joey as he said it.

"Oh God," Lucy breathed.

She started to say more, but Joey wanted to make sure all their cards were on the table first. "And even if you don't want to leave the farm and your family, we'll find a way to make this work, become farmers ourselves if that's what it takes because this—*you* —are what we want."

"I want that too," Lucy admitted, smiling. "So much."

Joey whooped, picking her up and tossing her over his shoulder.

Lucy half-heartedly beat on his back. "Put me down, you lunatic!"

Joey turned instead, heading toward the porch.

"What are you doing?" she asked, the shameless woman getting back a bit of her own by cupping his ass and squeezing as he walked.

Joey placed a firm smack on her ass in retaliation, chuckling at the wide-eyed, yet not horrified looks on her sisters' faces. Well, two faces. Remi was laughing so hard she was doubled over. "We're going to steal the keys to one of the cabins and figure out our future...in bed."

"Hey, Joey, Miles," Mila said, when they reached the porch.

Lucy wiggled as if to get down. Foolish woman. He didn't intend to let go of her until he had a promise that she would never —NEVER—walk away from them again. Sure, they'd been the ones to drive off this mountain, but only because he'd seen that shimmer of tears in her eyes, and he'd refused to make her cry.

"Hi. Mila, I was wondering if there were any cabins available for a week or two," Joey asked.

"Week or two?" Lucy asked, twisting and trying to lift herself up with her hands on his back.

Joey turned his head to look at her. "Yeah. Going to take us at least that long to make up for the past five days."

"Wow," Nora said softly.

"The cabin you guys stayed in before is vacant." Mila opened the screen door. "Let me go grab the key for you."

"These are Lucy's things," Remi pointed out helpfully. "She's all packed and ready for you."

"But only if you put me down," Lucy insisted. "I'm getting dizzy!"

Joey placed her on her feet, keeping a steadying hand on her elbow. "Just being careful. Don't want to lose you again."

The huge smile that filled Lucy's face went a long way toward erasing the last bit of doubt he harbored over her feelings.

"Never going to happen," she promised.

Joey swore he could hear both of her sisters sighing happily.

Mila came out of the house, key in hand. Miles stepped forward to take it from her, then grabbed Lucy's bags—all of them.

"I don't need the laptop and camera case," she said.

Miles didn't put them down. "We'll take them, just in case we feel the need to start working on our *Kiss and Tell* video."

This time, there was no doubt as to what Joey heard, as all three of Lucy's sisters all but swooned.

"Lu," Mila whispered, smiling almost as widely as her big sis.

Lucy took Joey's hand. "Come on." As the three of them

walked to the car, Lucy called out over her shoulder. "I'll text you guys later."

"Much later," Joey added, which prompted laughter from the front porch.

They threw Lucy's luggage in the trunk with theirs before climbing into the car. Joey shot Miles a pretend scowl in the rearview mirror when he claimed the backseat with Lucy. "I'm playing chauffeur?" he griped.

Miles hummed as he curled Lucy into his arms, cupping her cheek. "Mm-hmm. And take your time." That was when Miles began to kiss her.

Screw that, Joey thought as he kicked up dust driving too fast along the country lane. It only took a few minutes to arrive at the cabin, and Joey felt strangely at home the moment he saw it. While they'd stayed here less than a week, this was the place where they'd shared their first kiss with Lucy, the cabin feeling like the spot where his life truly began.

"Let's grab our stuff," Miles suggested as he walked to the trunk. "Something tells me once we get inside, we're not coming out for a while."

Joey slapped his friend on the back. "You got that right."

They each pulled their suitcases into the cabin, backpacks and duffels slung over their shoulders. He and Miles had packed enough for at least a few weeks, neither of them sure how their suit of Lucy would progress. Given her initial reaction to their arrival, Joey was optimistic that they'd wildly overpacked.

Once inside, Lucy started to tug her suitcase toward one of the bedrooms, and while Joey liked where her head was at—A LOT—he wanted to get the talking part over first. Because while they'd told her how they felt, he couldn't help but notice she hadn't shared *her* feelings. Not only that, but when they offered to be farmers, she hadn't exactly said no.

Joey had missed her like crazy, and while his cock was protesting the delay, he'd waited too damn long—thirty-seven years too long—to get to this point. He needed to be sure he was where he thought he was.

Lucy turned, surprised when he grasped her hand away from the suitcase, pulling her toward the couch instead.

"Wouldn't the bedroom be more comfortable?" she asked with an adorable grin.

"It would, and we'll get there. But I think we should talk for a few minutes."

Lucy sighed. "Okay. But...just so you know...blue bean."

The three of them laughed as Joey led her to the center of the couch, Miles claiming one side, Joey the other. A month ago, they were in these exact same spots, a million miles away from Joey's hopes and dreams for their future.

Right now, he prayed they weren't more than a few steps.

"Where were you going, honey?" Joey asked, tilting his head toward her suitcase.

"To Baltimore."

Best. Answer. Ever.

Miles placed a kiss on her shoulder. "Oh yeah? What changed your mind? Because you were dead set on staying on this farm a few days ago."

"My sisters changed my mind," she responded. "Or maybe it's more accurate to say they showed me the error of my thinking."

"Is it the threesome thing?" Joey asked. "Are you worried what people will say?"

Lucy was shaking her head before he finished his questions. "Not at all."

Joey tilted his head, trying to decide if she meant that or if she was saying it just because she thought that was what he wanted to hear.

"I swear." She drew a cross over her heart.

"What were you thinking about wrong?" Miles asked.

It made sense to Joey that Miles would home in on those words. He'd admitted on the way to the farm this morning that most of his issues with Rhiannon stemmed from his own wrong thinking or—as he described it—stubbornness. His heart wouldn't let her go, so it fooled his head into thinking he'd moved on and could handle being just friends, especially if that was the only way he could have her. It wasn't until his heart *truly* let go that he could see he'd never given up on her, not once in all these years.

Lucy's response to his question was simple, though confusing. "I was wrong about my reasons for not leaving."

"I thought you were staying for your family, for your job," Joey said.

Lucy shook her head. "Those were the excuses I used to avoid admitting the truth."

Miles twisted, crossing his ankle under his leg, facing her more fully. Joey did the same.

Lucy reclined slightly, resting her head on the back of the couch, looking toward the ceiling. "You know that my mom left for a year, right before she passed away."

"We know that," Miles confirmed.

"When she came back at the end of that year, I thought she planned to stay, that she was home for good. I was so excited. I started planning to do all those things we did before she left. Elaborate tea parties, thousand-piece puzzles with pictures of far-off places, traipsing around the farm taking pictures. My mom was an incredible photographer. She taught me all sorts of things about composition, color, lighting, stuff like that. I think those lessons tapped into my creative side and led to my interest in videography."

"Sounds like she was a good mom," Joey said, somewhat hesitantly. He knew Lucy's mom deserted the family, but listening to Lucy talk about her now, it was clear she'd loved the woman.

Lucy started to nod but stopped. "She was my best friend. When I was little, I swore I was going to grow up to be just like her."

Suddenly, things were becoming clearer. A quick glance at Miles proved he was putting two and two together as well.

"Lucy—" Joey started

She sat up straighter, cutting him off. "No one in my family has ever left. I mean, look at us. All adult children, all still living on the farm. And that doesn't even feel strange because they love it there, love being home, working the land, running the businesses."

"Weren't you happy here?" Miles asked.

"If you'd asked me a month ago, I would have said yes without a bit of hesitation. And I can see that I was happy *enough*. Then I went on the road with you guys, and I realized my true happiness can't be found on this farm. But I was afraid if I left…" Lucy ran her fingers through her hair, toying with the ends.

"You thought that made you like your mother?" Joey was trying to put the pieces together.

"She left us. I should hate her for that." Lucy's voice cracked.

"Should?" Miles pointed out the same word Joey was hung up on. "Lucy, you don't have to feel one way or another about your mom. You can feel it all. Any emotion that works for you. If you don't hate her, then great. If you love her, great. If you could care less, also great."

Lucy grimaced. "She died when I was ten, you would think I'd have sorted my shit out regarding Mom."

Joey reached out and took her hand. "No. I don't think you've had the time. Jesus, honey. You lost both your parents when you were a kid. As the big sister, you thought it was up to you to help take care of your younger siblings. Then your grandma got dementia—more caregiving. She died. More grieving. Your grandfather got cancer."

"More caregiving," she whispered. "More grieving."

Miles leaned toward her, giving her a soft kiss on the cheek. "Leaving with us obviously triggered some latent feelings you have regarding your mother."

"Before she left, my family had all sorts of nicknames for me. Always calling me Mom's mini-me or Little Diana. Aunt Claire always used to joke and say stuff like 'Oh, there's Diana and her shadow.' And Granddaddy used to claim I was the spit of her—said we were mirror images of each other. When she left, they stopped saying those things. I don't think they did it intentionally or to be mean. I think they were trying to protect me, trying not to remind me she wasn't here. But the thing is..."

Joey's heart ached for the young girl trying to find her way after losing her role model. "When they stopped using those nicknames, you took that as a negative thing. As their way of telling you *not* to be like her."

Lucy seemed surprised that he got it. "I thought if I left the farm, maybe my family would look at me differently."

Miles shook his head. "Lucy."

She raised her hand. "I know that's not true. Deep inside, I know it. Now. My sisters helped me see the light. And then they helped me pack."

Joey grinned. "I'm adding their names to my Christmas gift list."

"I didn't lie to you guys when I said the trip we took was the best time of my life," Lucy added. "It showed me just how big the difference between genuine happiness and happy enough *really* is. They're worlds apart."

"I like knowing I helped you discover that," Miles said. "Because God knows you did the same for me."

Lucy tilted her head. "Rhiannon?"

"I talked to her last night. She drove down to Baltimore," Miles confessed.

Lucy's eyes widened. "Wow. Those don't sound like the actions of a woman who just wants to be friends."

Miles chuckled. "You're right. They don't."

"What did you say to her?" Lucy asked.

"I said it was over. Then walked away. For good."

Lucy smiled widely, throwing her leg over Miles's so she was straddling him. "Good for you." She gave him a quick, hard kiss. Then peered over at Joey. "And good for us."

Miles gripped her ass, pushing her more firmly against his crotch. "Goddamn, I've missed you."

Lucy wrapped her arms around Miles's neck, bending her head to expand on the first kiss. Joey leaned his side against the back of the couch, soaking in the sight of the two of them. He'd foolishly let Miles convince him to walk away from this, from Lucy. He would never make that mistake again.

He'd known since the night he saw the two of them dancing in Whiskey Abbey that this was meant to be. There was no going back now.

Miles and Lucy kissed for several minutes, but Joey didn't attempt to join, happy to simply watch for now. When they parted, Lucy looked over at him, clearly surprised to find him still on the other side of the couch. Her reaction made sense. Miles was the one who typically played voyeur, Joey too tactile to remain apart without touching.

"So what were you going to say when you got to Baltimore?" he asked.

Lucy shifted off Miles's lap, crawling along the couch to him. Once she'd straddled his lap, she gave him a soft kiss on the side of his lips. "I was going to beg you to let me join you on the road again. I want to be adventurous."

"I like the idea of you begging," Joey purred. "Wonder if we can get you to do that for us now."

Lucy gave him a breathy laugh. "I don't think you'll have to try too hard."

"Ah, right," he said with a grin. "Blue bean."

"Can we go to the bedroom now?" she asked, her tone part whine, part desperation.

Joey rose with her in his arms, juggling her with his hands on her ass, making sure she was secure before heading toward the room. "Hell yeah."

Miles followed, the two of them working together to strip Lucy out of every piece of clothing.

Joey stepped behind her, wrapping his arms around her

midsection so that he could cup her breasts, lifting them up. "Give Miles a taste," he murmured in her ears.

Goose bumps erupted on her flesh as Lucy shivered with need, then she arched her back slightly, pushing her tits closer to Miles.

He sucked her nipples into his mouth, drawing on them roughly, betraying his own arousal.

Lucy gasped as Miles increased the pressure, but she didn't try to pull away. If anything, she inched closer. "Missed you so much," she said, her hands gripping the back of his head, holding him tight.

While retaining his grip on her breasts, Joey ran his lips along the side of her neck, kissing and sucking, leaving little love marks that she was certain to give him hell for tomorrow. Not that she seemed to mind getting them, if her little whimpers and moans were anything to go by.

Miles was the first to break, lifting his head and giving Lucy a long, slow kiss. "Ready to beg?"

Lucy trembled even as she nodded.

Joey moved her toward the bed, gently pushing her down until she was sitting on the edge. "Lay back and spread your legs."

"God. Yes," she hissed, doing exactly as Joey asked.

Once she was there, spread out like a delicious feast, he dropped to his knees beside the bed, lowering his face and running his tongue along her slit.

Her hands flew to his hair, tightening around the strands, pulling until his scalp stung. The pain sent more blood to his cock. Joey's plan to make her beg was backfiring because God knew he was seconds away from offering their beautiful woman the world on a silver platter just to get back inside her.

The sound of clothing hitting the floor told Joey that Miles was undressing, a weight on the other side of the mattress causing him to lift his eyes.

Miles crawled toward Lucy, kneeling next to her face. He gripped his thick cock in his hand, stroking the length of it slowly as she watched. He groaned when she licked her lips, which was invitation enough, but she still backed it up by crooking her finger.

Miles lifted off his haunches, lowering the head of his dick until it brushed against her lips. Joey watched, even as he continued to toy with her clit, the tip of his tongue spinning circles around the distended flesh without really touching her the way she needed.

He wanted to wait until the opportune moment, wanted to wait until Lucy was good and distracted by Miles's cock before he reminded her he was intent on hearing her pleas.

Miles teased her, drawing the head of his cock over her lips, painting them with drops of precome, without ever allowing her to take him inside. Her tongue darted out several times, stealing only quick swipes before Miles pulled it away again.

"What do you want, honey?" Miles asked in a deep, sexy voice.

"You," she said, reaching out for him.

He grasped her wrist, holding it away from him. Miles glanced down at Joey. "I didn't hear the magic word, did you?"

Joey snorted, shaking his head. "Nope. She must not really want it."

Lucy scowled, trying to shake her hand free from his grip. "I want it, Miles. Stop messing around and give it to me."

Miles held tight to her hand while continuing to stroke his own dick. Lucy started to lift her other hand, but Joey had been waiting for that, so he was ready. He grabbed it, pinning it tightly to the mattress by her side.

"Joey," she cried. "Dammit!"

He lifted his head. "Does that sound like begging?" he asked Miles.

"Nope. Not at all. Maybe we need to remind her what she's been missing out on."

Joey grinned, then lowered his head to her pussy once more. The buildup to the three of them becoming lovers had been slow, so the nights they'd spent merely kissing and touching and exploring were extremely instructive. As such, Joey knew exactly where and how to touch Lucy to evoke the words they were waiting to hear.

He took off the kid gloves when he sucked her clit into his mouth, driving two fingers inside her sopping-wet pussy. Joey had to release his grip on her hand, using it to press down on her stomach when her hips flew off the mattress.

"Oh my God!" she cried out. Miles had released her other hand, and now both of them rested above her head, where she was white-knuckling the duvet.

Joey continued to suck, tease, and nip her clit, thrusting his fingers in faster, harder. Like Miles, he'd become quite adept at finding her G-spot, something that was going to come in very handy right now.

He curled his fingers, and Lucy exploded, her body jerking roughly as her orgasm struck like lightning.

Joey hadn't intended to let her come so quickly, but it had been too long, and his ability to draw this out could be measured in inches rather than miles.

Miles smirked, shaking his head at him. Joey gave him a casual one-shoulder shrug, letting him know he was aware of his failure. Lucy hadn't come close to begging.

Joey ran his tongue along her slit as he pulled his fingers free. They were dripping with her arousal. So wet, in fact...

He drew one finger lower, twirling it around her ass. Lucy groaned but didn't attempt to pull away. With the exception of the night Miles had toyed with her anus, anal sex wasn't something they'd explored together.

The way Lucy tilted her hips upward, giving Joey better access, let him know she was not shying away from the idea. He pressed the tip of his finger inside, working it slowly with gentle back and forth motions, until it was completely lodged.

Miles was still stroking his own cock, his gaze riveted on what Joey was doing.

"That feels...different," she admitted, still breathless from her orgasm.

"Bad different?" Joey asked.

She shook her head. "No. Good different."

Lucy held Joey's gaze as he slowly fucked her ass with his finger. He wouldn't attempt more than that this time, but they were definitely going to explore this more fully...and soon.

"We're going to buy our girl a butt plug," Miles murmured.

Lucy giggled but didn't say no.

Unable to resist her a second longer, Joey rose, stripping out of his own clothes as Miles stroked her blonde hair, murmuring more of his deliciously dirty promises.

"I've got a whole list of toys in mind," he said. "We're going to clamp these sexy nipples," he pinched one as he spoke, Lucy whimpering from the brief spark of pleasurable pain. "And some straps for the bed. God, we're gonna tie you up one night, edge you until you feel like you're going to explode."

Lucy's breathing had evened out until Miles started making his list. Now she was panting again, her eyes nearly closed. "Yes," she whispered.

Joey reached down to grab his jeans, withdrawing a couple of condoms from his wallet. He wondered if they could talk Lucy into making an appointment with her doctor to get the birth control shot. He'd love to take her without anything between them.

Miles helped Lucy up onto the bed properly, shifting her to the middle. Then he resumed his place, kneeling by the side of her head. "You're going to suck on my dick while Joey takes you, Luce. But you're not going to make me come."

She narrowed her eyes as if to argue, but Miles cut her off.

"If you *do* make me come, Joey's going to pull out, we're going to flip you over, and we're going to spank that sweet little ass of yours until it's as bright red as these cheeks." He drew the back of one finger along the side of her flushed face.

Lucy tilted her head, a cute little crease forming between her eyes. "And then?"

"'And then' what?" Miles asked, confused.

"I was waiting for you to get to the punishment part."

Miles burst out laughing. "God. I had you pegged right from the beginning. You *are* trouble."

Joey loved watching the exchange between them, the easy give-and-take, the way Lucy was just as adept at trash-talking as they were.

"I was right too," Joey said. "I told you we fit." He drew on the condom, lifted Lucy's legs until they rested on his forearms and with one hard thrust, he found himself right back in heaven.

"*Fuck*," Joey said through gritted teeth, hating how damn quick this was going to be over. He'd spent every night since they'd left her, playing out one fantasy after another until the calluses on his palm had less to do with work and more to do with self-satiation.

Lucy's hips rose and fell from the bed in tandem with his thrusts. And while her tight, wet pussy gloved him perfectly, it wasn't just the fucking that was pushing him to an early end. It was the show Lucy and Miles were providing.

Lucy's head was turned to the right, her small hand wrapped around Miles's cock. It was so thick, her fingers didn't even touch. She'd taken the head of his dick inside, her cheeks hollowing out as she sucked on him. Her hums of appreciation obviously vibrated against Miles's dick, and his best friend's fingers tightened in Lucy's hair, tugging it the way she loved.

"Your mouth," Miles praised. "It's deadly, honey. Fucking deadly."

For several minutes, the only sounds in the room were their low moans of pleasure and their bodies slapping against each other.

When Joey felt as if he needed to come or die, he reached down, stroking Lucy's clit. Her lips popped off Miles's cock as she gasped. He leaned back, his gaze drifting to where Joey and Lucy were connected.

For a man who protested the idea of another guy in the bed, Miles had taken to sharing Lucy like a fish to water. Not only had he shed his own inhibitions about being watched, he'd also fully embraced his role as the observer.

"You two are so sexy together," Miles murmured. "You were made for us, honey."

Joey was grateful to Miles for providing the sweet talk because he didn't have enough air in his lungs to utter anything besides a string of curses and Lucy's name.

He feared for a second he'd reach the pinnacle before her, so he was relieved when, two panting breaths later, she hit the peak.

"Joey," she yelled. "Oh. Shit. Yes!"

Her inner muscles clenched around him in the world's most perfect vise grip, and he erupted as well, falling forward, his hands landing on the mattress by her shoulders. "Fuck. Luce! Honey. God*dammit.*"

Joey tried to suck in some much-needed air, even as his heart beat so hard he feared it would pound its way out of his chest. He wasn't sure how long he remained there, trying to recover, but when Miles placed a hand on his shoulder, he realized it was probably too long.

"You okay there, old man?" Miles taunted. His best friend took great pleasure in reminding Joey that he was five years older.

"Think you can do better?" he dared, simply because Miles wouldn't be able to resist the challenge and Lucy would benefit from that.

Joey pushed himself away from Lucy, falling to the bed beside her and clearing the way for Miles, who wasted no time taking his place. Joey twisted, pulling off the condom and carefully dropping it to the floor.

Miles and Lucy both shot him a look, as his tendency to be a slob was pointed out more than a few times in the RV.

"I'll clean it up in a minute," he said. "I swear."

Miles shook his head in disbelief, while Lucy giggled as she ran her fingertips along Miles's muscular arms. "I missed you," she whispered before looking at Joey. "Both of you."

Joey gave her a soft kiss on the cheek, resting his head on his hand as Miles slowly pushed his way inside her. Joey didn't consider himself a small man, his dick a bit longer than Miles's. But damn if he still wasn't a bit shocked whenever Miles managed to fit his thick cock inside her. She admitted one night that their dicks made her feel full, but not in an uncomfortable or painful way.

Miles, as always, opted for the slower, steadier pace, rocking his hips so that he was hitting her G-spot over and over. Joey watched, spellbound for several minutes, his cock—which should have been well sated—jerking slightly as he watched the two of them together. At this rate, Joey would be rock-hard again before they finished.

Despite already having two orgasms, Lucy was close. Joey had gotten accustomed to her little tells, the higher-pitched whimper, the almost Lamaze-like breathing as she struggled to fill her lungs, the way her chest flushed as brightly pink as her cheeks.

Miles was just as close. His tell was a lot simpler than Lucy's. Joey knew his friend was close when his finesse gave way to unadulterated need and he lost his steady rhythm, his hips pistoning into her harder and faster.

"Lucy," Miles said, his head bowed.

"Please," she said, finally offering them that magic word. "God, please!"

It worked.

Miles came with a loud curse. "Fuuuuck!"

At the same time, Lucy's body arched, her head thrown back in pleasure, her eyes closed tightly. "So good. Too good..."

Joey rested his palm over her heart, wanting to feel it race.

Miles withdrew after a few moments, heading to the bathroom to wash up. Joey followed suit, cleaning up after himself as promised.

Lucy remained in bed, her seemingly endless energy finally zapped. She lifted one hand toward them when they returned to the bedroom, but it fell back to the mattress heavily.

"How about an afternoon nap?" she suggested sleepily. "I haven't been..."

Joey crawled into bed next to her. "I've been sleeping like shit too."

"Ditto," Miles said as he reclaimed his side, the three of them cuddling under the covers.

Lucy placed her head on Joey's chest, wiggling her ass in a not-so-subtle hint for Miles to spoon her.

Joey sighed as a wave of pure joy washed through him, taking him down like a goddamn tsunami. Lucy had promised him the Storms were a force of nature, and there was no denying their little blonde tornado had cut a wide swath through them both, straight to their hearts.

Exchanging a glance with Miles, he could tell his friend felt exactly the same way. They shared a smile, Joey's wink prompting Miles to roll his eyes.

He placed a kiss on the top of Lucy's head, thinking she'd already fallen asleep. He was surprised when she lifted her head slightly.

"I love you," she whispered to him, before turning her head to offer Miles the same three words.

Life. Made.

J oey looked around Nonna and Nonno's living room, so overwhelmed with happiness, he was shocked he could hold it all in. It was Christmas Eve, his first spent with Miles *and* Lucy by his side. His partners were currently standing next to the dessert table, which was overflowing with biscotti, tiramisu, cannoli, almond cookies, olive oil cake, and at least a dozen other options. Miles and Lucy were clearly debating what to try. Knowing Miles's sweet tooth, he was probably wondering if he could help himself to a bit of all of it.

They'd spent Thanksgiving in Northern Virginia with the Storm family.

For the past couple of years, the two of them had lived in Joey's apartment here in Philadelphia through Thanksgiving and most of December, working for Moretti Brothers Restorations. Then Miles had returned to New York both years to spend Christmas with his mom and sister, returning right before New Year's Eve.

This year, they'd decided to start new traditions—as a throuple. He and Miles had remained with Lucy in that cozy cabin right through Thanksgiving and all the way to Cyber Monday.

After that, they'd hopped in his car and drove to Philadelphia, where they'd holed up in Joey's apartment for weeks, only coming up for air, food, and the occasional happy hour with his family.

The Storm family had reacted to their throuple status with mixed results. As Joey expected, her male cousins and Uncle Rex weren't pleased, their protective natures rising to the forefront. Their responses were very similar to his and his brothers that first time Layla came home with Finn and Miguel in tow.

Their attitudes began to thaw after he and Miles remained on Stormy Weather Farm, pitching in to help with the chores, not holding back when it came to their feelings for Lucy. The three of them were head over heels in love, and all the frosty looks in the world from Levi and Theo and the others hadn't chilled that a bit.

The night before Thanksgiving, Levi had pulled the two of them aside, saying that while he didn't fully understand what was going on between them and Lucy, there was no denying their intentions were good and their feelings genuine. Levi, like Joey, was closer to forty than thirty and still a bachelor. No doubt that was another reason Joey felt like the man was a kindred spirit. He sensed Levi was no more a fan of his single state than Joey had been, especially given the somewhat envious glances he'd flashed at him, Miles, and Lucy when he thought Joey wasn't looking.

After that initial peace offering, the other male Storms followed suit, and by the time they left the farm, Joey felt as if he'd acquired seven new male cousins, all of them trash-talking and giving each other shit the same way the Moretti males did.

Clearing that hurdle had been huge, but the three of them were aware there was an even larger one facing them.

Tomorrow, they planned to drive to New York to have Christmas dinner with Miles's mother and sister. Miles had initially bailed on the trip, explaining to his mom that he couldn't spend the holiday with Rhiannon. His mom had shocked him when she'd said if it was a choice between seeing her best friend and Rhiannon on the holiday, or her son, she chose him. Miles had been touched by the gesture, even though it took away his excuse to prolong introducing Joey and Lucy as his partners.

Miles was still convinced his mom wouldn't accept their relationship. Joey and Lucy had promised that whichever way the wind blew, they would be with him every step of the way. That vow appeared to do the trick because Miles had seemed much lighter since then, his anxiety alleviated.

His siblings and cousins had welcomed Lucy with open arms, including her in their gang as if she'd always been there. And once Joey told them about *Kiss and Tell*, they all became fans, begging Lucy to let them tell their stories. Despite the unbelievable number of hours Joey, Lucy, and Miles spent in bed, she'd managed to record several new episodes of the show, all of them including Joey's friends and family.

She'd filmed his cousin Liza, and her new husband, Matt, enthralled by their enemies-to-lovers tale.

She'd also done a show including Matt's brother, Gage, and his wife, Penny. Lucy admitted the couple gave Macie and Hank a run for their money when it came to the funniest retelling of a romance ever. She'd also returned home with a serious case of baby fever after spending an afternoon with Gage and Penny's adorable five-month-old daughter, Willow, something that had launched their own "baby talk."

Joey had been thrilled to learn that Lucy wanted children. He knew they were still in the very early days of this relationship, but at thirty-seven, Joey was feeling that tug to become a father big-time.

After hearing Liza and Penny were going to be on the show, Keeley had demanded her turn, dragging Gio and Rafe along for the ride. They'd filmed their episode in the haunted house Rafe had inherited from his grandfather, that the three of them had renovated into an inn.

Last week, Joey, Lucy, and Miles had traveled to Baltimore so that Lucy could meet Layla, who was spending Christmas with her in-laws this year. Lucy and Layla had become fast friends, bonding over the "ungodly" number of overprotective male relatives they each had.

While there, Lucy filmed Padraig and his romance writer wife, Emmy, for *Kiss and Tell*.

Since returning to Philadelphia, she'd been working on edits for that show, which were going slow because she couldn't watch the footage for long without crying. Padraig's journey to his happily ever after had been a painful one after the loss of his first wife.

"That dessert table is insane," Lucy exclaimed, plopping down on the couch next to him. "I'm sort of worried it's going to collapse under all the weight."

Miles claimed her opposite side, and as Joey expected, he appeared to have taken a sample of every single treat.

Joey reached across Lucy to grab something from Miles's plate. "Aw. You brought some for me. How sweet," he joked, laughing when Miles slapped his hand away.

"Mine," he grumbled.

Lucy lifted her plate, loaded down with a heaping helping of tiramisu—and two spoons. She winked at him as he grabbed a spoon, scooping some up and shoveling it into his mouth with a happy groan. Aunt Berta made the best tiramisu on the planet, though he'd never say that to Nonna, who liked to think hers was the best. The two of them demolished the dessert in record time.

"I want to go on record as saying," Lucy began, "that while being a Moretti prepared you for dinner with the Storms, the Storms did *not* prepare me for this." She gestured around the room, where the volume had continued to grow as the night wore on. Uncle Cesare and Nonno had pulled out their accordions, playing a lively tune that the smaller children were dancing to in the middle of the living room.

Joey's dad had pulled the Russo brothers, Gage, Conor, and Matt, into a discussion about cigars. Dad was showing them the box of cigars Tony had given him for Christmas, offering one to each of them, while Nonna shouted across the room for them to "smoke those smelly things outside."

Gianna and Penny were holding their daughters, chatting with Jess and Liza. Joey would bet a million dollars Liza would be pregnant or holding her own baby by this time next year. His brothers, Tony, Gio, and Luca, were gathered around the bar—of course—filling up their whiskey glasses, while debating which bourbon was the best.

They were surrounded by his family, and while Joey had always been grateful for his blessings, this was the first year he felt true happiness. Because he truly had it all.

He recalled Lucy's comment about being overwhelmed, wrapping his arm around her shoulders and leaning closer to her ear, so she and Miles could hear him. "Are you having fun?"

Her smile answered his question, so her words just felt like the icing on the cake. "Oh my God, yes. This is incredible. It's a lot to take in, but damn if every single part of it isn't super fun."

"You can say that again," Miles agreed, still chowing down on desserts.

Lucy reached out, swiping a tiny bit of chocolate off the corner of Miles's lips with her finger, licking it off in a seductive way that made him and Miles both groan.

"Trouble," Miles murmured, that nickname sticking just as much as honey had. "Maybe you should make sure you got it all. With your tongue."

Lucy never missed a beat, kissing him. Joey leaned forward so he could watch her tongue slide along Miles's lips in search of stray smears of chocolate. It made Joey wish he still had some dessert left.

That was when his eyes landed on Miles's forgotten plate... sitting unguarded on his lap as he kissed Lucy.

Snooze, ya lose.

Joey reached over and ran his finger through the icing of Miles's carrot cake, smearing some of the cream cheese frosting on his own lips.

"Oops," he said, when Miles and Lucy parted, drawing their attention. "I made a mess too."

Miles scowled when he glanced down at his plate. "Hey!"

Lucy just laughed, then did a very, very thorough job cleaning his lips.

As far as kisses went, it was one of the best ever.

So good, he couldn't wait to tell her...

"I love you, Lucy Storm," Joey murmured.

"*We* love you," Miles corrected, his chin resting on Lucy's shoulder. Joey would never get tired of hearing those words.

Or the next ones from Lucy...

"And I love you."

Want to read more about the Storm family? The Perfect Storm series begins with Levi!

Taken by Storm

And have you checked out all those hot Italian Stallions?

Down and Dirty

Hard and Fast

Rough and Ready

Wild and Wicked

Hot and Heavy

Naughty and Nice (a holiday novella)

Tempted and Taken

Steady and Strong

Kiss and Tell

Did you know there's an Italian Stallions playlist on Spotify? You can take a listen right HERE.

· · ·

Calling all fans of Mari Carr AND Facebook! There's a group for you. Come join Mari Carr's Facebook group for sneak peaks, cover reveals, contests and more! Join now.

And be sure to join Mari's mailing list to receive a **FREE** sexy novella, Midnight Wild.

About the Author

Virginia native Mari Carr is a New York Times and USA TODAY bestseller of contemporary romance novels. With over three million copies of her books sold, Mari was the winner of the Romance Writers of America's Passionate Plume award for her novella, Erotic Research. She has over a hundred published works, including her popular Wild Irish and Italian Stallions books, along with the Trinity Masters series she writes with Lila Dubois.

Follow Mari:
www.maricarr.com
mari@maricarr.com

Join her newsletter so you don't miss new releases and for exclusive subscriber-only content.